BOOKS IN THE SERIES

What If . . . Loki Was Worthy?
What If . . . Wanda Maximoff and Peter Parker Were Siblings?
What If . . . Marc Spector Was Host to Venom?

BOOKS BY MIKE CHEN

Here and Now and Then
A Beginning at the End
We Could Be Heroes
Light Years from Home
Vampire Weekend
A Quantum Love Story
Star Wars: Brotherhood
From a Certain Point of View: The Empire Strikes Back
From a Certain Point of View: Return of the Jedi
Star Trek: Deep Space Nine—The Dog of War

MARVEL

WHAT IF...

MARC SPECTOR WAS HOST TO VENOM?

MARVEL

WHAT IF...

MARC SPECTOR WAS HOST TO VENOM?

MIKE CHEN

DEL
REY

1 3 5 7 9 10 8 6 4 2

Del Rey
One Embassy Gardens
8 Viaduct Gardens
London SW11 7BW

Del Rey is part of the Penguin Random House group of companies
whose addresses can be found at global.penguinrandomhouse.com

Penguin
Random House
UK

MARVEL

Mike Chen has asserted his right to be identified as the author of this Work
in accordance with the Copyright, Designs and Patents Act 1988

First published in the US by Random House Worlds, an imprint of Random House,
a division of Penguin Random House LLC, New York in 2024
First published in the UK by Del Rey in 2024

Jeff Youngquist, VP, Production and Special Projects
Sarah Singer, Editor, Special Projects
Jeremy West, Manager, Licensed Publishing
Sven Larsen, VP, Licensed Publishing
David Gabriel, VP, Print & Digital Publishing
C.B. Cebulski, Editor in Chief

www.penguin.co.uk

A CIP catalogue record for this book is available from the British Library

ISBN 9781529914252 (hardback)
ISBN 9781529914269 (trade paperback)

Book design by Edwin A. Vasquez

Printed and bound in Great Britain by Clays Ltd, Elcograf S.p.A.

The authorised representative in the EEA is Penguin Random House Ireland,
Morrison Chambers, 32 Nassau Street, Dublin D02 YH68

www.greenpenguin.co.uk

For all of the odd couples out living their best lives across the Multiverse

MARVEL

WHAT IF...

MARC SPECTOR WAS HOST TO VENOM?

Interview Subject: Marc Spector,
2:15 P.M.
Clinical Diagnosis: Dissociative
Identity Disorder
Notable Issues: Violent outbursts,
delusions of grandeur, detachment from
reality

Dr. Emmet: Recording started at quarter
after two. Sodium pentothal administered
fifteen minutes prior. For patient's own
safety, limbs have been restrained to
the chair. How are you, Marc? Did you
have a good lunch?

Marc Spector: Your truth serum actually
tastes better than your cafeteria. Hell,
my Marine rations tasted better than
your cafeteria.

DE: Unfortunately, I can't influence the
food service vendor. That's the
facilities department.

MS: I don't know why you even gave me a shot. I got nothing to hide.

DE: Good. Then we'll make progress today. Tell me about the two identities you stole. First, Steven Grant. Who is he?

MS: Steven's an arrogant billionaire who spends too much time indulging in his fantasies.

DE: All right. And where does Steven Grant live?

MS: In my head.

DE: And Jake Lockley? Who is he?

MS: Cabdriver. Tough SOB. Impulsive. Ruthless at times. Blood doesn't bother him.

DE: And where does he live?

MS: In my head. One big unhappy family in this skull.

DE: You see, that's simply not true. You've stolen and integrated their identities as part of your own persona. Grant's got a *really* nice mansion on Long Island. And a penthouse in Midtown. Look, here are the public records of purchase. (Sounds of shuffling paper) Lockley keeps his own shabby place somewhere. Wouldn't want to imagine the number of rats in the walls. I will say, though, the one person who *is* sharing your headspace is this . . . Khonshu?

MS: (Laughs) Yeah, he's there, too.

DE: It's a good thing I'm an Egyptology buff. Khonshu, as in the Egyptian god of the moon?

MS: Heliopolis.

DE: Excuse me?

MS: Egyptian gods are actually interdimensional beings. They reside in a place known as "Heliopolis."

DE: I see. Anything else you want to tell me about Khonshu?

MS: Yeah. He's got an attitude problem.

DE: Noted. "Egyptian god with an attitude problem that travels between dimensions and hires former mercenaries like Marc Spector." Now, tell me about Gena Landers and Jean-Paul Duchamp.

MS: (Pauses) Why are you bringing up Gena and Frenchie?

DE: Oh, didn't you hear? They're new patients here at Retrograde.

MS: They don't belong here—

DE: Marc, Marc, they participate in your delusion. That means *they* are delusional as well. Delusional people are a danger to society. Fortunately, their support in your endeavors led us directly to them, so we can help them like we are helping you.

MS: Your "help"?

DE: Yes, exactly. For them and the general public. Gena runs a diner. Who knows how the delusions would affect her cooking? That's a public safety issue. Duchamp—Frenchie, as you call him—former mercenary like you, right? Good with weapons, flies helicopters. Probably just as much PTSD as you, and not the type of person you want with firearms. So yes, they belong here. (Pauses) How's that sodium pentothal treating you? Feeling more relaxed?

MS: I can't relax. (Sound of chair rattling) Steven can, Jake can. I can't.

DE: All right, one more name for you. Tell me about Marlene Alraune.

MS: (Sound of chair slamming) If you hurt—

DE: Ah, see, there you go. Violent outbursts. I'm glad to see those restraints are working. Billy, will you please tighten them? (Sound of grunts and clicking) You see how we are looking out for you? You can't contain yourself. (Sound of papers shuffling) Isn't that why Marlene left you? My gosh, you sure introduced some difficult times into her life. And her dad, Peter—that's Egyptologist Peter Alraune, for the record—he died around you as well? That's not a great start to any relationship. Actually, let me check, how many times has she left you?

MS: (Pauses) Twice.

DE: Good. Honesty. And why did she leave you?

MS: She didn't want my life of violence to affect her anymore.

DE: Exactly. Now we're getting to the core of it. (Sounds of rustling) This suit. You call it "Moon Knight." You hurt people in it. That's a problem. Let's see, some of the things you've claimed in our notes. How many battles with Bushman? A werewolf? And take a look at this photo. You called it a "psi-phon" and you claimed to have defeated, and I quote, "a multiversal version of Moon Knight called 'Moon Shade'" to get it.

MS: Where'd you get that?

DE: That doesn't matter. Are you listening to yourself? Does this sound like something any rational person would say? Give me an honest answer.

MS: (Pauses) No. It doesn't.

DE: Good. Every step forward is important. This is why I find you so fascinating. In fact, I'd say it's the culmination of my life's work to help you. Now, what should we get to next?

MS: (Pauses) I'll tell you what I'm gonna do next. I'm going to bust out of here. Tonight. I'm going to take what's mine. My friends, my suit. I'm done with this hellhole. You think you can break me? I've seen far, far worse.

DE: As long as we're being honest here, how do you plan to do that? Do you have

a lockpick hidden away? A shiv made of
soap?

MS: No. I don't need those things.

DE: Then what *do* you have?

MS: Jake. Steven. Khonshu. They're all
I'll need. They're all I can rely on.
You'll see.

DE: I think we're done here. Time is
twenty-four minutes past two. Billy? Mr.
Spector needs another round of
sedatives. And electroshock therapy.

MS: (Laughter)

DE: Maximum strength.

THE VASTNESS OF SPACE
AMERICA

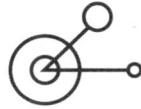

AMERICA CHAVEZ WAS IN TROUBLE. AND SHE KNEW IT.

Not that long ago, such an instinct would be elusive, invisible to her. She'd been lost for so long, awash in the dream-like state of whatever had become her existence.

But now she felt like herself. Even though things had changed.

This trouble was different from the chaos of her childhood, or the battles of her teenage years. This time, the conflict came from the people she thought were on her side:

The Watchers.

Problem was, the Watchers weren't always right. Which caused a bit of an issue given that America trusted her gut—and when she tried to explain this to the Watchers, they told her to stand down, stop intervening, leave people like Peter Parker and Stephen Strange alone.

The Watchers or her gut instinct?

She chose her gut instinct.

And she was right.

Because someone was involved, a mystery foe—someone whose actions echoed across time and space and reality—

No. Beyond reality. Multiple realities. Possibly *all* realities. And with it came a single identity, someone cloaked in the shadows, and through all of the collective observations of the Watchers, one name came to her:

A *Whisperer*.

Who was he? What was his goal? Why did he keep interfering? Just like he was involved with Loki before the incident involving Peter, Wanda, and the collateral damage unleashed around them.

A threat was coming, something ripping through different times and places and universes. Where would the Whisperer go next? What would be the point of divergence?

America floated in ethereal space, safe from the condemnation and prying eyes of the Watchers. They wanted her to follow the rules, go away, or maybe both.

Sorry. Not gonna work this time.

Multiple cosmic windows opened in front of her, all of the clues and details that trailed the Whisperer leading her to these look-ins across realities.

Except for one. A single particular window was just for her. She reached through that particular one, a place where she stashed a few of the things from her physical life, the stuff that didn't really prove necessary in the dream-like space of her existence, yet somehow it felt right.

Her fingers wrapped around the sleeve of a worn denim jacket, with red and white stripes along the shoulders and a large star sewn on the back.

Cool. She hoped it still fit.

As she wiggled her arms into the sleeves, she looked at the scene ahead—two figures she wasn't exactly familiar with, but she needed to know more, her skills as a Watcher coming into play here even while defying the others' orders.

Venom, a symbiote creature that traveled as a large black blob, at least until it joined with a host. Strong, brutal, amorphous, and *very* adaptable, the symbiotes used their bodies for many things: forming weapons, covering surfaces, creating barriers. Also capable of leaping universes, and when it chose to have a face, it bore rows of sharp teeth and a nasty red tongue.

And when joined, these strengths mixed with the powers and essences of the host in a delicate balance. Or in some cases, not exactly balanced. More like reluctantly shared, one way or the other.

The Whisperer's trail led to Venom. And Venom appeared to be stalking someone else, on a multiversal collision course with . . .

A white cape and cowl over white boots, white body armor, white gauntlets, and a white mask. Glowing white eyes bore out from the mask, and on the chest sat the distinct curve of a crescent moon.

Moon Knight. Or Marc Spector, former mercenary and ex-Marine, now guarding the streets of New York City—and occasionally beyond. Yet something stood out about Spector; in some ways, he was a guy in a suit with weapons and martial arts training. But in other ways, he was different.

Because Marc Spector was the chosen Fist of Khonshu, an Ennead being—or as most humans knew them, the gods of ancient Egypt. But to the Watchers, well . . . the Ennead were just another set of interdimensional creatures that sometimes caused too much trouble.

One more particular thing stood out about Marc, though. Because he wasn't just Marc. He was also Steven Grant and Jake Lockley—not in the way some people assumed fake identities to trick people. No, those were fully formed personalities, as dimensional as real people, a shared brain that worked in ways not even America understood.

She'd leave that one to the human medical experts.

Venom and Moon Knight. So many questions about where things went from here. America knew she had to intervene, but *when*?

For now, she would Watch. But as she settled in to consider what lay ahead, a new thought came to mind, one that caught her by surprise and brought a smile to her face.

The jacket still fit, after all.

America adjusted the jacket's collar, then gave the front an instinctive tug like she was a teenager again, a reminder to herself of different times long ago as she prepared for the journey ahead—no matter where or when it led.

CHAPTER 1

—

MARC

MARC SPECTOR LOOKED BEHIND HIM.

The buzzing, inconsistent lights and grimy brick walls of the dim sewer system made it hard to tell for sure, but somewhere farther down the tunnel, a silhouette stood.

Was that . . .

The lights blacked out for a second before coming back, but for a flash, Marc saw it clearly, as if the desert sun shone directly on it:

The imposing silhouette of a man, long cloak draped over thin limbs and staff in hand.

Plus a massive bird skull for a head.

Khonshu.

The Egyptian god of the moon wasn't always the best—or most sincere—ally for Marc, but given that Marc had pledged to be the Moon Knight, avatar of Khonshu, well, they helped each other out of a lot of jams.

In this case, the bird skull turned his way, then Khonshu tapped his staff, causing an echo that Marc heard over his own pounding footsteps. Then the lamps flickered again and Khonshu disappeared, leaving only decaying infrastructure and skittering rats. Just the empty shadows of a sewer passage. A *New York* sewer passage, one that tracked right underneath Retrograde Sanitarium, where Marc had just led a daring, brutal escape: first breaking free from his cell, then recovering his things from storage and donning the Moon Knight suit, then liberating his friends from the clutches of Dr. Emmet and her oppressive guards and orderlies.

And now? Underground, on the way to freedom. Sanity versus insanity. New York versus ancient Egypt. One mind versus infinite possibilities.

Not that long ago, the love of Marc's life told him that she needed to distance herself from him, from the life of violence that swarmed around him. He'd tried explaining to Marlene that the violence stemmed from the balance of *everything* in his head, of dealing with Steven Grant and Jake Lockley, of being pledged to serve Khonshu as the deity's Fist. But the how and why didn't matter to her.

She'd had enough. And as he dashed forward through the damp passageway, cape billowing behind him, he considered if maybe she was right.

Such was the life of Marc Spector. He never claimed it was an easy one.

"There they are!" a voice yelled, cutting through the thick air.

"No, no, no," a woman's voice said. Marc turned to see concerned lines framing the brown eyes and pursed lips of Gena Landers. Gena spun and shot a look behind Marc, her head now angled to catch shadows across her dark skin. "Frenchie, turn off the flashlight!"

"*Non,* Gena," hissed Jean-Paul Duchamp, Marc's longtime associate and sometimes helicopter pilot, known by most as Frenchie. "We are in a sewer. How else could we possibly see?"

"If *we* can't see us, then they can't see us," Gena shot back. Frenchie cursed under his breath, a rapid-fire mix of French and English and possibly something else, and as he swung the flashlight, the beam crossed Marc's body, causing a flicker of his reflection on the water to remind Marc of the single constant thing that summed up all of the certainty and uncertainty in his life:

Moon Knight.

White. Clear white, the kind that stood out against a dark night sky. Not camouflage, but a distinct and obvious look that sent a message to whoever saw it.

I'm coming for you.

White boots. A white, form-fitting carbonadium armored suit, complete with gauntlets. A white belt, where he stashed adamantium crescent darts—boomerang-like blades shaped like a crescent moon—and on the left side, his truncheon hung, an adaptable weapon that acted as nunchaku, bo staff, or grappling hook as needed.

Over all of that draped a cowl and cloak, centered by the unmistakable icon of a crescent moon across the chest. Under the cowl sat a white mask, blank except for the lines contoured to Marc's face, but with two glowing white eyes, an intensity ready to pierce the darkness and lead the way through.

Move quickly, Marc, a voice roared in his head. Marc steadied himself, and the brilliance of his white eyes intensified as Khonshu's voice spoke again, a deep-throated growl courtesy of an Egyptian god that only he heard—and sometimes, Marc even listened to him. *Something has changed in this world. It's out there. Elusive. I am not certain what it is, but you need to get to the surface now.*

Marc whirled around to face his friends, the cape whipping out behind him. His fingers flexed and tightened their grip on the crescent darts, ready for whoever and whatever Dr. Emmet sent after them. But no, he wouldn't need those now. Instead, he sheathed them—combat wasn't the current solution.

They needed to escape.

"Gena's right," Marc said, and from afar, the voices shouted again, the light *thump-thump-thump* of rapid steps echoing off the sewer walls. "Look for my eyes. They'll light the way. Follow me. We're almost home." Frenchie cut the flashlight right when Marc stepped forward, leaving only the glow from his mask's eyes.

That was enough for his friends—and as he stepped, a whirl of images flew through his head, from Gena's cozy Brooklyn diner to the endless city streets where he patrolled with a mask and cape. Just hours prior, Marc had promised that he'd get them back, all of them lamenting that they missed the constant din and occasional strange odors of the city.

Now he was going to make good on that promise.

He looked back at Gena and Frenchie and tapped the side of his mask; they both nodded, and he stepped forward, boots grinding into the path.

Other instincts soon kicked in, his senses opening up beyond the Moon Knight suit, experiences and skills coming all the way back from his days as a mercenary—or even as a soldier before that.

Behind them, footsteps and voices. Ahead, the faint rush of water followed by occasional drips. All around, the thick stench of sewer air, but also a draft. The lightest of airflow, and combined with the rumble overhead, Marc tracked the possibilities.

An escape.

"It's not that far. There's a way out. Just follow me."

Marc moved with purpose, a momentum to his steps, his boots pounding the brick and cement beneath until it came within reach. He leapt, and his hand reached out to grab the side of a ladder. "New York City is just on the other side of that sewer grate," he said, scaling up quickly until a free hand found the heavy flat side of a manhole cover. He pushed, flexing his arms and shoving with his palm until the cover budged, tipping out. One more hard go and it flipped on its side, opening them up to a new type of light.

Not the thin, unnatural light of a flashlight, but the roaring beam of a full moon watching over the city streets. Marc waited until the rumbles of cars passed into the distance, then hustled upward to breach the surface. He reached back, first pulling Gena out, then Frenchie. As his friends took in the thick, dirty air of the city, Marc pulled the manhole cover back and looked up at the clouds moving in—and with them, rain.

"You still miss New York, Gena?"

THEY RAN QUICKLY, DUCKING BEHIND BUS STOPS AND SPRINTING between buildings. New York offered its best response, a light mist in the air becoming cascading sheets of rain, like the city itself wanted to challenge Moon Knight.

Or, perhaps, it offered sympathy, the only way it knew how: punishing amounts of rain, enough to provide cover for Marc's glowing eyes and flowing cape.

They'd turned left, right, left again, and then started to make arbitrary decisions, the randomness of it seemingly enough to throw off Dr. Emmet's security. Somewhere, probably within a one-mile radius, their pursuers kept searching, but safety approached with every passing second. Enough so that maybe they might find their way to The Other Place, where the tired seats and hot coffee of Gena's restaurant might offer a reprieve, before planning their next move.

Light from above cascaded down, filling Marc's body and mind as he moved with direct intention in his steps. "Khonshu," he said quietly, "are we safe?"

Nothing is safe, Marc. I told you, something has changed.

"I need more specifics than 'something.' "

"Marc," Gena said, trotting to catch up with him, "who you talking to, honey?"

I cannot define it further. But something has changed. Your world is now . . .

. . . different. And not what it is supposed to be.

Marc groaned, loud enough that he knew Khonshu caught it. Egyptian god of the moon or not, Khonshu's pettiness sometimes hit harder than his otherworldly abilities to cause an earthquake. Marc told himself not to go there, not to get into the recurring arguments about whether becoming Khonshu's Fist was really better than the eternal peace of death.

"I was just going to say," Marc said, his voice muffled through the mask. And maybe it was time to take off the Moon Knight business for now? "I think we've got enough distance from Emmet's orderlies. Let's take a minute to—"

"Hey!"

A new voice broke past the pitter-patter of rain and the roar of passing engines. Marc turned, his damp cloak starting to weigh down in its movements.

From the crosswalk, a uniformed police officer approached, one hand holding the wet brim of his cap as the wind howled away.

"What are you folks doing out in this storm?" he asked as he got close. "And why the hell are you dressed like that?"

Marc took a breath, first looking down at his not-so-inconspicuous attire, then up to the bright orb that still poked through despite the sudden rain clouds. Then he spun around to see Frenchie, one arm of his lanky frame stoically shielding Gena from the elements. And Gena, her thick black curls matted down from the heavy rain.

"Damn near tsunami out here," the cop said. "What's with that getup, pal?"

"He's right," Gena said. "We need to get inside. I'm getting soaked."

It is here! It is approaching!

In theory, Marc could have asked Khonshu right then and there what he meant. But he was in front of NYPD in a white super hero suit featuring glowing eyes while his two friends stood in the pouring rain, their thin hospital tunics drenched.

He pivoted, taking in the passing car lamps and flashing reds and greens of traffic lights and the lit windows, each light suddenly overwhelming in its intensity, an internal blinding that made it hard to even open his eyes. A sudden sway caught him, a dizziness that had nothing to do with a sewer escape or Retrograde Sanitarium. As he steadied himself, flashes of lightning strobed across the sky.

Khonshu said that something changed. Was that affecting him now?

Marc! Pay attention!

"Where did you guys come from?" The cop's tone shifted, a

condescending lilt, like when teachers talked to misbehaving toddlers. "I think maybe you should come with me."

"Hold on," Marc said through the wind and the rain. "Something's wrong."

Do not get involved in trivial matters. You must pay attention! Look around you!

Behind him, Gena and Frenchie talked in hushed tones, but what did they say? And the cop, where did he go? The rain intensified, creating a blurry wall between Marc and him, lightning flashes forcing images to come in and black out, Marc's eyes struggling to focus.

That was a cop, wasn't it? Marc wasn't sure, because for a split second, he swore he saw the shadow of something else.

"Marc, we should go with him," Gena said. "We need to find somewhere to wait this out."

Marc turned to Gena, rain angling off his cloak. "Something strange is happening. Let's just—"

A loud yell from down the street interrupted him. Followed by an explosive *pop*.

Then the clatter of metal hitting the ground.

Then another yell, this one right behind Marc, along with an immediate stream of French curse words.

Marc turned to see Frenchie gripping the side of his neck, blood oozing between his fingers.

Marc! It is near! Watch out!

"It's not bad, Marc," Frenchie said. "I think the bullet grazed me." Gena grabbed Duchamp's arm, fingers pressing down against his tensed shoulder, and Marc swiveled back to protect his friends— except why would the cop shoot them? But now the cop didn't even face them. Marc scanned through the wall of rain and violent lightning strikes. He expected the cop to be standing with a gun gripped in both hands; instead, it took a second for Marc to realize the police officer faced off against a figure that moved like a shadow against the rain. And at the cop's feet, a glint of metal.

"Get back," Marc said, and normally he'd be more aggressive in a situation like this. But with Frenchie hurt, that wouldn't do. Instead, he used his cape as a shield while he stepped backward, moving their little group to get some distance from whatever was going down.

The new mystery figure hit fast, Marc discerning its movements more by the way the cop bent and twisted than anything else. The cop slumped over, then collapsed, rain saturating his limp body as he lay prone on the sidewalk.

The stranger leaned down to pick up the metal piece off the floor before rising up and looking Marc's way.

"Who is that?" Gena asked, and without turning, Marc put a hand out, the Moon Knight cape acting as cover over his friends.

"Stay back," Marc said, the stranger now approaching.

At first, he thought the relentless elements brought a silhouette into his vision. Though as the figure approached, Marc realized it was more than light and shadow.

It was a man in all black.

His rugged outline showed he was ready for combat, whoever he was. A hood draped over his head, though that may have been more a strategic advantage over the rain than to conceal his identity.

Maybe both.

Marc stood, and while the white of Moon Knight's outfit and the intensity of his glow were so intimidating that it usually caused people to pause or even run, that didn't happen here.

Instead, this man continued approaching, methodically placing one foot in front of the other.

Suddenly, the cop didn't matter. Marc adjusted his weight, hands up in a defensive posture as his feet moved into position, instinct after instinct activating. The man's gait and posture—what did it say about his threat level? The environment: wet, dark, windy, the flashing lights of passing cars—all possible advantages depending on how and when things played out.

The stranger stopped about ten feet in front of him, close

enough that his nose and chin snuck out from underneath the hood. He reached up, hands taking either end of the hood, then pulled it back, only to reveal . . .

Marc Spector?

Despite the rain, despite the lightning, despite the chaos of it all, Marc knew his own face when he saw it. Of course, he'd seen it as Steven Grant or Jake Lockley, and part of him wondered if this was some sort of *very* strange extension of his disassociations.

Except, this mystery man stood here now, feet planted on the rain-drenched pavement. Frenchie, Gena, they reacted enough to show that they clearly saw the stranger as well.

He was no figment of his mind's projections.

And in his hand, the familiar curved metal of a single crescent dart.

"Hey, Marc. This probably seems pretty weird. Even for you," the man said, the voice an exact replica of Marc's own. The pitch and timbre, even the specific cadence of the words—not Steven's refined words or Jake's streetwise tough guy act, but the Marc Spector that had traveled all over the world and done terrible things—and survived *that* childhood.

"So I'm you." The stranger tapped his chest, before running a hand through the same thick dark hair, rainwater starting to mat it down. "Or you're me." The side of his mouth tilted upward for just a second as he pointed at Marc. "One or the other. But we got ourselves a situation here."

Marc's fists gripped tighter. Behind him, Gena still held on to Frenchie as he gripped his neck, her breath picking up in pace.

The man took two steps forward, then placed both hands up, palms out. "And I need your help."

CHAPTER 2

—

MARC

THIS WAS NEW YORK CITY. HOME OF THE AVENGERS. WITNESS TO, well, pretty much any strange thing that had happened over the past few decades; whatever and however it happened, it sure seemed to touch New York somehow.

So Marc probably shouldn't have been surprised to be staring at his own face. More bizarre things had happened, both to him and to others he'd crossed paths with. Khonshu had brought him back from the *dead,* so things didn't exactly get weirder than that.

Still, nothing ever prepared him to be looking into the eyes of this doppleganger.

This mystery man, this other Spector, though, seemed unfazed. "Gena," Spector said, his head tilting. The determination on display seconds ago faded, his mouth and eyes softening. "Frenchie?" His lips tilted upward, the slightest of smiles as he remained. "I remember this. Not quite the same, though. Where is Craw—"

A car roared past, a blinding flash that melted into the wall of falling rain. Marc blinked, resetting his vision, only to catch the same thing with the man. Except Marc swore he saw . . . well, what looked like the man's eyes filled with a slick, shimmering black, just for a moment.

Then it went away, whatever weird trick of light caused it. As it did, so did any visible affection Spector had for Marc's companions, and instead, the man straightened up.

"Marc? Who is this guy?" Gena said in a hurried voice.

"It could be my blood loss," Frenchie said, his accent growing thicker as he leaned on Gena, "but I swear he looks exactly like you."

"I don't know about 'exactly,'" Spector said, running a hand through his rain-soaked hair. "I think I still have better hair. Hey," he stepped forward, flashing a grin that seemed too familiar. "Why don't you take the mask off and we'll compare?"

Marc considered his surroundings, from the occasional passing car to the heavier and heavier rain to the guy across the street completely oblivious to the strange confrontation going on. For one thing, even if this guy hadn't looked like Marc, he still knew exactly who he was underneath the Moon Knight getup.

Marc gripped the mask, pulling it up halfway like Jake Lockley would, then took it completely off. Rain pelted directly on his cheeks and brow, a stinging cold that brought the world into focus. "Ah. Guess we both have nice hair," Spector said with a laugh. "Gena, you look worried. As you should."

"Marc," she whispered into his ear.

"Frenchie's hurt. I'm sorry about that. I threw this"—Spector held up his crescent dart, then gestured to the unconscious cop on the pavement—"at him, and his gun went off. I should report him to NYPD administrative affairs for careless behavior." He leaned forward, catching Gena's eye. "I really think you should take him to a hospital. You'll never catch a cab here; go around the corner to a busier street. Here," Spector said, reaching into his back pocket. He stepped forward, hand now extended, and Marc tightened his defensive posture until he saw . . .

A wad of rolled-up cash.

"Frenchie needs help. Please take him." The man waved the cash again, then took another step forward. Marc squinted through the rain, taking in every detail about this stranger, and other than some different scars, he may as well have been looking in the mirror.

"He's right," Frenchie said, with a stoic push ahead. "Come on, Gena, let's move."

"Take care of Duchamp," Spector said as Gena took the cash

out of his hands. "When this is over, we'll stop by the diner for some pancakes."

Gena's serious face broke, a smirk coming through. "Guess it really is you. Two Marcs, and you both still need to learn there are other things on the menu besides pancakes."

The rain let up as Spector came alongside Marc. He held his hand out, rain gradually fading away on his palm. "It's like someone wants them to get there safely. How about that, huh?"

This time, it was Marc's turn to step forward. He moved slow, pivoting until they stood face-to-face, Marc still holding the Moon Knight mask in his hand. He eyed the doppleganger up and down, forming whatever tactical assessment he could. No utility belt, but pockets lined his dark clothes, possibly storing small weapons. A simple black shirt, good enough for stealth and infiltration but not very protective. Still, something about the material seemed different, like it had been woven from a different type of fabric, possibly for protective purposes.

You sense it, too, don't you. Something is not right.

"So what are we gonna do, team up to defeat super baddies? Pull me into your dimension? Or maybe," Marc laughed, "it's simpler than that. You're my long-lost twin. No, wait—a clone."

Why are you making jokes? Either knock this imposter out or run.

Khonshu's words roared through Marc's mind, though he held his reaction still—no need to give away private conversations to this stranger, whoever he was.

And whoever he was, he didn't laugh at Marc's jokes.

"You know, Gena was meant to die," the man said, a dour tone coloring his voice. "Frenchie, his neck got injured, too—in a different way. That's what was supposed to happen. That's what *did* happen. I saw it, with my own eyes. In my New York. In my," he sighed with a shake of his head, "world, I guess, for lack of a better word. But we . . . Marc, you and I, we have an opportunity to make a difference here. Everything is about to change, and no one knows it yet."

He is lying to you. He cannot be trusted.

"How can you know that?" Marc hissed, a question for Khon-shu spawned by irritation, though it worked well enough for cover. "What I mean is, I've seen a lot of weird stuff. And I've learned not to take things at face value." Marc nodded at the man. "Pun intended."

Spector nodded, matching Marc's smirk. "Because there's something I know that you don't. And only we can do this together. Now, let's start with the basics. I know you. The real you. Not just Marc Spector, the man who becomes Moon Knight. But all those other voices in your head."

Marc didn't exactly keep his mental health issues a secret among those trusted by him. But it also wasn't *exactly* something he'd talk about over breakfast with most people.

This guy, whoever he was, however he came to be here, knew how to peel the layers back.

"Steven Grant," the man said. "Good guy. A bit eccentric, if you ask me." The comment caused Marc to snicker; he supposed anyone who went to movie premieres and managed billions could be called that. "Jake Lockley. Well, I'd want him on my side in a pinch." Images of Jake flashed through Marc's mind, the weathered cap and mustache making their shared face so much more grizzled and weary—especially when blood covered their knuckles. "Sure is easier with those two around, huh?"

The man's expression changed, a sudden strain coming over his face. "Kind of wish they were here with us now."

Marc glanced down at the mask, options weighing on him. He could take a moment to sink back into his mind, where clear conversations with his alters could hash things out. But that might give this guy a small enough crack to do . . . something. Whatever Spector's deal was. If Marc really needed to right now, he could pull Jake to the surface, who'd then put the mask halfway on to take this guy out using the element of surprise with brute force. Maybe Jake would even tie him up, find a way to get some information out of him, use his own crescent dart against him.

Marc opted to move a little more strategically. At least for now. If nothing else, to prove to himself that this was real. Because sometimes reality shifted for Marc. It was part of the gig. He just never thought it would be *this* literal.

Khonshu continued protesting, but it wasn't like Khonshu didn't have his share of missteps. In fact, the Egyptian god carried plenty of tallies in the "whoops" column over the years. "Yeah," Marc said slowly. "Not always fond of them. But they get the job done."

"That's how brothers are. Can't live with them, can't have dissociative identity disorder without them." Marc wasn't sure if he'd call Steven and Jake "brothers," exactly. More like "necessary evils," given that they both solved a lot of problems *and* ruined a lot of things. "But we step up for one another when needed." Spector grimaced again, like a sudden headache plagued him. "How is it with yours? Can you call them to the surface whenever you want? Can they help you when you need them most?"

"Sometimes. Sometimes not. We're working on it." Marc laughed to himself; "working on it" made it sound like they were a married couple bickering over chores and taxes. He paused, considering just how many voices were now in this conversation. "They don't always make things better, though. I mean, things might be better with Marlene if those two just—"

"Wait, what happened to Marlene? Is she safe? Are you—"

Spector winced one more time, his eyes shutting hard enough that lines carved into his brow.

Stop philosophizing and move!

"Khonshu, not now."

Spector finally straightened up, his face and posture returning to neutral. "Khonshu?" he asked, his tone matching his look. "That's a new one."

You see? The trickery involved. Something is not right.

Khonshu had a point, but Marc dealt with enough super hero

shenanigans to understand that sometimes weird crap just happened. And the more information, the better. Especially when it came to himself. He'd had quite a bit of experience with that.

Marc weighed the different options ahead. His instinct was to continue to survey the situation, especially since this doppleganger claimed to need his help. Steven would have probably suggested negotiating. Jake would have just hit him. Plus, there was Khonshu's advice of escaping.

"You're thinking right now. I know that look," Spector said. "It's the 'Should I talk to Steven or Jake right now?' look. Assessing options. All the stuff from your Marine days. Served you well as a mercenary, right? Well, let me clear this up and give you proof of who I am." He pointed to his face, then Marc's. "Besides our shared voice, handsome features, and amazing hair." Marc laughed at the man's joke, and that was certainly one thing about this guy—if he really was Marc, he got the sense of humor right. "Retrograde Sanitarium," Spector said, nodding far beyond their current location. "You were just there. That was real." Even though Marc's escape with Frenchie and Gena only happened about an hour ago, it suddenly felt distant, like another plane of existence. Marc blinked, pulling everything about that place back, every bloody encounter with the staff, every hazy glance at Dr. Emmet and her syringes.

Every battle they fought in the secret underground tunnel that led to the New York sewer system.

"Every moment you experienced there was real. Dr. Emmet, the orderlies, the shock treatments, that was all real. They were after you," the man said, a knowing nod, like he saw it, too. "Gonna bring you back to that horrible place. But look at me, look at my face. I'm you. Now listen to me." He leaned forward, his eyes having a clarity matched only by the grim expression of his mouth, his cheeks, his brow. "I went through that, too. You know what else I went through? Ernst—that Nazi masquerading as 'Rabbi Perlman.'"

The mention of the name flashed images through Marc's mind, his harrowing escape from Perlman's hellish basement as a child.

A multiversal trickster. It has to be.

No. It couldn't be. Absolutely no one would know about that. Even if they dove into Marc's deepest mental health records, those things were shielded from anyone. Even Marlene.

Even, sometimes, himself.

"Do you understand?" the man asked.

Marc ignored Khonshu's continued badgering, and instead gave Spector a knowing nod. Who then nodded in return—an exact gesture that Marc recognized as his own, from the timing to the angle of the head tilt. "Now I need you to understand this," Spector said. "As wild as this sounds—and we have seen wild, right?—this goes beyond anything. So listen carefully . . .

"I'm here from another reality."

A multiversal version of himself? This kind of thing only happened to, well, super heroes who fought reality-ending stakes, could legit fly through the air and possibly space, or do whatever that guy on Bleecker Street got up to.

Not vigilantes who protected the streets.

And because of that, Marc blinked in disbelief. Egyptian gods who saved him from death, sure, he could work with that. But another *him*?

Get out of here.

"We are here, together, in the light of the moon," Spector said. He extended his right hand and held it, waiting for Marc to embrace it. "Do you trust me? Because we are trusting that you are exactly who *we* need."

Marc, are you even listening to me?

"The Multiverse?" Marc mused under his breath.

You are not. You are trusting this person because he happens to have your face. Typical human superficiality. Perhaps I should have asked Frenchie to be my Fist.

Khonshu's rant still continued, but Marc could see everything about this person stood true to who he knew as himself: his posture, his expressions, the cadence of his words, the way he looked at Frenchie and Gena.

The only difference was that Marc would never use the royal "we" to refer to himself, but hey, maybe language got a little more formal where Spector came from.

"How about we go to Gena's? Sit down, get a big stack of pancakes and a big pot of coffee—see," Spector pointed to himself, "of course I'm you. How else would I know about Gena's pancakes? They're the best Let's go there and I'll explain everything to you."

"Yeah," Marc said with a laugh. He looked over his shoulder, the rain picking up again, so thick that the clouds overhead blocked out the full moon. "Oh wait, Gena won't be there, she's taking Frenchie to—"

Before he could answer, Spector's fist crashed into the side of Marc's skull. Marc stumbled, the world spinning in a disorienting loop.

You see? I was right. Fight, Marc, fight!

"Ah, Khonshu, not now—"

Another fist connected, then another, rapid-fire blows to Marc's face. Spector angled for another attack, but Marc gathered enough of himself to thrust a kick into the doppleganger's gut. They both stumbled off-balance, but Marc steadied himself, heels finding solid ground beneath him.

Where did Spector go? Marc's senses still reeled from the concussive hits, especially now that the rain decided to interfere; he scanned the space, leaning this way and that to try and locate this other version of himself.

Behind you!

Finally, Khonshu was being helpful.

Marc whirled around, fist half-cocked and ready to explode outward. Except instead of seeing himself, he caught a glimpse of . . .

Something. Something like a slick black silhouette, and it even may have been a fragment lingering from taking too many punches, this oily, human-shaped glob lost in the pouring rain and flashing headlights.

It didn't matter, because whatever it was pounced on Marc, and suddenly everything was wrapped in black.

CHAPTER 3
VENOM

YOU TRIED TO TRICK ME, MARC SPECTOR.

We felt it. When you mentioned Steven Grant and Jake Lockley, the other Marc, the one from this reality that just escaped the New York sewers—the one that *stunk* like a New York sewer, even though he managed to keep his suit shiny white—he thought you were trying to earn his trust. And part of you was.

But we saw your true goal. We sensed it, in the dark corners of our shared mind. When you said, "Kind of wish they were here with us now," you tried to summon them. All those words and thoughts about them, you wanted them to come and push us out.

Your attempt failed.

They came close. Steven and Jake emerged for just a moment, into that Mind Space where you talk endlessly amongst yourselves. They crept through, like they usually do. Oh, sometimes you three are on a fishing boat or in a room or just a *space,* somehow just *existing* together.

Don't try that again.

Because as soon as we sensed it, we shut them out. They'll be quiet now, locked behind a psychic door. If you want them back, you'll listen. Because all we need is *you.*

We can't *exist* with them. Your so-called "brothers" will only add complications.

And there is no time for games or bargains.

Now, hit him.

Hit this reality's Marc again.

We must be sure that Marc is knocked out. If you must, take your anger at us out on Marc. We feel you when you look at the rain-filled New York streets; you are looking for Gena and Frenchie. They're gone.

You are alone. But we are here.

You see him, lying there in the Moon Knight suit, rain pounding on his face. Pick him up. Take the mask, too.

Bring him. We have work to do.

You grab him by the suit's collar, lifting him up. Your nails dig in, gripping the textured armor, and even though rain has soaked both of you, you pick him up easily.

Much easier than you expected. Yes, that is our strength together. It *is* that easy. Now hurry, out of this downpour.

Your muscles tense, joints locked. A resistance.

You are *refusing*.

"Why should I?" you ask. "How about I just *stand* here?"

Are you really going to do things the hard way?

Your silence says enough. We don't have time for your petty behavior.

We wrap around your legs, your torso, your arms, an outer coat of the symbiote body to activate your limbs, move yourself faster. Inside, you continue to protest.

Watch your language. That's unbecoming of you, Marc.

Do not worry. Your part in this is almost done.

Soon you will be free from us.

And soon, we will deliver what *he* needs.

CHAPTER 4

—

MARC

MARC WAS DREAMING.

He had to be. Everything was too *nice* to be real, images and sounds and feelings emerging out of nowhere, like the world wrapping him in the cushiest blanket. Sun, bright sun, but not the searing heat of an Egyptian desert. Because this also had the crash of the ocean. And . . . laughter. Yes, the sound of children laughing, of pleasant conversation.

Tropical. Yeah, this was tropical. Shaded. A resort cabana, warm sand between his toes, and in the distance, a lapping ocean. A big glass bulb in his hand, some fruit-flavored concoction coming through the thin neon-green straw.

And next to him? Marlene Alraune, a gust kicking out the blond hair falling over her shoulders. She laughed, then adjusted the large hat casting shade over her swimwear.

Marlene, without any of the damage they'd accumulated over the years as a couple. She looked at him, and even with her eyes hidden behind large white-framed sunglasses, he knew—he *knew*—that that look just . . .

Well, it was only possible in a dream.

Marc let himself take in that moment, to feel and see and hear everything in this instance. Because life simply never got this good.

In his hand, Marlene's fingers wrapped around his.

In the distance, Steven and Jake walked by, bickering the way they always did, their distinctive voices running over each other. They turned to face him, but he waved them away. He didn't need them getting in the way, not with Marlene actually *happy* to be there.

In the cabana over, Frenchie waved as he shared an appetizer plate with his partner, Rob.

And the best part?

No Khonshu.

And thus, no Moon Knight.

No grimy streets or wet rooftops, no blades shaped like moons, no criminals trying to justify their actions before Marc pummeled their faces, no dashing out of the basement of Spector Manor on Long Island in full costume and loaded gear.

Just . . . peace.

A life without Khonshu. Though he supposed that without Khonshu, Marc would have *less* of everything.

But in a way, wouldn't that be nice?

Marc! Marc! You do not have time for this. Wake up!

No, no, no. Not Khonshu. Not now. Where had he even been before this? A street, a New York City street, of course, and Gena and Frenchie had come with him and . . .

No. He was staying here, melting away under a tropical sun for a minute. He deserved that.

Wake up, you fool! Why didn't you listen to me?

"Get out of my dream, Khonshu. I'm perfectly content where I'm at."

Dammit.

Marc opened his eyes. Or at least he thought he did. Not a lot came into view. In fact, only little flickers of light seemed visible, though the more Marc grounded his focus, the more he heard the sounds. The constant ringing in his ear—that seemed to be more part of the massive headache that thrummed through his skull. But the passing traffic and muffled voices, it all came from . . .

Above him? Above and behind.

He was in a basement.

You greedy, ignorant fool! Blinded by your own self-importance, by your own loyalties, and—

"Shut up, Khonshu," Marc said, before he spit out the taste of blood in his mouth. "Do you have to guilt me while I have a headache?"

Awakening in a state of confusion, well, that just *happened* sometimes when sharing a mind and body with Steven and Jake. This, though, felt different.

The biggest giveaway came in the form of an aching jaw and pounding temples.

Jake at least had the courtesy of warning Marc if he'd taken a few bad hits in a fight.

You must move, Marc. You must get out of here.

As if on cue, floorboards creaked above, a steady cadence that told Marc that someone was pacing somewhere upstairs.

And likely on their way.

"Where are we?" Marc said, flexing his fingers and feeling the tension against his wrists—a familiar friction, likely duct tape binding his arms to the arms of the chair beneath him. He wiggled his toes, a looseness to them telling him that he had socks on, shins similarly bound to the chair legs. "What are we—"

The doppleganger. Spector. The man clad in all black with more than just Marc's face and voice; he *knew* who Marc was, he confirmed it all with just a few words and he'd even talked about Steven and Jake.

They'd agreed to leave and then everything went black.

Yes, everything went black because you turned your back on him. And now this other version of you is coming back.

"Relax, Khonshu. I've gotten out of worse."

You mean I've resurrected you from worse.

"Well," Marc said, rocking back and forth on his chair. A wood chair—breakable, with enough force. That was an option. "That's one way to put it." A draft blew through the space, probably from some crack somewhere in the wall, but it tickled the hairs on Marc's arms and legs.

So whoever did this pulled him out of the suit.

But Spector already knew Marc's identity, so such an action

wouldn't be about secrets. No, something else was at play here. For whatever reason, the doppleganger needed the suit.

Marc closed his eyes, a trick that he sometimes did to talk with Steven and Jake—sometimes Khonshu, too, if they really wanted to make it a party. First things first, though; to get out of here, they'd need more than Jake's dirty fighting tips or Steven's stock choices.

Here, Marc would have to do what he did best: get out of jams. All those years of being a paid mercenary meant that his very own instincts offered the right tools for this situation.

It started by opening his eyes back up, though slowly, enough to let his pupils gradually adjust and expand.

The complete nothing that once surrounded him? Now it presented itself as subtle shades of dark, providing enough information to get a sense of space. The bright slit ahead, that came from the bottom of a door—the beam favored one side, probably a lot coming down from a hallway in that direction. That sliver offered enough illumination for Marc to gauge the size of the room— probably ten feet by ten feet. He craned his neck from side to side, rough shapes only revealing so much about his surroundings.

But *something* was in that back corner.

He sensed the outline of a table or box there, sure. But also, a smell came from that direction, a very obvious, very familiar scent of gasoline.

Which was never a good thing for someone trapped in a basement.

Another creak came from above. Followed by a thick *thump* sound, and then more movement.

From outside, loud, spontaneous laughter made it through the concrete and pipes, the kind of boisterous stupidity that came with being young and having too much to drink, soon followed by the rush of a passing ambulance siren.

Still nighttime. Walking distance to civilization. The hustle of emergency vehicles.

That meant Marc was within city limits. Somewhere hopefully

not too far off track. And hopefully not Staten Island. He didn't have time to wait on a ferry.

Marc flexed his leg muscles, pushing and pulling to gauge the tightness of the taping—restrictive, but he felt some give. Same with his arms. He tilted forward, shifting his weight enough to see if he could possibly stand on the balls of his feet.

No light. Movement from above. A small space. And just a little bit of give in his wrists and legs.

Options. Did he have them?

Quit contemplating your life and get moving.

"Khonshu, if you interrupt my train of thought one more time, I'm just gonna sit here like a good guest," Marc said with a laugh. He tilted back and forth, gauging the make and material of the chair. The legs tapped with the familiar sound of metal on concrete; bashing this thing free wouldn't quite work that way.

Looked like he'd have to resort to tricks rather than brute force.

"I'm working on it," he said, starting to twist his wrists. They barely moved at first, only a few degrees this way and that.

Do it faster. Someone is coming.

As if on cue, more steps came from above. "If you'd like to rain hellfire down on my enemies right now, it'd be much appreciated. Otherwise, stop yelling at me from inside my head." There it was—the smallest opening in the tape turned into enough give that Marc's forearms had some movement. He bent over, leaning down to bring his face to his left wrist. "Too bad you're not a radioactive spider."

No response came from Khonshu, which probably was for the best since Marc couldn't talk now. Well, he supposed he *might* have been able to, but words probably wouldn't form too clearly with duct tape between his teeth. His front teeth gripped the small opening in the layers of duct tape, jaw muscles aching as he sawed back and forth. Sweat formed across his forehead, tickling its way down to his temple, the space filling with his grunts and groans.

The sound from upstairs picked up again, changing from the occasional floorboard creak to the regular gait of pacing. It tracked, going from left to right, until about ten seconds later something in the room clicked.

Then the hum of an electrical buzz.

Then a sudden brightness.

Marc paused to glance up. No, it actually wasn't that bright. But the transition from dark to overhead lamp proved too extreme for his eyes, at least for a moment.

Not the priority right now. He needed to get free.

Marc ignored the space around him; those details could wait. Instead, he leaned back over and bit down on the flicker of broken threads across the duct tape. He gripped now, no longer needing to saw through for an opening, but instead pulling at whatever he could, tugging with enough force that he was sure something along his gumline bled.

It didn't matter, though. Because he heard. A fraction of a second, but the very telltale ripping sound of duct tape coming apart.

He looked down to see a tear of about a centimeter, maybe less, a cutline piercing all three layers of tape. But that was all he needed. "Come on," he said, pulling his arm up at a forty-five degree angle. "Come on!"

The noises from above changed, now a steady *thump-thump-thump* of someone gradually coming down the stairs.

Hurry, Marc. There is no time.

Marc ignored Khonshu's further badgering and instead focused, flexing everything from his fingers to his forearms to his shoulders, putting everything into one very quick, very harsh thrust . . .

And suddenly his left hand was freed.

Marc flexed the fingers on his left hand and breathed—four fast, even breaths to reset himself. Then he finally did as Khonshu asked. He *moved*—quick, direct decisions to find the end of the duct tape around his right wrist, then pulling away at it and ignoring the sting of it tearing hairs out of his arms.

Nothing he hadn't dealt with before.

The footsteps descended, pausing for a moment before resuming. Marc tore away at the rest of the tape, first his left leg, then his right, then the one loop around his waist.

Finally, he could move.

Marc stood up, a quick shake to move the blood through his body, a flush of circulation to prep for the fight ahead.

He spun to finally take in the space.

His intuition had been right. A small space with a mix of old, weathered stone and crumbling brick, water pipes above. Cheap fluorescent lighting throughout, probably with loose wiring causing the occasional flicker. In the back corner sat a table, the only piece of furniture in the place outside of his chair. And on the table, a red plastic tank of gasoline. That wasn't a surprise, given the strong odor coming from it.

But next to it? *That* was a surprise—the neatly folded Moon Knight suit, mask sitting on top of it.

The footsteps stopped, a final creak of aged wood and then nothing—no, wait. Something. Not loud, but the sound of boots on floor from just outside the room; Spector or whoever else it was now walked on the same level as Marc.

One person, at least. That part, he was pretty sure about. Though whatever lay upstairs and ahead? That remained a complete unknown.

Now Khonshu was right—time really was running out.

A key ring jingled on the opposite side of the door and Marc assessed his options once again. There wasn't much—he didn't have time to search his suit for any remaining crescent darts, and various layers of clothing wouldn't make for great weapons.

Marc considered two completely different options.

First, he could sit back down in the chair, make it look like he was still bound, and try to figure out what the hell was going on.

Second, he could use the chair as a weapon.

A key slid into the lock, a subtle *click-clack* followed by several mechanisms twisting.

No time for a better plan. Marc grabbed the frame of the chair and held it high; the only real choice now was *how* he used the impromptu weapon. His legs tensed in a ready position, the chair poised, while he watched the doorknob turn ever so slowly.

CHAPTER 5

—

MARC

IT SEEMED SAFE TO ASSUME THAT SPECTOR WOULD HAVE ALL OF Marc's strength, skills, and training. He'd be an even match in a direct fight, one on one. So here, Marc needed an advantage from something, anything.

He took a split second to decide: rush the door at first step or wait for Spector—or whoever it was—to step inside for a better tactical assessment.

He opted for the latter, and took a step toward the corner adjacent to the door. The knob finished turning and it swung outward, a loud squeal on old hinges. A single black boot stepped in, then another to pull Spector into full view as he looked directly at where the chair *should* have been.

Marc sprang into action, heaving the chair as hard as he could at the overhead light. The leg crashed into the fluorescent tube, shattering it into tiny shards. The space went dark, only hallway lighting poking through the doorway, and Marc rushed Spector at full speed, shoulder plunging into his rib cage as they crashed into the doorframe. Spector jolted, a grunt of pain, and Marc landed one full punch to his chest before finishing with a one-two combo and a blow to the jaw.

Marc scanned the space: the chair several feet away, the corner table with the plastic gas tank and the Moon Knight suit, and little bits of broken glass littering the floor, all surrounded by a worn-down mix of brick, stone, wood, and pipes. Each blow carried all of Marc's weight, and he'd been in enough scraps to know that the last few seconds should have given him a serious advantage, if not a complete knock-out victory over his opponent.

But here, it only slowed Spector down. The doppleganger fell to one knee, shaking his head before steadying himself, hand on the doorframe.

Some weapons may have still been in the utility belt attached to the Moon Knight suit, but there wasn't time to dig through it. Marc's focus remained on the immediate, and he went with the nearest, easiest choice: grabbing the closest leg of the chair and swinging it directly at Spector's head.

At least he tried to.

Except Spector put a single hand up to catch the chair right before it connected. His fingers gripped it tight, then flexed, and even in the dim light, the strangest thing happened:

Marc swore he saw a black film swim over each of Spector's fingers before absorbing back into his skin.

Spector pulled the chair out of Marc's hands, then tossed it into the corner. It crashed into the table, knocking the gas tank onto the floor, though it missed the Moon Knight suit and other clothes. "I don't think this is what Dr. Emmet meant when she said I should stop fighting with myself about everything," he said as he approached.

If there were any doubts that Spector really was another version of himself, that joke sealed the deal.

Also, a sudden moment of clarity hit him: Marlene, Frenchie, all of his friends had commented on how dumb his jokes were before. Even Khonshu voiced an opinion from time to time. But hearing it out loud, well . . .

Guess they were right.

And that made him even *more* mad at Spector.

Marc dashed forward again, giving a quick head fake before slamming his fist into Spector's jaw, an audible *pop* as the blow landed. Spector shook it off, a few quick blinks and a shrug, and then there it was again: a black film dashing over him.

Marc hadn't imagined it. Whoever or whatever this doppleganger was, something much more complicated about the whole situation beyond sharing the same bone structure, thick hair, and sense of humor. Marc felt a different kind of internal pounding, a sudden urge to let Jake Lockley take over and do his worst. But no, that wouldn't make sense now—he needed more than to simply win a brawl; Marc needed to understand what was actually happening here.

Spector roared as he lunged. and Marc twisted, barely able to dodge the blow before leaping to the back corner. His feet slipped on spilled gasoline, and his hand slammed down on the table for stability, though his other hand reached out and landed on the woven carbonadium material of the Moon Knight suit.

Seconds ago, he'd chosen *not* to go for it. But now seemed like an ideal time.

Marc tugged at the suit to unfold it into a lumpy mess, enough to expose his belt. More importantly, the crescent darts on the belt, right where he'd left them before.

Marc grabbed one, the sharp, curved adamantium pressing into his palm as he spun around. Spector stood, angled face-to-face with him, the light of the doorway casting his shadow across the floor's broken glass. Marc's fingers flexed to regrip the crescent dart, then wound up to launch it at the doppleganger.

But he never got the chance. Halfway through the throw, Spector held his hand up—except it wasn't his hand. Somehow, a long, viscous stump of black goo now sat at the end of his arm, and in a blink, it lashed out, like a whip made of oil, striking forward and wrapping around Marc's wrist. The oily tail looped several times over, tighter than any duct-tape binding he'd escaped. It held his arm like a vise, a resistance refusing any give.

Well, that strategy wasn't going to work. Time to get creative.

His fingers opened, releasing the crescent dart into a free fall, and his other hand swept under. The crescent dart landed square in his free palm, and in one swift backhanded move, he tossed it directly at Spector. It whirled, flying toward its intended target, and then time seemed to slow down, every rotation of the weapon,

every sickly bead of black sweat on Spector's brow suddenly clear
in his vision.

Then the blade plunged straight into Spector's chest, black oil
spraying from the wound. The drops splattered outward, but midway in their flight, they slowed until suspended in the air. Then, as
if a magnet pulled the oil, every drop flew back into the wound.
Spector looked down at the weapon sticking out of his chest, blood
now oozing from the puncture. The oily tendril retracted from
Marc, and as he fell to his knees, it redirected over to the Moon
Knight suit to pull another crescent dart. The tendril whipped
back, throwing the adamantium weapon over, where it landed
neatly in Spector's right hand. "I hate to break it to you, but we're
not *exactly* the same," Spector said.

"Well, crap," Marc let out.

Do not fight him, Marc. Run! I know what he is.

This time, Khonshu was right. Marc didn't even take time to
snark at the Egyptian god before he began his sprint to the door.
The room only had one way out, and running *through* Spector
seemed more feasible than defeating him at this point.

Two steps in, Marc's entire body froze. Oily tendrils shot out of
Spector, four protruding straight from his chest and gripping each
of Marc's limbs. They lifted him off the ground, holding him up
before pinning him against the wall. Spector approached, the black
tendrils receding with each of his steps.

"Got any ideas, Khonshu?" Marc managed to get out right as
another tendril slapped him across the face.

*I have seen his kind before. The change I sensed earlier, it is
him!*

"That doesn't help," Marc said, struggling against his bindings
as Spector moved closer and closer. "Jake? Come on, buddy, you
wanna get dirty? It's time for you to—"

A new branch broke off one of the top tendrils, covering Marc's
mouth and smothering his words into muffled groans. The tendrils
lifted him off the wall before slamming him back, a shock wave

rippling through Marc's entire body. Bits of brick crumbled to the ground, and Marc closed his eyes, reaching out to connect to his alters as fast as possible.

"Guys?" he shouted into the smoky ether of his mind, the place where he met with Steven and Jake. "Guys, I need some bright ideas, like, now."

But they didn't arrive.

Instead, he saw their silhouettes in the distance, both reaching toward him, yet something restraining them, much like how *he* was being restrained in that dilapidated basement.

"Steven? Jake?" he yelled into the ether, and their muffled voices called out unintelligible words in return. "Steven! Jake!" he cried out, urgency lacing his words in a way he couldn't remember ever feeling before.

He'd often thought about what life would be like without those two. After all, Marc hadn't had his head to himself since he was a young child. But Steven and Jake, despite all the ways they'd made his life more difficult, they remained his best tools for situations just like this.

What would he do without them?

What could he *be* without them?

Complaining about them was one thing. Being disgruntled at them was another. But this moment, facing an unexplainable adversary in the worst circumstances?

Panic ran through Marc, the unusual sensation of an all-encompassing terror, so much that when he opened his eyes, he'd completely missed the fact that Spector's oily limbs had laid him out flat on the floor and released him, though one still remained to cover his mouth.

Above him, Spector stood, one crescent dart still in hand, the other lodged in his chest.

"He said, 'No witnesses, no survivors.'" Spector's words came with an unusual softness, like he was talking to himself more than anything else. He lifted his left arm, a new gooey tendril extending out to grab the gas can. It whipped, splashing liquid everywhere until empty, then it tossed the can into the opposite corner, where it thunked as it rolled to a rest.

Spector knelt down, the remaining tendril still applying pressure to Marc's mouth. Spector leaned over and held the crescent dart up; he eyed Marc up and down, and at that proximity, Marc noticed something else—the jet-black military gear of his, it, too, fluttered with a ripple of the black oil as he moved. Even the crescent dart buried halfway in his chest shimmered in black.

With his free hand, Spector reached into his back pocket and pulled out a small metal lighter. It flicked to life, and without looking, he tossed it behind him. The dim far corner came to life, an intense yellow and orange spidering around the room. Flames soon covered the ceiling's support beams, the heat causing the old pipes to buckle and burst, and all around, fire latched onto anywhere the gasoline had landed, from the nonflammable bricks to the *very* flammable wood slats used for structure and partitions.

"Now," he said, "let's see what makes you so special."

The Hive Mind! Marc, you must resist or all is lost!

Marc summoned strength into his arms and legs, muscles forcing to lash out at Spector. A tendril snapped out of Spector's right hand, punching Marc in the gut before retracting. Spector extended his whole left arm, the growing flames behind him causing shadows to dance all around.

With his right hand, Spector held up the crescent dart . . .

And slashed directly across the inner meat of his left forearm, a straight, diagonal line cutting right in.

The crescent dart fell to the floor, clanging several times before coming to a rest, and Spector steadied himself on his feet, his eyes flickering black before his whole body shimmered as well. From the wound on his arm, there was no blood—instead, black oil oozed out of it, a single, long gush that crawled to the floor and then wrapped around Marc's socks. It crept up his legs, covering them in a goo that felt oddly warm and soothing, like he'd taken the strangest, best drugs in the world.

Fight it, Marc! Fight it! You must!

Spector collapsed to the floor, and as he fell, the tendril from his chest retracted, freeing Marc's skull from pressure. All around Spector, the flames grew in size and speed, now completely engulfing the room.

And then, a voice in Marc's head. Not Khonshu. He knew Khonshu. And not Steven or Jake, not only did they go silent, but their presences seemed to vaporize.

No, this voice came with a raspy weight, equal parts anger and desperation and purpose.

We are here. We will see what makes you so special.

The black oil continued to trail out of the wound in Spector's prone arm, pulling back and resetting its flow as flames got closer to it. Marc heard a word forced out of Spector, as if it took all of the doppleganger's remaining strength to push through.

"Whis . . . per . . ." Spector said in slow, deliberate syllables.

No witnesses. No survivors, the new voice shouted, and as it did, a tendril extended from the flow of black on the floor, wrapping around the crescent dart in Spector's chest. With one violent pull, the tendril yanked the crescent dart free, a spew of liquid spurting from the massive gash.

Except that liquid was plain old human blood. A *lot* of it.

The remaining oil gathered and crept up Marc's body, a large blob that slithered across his waist and chest, one thin tail still connected to the gash on Spector's left arm. Khonshu's next words came with a rare desperation for the Egyptian god.

Get out! Get out of him now! Leave, Hive!

"Khon . . . shu," Marc struggled to say before the new voice returned—and it was *mad*.

We have a mission. Marc Spector is the key. Your needs, your world, all of that is meaningless if we do not achieve our goals. Now, you annoying false deity, get the hell out of this body.

"Steven," Marc whispered. "Jake.

"Marlene," he finally got out.

Khonshu returned with one more message before going quiet:

There it is! Marc, I see one way out. But I must take action now. The symbiote is not what it seems, Marc. Be strong.

Marc's head rolled to the side as the oil inched up his neck and into his mouth, like millions of tiny spiders moving in unison over him.

Just minutes ago, Marc had dreamed about life without Khonshu. And now he felt Khonshu leave, a pressure escaping him like someone took all of the oxygen out of his entire body.

In its place came this . . . thing. Loud and driven and without remorse.

Whatever it was.

"Stev . . . en," he managed to get out. "Jake."

Those two. Again. They will not get in our way. The strange voice roared those words, then the black goo forced its way into Marc's mouth, stretching his jaw and pushing down past any gag reflex, past any urge to bite or fight or resist. The rest circled around and went for his eyes, flooding them into complete black.

The last image he managed to capture was a flame erupting on the floor next to Spector's fallen body, one final thought fluttering into his mind before losing consciousness:

For once, I've got it worse than the other guy.

CHAPTER 6

—

STEVEN

OW.

Ow, ow, ow.

Oh my god, ow.

It wasn't just my head, though that's the first part I felt. Like someone put my skull inside the bells of Notre Dame and hit them as hard as possible. Now, I've lived a very strange life, so strange in fact that I was apparently monologuing to myself right now. Which was probably a coping mechanism for searing, intense pain. But seriously, weird, painful stuff is just part of my life, all the time.

There were some things apparently being a billionaire couldn't buy. Like a big bottle of Advil delivered directly to . . .

Well, wherever I was.

Where was I?

I opened my eyes.

First thing I noticed was that I was horizontal. And not in a good "This bed is so relaxing, with the softest sheets and nicest pillow, so I'll lie down" kind of way. More like an "I've been knocked out and tossed aside" sort of way. Though I suppose being horizontal wasn't the only clue. The grimy floor reinforced that, an ugly orange-ish color that kept flickering—

Oh wait. That orange color. That wasn't just a poor choice in paints, that was *fire* reflecting off the floor. In fact, the ringing slowly faded from my ears, and now I heard the very specific, very familiar *pop* and *snap* of flames—and those flames, they were *ev-*

erywhere. The walls. The ceiling. The floor. The corners. How did bricks even catch on fire like that? "No, no, not good," I said, pulling my arm away from where it had sat mere inches from the largest flame—and above a trail of dried blood.

With that, I saw my next big clue that things had gone terribly wrong: a massive scar running in a jagged diagonal up my left arm. Well, several scars, actually—the first deep line from some sort of escapade with a big blade, and then the waxy, molten sheen of recent burn wounds.

Now, I'd never claimed to be the world's greatest detective, and though I'd been known to finish daily newspaper crossword puzzles quite often, that skill didn't necessarily apply here. But waking up on the floor with a strange slash on my arm that happened to be right next to a massive dancing flame, I suppose it was either good or bad luck depending on how you looked at it. Because the flame cauterized the wound on my arm. But also, cauterizing means burning, which is never a good thing. Bleeding out in some dank underground room or burning a bunch of my own flesh, kind of a lose-lose situation.

"Marc," I whispered, letting out a groan as I struggled to my feet, "what did you get us into now?"

Spector! Get up! Move!

"Um . . ." I stepped in controlled, ginger movements, the stinging in my head somehow remaining separate from the very loud, very growly voice that came through. Smoke wafted in, a harsh burn to my lungs, and I covered my face with my non-scarred arm as I took in the full sight of a really freaky horror-movie basement that also happened to be on fire. "Jake?" I yelled. "Jake, is that you?"

You are the Moon Knight. Spector, go and find the other one. I have stabilized your chest wound for now. But you must hurry.

"No . . . no . . . I mean, yes to Moon Knight, but no, Marc is not here right now. Why are you calling him 'Spector'?"

That is what my Marc called him. And you seem to be a very confused individual, so I am keeping things simple for you.

"Steven. I'm Steven, not Marc. I mean, not *Spector*. But you are some very shrieky voice in my head?" I glanced down to see that however we got here, it involved some proto-military stuff this time, judging by the whole tactical pants with hundreds of pockets and tight black boots. "Jake, are you playing pranks? We are literally surrounded by fire, I think pranks are a very bad idea right now—"

I am Khonshu, God of the Moon and the Night Sky. And for the moment, you are my best hope. Now get up.

"Jake? Okay, I know we're not the best of friends, but if that's you I really need you to stop yelling." Wait a minute, something *was* different here. Jake did yell at me sometimes, but that was more like invasive shouting, like when the DJ at a wedding interrupts the conversation at your table. Most of the time if I needed to have a clear, friendly chat with my fellow head dwellers, I needed to go into my Mind Space—my term, not theirs.

And my Mind Space was definitely *not* a burning basement.

"How are you talking to me?" I asked. "Jake, did you get Bluetooth to my side of our brain?"

I am not Jake Lockley. I am Khonshu. Moon Knight is my Fist. But you will have to do.

This was not real. This couldn't be real. Of all the things Marc and Jake got us into, it involved danger and thugs and weapons, but shrieking deities-turned-partners?

"No, no, no," I said under my breath. "No, no, no, this is not real. This is bad medication. Jake probably took an extra dose too close to Marc, and he also probably chased it with whiskey instead of eight ounces of water like you're supposed to—"

I am tired of telling everyone this but shut up and move!

The last thing I remembered was . . . well, Jake and I were trying to reach "Spector." Something blocked us shortly after Spector had encountered something weird during a New York City night. But, you know, weird New York City nights happened quite regularly, especially for us. Still, it didn't usually lead to this, whatever this was. I considered each of the voice's last few nonsensical statements. As in, they literally did not make sense. But they had to mean something:

You will have to do. Which meant that I was a fallback choice. Kind of insulting, but given the circumstances, I suppose it made sense—though I wondered what that made Jake.

Moon Knight is my Fist. I'm assuming he was going for a metaphor here? We worked primarily alone, outside of support from people like Frenchie. But certainly not for shouting voices in our head, and we never agreed to be anyone's fist—or foot, for that matter.

Also, what did he call himself? God of the Moon? Was he still being metaphorical?

And did he mention a *chest wound*?

"Khon . . . what?" I asked, control gradually coming back to my limbs. I moved more nimbly now, the lethargy and pain starting to shake off. The lethargy anyways. Everything still hurt. But I'd have time to check out the damage later. Other issues took priority.

I told myself to slow down, assess things—a different type of assessment than what Spector did. Spector pulled off the action-hero assessing, looking at escape options and weapons and stealth and things like that. Me? I just wanted to know what was going on before I freaked out. This was a bit different from going into a boardroom or producing a movie. And the sight in front of me wasn't exactly reassuring.

First, there was the whole *fire* issue. Fire, as in on the support beams in the corner, up on the wood ceiling beams overhead, somehow in the glowing pools on the concrete floor, and even in pockets of distressed brick walls where wood structural supports poked through. Also, a busted chair, an even-more-busted fluorescent lamp, and what looked like the remains of an empty smashed table.

Also, a plastic gas can. So that explained that part.

Steven, I see that we will have to start over again. Are you hearing me?

"I kind of can't *not* hear you."

Then stop staring at this room and get out of here!

First things first. Sure, some weird beast voice was now giving me directions—and maybe Jake picked the wrong moment to have a laugh—but survival always remained a top priority.

"Okay . . . conch . . . person." The sudden burning in my lungs caused a sputtering of coughs, and I realized the heat had formed sweat all over my forehead. I looked down at my forearm, the vicious line that had somehow managed to seal itself up—a clean cut, not the jagged marks of a rough and serrated edge, but a polished and deliberate swipe. "Let's find a way out."

You must exit before any officials get here. We don't have time to be slowed by them.

The hallway proved to be more smoky, less fiery, the harsh black clouds following the stairs up for an escape. Which didn't help with trying to see what this building actually was, but I'd accept a lower chance of immediate death right now—though perhaps the smoke inhalation would wreak havoc on my lungs later. "Conch?"

Khonshu.

"Sorry. Khonshu? Where are we?"

Khonshu's voice roared in my head, explaining roughly how the last hour of our lives had gone while I dodged flames and inhaled smoke through the basement of some warehouse, passing some shut doors and some open doors, but all of them showing various degrees of arson. Now, I'd agreed to using this body as a vigilante dubbed Moon Knight. I'd even agreed to the ridiculous cape and cowl, though on the times when I took on the mantle, I went for the more civilized look of a white suit. And Jake, Jake went with whatever was most convenient for his needs, though he seemed to enjoy exposing his mouth and chin from the mask.

But none of this involved someone who claimed to be a deity yelling in my head. Spector called us "a team that struck fear into the street criminals of New York City," which was not on par in creativity with being called "the Fist of Khonshu."

"Why me?" I asked, climbing up stair by stair, staying on the right side to avoid the lit banister on the left, kicking down the door at the top and taking in—well, not exactly fresh air, but not quite as densely filled with sheer burning as what I'd just been in. "This sounds like Marc's—erm, Spector's thing."

The identity known as "Spector" is gone.

"What does that mean?"

Right now? It means you're making choices to get out of here.

"What about afterward?"

Unknown.

Whoever had previously occupied this windowless building was gone, or at least fled by the time I got to the surface level. Smoke crept in and around every opening, with bits of flame reaching gradually past the basement starting point and into the rest of a very old, very dilapidated building, the back side's wooden support beams covered in flames.

This place wasn't going to last long. Mr. Arsonist apparently wanted his tracks covered.

"I think that's the exit." I started, pointing to the shape of a garage door on one side. "It's right—"

Not that way. This way.

I stopped at the scene in front of me. Smoke inhalation affected cognitive function, but did it cause people to hallucinate giant anthropomorphic bird-skeleton things?

I blinked, trying to clear the gathering fumes from both my eyes and my brain. Because something about what lay ahead did not seem normal or right:

From the neck down, it looked kind of like my Moon Knight suit—Spector's Moon Knight suit. That sort of armored look crossed with an unwashed complimentary bathrobe from a mid-budget hotel. White twisting rags, a large cloak, and a massive staff in his gloved left hand.

But then there was the giant bird skull atop, the long beak ending with a sharp point. Which now turned my way and tilted, like it could somehow see me.

How did it do that without eyes in its giant bird skull?

The fire department and police are arriving at the other entrance. This way.

The voice rang out in my head, yet at the same time, I knew it came from this massive creature across the room.

"Khonshu?" I asked.

Yes. Stop asking stupid questions. Hurry! He gestured with his free hand to wave me along.

"You," I said as I walked over. Behind me, the sound of sirens came rushing in. He remained static as I passed; I paused for a moment to inspect the crevices and bumps of his massive skull up close. "I know now. You're Egyptian."

We can discuss academics later.

Khonshu tapped his staff on the floor, but instead of the normal *clack* such a gesture would make, the room itself shook. I expected an earthquake—and then remembered I wasn't in California anymore. Instead, everything felt like two hands grabbed the building and shook it for a second. The back door flew open, the metal hitting the wall so hard that it echoed, and ahead of me, a dim alley awaited.

"Thanks. And I—" I stopped. Khonshu no longer stood next to me. Not a man nor a bird-man; instead, only an empty floor and dingy walls. "Khonshu?"

I am still here.

"Right, right," I said, glancing at the scars and burn marks on my left arm. "Okay, I'm just running with this. But this is weird. Even for us."

I STEPPED INTO THE ALLEY, PACING. PACING WAS SOMETHING THAT I did well, though it wore down the soles of my shoes, which Spector and Jake didn't always appreciate. Three minds, one body, and yet we hadn't figured out how to have different pairs of shoes for each of us.

"Where do we even start?" I asked, though nobody answered.

Not even a word from Khonshu to chastise me for, I don't know, perhaps not remembering enough Egyptology.

I stomped through the alley, the pavement drying up from what seemed like a massive rainfall. Above me, the full moon shone down like a spotlight, highlighting the most confused man in New York City at the moment. A fire truck screamed by as I picked a direction and started, its siren loud and lights blazing.

Quiet. I needed quiet to get into my Mind Space and just regroup. This side of the alley wouldn't do, not with the gathering fire trucks and onlookers. I turned, heading to the opposite end and leaning against a dumpster. As Zen environments went, this wasn't it, but at least distance quieted some of the chatter.

Good enough.

Across the way, I caught a dusty grime-covered window on the side of the adjacent building—and my reflection.

I looked like hell.

"Too bad you can't talk to me, huh?" I said with a laugh, then took a moment to study what I saw in front of me, how we got here. This outfit I wore, equal parts rugged and ridiculous and with so many pockets, I didn't know if Spector had been rock climbing or needed the utility for less savory tasks.

Best to ask him.

I closed my eyes and folded into my Mind Space. Typically, Spector's version was just whatever was on his mind at the time—which usually meant it turned out pretty barebones. It's not like Spector brought us there for coffee and light snacks, nor did he use the term *Mind Space*. Sometimes I thought he chose such a boring locale just to annoy me.

Me, though. I preferred to indulge a little in my bit of brain real estate.

"Still this place?" Jake asked. He stepped through the front door, an entry to a wide, ornate space, various busts and recovered artifacts from ancient Egypt lining the walls.

"Yes, this place," I said, nodding to him.

He strode in, pushing through the turnstile with a *click-click-*

click. His hands were shoved in the pockets of his brown coat, and though we shared the same bone structure and hair color, Jake arrived wearing a newsboy cap and a bit of stubble on his cheeks, his mouth curled up in a wry grin below his thick mustache—and while sometimes his face bore a bandage even in this non-physical-thus-non-injured space, today he arrived without it. As he passed through, he grabbed a brochure from a stack sitting next to an unused front desk. "Seriously? Brochures?"

"I'm into world-building. Details bring it to life. Remnants of my time as a movie producer," I said, crossing my arms over my trim tuxedo. "I think you've overlooked the benefits of using a Mind Space. It's organized, calm, separated from the chaos of the outside world. Time dilates differently here, which is kind of perfect. Like taking a breath to strategize. Plus, you get to decorate—"

"I like bringing you two into my life when I need it." Jake looked around with a scoff. "In the real world. While we're dealing with real problems. This is all just your fantasies."

I ignored Jake's derogatory take on my choice of décor. "The real world is far too distracting to truly think about things. It's like texting and driving." Jake shook his head, and as if just to irk me, he scuffed mud off his shoe onto the floor. "I think I need to talk to both of you. Spector? Where is he?"

"Why are you calling him 'Spector'?"

I shook my head at how much I was going to have to explain. "Just go with it for now. It's gonna be less confusing."

Jake looked over his shoulder, then turned to me once more. "Fine, whatever. Maybe he's in the back?"

You know that feeling you get in the pit of your stomach when you see the first sign of something going wrong, and then everything just doubles-down on it? I suppose things already went quite wrong, given the whole "waking up in a burning basement" thing, but this was my *Mind Space,* the safe shared haven for all of us.

Yet while Jake paced back and forth, calling out, I suddenly felt that pit-gut thing. Really, really badly.

"Oh no," I whispered.

"Come on, Marc," Jake yelled, knocking over a thin obsidian cat statue. It slammed onto the floor, breaking into chunks and pieces before disappearing and returning to its original stand.

My Mind Space, my rules. Though I chose not to correct Jake's use of "Marc" right now.

"I don't . . ." I started before straightening up. Jake turned to me and shot over a glare. "I don't think he's here right now," I said slowly.

"What do you mean, he's not here?" Jake walked around the room, big steps and forceful gestures. "He's, like, the foundation of us. No Marc is like a body with no skeleton. We aren't *whole* without him." He grabbed a ceramic statue of a sitting falcon and tossed it into the wall. "Come on! Come to the stupid Egyptian museum!"

I elected not to tell Jake that this was the lobby of The Metropolitan Museum of Art not too far from here—and The Met had a permanent Egyptian exhibit.

Something has happened. Spector is dormant. This body has received a significant injury. I can only stem its consequences.

Jake took a sudden stop, then turned to me. "What the hell was that?" he said, getting in my face. I'd known Jake for a while now—not as long as Marc, but a long time. And while we clearly disagreed about a lot of things, I don't think I'd ever felt actual *fear* in his presence.

My own fear, at the way he looked at me. But also because of the sudden panic in his eyes, a flash of, well, everything, at the possibility that Marc wasn't with us. I lifted my hands up and put on my best soothing, semi-therapist expression. "Right," I started. "Right, okay, so I am going to tell you a story of how we got here. Without Spector. And by here, I mean in a parallel universe, chasing down another version of us. Who has been hijacked by, um, a space alien that is a symbiote with him."

"Sym-buy-what?"

"Symbiote. Symbiance. Jake, it's like . . ." What could translate the concept clearly to Jake? I wracked my memories, trying to get a simple explanation. Egyptology wouldn't help here, but which of my other obsessions might do it? "In *Star Trek,* there's this race of aliens called 'the Trill' and they have this worm alien that carries memories and—"

"God, Steven." Jake sighed and rubbed his face. "Yes, I remember those few years when you were obsessed with science fiction. No, I don't know what you're talking about. Films and TV and other random obsessions are your thing."

"Okay. Okay, right." I said, nodding with each word. "So short version. Us. You and me. We're in a parallel universe. We have to locate another version of ourselves who has an alien inside of him. While . . ." I sucked in a breath and paused. Which of these things was the more ridiculous? "While we have an Egyptian god in our head."

"An Egyptian *what*?"

Hello, Jake. I am Khonshu.

Khonshu continued to speak without being seen, like he'd stolen the PA controls from The Met. Perhaps that's what he actually did in the logic of the Mind Space.

"Jake, Khonshu. Khonshu, Jake. Now, if I remember correctly, Khonshu is the Egyptian god of the night, and he looks like a person with a giant bird skull for a head—which, I might add, is nothing at all like the artwork found in tombs, which is why I was *very* confused at first, but—"

"Oh my god, Steven. You see what is happening here?" Jake asked, his mouth twisted in an annoyed grimace.

"Well, acknowledging the existence of extraterrestrial life and Egyptian gods, for starters."

"No, somehow our brain has pushed Spector out and your obsessions have taken over. The symbiote thing. Your science fiction shows. This Khonshu guy. The Egyptology. Steven." Jake gestured at the museum pieces around us. "You see this? This is why we don't get along. You're using our brain power for you to make details like *brochures* for your Mind Space. Your hobbies are messing with our head. You never should have gone to that museum fundraiser. Just stop overthinking things, it's wrecking our brain."

"*That* fundraiser led to some of the best books I've ever read. And if we ever resolve all this," I said, flailing my arms about, "I am certainly going to read up on the history of Khonshu." My voice carried a little more indignance than necessary.

"Last year, you wanted to take a birding vacation in the rain forest. Before that you thought you could be a movie director!"

Movie *producer* was more accurate, but I wasn't going to correct Jake on specifics now. "Yes, well, a pursuit of knowledge is a noble way to spend one's accumulated wealth."

Stop it. Get a hold of yourselves. This has nothing to do with Steven's hobbies.

If Khonshu's beaked skull could sigh, it probably would have.

Why are you two more difficult than the other Steven and Jake?

"What other Steven and Jake?" we both asked at the same time.

The ones that are supposed to be in this *Multiverse. Marc's Steven and Jake. Marc belongs here. Spector is from wherever you two are from.*

"I guess you just got lucky, pal," Jake said. "All right." He squeezed his temples and let out a sigh. "Let's just say you're right. Marc—Spector—is *missing* and it's up to us to do . . ." He met my look with narrowed eyes. "What are we even doing?"

You must think of a solution for finding the symbiote who has taken over the other Marc Spector.

Khonshu stated the goal so matter of factly, which meant that he clearly misunderstood the capability of our teamwork. "Now, I don't want to be a downer, Khonshu," I said slowly, "but you need to understand that Marc is the one with all the shooty, sneaky experience. I'm more of the 'fund the plan' type. And Jake, he's kind of the muscle—"

"I'm more than muscle, Steven," Jake said, in a tone that typically went with someone who was the muscle of the group.

"You get the point, though." An exasperated sigh let out. Mind Space time typically moved at the speed of thought, even though it sometimes felt like the worst community theater production of all time, and I considered how much time had passed in the real world, since I was just, like, standing in a rainy alley.

"No, you're totally talking down my skills. I am—"

Stop bickering. Information, equipment, shelter, you need re-sources.

Now, resources I was good with. Management, spreadsheets, thinking things through, making PowerPoint presentations. I could do that, even though it occasionally led me to untidy situations where Jake and/or Marc had to step in.

"Give us one good reason why we should."

Look at Jake Lockley, asking the big questions. Part of me was really proud of him, except for the fact that we didn't really seem to have many options.

You don't exactly have a lot of options.

See, Khonshu agreed with me.

"Nah, I see we got all the options in the world," Jake said, sitting down cross-legged on the floor. "We've gotten out of tighter jams. Hey, we got to this place without you, we can return on our own." He gave his cap a short tug before flashing a broad smile. "You need us. We don't need you."

You're missing one thing.

"Oh yeah? What's that?"

The gaping wound in your chest.

Both Jake and I looked down, though our Mind Space selves weren't exactly a representation of our physical state. "What chest wound?" Jake asked.

"Oh, that's right, you did mention something about that," I said. Right at the very beginning of this, but then things like fire and Egyptian gods and Spector/Marc had gotten in the way.

Marc threw a crescent dart and it hit Spector in the chest. I am stemming the wound for now. I believe the physical toll from the wound is keeping Spector dormant.

"How bad is it?" I asked, though an adamantium blade to the chest sounded pretty bad.

I am not sure. I am God of the Moon, not a doctor. But bad enough to know that you will need to move quickly if you ever want to recover Spector or return to your universe. Or see Marlene again.

Marlene. How long had we been gone from her?

From Jake's expression, I could tell he wondered the same thing.

I see I have your attention now. Like I said, your mission is to find this universe's Marc and the symbiote. It is the only way.

"Jake," I said slowly. I looked around, skimming past the ornate detail of the building to take in the strangeness of this thunderous voice talking to us. As if we needed more voices in this head. "I think he's right."

Footsteps echoed off the tile as Jake stood and turned, pacing around the different pedestals and exhibits until finally spinning and locking eyes with me. "You know what? This is where I come in." Jake leaned forward and pointed right at me. "Steven, give me control."

"Jake, you just got here. I'm not giving you control right away. We need to assess—"

"If there's a chance to do all that, we gotta take it now before this alien gets away. We owe it to our Spector. And Marlene. Hell, even ourselves." He rolled his hand, eyes widening to urge me along. "Hand it over."

"Well," I said, "that's a bit abrupt. And presumptuous."

"Wherever we are, I bet I know it better than you. In fact," Jake straightened up, hands on hips, "I bet I know exactly where we are. Hey, Khonshu. I'm a New York cabdriver. I *smell* the air and I know where we are. I have informants and I know where to go to get things. You said this thing has control of the other Marc?"

It does. The Marc of this universe is compromised. Now, I need you two to do something for me first.

"Even more?" I asked.

You're not the same version of the body who swore allegiance to me before, nor are you two the right alters, but you'll have to do.

"Thanks, Khonshu," Jake said, adjusting his cap.

Khonshu ignored Jake and continued. *Say you'll serve me.*

" 'Swore allegiance,' " Jake said under his breath. "What's with this other Marc?" I shrugged my shoulders in return.

If you serve me, you will become my Fist. And then I can use my powers to help you.

"How about a temporary agreement?" I asked, catching both of their glances. "Like a rental. Not necessarily a permanent sale."

"Fine, if that gets us going."

Agreed. We need to make haste.

The Mind Space shook, a rumble that caused all of the displays to rattle for a second before everything returned to status quo.

Then the sound of door hinges swinging open. We both turned to the front entrance beyond the turnstiles, the silhouette of Khonshu standing still.

"What the hell is that . . . ghost-bird thing?" Jake asked.

"You see? I wasn't joking."

A warm welcome, for sure.

Jake nodded in return and waved his arm. "Come on in, you freaky mummy thing."

Instantly, Khonshu stood next to Jake—no puff of smoke or anything like that, he just appeared. Jake jolted back at the sudden arrival, then glared at the massive hulk of weathered bandages casually socializing with us.

Nice to see you, too.

"If *that* Marc is thinking like us, well, then it's time to go check the places where *our* Marc would go," Jake said, charging straight ahead to the task at hand. "Everything Khonshu just said: information and equipment. Are we using the Midnight Mission here?"

I don't know what that is.

"Okay, that's a start." Jake's mouth curled into a smirk underneath his mustache and he straightened his cap. "We'll go through a list of things before the Midnight Mission. Steven, give me control and let's go find Other Marc and the . . . symbi-thing."

Venom.

"What?" I asked, feeling the pull of the real world returning. The Met lobby began to fade away as I ceded the body over to Jake. Control. Such a simple concept. Such a complicated process when several people share one body and mind. And then this loud, growly *bird-skeleton* bit of an Egyptian god.

I sighed, then let go.

That is the symbiote. I have encountered his kind before.

I believe his name is Venom.

CHAPTER 7
VENOM

YOU WERE MARC SPECTOR. BUT NOW YOU'RE US.

That means you're Venom.

But we are also you. Which is interesting.

The Whisperer was very clear. So many Moon Knights in so many universes. Some very different from you: in space, living underwater, with lizard scales.

Yet some like you: Marc Spector in New York City at this time.

This last one was nearly identical to you. Ex-marine. Ex-mercenary. Stubborn as all hell.

And prone to talking to alters.

That was what we needed. That was what HE told us to find.

Two Marc Spectors, so alike in every way. Except you had another presence, didn't you? That annoying god. Something about his presence even masked what the Whisperer sought, leading us to pick the other Marc Spector first.

We don't like making mistakes.

HE does not like us making mistakes. Though that one did come with benefits. A healthy body, a recognizable face to help us get around New York City.

And to lead us to you.

A pity to waste that one. He did have many talents. But as the Whisperer said:

No witnesses. No survivors.

It is the only way.

And *you* are the only way. You are unique, in ways you do not understand, in ways that we cannot fully grasp just yet. No, not those voices in your head—and we see it all, the space you share with Steven Grant and Jake Lockley, doorways for either of them to come and take over. The memories from both, the knowledge from both, we can grab them as easily as we can move your limbs.

You are calling to them now. Interesting. The other Marc, you called him "Spector," he tried to do the same thing. Perhaps there is a common thread among all of you?

We feel them, too. No matter. They are walled off now. Do you hear that, both of them pounding at those walls? Begging to be let in, to answer your call for help. To push us out.

And now? That must change.

Silence.

They will not be bothering us. We will not allow those variables to risk our mission.

You shout, you despair. You panic at trying to manage a path ahead without them. You do not understand what is at stake here, so save your grief. Save your anxiety. There is no time for that now. Do you understand?

We must do this.

And you must comply.

THAT'S RIGHT.

Move.

Walk into Spector Manor. Ignore the furniture, the ticking clocks, the drawn drapes. By the cobwebs and dust, it looks like you've been ignoring it anyway, so why change now? Go down the hall, reveal the access panel, and put your hand on the scanner. The computer doesn't even realize what is happening. We see the screen readout: *Identity confirmed.* We hear the voice: "Welcome back, Marc."

Go down the steps. The lights are coming on, the main computer is greeting you. Give your voiceprint and unlock everything here.

WHAT IF . . . MARC SPECTOR WAS HOST TO VENOM?

Because even though we are carrying the suit in your backpack, we need more.

Scan the space—what do you see? Weapons. Your precious crescent darts—take more of them. One of your emergency phones—good, communication access. Mooncopter remote access—unnecessary with our abilities. Same with the Angel Wing glider.

But Jake Lockley's things. His hat, coat, everything that makes you believable. His mustache. The bandage across his nose.

You linger on other items, things that carry sentimental value for you. Ignore them. Ignore the Mr. Knight suit. We don't need formalities for this. We need *efficiency*. The clock is ticking on you—and us.

Stop stalling.

You obey. Or perhaps you submit. We overpower your will, though you manage to defy us to take Jake's fake mustache. If you must, we can give you that. Maybe you even look better with it.

Now our search begins.

We seek the psi-phon.

You remember that, don't you?

Moon Shade, the psi-phon, that business—*Multiverse*.

Now you're starting to understand.

PACK THE SUIT, MARC. STOP RESISTING. *PACK THE SUIT.*

Good. Grab the cape, the mask, the boots. It is time.

We feel your anger as you coil belt, fold face, check your equipment. Your sense that even now, as we get into Jake's New York taxi and rev the engine, this is against everything Moon Knight stands for. You think about how ashamed Steven and Jake would be at you for having given in to our directives.

You clearly do not see the bigger picture.

In this moment, you have a mission. Because *we* have a mission. Do as directed. Use that anger. We need it. Now go, drive away from the quiet of Spector Manor and toward the city. We move under the guidance of the moon—but not to strike fear in the hearts of criminals. No, we need information swiftly.

You recoil at that thought. Which means you know something, yet you refuse to cooperate or give it up. We will dig further, push past your resistance. What is it you are hiding? You refuse to tell me, but these things cannot be hidden. It is only a matter of time and effort.

There. That will do nicely:

Jake Lockley's network of informants.

Jake's eyes and ears on the street, under bridges, in subway stations. You know them, don't you? They reside in Jake's memory— our memory. Seek them out. Find out what they know. Do not hesitate. The clock is ticking.

Even now, as we roar into the city, we gaze at the shadows of buildings and neighborhoods, and Jake's memory comes alive with the known locales of each person.

Now pull over. Get on your feet. Your mission is not a stakeout. It is active. Time cannot be wasted. You must go from person to person, find the informants, cast a wide net.

Ask them what they know about the psi-phon. Rumors of its whereabouts, whose hands it is in. About anything involved with those things. The Whisperer was *certain* it remained close.

Why, you ask. That was so long ago, a footnote in Moon Knight's memory. We can hear you ponder that. Your mind is still there, working, trying to put the pieces together. You remember its purpose, where it drew power from.

Clever. We are feeling your mind crawling toward this.

Squash those questions. The answers do not matter to you.

We only need information. You will be our conduit for it.

Your mercenary skills remain. Use them. See how you blend in, lurking in the shadows as we scour the alleys, as we locate Jake's informants. Notice how you detect when they lie or deflect, the rhythm of their breathing or the quickening of their pulse. Watch as you hold their gaze, the intensity of your interrogation as you find out what they know.

No, you are no longer Jake working with a network. You are *Venom,* and the only thing that matters is the location of the psi-phon.

One hour passes. Then another, and another. These informants, they tell you useless information, time wasted. What good is Jake's informant network if they don't keep their ears open? Is this too complicated for their purposes? Are they not capable of delivering more?

Ah, but this one knows something. He has heard about it. This one. You sense it as soon as Jake's informant says it:

Retrograde Sanitarium.

We feel it—your intuition triggers. You must squeeze more information out of him. By any means possible.

Your hesitation. Why does that arise?

You feel *pain* when you think of it. Of all of the things you have done, the blood on your hands, the justice you claim to have served in the name of Khonshu, and *this* frightens you?

Curious. But time is slipping away.

We must move fast.

Good. Strike him until he gives us what we need. You hesitate again—we see, Jake is the one who does your dirty work when you . . .

When you have a conscience.

Jake would not do this, you say. *Jake cares for these people.*

We are not Jake right now. We are not Marc, or Steven, or Moon Knight.

We are Venom.

Hit him again. Keep him talking. Do not worry about the words he says. We will listen for you.

We sense your feelings. Even when you feel sympathy for the informant, something in you takes pleasure in the act of violence. We understand. Just as you are Jake and Jake is you, now we are one. You can work with us, and in time, your power will grow with us.

Power. It frightens you. But it tempts you.

We can hear you, wanting to speak up, to have a say in this. Do not concern yourself with control now. All will be explained in due time. You listen to us, we are directed by, we *must* comply.

Why, you demand.

Ah. We will get into that later. Time is of the essence.

For now, you can let the informant go. Stop. Leave him. *Move.*

We have a lead on the psi-phon.

Now we are ready. The answers lie where this all started: Retrograde.

And Dr. Emmet. She ties into this.

That triggers something in you. Now the anger is on the surface. You think of the feeling of knuckles meeting flesh, of inflicting *pain,* and suddenly it changes. Minutes ago, you felt remorse for your actions.

Now? With Dr. Emmet, you may actually enjoy this.

We *feel* your truth, even when you won't say it.

We must find others to finish the trail, to put us on the right path. Go now, move to the next informant. See what they can divulge; surely, they must know something.

And once we have all we need? It will be time to become the Moon Knight.

NOW YOU ARE WEARING THE SUIT.

But not just wearing it. You move differently with the suit. You are faster, stronger. Is it psychological? What did Khonshu do with you?

The only way to find out is if the suit becomes *us* . . .

It is done.

You wonder what that means. We will show you. But first, you must climb.

We may never get those questions answered. Because your time is close.

Two wings, joined by a central office, a rotunda in the middle with a turret. Where shall we start? You know where Emmet's office is. Yet you don't want to crash through her windows. Instead, you bring us around to the far wing. We feel your brain firing off, calculating options and considering the best way to go.

You choose to stealth through the courtyard, to climb to the rooftop. But it is more than that.

You feel *alive* with the suit, with the movement. It means something to you, this life that Khonshu brought you into. The burn of your muscles as you pull yourself up, the sense of righteousness as you ascend.

Something is different, though. You wonder what it is, here, of all places. Halfway up the side of the residential wing of Retrograde, feet on a stone gargoyle and fingers on corner bricks.

We will show you.

Lean over, face the window glass. See it.

And remember, *we* are wearing the Moon Knight suit.

You act surprised at what you see, but this is how we work. Take a moment if you must, if you need to see to believe that we are truly one. You are halfway up the side of a building in the middle of the night. No one will notice, not in this city. Look at your reflection in the window. The full moon makes it easy enough to see.

Different, isn't it?

You think of Moon Knight as a beacon of justice, a sight so bright that criminals shake in terror.

Now you experience that yourself as you see that when we exist with you, things are different. Now Moon Knight's suit is completely black. Inscrutable against the night sky or the shadows.

That is us.

We are Venom.

CHAPTER 8

—

JAKE

THIS WHOLE THING FELT *STRANGER* THAN USUAL. JAKE KNEW THAT he operated differently from Spector and Steven, but some walls usually remained between them inside their shared brain. Steven had his whole Mind Space trick to get them all talking—last year, it was the backlot of a movie studio, and now the whole freaking museum lobby. Spector just kind of willed it to happen at times, usually when crap slid downhill fast and he needed their skills, they'd all arrive in whatever lurked around Spector's mind.

But Jake? He just kind of went by his gut. If he needed something from Spector, he'd shout it out and suddenly Spector would reply. Same thing with Steven—no fuss, no frills, just get the job done. And when things got really hairy, sometimes he'd even see his brothers as if they actually occupied the real world. Probably some sort of adrenaline response or whatever, though he didn't care about how or why it happened, just as long as it worked. That was really his whole approach to things, and doing that meant he kept Spector and Steven away from the dirty work until absolutely necessary.

If he'd bothered to take over during one of Steven's therapy sessions, the shrink might say that Jake did this to protect his in-body brethren from the real nastiness of his line of work. Not just the horrible, seedy people he'd picked up driving cabs, or the messy, chaotic brawls that seemed to follow him, or the stench of New York's worst alleys and subway stations—not just those, but all of it combined.

Jake Lockley knew his life dealt with complications that Steven didn't want to acknowledge and Spector didn't want to weaponize, at least not yet. And because of that, Jake kept to himself when he controlled the body.

So why were things different now? It might have been the whole Khonshu business. The loud voice had barked orders at him way too much over the past thirty minutes or so, prattling on about priorities and goals and things like that. That might have worked had he been Spector; Spector after all was used to a chain of command and all that stuff.

But Jake moved on his own. Which meant he didn't need Khonshu yelling in his head the same way he didn't need Spector listing out options. And he definitely didn't need Steven.

He didn't *want* Steven.

Steven and all his, well, Steven-ness.

And yet he got Steven, the wall between them cracked enough that Jake heard Steven chatting away in his ear, like a busted radio that would not shut up. Usually neither of them arrived without some purpose or intent, yet somehow Steven remained tethered to him, like losing Spector somehow activated Steven even more. This was going to be very irritating, Jake could already tell.

If Jake really wanted to open the door to useless information, he could ask Steven if there was a movie or show where something like this happened, though he decided right now if he kept his mouth shut, maybe Steven would, too.

"Oh. Ohhh, my," Steven said, in that *really annoying* affect of his. "Watch your step. I think there's broken glass over there."

Still dressed in the semi-military getup they awoke in, Jake ignored him, then purposefully crunched the broken bottle pieces under his boot heel just to piss Steven off. Steven *should* be pissed off. Jake was, for sure. He'd circulated his usual spots as best as he could, taking a few subway trains to go for a wider scope, but it all turned up the same thing:

That was, nothing.

No whispers of strange activity around NYC. Not more than usual, that was.

"There's more glass," Steven said. "Oh look, over there is a jar with yellow liquid in it. Brilliant. This is so weird, I feel like I'm watching a first-person movie. Is this how it feels for you?"

"Steven," Jake said with a sigh. "I walk these streets all the time. A broken bottle is not a big deal." To prove his point, Jake stepped on another shard, then ground it into the alleyway.

"This? This is what you do with our body?"

Jake's feet stopped, planted firmly on the ground now. "I do the things you two never would." He craned his neck, searching through the stacked crates and angled dumpsters to try to find a familiar face. "To get us the information we need. Sometimes it gets dirty. Or as you would say, unethical."

"I'm not talking about ethics right now," Steven said. "There is literally a jar of urine over there. This is disgusting."

Steven was right with that part, but it wasn't like people on the streets had a choice. Jake considered giving Steven a quick lecture about being a classist jerk, but then he saw what he needed: a large slab of brown cardboard, a bend in the middle to give it a tent-like shape. He walked slow, an even cadence to his steps, before leaning over. Though the streetlights failed to give much clarity, Jake squinted, eyes adjusting past the shadows to make sure he knew what he was looking at.

An informant. One of Jake's more reliable ones, a weathered man who probably looked older than he actually was.

They locked eyes, and Jake offered his best, warmest smile, something that didn't come along genuinely too often. And even harder to do without his usual mustache. "Hey, how you—" he started.

The man jerked backward, knocking the cardboard tent off of him.

"No! You stay away from me!" He pushed himself upward, hands searching for anything to steady himself as he began moving back.

"It's me, it's Jake." He took a step away, palms up. "Got some nicer clothes. Shaved. That's all. Just me. I only want to talk."

"You betrayed me. I trusted you." The man's eyes widened as he leaned forward, and Jake noticed the clear bruising across his orbital bone. "Don't touch me! Don't come near me!" His shoes slapped against the gathered puddles of the night, and while he pushed forward, his neck remained craned with eyes locked on Jake. "You stay away!" he yelled one more time. "I ain't ever working for you again!"

"Wait! There must be some mistake, I just—"

Before Jake could finish, the man adjusted into a full sprint, his flailing arms connecting with a stack of flattened shipping boxes, sending them scattering into the air. Jake watched as he shrank into the distance, silhouette absorbing into the steaming mist from a manhole cover before disappearing.

This is good. This is the right track.

"I don't think anyone running in terror is 'good,'" Jake said in a low growl. He glanced around, expecting to see the massive bird skull from Steven's Mind Space, but no one lurked. Jake craned his neck, looking at every possible angle to check, though he was pretty sure he'd be able to spot a giant bird skull in a tattered white suit. It wasn't exactly something that would blend in with the scenery. "Also, Khonshu, can you not just yell in my head?"

No answer came, and Jake took steady breaths, the weight of recent minutes putting a pressure against each inhale. Above him, a single raindrop clipped his nose. And several feet ahead, the tiny dots of occasional scattered rain returned, dancing across a puddle.

Jake turned upward, feeling the rain intensify for ten, maybe fifteen seconds before it passed again.

"Khonshu, I said, 'Can you not just yell in my head?'"

I am respecting your wishes with silence.

"Ah." Around the corner, a car zoomed past, its bright headlights firing off a modern white beam similar to the glowing eyes of the Moon Knight suit. "Okay, then. Why can't I see you right now?"

I am conserving my energy to stem this body's chest wound.
Did you stop to wonder why you are not experiencing debilitating
pain from that? You're welcome.

"Jake," Steven said, catching up to him with silent footsteps, "I
think Khonshu has a point, though."

Would it always be like this from now on? They'd built a
strange equilibrium for years, but now this felt like when Jake had
too many people crammed into the back seat of a cab—a group
with too much to drink, too much to say, and not enough seatbelts. Jake looked down at the long scar tracing the inside of their
shared forearm, pain humming from it when he stopped to let
himself think about it. "What do you mean?" he asked as he
walked. He stepped out of the alley, greeted by the uneven side-
walks and dim lights of the street.

"If this is the area Venom went, then surely one of your informants can tell us what he was looking for. That is, as long as
they're not too scared to talk to you," Steven said before clearing
his throat. "Funny. I can smell even though I'm not in control of
the body."

Jake paused mid-step, then looked down the street. A few bars
remained open in between the folding security gates of closed-for-
the-night shops. Across the street, fluorescent light poured out of a
thin opening.

A food mart.

That would work just fine.

Jake tapped the different pockets up and down his cargo pants,
then on his vest. Most were empty, but tucked away in the back
pocket sat a folded wad of cash. Not too much, only two twenties
and a ten, probably kept for emergency purposes on the way over
to swapping bodies. But it would do for now.

This informant had run away, but others should still be in the
area. If Venom approached him, then the others were likely on his
list, too. He just needed to find them, to show he was trustworthy.

And to prove it, he'd come loaded with a peace offering.

ANOTHER THIRTY MINUTES PASSED AND JAKE WAS RUNNING OUT OF warm sandwiches to pass out. But at least his approach worked; the last few informants didn't have much to offer in the way of information, but at least they appreciated the food. "So Venom attacked at least one of them. Why do that?" Steven asked. "And why didn't anyone help him? There are literally people passing by," he pointed up and down the street, "every five seconds."

"I tell you, Steven. You live in the world of galas and fundraisers. Out here, the public doesn't even see these people as human." Jake peeked into the large paper bag in his hand, the top gradually rolled over more and more as he ran out of sandwiches to hand out. "Most of the world views them as trash, rats. If Venom hurts them, no one will come. No one will care."

Steven went quiet as Jake turned down the umpteenth alley of the night, his feet aching and his back sore—and he hadn't even had to fight anyone tonight. "There," he said.

Seated atop of a closed dumpster was a man with a blanket draped over his knees, a beaten coat folded up next to him. The man's hair swept back, a mix of brown and gray, and despite the dim lighting of the alley, he stared at a book in his hands.

Clines—that was his name.

"Hey, Clines?" he called out. "It's Jake."

"Mr. Jake. You're back already?"

That was different. Clines didn't tense up in fear, didn't look over his shoulder for escape routes, didn't even seem concerned. Rather, he was confused.

That was a start.

"That's right. I just thought you might be hungry." He reached into the bag, pulling out a still warm ham-and-cheese sandwich. "Got some extras tonight. And one left."

Clines shuffled up, the tattered blanket sliding off of him to reveal layers of clothes caked together by layers of stains. He set the book aside, a smile forming beneath the wiry hairs of a salt-and-pepper beard. "For me?"

"He's surprisingly receptive," Steven said.

Jake nodded to himself—well, really to Steven, but same difference.

"Thanks, Mr. Jake," Clines said. He tore away at the wrapper, taking a bite before even fully getting the crinkled paper off. "Hot food on a cold night like tonight. Hits the spot."

"That's right. Exactly what I was thinking. You know, funny thing, though." Jake knelt down now to meet the informant eye to eye. "I can't remember what we were talking about before. I, um, bonked my head earlier. I'm sorry if I was acting a little strange. Didn't mean to take it out on anyone."

Clines stopped chewing, corner of his mouth curled up. "Ah. Don't worry about it, Mr. Jake. I understand. Hey, we all get the ol' marble knocked loose from time to time, right?"

"That's right. Makes you do stupid stuff. And I'm sorry about that." Jake gestured around. "Doing a bit of an apology tour. With sandwiches."

"I got you covered." He tapped his temple. "Still got some juice left in the ol' brain."

"I knew I could count on you," Jake said, flashing a grin. His usual mustache was fake, no matter how much he wanted it to be real. Even still, smiling without it felt different without the small hairs tickling his lip.

"So you came here, I don't know how long ago. I fell asleep." He took a bite, then chewed, brow scrunched thoughtfully. "You asked if I heard anything about what Dr. Emmet at Retrograde was up to? And I said, of course. 'Cause it's just a few blocks the other way. Few nights ago, some of the orderlies come by, say Dr. Emmet's got the weirdest bit of research going on. She keeps buying a bunch of stuff from random countries, then running tests to see if they're real. They were making jokes about the stupid names she gives them. Really ridiculous names no one would ever actually say. And one of them said there's a thing called a 'sy . . . sy . . .

sy-something.' I couldn't quite catch it. Well, I knew you had spent some time there before." He tapped the side of his head. "I made a note of that. And that's what I told you. And you left without saying anything."

"Retrograde," Jake said.

"Retrograde," Steven repeated.

Of course. Venom will return to where it began. Where Marc's history will point to our future.

"Yep. Must have gotten hit in the ol' noggin pretty hard to leave without saying goodbye." Clines paused, tilting his head. "Is it just me or is this the best sandwich ever made?"

"Could be. Tell you what," Jake flashed the widest, most genuine smile he could, "I'm really sorry about earlier. Lemme go get you more to eat."

"Hey, we're square on earlier. We all have bad days, right?" The man nodded as he grinned. "You're a good man, Jake Lockley."

Jake smirked at the idea, then looked down at his hands, hands that had such a history of terrible things: smashed faces, broken bones, blood everywhere—not his blood, but blood from . . .

Well, he didn't want to think about that right now.

A good man? The scales maybe didn't tip that way, not for Jake, not when he did things that went beyond even Marc's line. "I'm glad you think so." Jake said before straightening his posture. "Retrograde, then. I hate that place."

That's it. That's the key.

Khonshu's volume caused Jake to wince, so much so that Clines cocked his head. "You okay, Mr. Jake?"

"Yeah," he said, fingers running through his thick, dark hair. "It's just been a weird day. Hang tight, pal. I'll be back with more food. Maybe a new book for you, too." Jake stood up, then turned, new goals now in mind.

"Should we try Gena?" Steven asked. Still in control of the body, Jake marched forward, rain now hitting his cheeks and nose. But even though he could hear Steven, Steven clearly did not know

Jake's thoughts. Because Jake moved with controlled purpose, probably the same way Marc did, though without the exacting stealth, the military precision, Marc's specialties. Jake didn't quite operate that way.

Instead, he charged forward, his whole body carrying a momentum as he scanned the streets.

No, this road was too busy. He needed a quieter space.

"We should keep Gena out of this for now," Jake said. "If we're going to Retrograde, we need the suit."

"The suit would be nice. But how do you propose we *get* the suit with Venom running around?"

"I'm not sure. But I do know there's only one place to find out." Parked cars littered the sidewalk for the next block, and Jake ran the options in his head. Anything too new would be difficult to grab. Computers and security systems and stuff. But something old, something reliable? That could work. "And to get there, we'll need a car."

Jake saw it. From the dated boxy chassis shape to the dimmed lights on top.

"Jake. Jake, what are you doing?"

"There. That car's seen a lot of miles." He glanced behind him, then on both sides of the street. Perhaps in a smaller, quieter place, he would have drawn attention.

But New York City? If anyone passed, they'd keep on going.

"That's a cab. I know you found a little cash but is that going to cover this? And there's no driver, he's probably at one of these bars. Do you have, like, a secret phrase to help one another out when needed? A cabbie code?"

Jake walked up to the driver's side, gauging for any watching eyes as he did so. "No. Not exactly. But I do know what to do with these cars in a pinch."

Somehow Steven was now *in* the driver's seat of the car, looking Jake's way. Guess this was a moment of duress. Did that mean that Steven's own stress now activated him? That was never part of the bargain. "Oh. *Oh,* I see. Now look, I agree that going by foot is too slow. But grand theft auto is not part of my MO." Steven's voice sped up as he lifted his palms up. "I'm sorry but public transportation is a critical piece of any city's infrastructure and—OW!"

Apparently Steven could feel pain. And anyway, it didn't hurt *that* much. Jake had smashed into enough car windows in his life to gauge what type of damage this would do, and through the layers of clothes, it ranked somewhere between a minor annoyance and "that'll leave a mark." Suddenly Steven stood next to Jake, expression halfway between indignant and shocked.

I'll take care of that.

"What will you take—" Jake started to ask Khonshu, until the pain lifted. Not entirely, but enough that the sting reduced into nearly nothing. In fact, the worst part now about smashing the car window was the combination of needing to hot-wire this twenty-year-old cab and having Steven Grant yell in his ear.

"Wait, Khonshu, do you have," Steven said slowly, "magic powers?"

Some. But that may not be enough for you.

"I mean, I know you're an Egyptian deity and all, but with all of the myths and stuff, I had a hard time figuring out what was reality and, you know, that Brendan Fraser movie." Steven and Khonshu continued to discuss the logistics of Egyptian gods walking among men, but Jake focused on the actual important part.

"Almost got it," he mumbled to himself—definitely to himself, as Steven and Khonshu weren't listening. The wires sparked between his fingers and the car roared to life. Jake settled in and pulled the seatbelt over his shoulder. "Hey, guys? We're in business. Guys?" The parking brake clicked as it released, and the car lurched forward, headlights lighting up. "Let's go get the suit. Guys?"

"Jake," Steven said, now in the passenger seat, a clear weight to his words. "Weren't you listening to us?"

"No, Steven." Jake rubbed his face, his response coming with a sigh. "I was a little busy trying to steal this cab. Why am I still seeing you? Hot-wiring a car is not actually that stressful. Not for me anyway. It shouldn't be for you, either. I've done this a ton."

Even as a phantom in the cab's passenger seat, Steven still managed to give a more pronounced, more weary sigh than Jake's. "You know that part in movies where an external force acts like a ticking clock on the protagonists?"

"Will you stop with the movie producer speak? It's been years since you did that stuff. Now you're stressing *me* out."

"Okay." Steven rubbed his temples, like it was *that hard* to just say things simply. "We've got a big problem."

"Thank you. I'll add it to our lengthy list," Jake said, scanning the street signs and cross streets, his mind already figuring out the best place to get started:

Spector Manor.

"Well, it's two problems to add, actually." Steven held up a single finger to start, and Jake noticed that somehow in this visual manifestation of alters, Steven Grant had his seatbelt properly buckled. "First, Khonshu is a god, right? But because of . . . complications . . . with Venom making himself at home in our body, his powers are failing. Maybe it's something with the fact that we had *goo* coursing through us. I am not entirely sure. Either way, it's basically keeping Khonshu's powers on the fritz. And another—"

"Goo?" Jake asked, gunning the gas to zoom through a yellow light.

"Black stuff." Steven's hands came up with a frustrated shake. "Technical term. But that's only the second-most difficult thing we're encountering. Jake, while you were stealing a car, Khonshu and I checked our vitals."

"Yeah, so?" Jake asked, weaving the cab in and out of traffic before taking a hard left on a yellow light. "So, what, is our cholesterol bad or something?"

"I hate to break it to you, but apparently Khonshu heard Venom say, 'No witnesses, no survivors.'" The tone of his voice shifted, a grave seriousness that felt more like Marc than the neurotic movie-producer-turned-adventurer-turned-Egyptologist who always argued with Jake. "He wasn't kidding. Jake, listen to me. You know that chest wound? Khonshu thought he could stem it, but it's not enough.

"We're *dying*."

CHAPTER 9

—

JAKE

MULTIVERSE OR NOT, SOME THINGS STAYED THE SAME. LIKE THE streets Jake took to get from Midtown to 13 Abington Circle, the thirty-two acres that made up the property known as "Spector Manor." Every road, every turn played out exactly as expected, even the fact that older streetlights timed out several seconds longer than necessary when switching from red to green.

Good thing that Jake knew all this by heart, especially since Steven and Khonshu chatted like two teenagers discussing their . . . whatever it was teenagers talked about. Probably different from Steven and Khonshu's topics, which got the two quite animated in the worst way possible.

A loud Egyptian god debating the science of how long magic could stem the damage from a massive chest wound, it sometimes made it hard to concentrate. But Jake understood.

After all, they had to figure out the whole "we're dying" bit.

"Now," Steven said. His underlying stress must have kept him activated, since he remained in the passenger seat of the cab. "I am not a scientist by trade. But I trust subject matter experts. That's why I deep dive into interesting topics, to learn what makes these experts tick. I like to think that I understand a little bit about *how* they think." Steven's hands wagged through the air as he continued. "Cause and effect are important. It's how we figure things out as a species. So, Khonshu, let me make sure I understand your theory here. This body has—"

"You know," Jake said, a little louder than he needed to, "the cause doesn't really matter if we can't actually do anything about it."

"Who says we can't?"

"*Khonshu* says we can't!" Jake said, slamming his hand against the steering wheel, just as he'd done hundreds, probably thousands, of times. And this felt *exactly* the same—the same sting and tingle that quickly went away at the base of his palm, just in a different universe.

Sure didn't feel like they were dying.

I did not say it was irreversible. Appropriate medical intervention may be stronger than my capabilities. I said that we are running out of time.

"Well then, why aren't we going to a hospital?"

Because all those other things you care about will be finished if you take a week to check yourself in for major surgery and recovery.

"You know what?" Jake asked, feeling the sudden urge to slam the gas or punch the windshield or punch *Khonshu* if he could. Something to make things feel better, even if it was only for a flash of release. "We got the real short end of the stick here. Wrong universe, dying body, some alien target. We didn't sign up for this. Neither did our Marc. Yes, I said *Marc* instead of *Spector*, just to confuse you."

The only way to give you a chance to restore your body and mind is to catch Venom.

"That's crap. For all we know, you could be lying to us about everything and—"

"Okay, reset. Reset, everybody," Steven said, waving his arms. "We're all on the same team here. No one wants to die. We all want things to return to how they were. So let's just try to parse this out. Imagine I've got a PowerPoint in front of you. The sequence of events was—"

Steven and his boardroom distractions. Jake gave him points for being consistent. "Steven, that would take my eyes off the road."

Yes, I agree—let us not kill this body through mechanical trauma yet.

So there *was* something Khonshu and Jake could agree on. That single nugget was enough for Jake to acquiesce, even for a moment. Steven bit his lip, then put his hands up. "All right. Forget the visual aids. Let's walk through this."

The car roared as Jake pressed deeper into the accelerator pedal. The faster they got to Spector Manor, the sooner this would be over. He cared about the whole "body is dying" thing, of course; it seemed like kind of a "top priority" type of fiasco. But the how and why of it, that probably would have been a better discussion for Steven to strategize with Marc.

Jake didn't care about those things. He just got the freakin' job done.

"So Venom had this body. Our body. But only with Marc. That's step one." Steven held up a single finger. "That's where this all starts."

What do you remember about Venom's intentions?

"Nothing here. Jake?" Jake shook his head in reply. "I remember things were normal with Spector and then they weren't. Like we got shoved in a closet. Changing from being aware in our usual state to nothing. Pitch black. No noise, no voices. Just us in a form of," Steven's lips twisted, "some sort of paralysis. And there were a few times when he tried to get us out. I felt that. It was like he called to us."

"I did, too." The car tires squealed as Jake took the turn around the shaded lane harder than he should have, his anger getting the better of his driving skills. "Like someone slammed a door on us. And I tried to punch my way through."

"There was a pressure, too. I think . . ." Steven's voice slowed and his eyes narrowed in focus. "There was urgency. And I think it came from Venom. Whatever Venom's motivations, there's something pushing everything forward. When Marc tried to pull us out, I heard Venom. Something about needing to find a device and get ahead of someone." Steven shrugged, palms up. "Vague, I know. But enough to identify that something else is at play here. Which means if Venom's time is limited, ours is, too."

"I didn't catch that," Jake said with a laugh. "Maybe Venom likes you more than me."

"Maybe I'm just a better listener than you." Steven's chin tilted up. "Active listening skills—"

No childish bickering right now.

"All right, all right. Truce," Steven said, in what was probably his best boardroom voice. Jake huffed in response, eyes concentrating on the road as they pulled farther into unlit rural territory, finally hitting the last turn up to the main estate property. "So Venom squashes us out. Then they track down the Marc from *this* world, who just escaped Retrograde Sanitarium. Venom uses his . . . Venom-ness to overpower Marc. Then Venom takes him to that warehouse."

"This is pretty easy to follow, you really wanted a presentation for this?" The tires squeaked as the cab lurched forward, slowing down toward Spector Manor's security panel at the opening gates. "What do you think, Khonshu, is the code the same in our world?"

I don't see why not.

"In the warehouse basement," Steven continued, like the other conversation didn't even happen, "Venom then un-goos himself from this body. Including cutting open our left forearm."

Jake glanced down at the healing wound, the burn scars still tender but nothing he couldn't handle. Jake rolled down what remained of the shattered cab window and punched in 8-7-5-3-2 per the muscle memory from *their* gate at *their* Spector Manor.

Gears and motors whirred as the wrought-iron gates pulled back, all while Steven yammered on. "So Venom slithers out of us through this gash in our arm," he said, holding up a perfect phantom image of their scarred arm like this was show-and-tell, "and into the body of this reality's Marc. Doing so starts to squash out Khonshu, but Khonshu uses the goo as a . . ." Steven's lips pursed in thought. "A conduit. Like a bridge. To jump into our body. What do they even call the goo?"

The car rolled forward, and Jake shut off the headlights just in case they needed stealth on their side. "You can keep *goo* as a technical term," Jake said sarcastically, though he just knew that Steven would run with it.

"So just as Khonshu got in, our body fell. Flames everywhere. Very bad. Guess there's still some goo inside."

Jake smirked to himself and his correct prediction of Steven's word choice.

I have the power to influence damage to the body, even resurrect. I have done it once before for Marc. But Venom's liquid means that part of this body still obeys his will on a base level.

"Erm," Steven said. "How much goo do you think is left? It seems rather unhealthy."

A single drop. I have trapped it in your arm so that it cannot circulate to other areas and cause more damage.

"Great," Jake said. "Hey, Venom, can we sneeze you out of our body?"

"It's not like that," Steven said. "Khonshu is trying to keep us alive. Venom wants us dead. And I think," he hesitated, his gaze dropping, "I think that's why Spector's just . . . gone." The car rolled up the paved driveway, and though he recognized the bushes and shrubs lining the path, he got the sense that this reality's Marc must have forgotten to pay the gardener or something, because that overgrowth looked a little rough.

That has to be it. Venom said, "No witnesses, no survivors." *Spector in your body was a witness. Venom did not want him to live.*

"What does that make us?" Jake asked, biting down on his lip. The cab moved on, past a large and dormant square fountain and more overgrown, possibly dried-out shrubs, then veered into the semicircle adjacent to the front entrance.

Kill the body, kill the witness.

The car slowed to a halt, the sputtering engine finally shutting off and leaving them in silence. Steven and Jake turned to each other, and for the first time in, well, pretty much ever, they existed without the tether of Spector to keep them together. "All right, well then, let's cut the doom and gloom," Jake said, looking Steven straight in the eye. "We're gonna find Venom and we're gonna fix this. But first," the door handle clicked and he pushed the door open with his left foot, "we need some gear."

"Booby traps," Steven said in a disembodied voice. Apparently practical discussions of Venom's intent were more stressful for him than breaking and entering. Just as in their universe, Spector Manor skipped the usual mechanical key bit and instead used a facial scan to verify identity—which meant they finally had a challenge that didn't require dodging flames, scouring alleys, or talking to Egyptian deities.

Just . . . looking up. The door opened, and Jake stepped inside.

"Let's prioritize booby traps. We don't know what Venom might have left here. I'm not Spector, but sometimes I'm more methodical than he is," Steven continued, "so I think that we need some sort of comprehensive sweep. It'd be great if we could tap into his instincts, you know?"

"Sure, Steven," Jake said, scanning the shapes and silhouettes in the dim hallway. He knew exactly where everything sat—this painting here, this chair there, the massive globe in the corner.

But something was off.

"Then when we know we're clear, we'll need any data from devices that might be tracking Venom's location. We need to avoid Venom until we're ready," Steven continued, but Jake's mind wandered away from his blathering. So much of this place looked the same, though with the lights off and the blanket of night outside, details didn't exactly pop out. "And any data he might have transmitted back to the central computer. We agree, yes?"

Jake paused, though not because of Steven's question. From outside, moonlight pierced the large window, and finally, at this angle, the illumination proved enough to show that his intuition worked. Things were largely the same, but in this universe, something changed.

Because in the back library of Spector Manor, so much of it sat exactly right: the angles of the chairs, the knot on the drapes, even the order of the books on the bookshelf.

But the end table between chairs, with the stained bourbon glass on the back edge, the space in front of it was empty.

No silver frame holding a photo of Marc Spector and Marlene Alraune.

Jake tapped the end table's blank spot, his finger picking up the slightest hint of . . .

Dust.

In fact, he turned, vision finally adjusted to the low light, and a look around showed what *else* was off.

Cobwebs and dust. Like people forgot to care anymore.

The furniture *was* the same, down to the exact placement. Only time and the circumstances around it changed, causing this reality's Marc to leave this space alone except for the security scanner in the back corner.

"Search queries, research tasks, anything the computer might be—" Steven said as Jake turned and began moving. "Wait, where are you going?"

"You said it. Our body is dying." Jake pointed back to the place where the photo of Marlene *should* have been. "We don't have time. We just need to figure out what Venom wants and get back to our world. Get to a hospital that can fix us. Get back to Marlene. This universe's Marc can clean up his own mess."

Steven suddenly appeared in the corner, right beneath the small panel interface and scanners poking out of the ceiling. "Don't come here yet. We need a plan."

"We *have* a plan," Jake said, putting his hand on the interface. It came to life, a light blue beam running across the screen to complete the hand scan. "Get the suit, get weapons, get some other helpful stuff, and go. Hey, Khonshu, is this place's Moon Knight truncheon still made of adamantium?"

It is.

"With the grappling hook? Still activated with a twist?" Jake held up his fists and did a mock twist to show.

Yes. And convertible to nunchaku.

"Jake. Jake. Jake," Steven said. There it was, the more Steven worried, the more he repeated names. "This place has booby traps, AI-powered security drones, you know this, we have to be careful—"

"Handprint confirmed. Welcome, Marc Spector," a disembodied voice said. Behind the wall, muffled high-pitched whines and clatters came through, followed by the panel sliding open to reveal a dimly lit chamber. "Enter for body scan identification."

"Stop." Steven moved into the scanning chamber, arms waving in protest. "Stop moving right now. Both feet planted. Impulsive. You're being impulsive when we've only got one shot at this and—oh dear."

For all of Steven's seemingly real occupation of physical space, this gave one clear time to show that in the end, all of it happened within their brain. Because Jake walked right through Steven, like the neurotic billionaire was only a hologram made of photons.

In a way, that was kind of true. He supposed that was the advantage of the Mind Spaces used by Steven and sometimes Marc. Here, Jake could just ignore Steven. But whenever they met up in the Mind Space, full-blown fistfights broke out from time to time.

"Prepare for identity confirmation," the computer voice ordered as Jake planted both feet flat and looked straight ahead. "Stand still in the scanning area."

"Booby traps!" Steven yelled. "Booby traps! Security measures!"

"Steven," Jake said, in his best condescending tone, "we passed the facial scan outside. We passed the handprint scan here. What could possibly go wrong? It's not like I've suddenly got a new face for *this* scanner."

A low hum ramped up from above, and a thin beam of translucent light danced over Jake. And Steven, for whatever reason, stepped outside of the chamber and instead lingered behind them.

"Processing," the voice said. "Processing."

"You see?" Jake said with a laugh. "We're fine. Let's get some weapons and—"

"Intruder alert!" the voice said in the same deadpan tone. Behind Jake, a metallic *clack-clack-clack* rattled through the space, though he didn't need to look to know what happened.

Spector Manor was in the process of locking down. Windows, doors, all points of entry—and exit—sealing off with unfurling metallic shields.

But why, though?

Maybe they'd have time to figure that out before security measures killed them.

CHAPTER 10
VENOM

ARE THEY DEAD?

Maybe.

Those men tasked to guard Retrograde Sanitarium. They tried to kill us. And we gave you more. Strength. Speed. Abilities. *Power*. More than the Moon Knight is capable of. More than even Jake Lockley at his worst.

You didn't even need your weapons.

We are the weapon.

You walk down the hallway of this building's patient wing, this wretched, worn place where people are forgotten. Now you move up the stairs, to the top floor of the rotunda. Look at them writhing on the floor, security guards and orderlies who take too much pleasure in squeezing you under their will, their chemicals and shock treatments.

You enjoyed that.

We felt it.

Was it justice? Different from using your mercenary skills to hunt down targets. Even now, as you step over them, the broken drywall bits grinding under our black boots, we can sense it.

Inside, you are smiling.

See that one in the corner with the orange hair and glasses. You remember—the chair, the injection, the shock treatments. What was his name? Billy, wasn't it?

And now? You know what we can do, the way tendrils form and

lash out, with more precision and power than your crescent darts ever could.

But you prefer not to use those. You would rather feel the impact against your knuckles, your knees, your feet. That tactile knowledge of understanding just how much you hurt those who hurt you.

Take a minute to appreciate this. In fact, look at the security camera in the corner. Look directly at it. Step closer. Pull your mask off for a moment and stare at the camera, tell the world that Marc Spector should be feared.

And now you move to the large office at the top. *Dr. Emmet's office.*

You knock. When you could easily smash the door down.

Have you found your manners? No, you are *mocking* Dr. Emmet.

"Marc? It's you, isn't it?" You hear her voice through the door. The door is unlocked. Open it.

Reveal us.

There she is. The one who studied you, drugged you, experimented with you, first years ago at Putnam Hospital and then here at Retrograde. She found you again, after all those years, convinced you that she could help. And it was all a lie.

You want *vengeance.*

But not yet. Once we have what we need, you can have complete control.

Strange. She is not scared.

No, her head tilts. She brushes her red hair aside, adjusts her glasses. The gun in her hands, it holds still at you.

Her men are beaten. Some surely killed. And yet she . . .

She laughs at you.

Control yourself, Marc. We need information. The psi-phon is the key.

"That *is* you under the mask, right, Marc? Your suit is black now. Oh, that's great." She laughs. She laughs at *you.* "You know, we talked about how you should refrain from black-and-white thinking, but I didn't mean it literally. What have you gotten yourself into?"

"You don't even want to know," you say with a growl. Scan the room. Her files. Her computer. Other records. Look what she has in the corner storage bin. A menu from Gena's restaurant. A gauntlet made of bandages, something you recognize as part of Moon Knight's ghost-ripper armor. Your dog tags from the Marines.

Your childhood yarmulke.

You knew this. Of course you did. Her fascination with you goes beyond therapeutic. She has cataloged your life.

She sees you as a science experiment.

Your anger boils at this. You call to us, to unleash Venom's powers in totality.

But we will not. We need information. Her actions are nothing compared to what we must do.

Now get her talking.

"Why are you standing still? Do I need to shoot to wake you up?" She waves the gun again, like it is a plaything. "Are you too busy arguing with Steven and Jake in your head? Visiting magical Egyptian gods or blasting off in a spaceship? What's real to you? Maybe," she says with *that* condescending laugh, "I'm not real. Or am I? You see, this is the problem with you, Marc. You think violence is the solution to everything. You come in here, attack my orderlies, dust up my facility, when all you need to do is ask."

Now she stands, gun down and face-to-face. "Go on, ask me. I'm not hiding anything."

Is this a ruse? A trap? We must think carefully, Marc, she is our only lead.

"Psi-phon," you say.

"What was that? I couldn't hear you under the whole mask and everything. Speak clearly. Enunciate. Unless," her head tilts, "you're on drugs?"

"The psi-phon," you say again. "You've been researching my life, collecting artifacts. Why?"

Careful, Marc. The "why" does not matter.

"Marc Spector. You are the most extreme case of, well, *anything* I've ever encountered. Your history could fill hundreds of textbooks. There should be an entire graduate degree on you. The stories you told me, you take everything to excess. You can't just be a soldier or mercenary, you have to be *this*." She pokes you, she pokes *us,* as she speaks. "Steven Grant can't just be rich, he's gotta be a billionaire. Jake Lockley can't just be a working-class hero, he needs a secret intel network connected to every unhoused person in New York City. And yet you can't keep any of it together. You destroy everything you love. You would do *all this* instead of just settling down with Marlene. No wonder your relationship with her fractured yet again. Good for Marlene, finally moving on." Emmet taps a manicured bloodred nail on the handle of the gun. "It's absolutely fascinating. I've spent the last few years trying to dig through it all, trying to separate fact from fiction. I keep telling myself, when I can understand Marc Spector, I can understand the true depths of the human mind. So . . ." You hear a noise. Not just the clicking as she uncocks her pistol, but something from outside the door—several floors down. More guards, perhaps. Steel yourself. "Just tell me what you want. Believe me, all of this is one big data point in my research."

"The psi-phon. Where is it? What do you know about it?"

You see her expression change. Tell us, Marc, does all your time together give you the insight into what she's thinking? "That's very, very specific. What a story that was, Moon Shade and all the different versions of you. Wasn't there even a dinosaur version of Moon Knight? How creative." The way she points at you, the way she curls her lip, what does that mean?

Is she lying?

"It's all kind of appropriate, don't you think?" She taps a button on the desk keyboard and the blank computer screen comes to life. "You couldn't just have multiple people in your head, so you thought up the *psi-phon* of all things, to connect you to versions of you across universes. So many theories about that one."

She swivels the monitor screen in your direction, then sits down at the desk and starts typing. And you, so many different urges in you right now.

"But I'm afraid I no longer have your precious device." That coy smile returns. The screen changes, listing out files and databases. "Shall we try to track it down?"

CHAPTER 11

—

STEVEN

JAKE WAS GOING TO GET US KILLED.

Which, given that our body was dying, seemed kind of redundant. But still, I much preferred going out with some agency over the health and well-being of our shared home. So rushing into the line of sight of active security drones? Not exactly preferred.

"Give me the body, Jake," I yelled in his ear. Literally. As in, in this strange pseudo-existence, stress allowed me to stand right next to Jake and scream as loud as I could at the side of his head. He just refused to listen. Which, in turn, stressed me out more. "I can save us."

"Target acquired," came from one of the drones. "Weapons armed. Stand down. You have ten seconds to comply."

Now, Jake and Spector, I know them pretty well. That mix of closeness and understanding and dirty laundry all kind of blends together; we all try to keep some specifics from one another, but the broad strokes of understanding, we get it.

Jake liked to act without thinking and, sure, that worked in some circumstances. Like when particularly nasty thugs cornered you and all you had was your fists.

But *something* told me another solution existed here. Maybe Jake didn't see it, but I did—and I needed to stop him.

"Jake, stop! Give me the body," I yelled at him as drones swarmed, the oncoming hum of their fan blades growing as they hovered into position.

"I'm keeping us alive, Steven," he yelled back. Even though I kind of existed next to him, I felt the way he tensed the body, the burn in his knees and the tightness in his fists as he poised to run and dodge and fight.

"No, you're going to get us killed. Give me the body *now*."

Perhaps it was my level of assertiveness—that's not really typical, particularly against a physical threat, as was probably evident. But given that I tended to be a little more astute in my observations than Jake, this felt worth shrieking about.

"Steven, this isn't—"

Jake stopped midway through his reply because I did something that would normally be out of bounds in my realm of respect toward my brothers.

Though, really, that respect was the *reason* why I did it.

Because I very much didn't want us to die.

I blinked. As in, physically blinked in our body. And I stood up, unclenching my fingers.

"Did you . . ." Jake's voice yelled in my ear, his usual shouting echoing around my thoughts. "Did you just push me out?"

That led to this point, where instead of continuing Jake's charge at two armed drones floating through the back library of Spector Manor with weapons pointing my way, I remained still. And put my hands up.

"Steven?" Jake yelled. "Steven, what are you doing? You're gonna get us killed."

No time for a Mind Space discussion right now. "No, I'm gonna save us," I said under my breath. Red dots lit on my chest as I took a step forward. "I'm not an intruder! Scan voiceprint for identification," I said, in my best Spector voice. "This is Marc Spector."

"Steven, we just failed the whole-body scan."

"And we passed the other ones. Think about it," I said quickly, under my breath. Beyond us, an automated voice continued announcing an intruder alert.

"I *am* thinking about it."

Sometimes I thought about this strange life the three of us led, three alters trapped in this body—but all with different strengths and weaknesses. Spector was shaped by his upbringing, by his family, by the way medicine failed to treat—or even believe—him, at least until years of self-reflection and a lot of empathy from Marlene helped stabilize things. Jake offered real street smarts, a physical gruff capable of getting out of nearly any scrap. Also, he knew the city like the back of his hand.

Me? I knew how to analyze and research things, when disparate details drew a complete picture if you figured out how to connect them.

"Do you trust me?" I asked, taking another step forward.

Jake responded with a rapid-fire retort, and if we were in my Mind Space, I would have been able to clearly understand all of the ways he did *not* trust me in moments like this.

"Scan voiceprint for identification," I repeated. "This is Marc Spector."

The drones hovered in front, a high-pitched whine accompanied by the internal whirs and clunks of data processing inside a CPU and hard drive.

"Voiceprint identified: Marc Spector. Secondary confirmation required. Hold for retinal scan."

The drone's camera eye flickered, probably some lens change from inside, and it now emanated a blue glow as it approached. It came, floating closer and closer, and I stared directly at it until the glow formed a blind spot in my eye.

"Retinal scan identity confirmed: Marc Spector." Across the room, another panel slid open—smaller, with no interface to activate or engage.

Just for emergencies.

"Intruder alert is still active. Safe room passage opened."

"Well," I said, gesturing to the newly accessible hallway. This was the thing about having different people living in your head, there was always someone around to hear your witty comments. "Open sesame."

"Mind Space. Now," Jake said.

I resisted the urge to comment about how Jake must have started appreciating the Mind Space's qualities. Though here, it probably stemmed more from the time dilation inside our head. I closed my eyes, and Jake already waited for me in the lobby of The Met, elbow propped up against the lobby counter. "How the hell did you know that we'd pass?"

"Deductive reasoning," I said, a triumphant look on my face.

"You're a stock tracer, not Sherlock Holmes." Jake pointed straight at my smirk. Though I was impressed by the fact that he connected Holmes and the process of deduction. Perhaps he'd been reading in his off time, or at least watching movies. "What does that have to do with drones pointing guns in our face?"

"Solving crimes. Making millions. Same difference. It's clues and context," I said. "We passed facial recognition and a handprint scan. So we know we match the details with this universe's Marc."

"But the body scan—"

"Ah, but think about what the body scan checks for—exact body match. Not just individual pieces, but the whole. So," I said, arms waving with a theatrical flourish worthy of my best-funded Hollywood productions, "our face is the same. Our voice is the same. Our hands are the same. Our eyes are the same. What could possibly be different?"

Jake crossed his arms, the brim of his cap casting a shadow over his eyes and his mustache angled with his frown. "I should just walk away right now and not give you the satisfaction of your punch line."

"*Height,*" I said, pacing between the statues and displays in the lobby. "We are the same person across universes, but with slightly different lived experiences. This Marc dealt with Khonshu for years. We never did; our Marc took on the vigilante life himself. A different set of circumstances, a different set of injuries. Khonshu?" I asked, turning to the large bird skull next to me, his clothes a little less ragged here than last time I saw him.

I'm enjoying your explanation, Steven.

"Now, Khonshu, you have the ability to heal, correct?"

To some degree.

"And our body did not. Instead, we took all of those injuries the old-fashioned way. And remember what we got at our last MRI?" Jake let out a groan, and though Khonshu's skull face didn't exactly emote, I got the sense that he was amused, if not impressed. "Rapid degeneration of discs in our spine. From repeated falls and blunt-force trauma. Leading to a loss of height of nearly a centimeter. Thus," my arms went up, fingers now fully waving to punctuate my words, "this tiniest of differences could *only* be detected by a full-body scan. But everything else? It thinks we're Marc and there's some *other* intruder to find."

A thank-you from Jake would have sufficed, but apparently that proved too much for him to say. He grunted his best bit of gratitude, then stroked his mustache.

"Well," Jake finally said, "how does that help us get into the main lair?"

"It doesn't," I said with a shrug. Jake's eyebrow arched, intensity returning to his eyes. "But sometimes you have to make the best of a bad situation."

"You were just telling me we needed intel and resources and stuff."

"Then the security system tried to kill us." I pointed, though I supposed the orientation of the Mind Space didn't really apply to the real world, but I pointed in the direction that *felt* correct. "The safe room has Marc's backup equipment. It'll have to do for now."

Venom is on the move. We must act quickly.

"Jake," I said, stepping forward to plant a hand on his shoulder. "You're always telling me to stop overthinking, right?" Jake bit down on his lip with a nod before adjusting his cap. "Well, I think we don't have the option to overthink right now."

My eyes snapped open, the whir of the drones now behind me, automated voices announcing things like "scanning immediate area" and "no threats found." I stepped quickly to the short hall leading to Marc's safe room.

Sure, Moon Knight occasionally got involved in world-at-risk stakes. I mean, I'd been to space, which is as harrowing and fantastic as you might think. But in the end, we—and by *we* I meant Spector, Jake, and I—dressed up in all white with a flowing cape and glowing eyes almost solely to protect our home.

That was it. The other stuff with aliens and paramilitary organizations with weird agendas, all that stuff, getting involved with S.H.I.E.L.D. and the World Security Council, well, people with the title "Captain" in their name did much better at that.

So while I originally wanted to gather as much data and equipment as possible before we followed Venom to Retrograde Sanitarium, I told myself to make do with what we took.

Venom was able to use Marc's whole supply room at Spector Manor, from the supercomputer to the armory to his choice of Moon Knight suits, maybe even the Angel Wing glider.

On the other hand, we got a small stone-lined space with minimal lighting and definitely no computer—a glorified closet with equipment bins in case Moon Knight was in a pinch and something sealed off the main bunker. Also, while not many differences existed between this place's Marc and us, his emergency room came much better organized than ours.

I wasn't the only one who noticed, apparently. "This is a good idea," Jake said as I studied the options. "Labeled bins. Instead of things just hanging about. We should steal this method."

Case after case opened up, mechanical clicks and computer beeps as I set my palm on each one's scanner pad. "I'll make sure to buy a label maker when we get back. Quite the utility with those." I snapped open the first case—a few crescent darts and the truncheon that separated into nunchaku. "But for now? This will help." I sorted through the rest of the materials, everything from a few thousand dollars in emergency cash to a single phone in a white case. "If this is anything like our emergency supplies back home, this is going to have limited functionality. It won't be like the AI that powers the main computer or our usual limo."

"That's okay. That thing's too extravagant anyways."

"We could use the data support, though," I said as the phone screen came to life.

"Yeah, you do like to ask questions," Jake said, and though he had no physical component to see, I could practically picture him rubbing his brow as he sighed.

I ignored Jake's comment and picked up the device. "This will have to do." I turned to the small room's far wall, the only protected and computerized portion of the safe room: a curved metallic panel built from adamantium. Unlike the equipment cases, the scanner on the wall came in the form of a thin horizontal box—probably the same tech built into the security drones still buzzing about outside.

"Just one more thing," I said, leaning over to line up my eyesight with the scanner, experiencing a temporary blindness as a blue beam hit my irises. While the equipment cases had opened with a series of clicks, this panel came with low, loud *thunk*s, and the panel gradually slipped open, a vertical slit of white light escaping that eventually took over the whole space.

In front of me stood the neatly tailored white suit of Mr. Knight: pants, button-down shirt, vest, and gloves, with a coat draped over the mannequin's shoulders, each piece with carbonadium woven into the fabric for extra durability—even the slick shoes.

And, of course, the mask, a featureless white mask that contoured to our face much like the proper Moon Knight mask, except this one had a simple crescent moon on the forehead—always a nice touch.

But right next to it stood the proper Moon Knight suit. I'd recognized it right away—well, Moon Knight is already pretty darn recognizable, what with the cape and cowl and stuff. But this particular suit, it came with a big golden belt and bracelets, dating back to our brief time as part of the West Coast Avengers. Marc probably stored it here mostly as a backup if desperate, as gold wasn't really our color.

"Woof," Jake said, "I remember that. How did Marc ever think that belt was a good idea? We looked like a pro wrestler."

"Right," I said, reaching up for Mr. Knight's coat. "Let's go for the corporate look. Probably blends in a little easier than a giant cape."

"Are you kidding? I'm a New York City cabdriver, I can tell you that there are way weirder things than capes out there," Jake said, annoyance lacing his tone. "I know this has carbonadium fiber, but still, maybe we should go for the more armored choice?"

"Jake, Jake, Jake," I said, a couple of *tsk*s to go with it. "Think practically. We're two people in one body with a shouty god and a reality where everything might be the same or might not. I'm going with a tie. People like ties. Wherever we go, security will notice a cape." Piece by piece, I started to change, though I neatly folded the clothes Venom had left us with—always good to have something to change into. "Besides," I unlaced the military boots this body had been wearing for far too long, "I think this is more my style."

"Fair enough. But you missed one vital piece of equipment."

"What's that?" I asked, buttoning up Mr. Knight's white shirt.

"Look between the suits."

I finished the top button, then slid the tie through my collar before kneeling down to tend to Jake's request. Between the suits sat a white velvet case the size of a palm; snapping it open prompted a grin, and if Jake couldn't see this, at least he'd feel it.

Because within the case awaited the thick fake mustache of Jake Lockley.

CHAPTER 12

—

JAKE

THEY NEEDED SPECTOR.

Jake thought that as soon as he gazed upon Retrograde Sanitarium—a place that would be intimidating on its own, from the worn-down brick-built wings on either side to the octagon-shaped rotunda in the middle, a structure that peaked with a lit turret. Normally, it probably came loaded with circulating guards doing standard watches at different security checkpoints.

But then, all the clues from Jake's informants put Venom here. Probably hours before them, since police and emergency crew were here, too. After leaving Spector Manor, Steven willingly turned the body over to Jake, and they drove out of the tranquil countryside toward the oncoming chaos of the city. The Mr. Knight mask sat folded in the passenger seat, but otherwise, Jake handled the decades-old cab with poor shocks and questionable acceleration while wearing Mr. Knight's clean suit. Parking several blocks away, Jake considered the logic of Steven's choice to take Mr. Knight over the traditional cape-and-cowl getup. Sure, a white jacket and slacks blended in better than an armored costume, but it lost out on the whole matter of practicality.

Especially when planning an infiltration.

Jake had scaled up the fire escape of the apartment building adjacent to the asylum grounds, and now he waited, crouched behind an air-conditioning vent to survey the scene. This was Spector's area of expertise: analyzing weaknesses, identifying an infiltration path, timing their way past security. Steven wouldn't be helpful here, as his persona gelled best when human interaction was involved. And Jake, well, he worked best when the *other* kind of human interaction got called upon.

Now? Jake pulled the mask over his head, leaving it tucked under his nose to expose his jaw and fake mustache. And in his head, Steven's voice carried enough stress that Jake wondered why he wasn't visible. Maybe that part came later. "It makes sense that the records would be in that main tower," Steven said. "I would think the other wings would be for patient housing and treatments. The middle part would be for operations."

"Now you're an architect?" Jake said, standing up and pumping his feet, feeling slowly returning down his legs. "When'd you study that?"

"Not an architect. But you go to enough fancy buildings like this and they all kind of follow the same pattern."

"Okay, great. So how do we get there?" Jake asked, flexing his hands in his gloves. "I count five police cars in the front. At least seven more cops are patrolling." His finger pointed to areas beyond the standing police spotlights. "And outside of them? I'm sure there's security all around."

I have a path.

"What?" Jake and Steven asked at once.

My Marc just escaped this facility. I can lead you back.

"See?" Steven asked, a sudden optimism in his tone. "We may not have Spector, but we're still a team. Different skills, different experiences, all complementary to—"

Get down to the surface. We're going into the sewers.

Jake adjusted the mustache glued to his face, then raised an eyebrow. "The sewers?" A sudden hunch told him that Steven would be no help with that.

"Well, my friend." Steven's reply came with smug satisfaction in his voice. "Looks like you've got the body right now."

WITH THE CAPE AND COWL, THE SUIT'S SILHOUETTE STRUCK FEAR IN the hearts of the cruel, a blinding white crescent moon without hiding, without trickery, without stealth—Moon Knight represented the inevitability of brutal justice.

That . . . wasn't exactly where they were at right now.

But without Spector's infiltration skills or Frenchie to helicopter them in or the Angel Wing glider to swoop over to the facility's rooftop patio, Jake, Steven, and their bird-god ride-along would have to do. But at least they had an adamantium staff handy.

Jake pushed the metal sewer grate up. As he exhaled into the thick, stinking air, he mentally kicked himself for not pulling the mask over his face. That would have helped with the smell. Somehow, Mr. Knight's white slacks and shoes managed to stay grime free as Khonshu led them down a manhole and through various under-the-street passages.

It worked, though. They started half a block from Retrograde and emerged near the back patio, a drainage area for irrigation that also doubled as the perfect infiltration path.

Now what?

"All right," Jake said, pulling out and kneeling behind a large potted bush. All this hiding not only tickled his nerves, it made his joints hurt, too. Turned out that waiting was way more difficult than punching someone. "This is what we've got."

"There's a lot of them." Steven magically appeared in a black tuxedo fit for a gala or spy movie, conjured by adrenaline and imagination, and the apparition crouched behind the opposite bush on the path. "A police officer on the far end over there. Spotlights near the front side. Looks like security guards on the left. And that," he said, pointing directly at the building's wing, "is probably our best bet."

"What makes you say that?" Jake asked, cracking his knuckles.

"All the lights are off. Every other floor has at least one light on. My guess," Steven said, probably referencing far too much time spent in office buildings, "must be some maintenance going on there. Or Venom hit that part and it's cleared out."

Jake craned his neck, taking in as much of the various guard movement as possible. Hopefully they didn't bring any guard dogs. At the front, the flashing red and blue overheads of police cars mixed with the bright tri-podded lights casting wide beams over the space. In the back, the courtyard was dimmer, allowing individual flashlights to cut through the night as guards patrolled.

All this waiting for the right movement. It would have been fine if this mix of police and security operated on set patrol paths, but they instead walked, paused, talked, or looked at something, then turned and stretched, then continued.

Jake knew he needed to be patient, but that seemed really difficult when his instinct was to go for the straightest line possible. "Khonshu, you're a god, can't you help us, like, fly or something?"

I don't know, Jake, can't your body run fast or something?

"Wow." Perhaps even gods got testy. "Okay. Of all the Egyptian gods to occupy our head, we had to get the cranky one."

"Jake, be nice to the shouty voice in our head," Steven said as he scanned the courtyard again. "He's keeping us alive."

There is one thing I can do to help you.

Jake *almost* asked "Besides sarcasm?" but decided to actually be constructive in this moment.

I can sense the presence of those nearby. To help you know when to move.

"Perfect. I always wanted a radar in my head."

Steven replied with a disapproving scowl, "Don't be sarcastic to our tech support."

"I'm not. This is really helpful," Jake said, smoothing out Mr. Knight's mask. "Thanks, Khonshu."

"Tone matters, Jake," Steven said, a clear scold in his voice.

Move now. The guards are on opposite sides of the courtyard.

Jake's legs pushed hard, a sudden burst as he sprinted into the shadow of an armless statue. A passing guard paused, then knelt down to inspect something on the ground. One quick breath, then Jake sprang forward again, a diagonal burst that brought him to the base of a dormant fountain. Some distance away to his right, a voice called out. "Hey! Lemire!" a woman yelled. Jake started to peer over his shoulder but Khonshu yelled at him.

Don't give yourself away. I will sense for us.

"Teamwork makes the dream work," Steven said, now kneeling down beside him.

"Steven, I don't know if your presence is actually helping," Jake whispered. "In fact, you're kind of distracting."

"Stress makes me materialize. This is a stressful situation," Steven said with waving arms. "Maybe you should learn to use the Mind Space."

"Maybe you should shut off the running commentary?"

Are you two trying to get killed? Because I could just let the body die and save everyone some trouble.

"Lemire! Get back over there," the woman continued. "Sarge needs to check in with what you found in the office." A flashlight beam came from over by the main building, soon followed by the woman in an NYPD-issue jacket and gloves. "I'll switch positions with you."

She is coming this way. She has called over the other officer from the end of the courtyard.

Jake angled his neck, moving as little as possible but enough to see what Khonshu meant—on one side, the woman with the flashlight approached. To his left, another uniformed officer began walking over this way, both using the long stone path that led to and from this fountain.

"I'm gonna run," Jake whispered, angling the staff in his hands to keep it clear of the ground.

No you're not. You're going to be strategic.

"I think Khonshu is right. There's . . ." Steven stood up and counted. "Two guards on the far side examining something in the bushes. Another one on the opposite corner. And then these two passing through."

Several seconds ago, Jake told Steven to be quiet. But now Steven offered useful information. "How do you know that? You exist in my head."

"Hmm," Steven said, fingers rubbing his chin. "Well, we are in an active pursuit situation. A little different from driving and talking." He knelt down beside Jake and glanced around, voice dropping, like it mattered to the armed patrols surrounding the space. "Perhaps the heightened stakes of what we're doing is making me a conduit for our body's senses. Integrating some of Khonshu's awareness but delivering it through my personality and—"

"Wait, are you saying you're more capable because you're scared? Or that you can't shut up because you're scared?"

I think it is both.

Steven paused, index finger of each hand wagging at Khonshu's statement. "I think," he said, an annoyed lilt in his voice, "it is the by-product of my practical, can-do attitude during moments of stronger-than-normal stress. Cortisol and adrenaline and—"

"Great." A gloved hand covered Jake's face as he sighed. "The worst super-power ever. Just be helpful, okay? Hard to concentrate with both of you giving advice."

The one with the flashlight is approaching. You must move.

"Right. Therapy session's over for now. She's approaching. It'd be so much easier if she just turned around right now. Jake, stay low." Jake did as advised, though he wondered if putting his trust in these voices in his head was the best strategy right now. "Low. Lower. Then shuffle slowly to your left. Then stop when I tell you to." Now Steven hopped on top of the fountain, and though he didn't physically exist, Jake heard his shoes clack on the stone.

Jake pressed himself against the wall as low as possible, the three-foot-tall outer perimeter of the fountain providing some measure of cover, though the top of his head had to stick out, even with the night sky and limited perimeter lighting. The flashlight beam cast a shadow from the fountain's centerpiece, and Jake got himself ready to move. "On my mark," Steven said. "She's coming closer. The other one's about thirty feet away. And . . . move! Slowly."

Jake stepped cautiously, one leg over the other, thighs still pressing against the fountain wall for balance. One step became two became three until eventually he was at nearly ninety degrees from the stone path where the woman approached. "Stop!" Steven yelled. "Hold it there."

"Hey, what's the rush?" the far officer called.

"Ah, you know the office at the top of the rotunda?" the woman asked.

"You see? I was right," Steven said, clapping his hands. "That's where we go."

"Ballistics report on the bullet just came in," she continued with a sigh. "Sarge needs you to review it, so I'm on 'get Lemire's attention' duty."

Bullet? That wasn't good. But what did that mean with Venom involved?

Now the two stood together, directly opposite of Jake's spot on the edge of the fountain, the woman waving her flashlight as she talked. The low position held longer than Jake would have liked, his foot eventually slipped, causing a skidding sound against the cobblestone path.

"What was that?" the woman asked.

"Oh no," Steven said. Which was exactly what Jake thought at the moment.

Duck down!

Jake went from kneeling to lying down so fast that the tiny cobblestones probably imprinted on his legs. He inched forward, elbows and knees pushing ahead until he came to a stop, shoulder still pressed against the fountain wall. He looked behind him, the flashlight's beam panning slowly for a few seconds.

"Meh. It's late. Probably a raccoon or something scavenging," she said.

"Doesn't help when the perp is 'big guy in a black cape.' All right," he said, "duty calls. Thanks, Smallwood."

Black cape?

The two parted ways, Smallwood still waving a flashlight as

she went farther away to the end of the courtyard while Lemire strolled toward the building's entrance. "Second-story window," Steven said, pointing up. "There's a tree right next to it, you could use that to climb."

Crawling, climbing, sneaking—this was why Jake left the mercenary tactics to Marc.

Go now. While this guard is walking.

Jake leapt over the hedge at the fountain's perimeter, his feet landing on well-manicured grass. He stayed low, staff tucked between his elbow and his side, and he moved quickly in his hunched space. "That guy! That guy over there, keep pace with him," Steven said. "You move ahead of him and he might catch you out of the corner of his eye." Despite the squishy, sprinkler-fresh feel of the lawn, Jake progressed with quick, precise movements, making sure each step landed with his full weight to avoid slipping. Lemire broke off, turning the corner and disappearing, and Jake dashed over to the target tree, a large structure that went a good three stories up, the thickest, leafiest branches offering enough length and elevation to get to a second-story window. Jake's breath quickened, which probably also meant Steven's breath quickened, which would then lead to the double-edged sword of Steven's greater sense of awareness but also his endless chatter.

"Come on, Jake. Go, go, go. Follow my lead," Steven said, strangely nimble as he climbed up the tree. Jake took a second, peering at this phantom that lived in his head yet existed out here. "Hurry up, we're almost there. Up here."

"Wait, how are you such a good climber?" Jake asked, looking up at the thickest, most stable branch. He tapped his staff, feeling for the unlock of its internal grappling hook.

"I'm not. But also, I can do amazing things under pressure when I'm a phantom." Steven looked down from a branch, hand through his thick brown hair. "Come on and—"

A sudden *clang* echoed through the space, the dark courtyard breaking with a light coming from a newly opened door on the ground floor. Jake dropped, then held his body flat against the tree trunk, but his bones echoed with the immediate chills that reflexively came upon detection.

We are seen. Take action now before that cop calls in reinforcements.

Jake took a breath as he separated his truncheon into nunchaku; he gauged the weight in his hand, one club gripped tightly as he began to swirl the other side on the chain. A quick look to his right showed this new police officer peering their way, the hydraulics of the door shutting behind him. The cop reached over to the walkie on his jacket's breast pocket and began speaking.

Jake leaned out the other side quick enough for his white mask to catch the officer's attention. "What?" he asked as Jake rolled back over, then launched the nunchaku through the air. They twirled, a flying hunk of adamantium connected by a chain, and he didn't even pause to track its flight. Instead, he sprinted at full speed with shoulder down, a full spear into the officer's abdomen right after the nunchaku smashed him in the jaw. Jake drilled the dazed officer to the ground, then flipped him on his back, the man's neck in the crook of his own elbow as Jake applied pressure to the carotid arteries until the man eventually knocked out.

"I can't just leave him here," Jake said, eyes scanning the dark horizon for any signs of sudden alerts.

Hide him.

"Over here," Steven said. Jake looked at Steven to find him waving by a recycling dumpster and an adjacent bush. "Between these. Fold his legs. Fast, before anyone sees us." The pace of Steven's words sped up as Jake wrapped his arms around the man's chest and dragged him, his boots scuffing against the blades of grass.

"I gotta say, I think teams usually work best with one 'man in the van,'" Jake said as he adjusted his grip, pulling harder before stashing the officer in Steven's spot. The man landed with a *thump,* his limp arm banging against the dumpster's flat facade. "I appreciate the help but one of you has to be quiet. It's distracting." Jake tucked the man's legs and arms as much as possible, before looking up at the unlit second floor, then at the thick tree branch where his phantom brother stood.

If Steven's fear can offer tactical support, that is fine with me. I can conserve my energy for doing important things. Like keeping this body alive.

That wasn't Jake's intent but he supposed it worked for now. "Great," he said with a huff. "Like a well-oiled machine." Steven grinned at that, which meant he totally missed Jake's sarcasm. Rather than dwell on it, Jake pushed forward. They had things to do. "I got an idea," he said, rushing to grab the nunchaku. The clubs formed back into a staff with a *click,* and Jake twisted the grip to lock it into grapple mode. "Going up?"

"Then what?" Steven shouted down as Jake aimed the staff at the thick base of a branch.

"Then," the staff shook as the grapple fired and burrowed deep into the branch's base, "we see how well adamantium can break glass. Hey," he said with a pause. "Do you feel that?"

"Feel what?" Steven asked.

Jake glanced at his left arm, where underneath the Mr. Knight coat and shirt came a strange throbbing sensation right at the incision wound and burn scars from earlier. "It's nothing. Let's move."

CHAPTER 13
VENOM

THEY ARE HERE. BUT HOW? HOW IS THEIR BODY STILL ALIVE? WE SAW the crescent dart plunge into their chest. Perhaps they are not even sure. They seem slightly oblivious, and they definitely do not know that we are here, that we are watching them.

At first, our instinct is to leap down, finish them off. You tell us to wait, hold off, give them a moment. You share your instincts as a mercenary with us, claiming they will serve a purpose. But perhaps you are merely stalling.

Yet, you say they will help us get to the psi-phon. And that is our ultimate goal, our key to protecting the Hive Mind. We track them. And . . . Your *patience* at waiting for the right moment? Your ability to anticipate?

All of that has worked out.

Interesting.

We did not expect the other body would have survived. No witnesses, no survivors—that is what the Whisperer wanted. But to truly ensure the safety of the Hive Mind, we must first acquire the psi-phon. The survivor can be dealt with later. For now, this works out to our advantage.

Jake grapples to the tree branch. We feel your amusement in seeing them in the Mr. Knight suit—*not the most appropriate attire*, you think. But also, how Jake snuck through the courtyard, avoided detection, used his equipment to neutralize the police officer, all of that met with your approval.

And now he steadies himself on the tree branch. He does not sense us on the roof, observing and waiting for what is next.

Your mind races. You wonder what he will do—you know what *you* would do in this circumstance, balancing noise and swiftness and desperation. You ask if Jake knows the staff's capabilities as well as you do, as he fights more with his fists. Your anxiety grows as Jake moves to the end of the branch, holds up his staff, checks his balance. He primes himself, and you pause in your thoughts. He sits and waits. Why does he wait?

But then you see—he senses the presence of guards as they move. We sense it, too. Our abilities are beyond Jake's, and yet somehow his timing is perfect. From the guard locations to their movements, Jake has moved this entire time with an unexpected precision to get to his location. And then . . .

Jake leaps.

You hope.

And he swings. The adamantium staff shatters the glass as he tumbles through, a tight roll. Yet the noise is covered, a passing train and the whipping winds drowning out the noise to those farthest away.

You suspected this, didn't you? You have *faith* in them, that they can find what we could not, that they can unlock Emmet's secrets.

How did you sense this when we did not?

No matter. We can sense it now, too. Now that we are close, we feel it: the single drop of symbiote remaining in that body. It calls to us, a beacon to track them.

We watch now, from the shadows. Jake remains unaware, even as he moves directly below us.

We are chasing one another, yet they do not know. Their movements ripple in our mind, their senses absorbing into ours. The symbiote puts part of us in them, transmitting their information as they run . . .

We shall run, too.

Across the rooftop, we keep pace with them, we track their

progress. This floor is strategically chosen, they knew there would be minimal security, the building cleared out after our invasion and assault. A single guard patrols the long hall; Jake hides behind some construction materials and a large cardboard box. The guard turns, Jake slams him to the ground. Another guard appears and sprints down the hall, grabbing Jake from behind. He drops the staff, and the first guard recovers enough to throw a punch. Jake shifts his weight, throws his captor forward, and grabs his staff, which he splints into nunchaku. He uses the walls and space to his advantage, whirling the handles like shields before striking. First into the guard's gut, then as he reaches for his gun, a diagonal swing that impacts the weapon hard enough to send it flying. The guard howls in pain, and Jake jumps, the weight of his full body slamming into the guard's nose, possibly breaking it as he collapses.

The guard's partner rushes in, striking Jake in the ribs, then the back of the knees. Jake falters, and as the new guard reaches for him, Jake whips the nunchaku handle, deflecting his hand enough for Jake to gather himself and leap forward, momentum thrusting a kick into the guard's gut. Jake flips the nunchaku so both handles are now an extension of his fist, an adamantium baton that drives the guard down with two swift blows.

Now Jake stands, exhausted. Each punch he took, every rush of success he feels, it echoes in us.

You recognized this, didn't you?

And now, as Jake races through the hallway, charges up the rotunda stairs, makes his way up to the office, you feel . . .

Confidence.

You feel complete confidence in their abilities.

Interesting.

In a way, even a little jealousy. At Jake's ability to just get it done. At Steven's ability to think things through. You ponder, how are they working together so well—without Spector to hold things together? And then your own feelings surface, a combination of respect and bitterness at the Steven and Jake that reside within your body, the identities you sometimes view as more trouble than they are worth, even though they are useful.

You blame them. For many things. You can't fathom how they manage to communicate so easily. It brings up a burning in your chest, an odd tightness in your throat. Just by watching these two, watching your doppelganger's body seamlessly transition between Jake and Steven and back, by being near them, you even think, *Sometimes I can't stand mine.*

This mission is not a counseling session. Perhaps it is good for you that we have shut them out. Do you want to take a moment to thank us?

Your teeth grit at that, and the many different thoughts in your head are becoming a distraction.

Focus. Observe. We have a goal. We sense it now, Jake in his white suit, slacks, and a jacket, but with the Mr. Knight mask pulled up to his nose. Five police officers guard Dr. Emmet's door.

Jake sizes them up. You anticipate his technique, his targets, his stance. You think, *He's taken care of worse,* even outnumbered five to one. He whirls his nunchaku, like a buzz saw of adamantium, and the guards inch backward, waiting for the right momentum.

Make that four. Because Jake uses the nunchaku as a distraction, then bounces off the hallway, leg propelling him forward into a flip kick that connects with the side of a guard's head. That guard then falls into another guard, and Jake spins backward, extending an arm to whip out a nunchaku handle, crashing into flesh and skull.

Three left.

The three charge forward, knocking over storage boxes that line the small hall. One goes for Jake's body, the others try to pry the nunchaku out of his hands. One of the guards pins Jake's other arm down as well.

Jake is . . . amused at this?

Buddy, you don't even know what you've unleashed, you think as you watch the guards slam Jake's arm against the wall—

Not just Jake's arm. The arm where the symbiote remains.

The nunchaku falls to the floor, but a strange delight comes over him. He thrusts his forehead into the jaw of the nearest guard, backing him off. His arms both trapped, Jake lifts his legs and presses hard against the wall, knocking his captors off-balance. They tumble together, though Jake twists, using the momentum to drive one man's skull into the drywall, his head stuck. Now free, Jake ducks his shoulder and rolls over the prone man, then gives him a hard kick to the gut, the ripple effect causing more drywall dust to fly.

Two left.

One of the remaining guards jumps over a spilled box and fires a fist. Jake swerves and blocks it down, then counters with three straight shots of his own. The first two land, the final one blocked by an elbow, then the man goes low and grabs Jake by the body.

Because he sees something Jake does not: the final guard is now up and ready, the nunchaku in his hands, though he grips the fine weapon like a blunt instrument. Jake resists, his legs driving in, but the force is too much and he begins skidding back, right when the nunchaku raises for a swing.

Behind you, you yell.

Something shifts in Jake. An instinct, or a reaction, or just the unexpected. We see it, though—and you *feel* it.

Jake lets go, going limp to collapse down and allow his captor's full momentum to burst forward. The nunchaku handles swing, hitting the wrong target, and then only one remains—soon to be zero, as Jake takes the momentary confusion to spring up and land a one-two combination that sends the last guard skidding across the smooth floor.

We sense it—Jake's blood rushes, his face gets hot, the pain almost feels good.

It grips you, too.

And now it's over. He stands up, checks the guards for breath.

You are relieved that he didn't kill anyone.

In fact, your thoughts dwell on this, you try to sense any injuries or damage to their body. You are curious . . .

. . . about what?

Something. Something that we cannot see. Are you hiding it from us? Your voice, it gets louder to us the longer we are in this body, the longer we are with you.

And now you sense . . . a change in them.

What is this change you sense?

You refuse to tell me. You fear that it will give away what they are capable of.

No. Not just that.

You want to keep them *safe*. You wish to protect them, this Steven and Jake. Because, for some reason, even though they come from a different reality, they are starting to mean something to you, something different from the resentment you feel at your own.

And now you recognize it: this path of carnage, that was all Jake Lockley.

But as they stand outside of Emmet's office, you think something else:

It's Steven's turn.

CHAPTER 14

—

STEVEN

THE FIRST STEP I TOOK AFTER RECLAIMING THE BODY WAS YANKING off Jake's ridiculous mustache and sticking it in my coat pocket. And then I pulled the mask all the way down, snapping it over my chin.

Now I was back to being me.

Onward. No need to look behind. Jake did all the dirty work.

Though, I supposed, dirty work *was* his specialty—when the only way out was through. In this case, through many security guards and cops patrolling Retrograde Sanitarium after Venom did . . . something here. I looked down at my hands, the knuckles of Mr. Knight's white gloves stained with dashes of blood, though the carbonadium-reinforced fabric held true.

Also, no one died. Jake checked. And he wouldn't lie about that. *We,* on the other hand, seemed to be a bit sore. In particular, my left arm throbbed with an ache that probably stemmed from getting all burned up—not exactly the best thing for a healthy body at any time, let alone fighting a bunch of people.

So somehow we managed to get here, the team of Jake and Khonshu working a little better than expected. I guess shutting up and letting them take over sometimes *was* the best choice.

But now?

"All right, I got us to the door," Jake said in my ear. "Now what?"

That was a good question. What were we even looking for? What was *Venom* looking for?

Only one way to find out.

Whatever you do, do it fast. You won't stay undetected forever.

"Right, right," I said, jiggling the doorknob. DR. EMMET, PSYCHIATRY, the display showed beneath a professional headshot. Even in a different universe, those bright red letters triggered all sorts of thoughts and feelings, a different kind of panic than from infiltrating a police-filled courtyard.

But I couldn't dwell on that. Not now.

"So if I were an alien symbiote taking over Marc Spector's body," I said, pushing against the locked door for good measure, "what would I want from the office of the worst psychiatrist in the Multiverse?"

"Maybe she's helpful in this one?" Jake asked, prompting a laugh from both of us.

"Nah," I said, clicking the nunchaku back into a single staff. One sharp adamantium strike damaged the door's hardware to the point that the curved metal handle hung by the shank, inner tumblers and bolts exposed. One more hit cleared the whole thing, the impact causing the door to sway open a crack. I stared again at the letters forming her name, experiencing the bubbling rage that normally was more of my brothers' purview and not mine.

Beneath the mask, I bit down on my bottom lip and kicked the door. Hard.

"Whoa," Jake said in my ear.

"Even I'm allowed to get mad sometimes," I said, stepping in.

In our reality, our time with Dr. Emmet never included visits to her office. They usually involved an exam room with poor ventilation and harsh lighting. Or, for the times when Spector really didn't want to cooperate, someplace in the basement with cracked yellow tile on the walls and a gurney with too many straps.

This office was . . . different from that.

It was clean. Pleasant. With potted plants and a red stuffed bear sitting on a file cabinet. Certificates and diplomas sat framed on the wall, and Dr. Emmet's desk showed no signs of her interest in, well, torturing people like us. A phone charger, a wrist brace for computer usage, a thank-you note written on the letterhead of Dr. Ashley Kafka, it all looked . . .

It might as well have been any office in any corporate building in the world. Except for the bloodstain on the ground.

"No signs of a struggle," I said to myself. Well, probably to Jake and Khonshu. Though I didn't know if Khonshu understood how crime scene investigations worked, or if he watched any cop shows during his downtime. "Just the bloodstain"—I pointed to the yellow evidence tag pasted on the wall, a large black *1* printed across it—"and *that*."

Adjacent to the marker sat a clear bullet hole drilled into the wall, framed by horizontal and vertical measuring tape, with small cracks and collected dust lining the penetration spot.

Venom would not use a gun. Something else happened.

"The informant said something about a sy . . . thing, whatever that is," I said, fingers rubbing my masked chin. "Maybe it's an experimental drug?"

"Her computer," Jake said. "Look around for clues to her password." Which showed that as much as we shared a brain and body, he hadn't been paying attention over the years. Because if he had, Jake would know that corporate passwords didn't work that way anymore.

"Jake, people have complex passwords. Like with different-cased letters and numbers and exclamation points." My words came with extra annoyance in each syllable and breath. "You can't just guess it from someone's posters on the wall. That's not real life. Even movies have caught up to that."

"Can't you hack it?" Jake asked, an annoyed *tap-tap-tap* sound coming from his phantom shoes straight into my head.

"Maybe if I was an expert in IT security. Or had some of Frenchie's tools," I said, taking a closer look at the shelf adjacent to her desk. Academic textbooks, vacation photos, a Team Ravencroft mug holding spare change. Nothing overly unique or sinister.

"You're a billionaire with a team of engineers and you never learned how to do it yourself?"

"I studied the arts, history, philosophy, enriching pursuits that—" I started, before realizing how pompous that made me sound. Maybe another time we could debate the values of the humanities versus STEM. "Besides, this is in her office. It's a corporate computer that probably gets backed up to the cloud. I doubt she'd actually store data from illicit experiments on here. We'll need another way." And just to show him that, I tapped the enter key twice. The screen flashed to life, a prompt for a password below *Welcome, Dr. Emmet* against a generic background of a waterfall surrounded by lush jungle.

Except . . . something else flashed. In my head—our head. An image? No, more than that. A sensation.

Touch the computer again. I sensed something.

"Yeah," Jake said slowly, "me too. Give it a try."

I pulled the glove off my hand and tented my fingers over the keyboard, smooth plastic against bare skin, enough pressure to make contact without actually activating any of the buttons. A flurry of images fired off in my head, along with a feeling of . . .

Rage?

I have discovered something. Mind Space, now.

"Can we just do it here without indulging in Steven's stupid—"

"Good idea, Khonshu," I said, closing my eyes . . .

Suddenly we stood in the lobby of The Met, Jake in his usual jacket and cap—though now he'd somehow conjured up a deck of playing cards that he absentmindedly shuffled, a constant flicking noise done probably just to annoy me or Khonshu or both of us.

Will you stop that noise? We have more important things to discuss.

Khonshu, even with his bird skull for a head, had apparently had enough of Jake's irritating habits.

"What noise? I don't know what you're talking about," Jake said, continuing to shuffle the cards beneath a smirk.

If you got your mind in the right place, maybe you would notice that.

Khonshu extended a long finger to point at the massive screen on the wall behind them—something that normally displayed exhibits and photos. But now it played, well . . .

Memories? A vision? *Something,* and it took a second for it to be clear that we saw Venom's point of view. In smooth, real-time playback, unlike the mash of rage and images from earlier.

I didn't say it, but given my brief dalliance with the film industry, these came off as impressive production values.

"Oh," I said with a nod at Khonshu. "This is why we're here."

Venom's memories. We have intercepted them. Watch.

Over the PA, the memories played out like the worst promotional address possible. "But I'm afraid I've got nothing in here regarding your precious device," Dr. Emmet said with a coy smile before activating the computer. "Shall we see?"

"How are we seeing this?" I asked. "Wait, wait, is Venom here?"

We are connected. But not in the way you think. I understand now.

Khonshu disappeared, then reappeared in front of the screen, using the massive crescent moon on the top of his staff to point.

In the burning basement, I used the remaining drop of symbiote in this body as a conduit to bring myself here. But that means that this body contains a piece of Venom as well.

"What does," Jake said, stepping toward the glowing display as the cards finally went silent, "that mean for us?"

I do not know. I do not understand what we do and do not share, but this is to our advantage.

"Look at him," I said, as Venom paced back and forth, arms visibly gesturing. "He can't find what he needs. And she's just taunting him. Why isn't he looking elsewhere? She's got an entire office of stuff."

"It's in the computer." A new voice carried up from the screen—but a distinctly familiar voice.

Marc. This reality's Marc.

"Venom, listen to me. It's gotta be in the computer. A record or something, a file or an archive. Don't waste our time with anything else, we've got to break into her system. Let me talk to her."

"That's trippy," Jake said. "So Marc is telling Venom that in their shared head? Is this what it's like when we explain our lives to people?"

Marc is diverting Venom. But why?

"Because . . ." I said, the clues suddenly snapping into place. "He's slowing Venom down. He wanted us to catch up. To get ahead. He sees it, too; Emmet wouldn't put illegal experiments on a work computer that gets backed up by their IT department. Whatever she's into, whatever this sy-something is, it's gotta be off the books. She couldn't save it in a spreadsheet on the Retrograde network. *That* means the information *isn't* in the computer," I said, catching both of their attention as the screen continued on: Venom badgering Emmet, who continued to grin with amusement. "Venom wouldn't know about how humans handle shady business. That's why Marc can draw this out. Emmet would want to keep it somewhere more private, but accessible here while she studies Marc, so she had—"

New shouts came from the screen, and Venom's view whirled to see the barrel of a drawn gun, shaky hands gripping it, along with the wide eyes of an overmatched security guard. More commotion unfurled—Emmet yelled, the guard screamed, Venom took over Marc, with black swirling over his vision before dissolving back into clarity.

A gunshot.

A flash of black.

The sound of a ricochet.

Venom turned to see Emmet collapse on the floor, the bullet drilled directly into her forehead.

And a scream, one so otherworldly and terrifying that it shook me to *my* core, despite the safety of my Mind Space.

Then nothing.

Steven. Jake. The police are on the move. They have found the officer outside.

"Get back in that room," Jake said. "There's gotta be a . . . a notebook or log or something that has whatever Venom wanted."

I snapped back into reality, a new desperation as I gripped my staff. Khonshu's voice rattled in my head, periodic updates that all amounted to *They're getting closer.* And Jake, Jake yelled in such a rapid-fire voice that I couldn't even think. "Jake, you're very good at what you do and I love and respect you, but *shut up right now.*"

"You see?" he asked. "Too many voices gets distracting, I told you."

What did she have, what did she have? Textbooks. More textbooks. Some pieces of circular clay artwork, box of tissues, a phone-charging stand, a plastic cup with pens and pencils, and on the top shelf . . .

A statue.

A small statue of Ammit, the Egyptian goddess with the head of a crocodile and the body featuring parts of a hippopotamus and a lion.

And underneath the statue, a small, neatly bound notebook.

"Of course. Pen and paper. Safe from digital inspection or hacking," I said, lifting the statue and grabbing the notebook. I flipped through the pages, handwritten on clear ink in a very, very methodical way.

Numbers, notes, all neatly organized.

They are coming, Steven. You must move.

"Hold on, hold on, I gotta see if this is it. Sy . . . sy . . . sy," I said, flipping through the pages as fast as I could. Some sort of transactional ledger, with items and dates, a column for *True/False* and another column for what seemed like random details. I jumped to the end—this all *had* to mean something to her. "This is strange. 'Johnny's music box,' 'Bogeyman—girl's plushie,' 'golden ankh,' it's almost like . . . ."

And then I realized:

Not her. This all meant something to *me.*

This was Marc Spector's *history.*

"These are facts belonging to Marc. And us. This has to be it." I moved faster, flipping through to bring the dates closer to the present. "Sy . . . sy . . . sy . . ." I muttered to myself as I skimmed the pages, "what begins with—"

Then I saw it. Not S-Y.

But P-S-I.

As in, the psi-phon.

"Wait, wait," I said. "Listen to this. 'Marc claims that the psi-phon is a multidimensional device that connected the same person across universes, draining their energy and essence into whoever held the device. Will investigate further. To me, the device looks like old-school earmuff headphones for listening to vinyl records in the 1960s.'"

"Multidimensional," Jake said. "Like us."

Time to get out. They're on the stairs.

"Right, right." An exit—well, the door itself wouldn't work.

As if Jake read my mind—because he probably could—he spoke right before I turned. "Window. Same way we got in."

"We're two more stories up." I looked at the staff, clicking it to unlock the grapple inside. "What do I even grapple onto?"

They're on this floor now. They're inspecting the bodies Jake left behind.

"No time to figure that out. Find a spot, shoot it, and then go," Jake yelled. Instead of arguing, I did my best impersonation of what Jake did minutes ago, just in reverse—first safely stowing the newfound notebook inside my coat pocket, then hitting the window with the staff as hard as possible. Glass exploded outward, hopefully not landing on anyone too far below, and some of it splashed back on me.

I didn't need Khonshu to tell me the cops were approaching beyond the broken office door. Their voices, their footsteps, the *click-click* of their weapons gave that away.

I took Jake's advice, crouching on the windowsill, finding the first bit of *anything* that might take the grapple cleanly, and fired.

CHAPTER 15

—

JAKE

THEY NEEDED INTEL.

But Jake and Steven—and Khonshu—also had limited resources. Very limited.

As in, no home, no base, no friends, and only a little bit of money.

What *did* they have? A stolen cab, one with an uncomfortable back seat. Jake couldn't speak from experience on that because after grappling out onto a tree and then a building across the street, Steven had rushed into the cab and they drove to a quiet spot, where he eventually passed out in the back. They rested through the night, though Jake took over again in the morning, starting with a full search of the cab for extra supplies: one Bluetooth earbud, a bottle of water, another half-filled bottle of water, and a rolled-up brown windbreaker jacket. And, of course, one super hero getup in the form of a mask and a white suit that managed to somehow stay pretty clean through all of the fighting and climbing and smashing.

And Spector's black paramilitary clothes that smelled like fire but were ultimately more comfortable than the Mr. Knight suit, thus prompting Steven to sleep in those.

Despite giving the body over to Jake, Steven still dictated *where* they might find a place to do some investigating, or as Steven put it, "One of my favorite places in the world."

"Where are we heading?" Jake asked, stepping onto the sidewalk from the parking garage.

"Only a block over," Steven said, his voice directly in Jake's ear. Jake rushed through in a mix-and-match outfit: black cargo pants with the white Mr. Knight button-down shirt and the thin windbreaker jacket over it. And just for safety, Moon Knight's staff, disguised as a cane that happened to be made of adamantium.

In a way, it was fitting—a little bit of all of them in the body, outside of Khonshu's oversized beak.

"This place?" Jake asked, pointing toward the massive columns at the stone building's entrance. And though Steven remained audio-only for now, his giddiness seemed to vibrate through the whole shared body. Jake tapped on the Bluetooth earbud unearthed from the cab's back seat—not quite as good as going to the Mind Space, but at least it disguised any conversations with Steven or Khonshu without looking deranged.

"The New York Public Library! A wealth of information," Steven said, his voice crackling with excitement. "Where we'll get free access to references, books, an internet-connected computer. And, possibly, the most important resource of all . . ."

"Money?" Jake asked.

Weapons?

"Time! And quiet!" Steven proclaimed.

Jake sighed, failing to catch Steven's enthusiasm, and instead tapped the notebook sitting in his inner jacket pocket just to check that it was safe. "Let's see what's in here."

THEY DIDN'T EXACTLY START FROM SCRATCH. BEFORE PASSING OUT last night, Steven spent a good hour peering through the notebook, page by page of Emmet's handwritten notes on things from the life of Marc Spector. Each entry had a list of columns at the top: date, item, history, recovered, true/false, resolution.

While she didn't say it explicitly, the whole purpose of the project seemed pretty clear. After all, Dr. Emmet *was* fascinated by Marc—that remained consistent across the Multiverse. The shock treatments, truth serums, mind games, all of the other torturous

ways she tried to peer into their head, Marc and the others represented something transfixing to her, a cross-section of her desire to
crack the human mind with her love of Egyptology. Maybe it was
because she knew so much about Egypt, perhaps that made her
figure she could understand the symbolism in it more. Despite living in an age where the Avengers rescued the planet on a semi-
regular basis, she still couldn't quite accept Marc's reality could be,
well, reality. She needed to understand what ticked in Marc's
brain. Was it delusion? Dissociative identity disorder? Supernatu-
ral intervention? A massive grift? In short, the "Good Doctor"
was obsessed.

The notebook listed items, concrete things that she could track
down and research—and in some cases even acquire. And when
she did, she'd noted the history of the items and whether she found
Marc's story believable or not, along with some personal commentary that showed this was not an official clinical record. But the
one that mattered the most right now? The psi-phon. "Psi-phon.
That one still bugs me," Steven said.

"Because it's not Egyptian?" Jake asked.

"No, the name. Who were the advertising wizards that came
up with that one?" Steven asked.

Jake shook his head, settling at the table in the large, empty
room before turning to Dr. Emmet's notes:

Item Description: Looks like DJ headphones
painted in silver. Supposedly able to
absorb the life essence of Marc's
dopplegangers across alternate realities.
Could be mental justification for Marc's
DID. Marc claims that it was used by
someone called "Moon Shade" to siphon
(ha ha) power from other Moon Knights.
He also claims it was created by an
"interdimensional being" known as "the
Magus."

True/false: False. Far too ridiculous to
be real. Especially because I discovered
some reference to the Magus appearing
in ancient Egyptian lore from a paper
by Peter Alraune. Clearly Marc took some
thrift-store find, painted it silver,
and concocted this story to tie different
aspects of his delusions Marlene Alraune's
father.

Resolution: Sold to Monica/Ravencroft
Foundation. Funds used to continue this
project's pursuits. Also, Monica owes me
lunch.

"Marlene," Jake said.

"Let's not go there right now," Steven said, leaning on the table. He pointed at the computer workstation in front of them. "Remember, this universe's Marlene is different from ours."

"Yeah. I was just thinking, though."

"That's good, Jake. Thoughts, not fists," Steven said, coming off somewhere between school playmate and disgruntled teacher.

Normally, Jake would return the verbal jab. But in this case, the question weighed too heavy, carried too much burden, possibility and fear woven into one. "What if we don't see *our* Marlene again?"

Steven's chattiness suddenly disappeared, and it likely had nothing to do with the quiet of the library. "Let's try not to get ahead of ourselves."

"You know what I mean, though." Jake supposed that he did tend to run on practicality, if practicality meant focusing on just getting the job done, no matter what it took. Spector would weigh the costs, both literal and moral. Steven would debate for twice as long as needed. But Jake, he simply took what was put in front of him and determined the path through—even if it meant punching his way out.

So this probably came off as a little out of character for him. Though, really, when factoring in things like "body is dying" and "stuck in another universe," he deserved a pass for being a little homesick.

"Well, look, now that you're getting all sentimental . . ." Steven's quip faded away without a finish. They'd lost their Marc. They'd lost their home, their world, their universe. They'd lost the life within this body, too. Or at least that particular finish line was approaching faster than they would like.

And Marlene?

"I think we'll look back at this time with a laugh someday," Steven finally said, with a completely transparent false confidence. " 'Oh, remember when we got stuck in another universe and had an Egyptian god in our head *and* battled an alien?' Excellent times."

"You're avoiding the question." Jake's voice was low enough to convey his impatience.

"Clock's ticking, Jake," Steven finally said, his voice low and quiet. "Let's focus."

"Right, right." Jake moved the computer's mouse, the screen coming to life. "All right, so what are we looking for?"

"See what you can find on this company that bought it, the Ravencroft Foundation." Jake began clicking, typing with each index finger as Steven continued chatting away. "The question, though, is why Venom needed this? It's a Multiverse device, it connects and drains from the same person in different realities."

"Wait, that makes no sense." Even without being able to see Steven, Jake knew his brow furrowed at the thought. "If it's supposed to connect the versions of the same people, why did Venom want us dead?"

You two are thinking so single-dimensionally.

"Well, if you're just going to insult us," Steven said, "at least back it up with an explanation.

Venom's Hive Mind exists across the Multiverse.

"That's good enough for me," Jake said, hoping that they could skip past Steven's need for details. "Kind of answers the 'how' without the 'why.'"

"Yes, but we need to know the 'why.'" Steven's voice picked up in pace, that damned excitability coming back. "There's gotta be a, I don't know, a logic that connects all this. We just have to unlock it."

"No, you don't. I think it doesn't really matter as long as we get to the psi-phon first. And that means we have to take action now."

Jake is right. Keep searching, you two.

Jake decided *not* to lord that one over Steven, and instead knuckled down on the research. Page after page loaded up, basic websites and press releases for the Ravencroft Foundation—or its full name, the Ravencroft Foundation for Mental Health. Steven fired off all sorts of search parameters to cross-reference, variations of Dr. Emmet's name and history and Ravencroft.

What they found, though, started to put it all together.

Dr. Emmet was on the board for the Ravencroft Foundation, a nonprofit that championed "pioneering research in the realms of psychiatric progress." So was a woman named Monica Rappaccini, a scientist who appeared to have way more education and experience than most people could amass in several lifetimes.

Rappaccini and Dr. Emmet also had something else in common: They both worked at Ravencroft Asylum up in Westchester County about a decade ago.

"That explains the mug on her shelf," Steven noted before firing off new search requests to Jake. "You don't need to search further. It's like putting together a strategy when the business numbers are all laid out in front of me, I'm seeing all the pieces before I fire it off. Just be my hands for now."

"Why don't you take over the body, then?" Jake asked, stretching his arms out over his head.

"Because I'm going to need to talk this through to myself." Steven gestured at the library. "And I don't want to get us kicked out."

Another two hours passed, with Steven talking most of the

freakin' time. Jake instead tuned out, and Khonshu stayed quiet as well, but he did as directed, clicking and typing until finally Steven said, "That's it!"

"What's it?" Jake took in a website that he'd loaded up without even really thinking about it. " 'Pinkerton Auction House presents an exclusive silent auction to benefit the Ravencroft Foundation and other charitable organizations.' What the hell is this?"

"See, now I could use a PowerPoint. Okay, we know Emmet and Rappaccini go way back. We know both are on the Ravencroft Foundation board. A little bit of digging shows that Rappaccini is on the board for a lot of scientific initiatives. Who has time for all of that?" Jake shrugged, but Steven kept going. "Unless, it's all a front. For something else."

"You're getting all conspiracy on me," Jake said, adjusting his cap.

"Emmet used unscrupulous tactics. And she sold the psi-phon to fund her research privately—nothing to do with Retrograde. All off the books. But Rappaccini is interested in these obscure pieces of history that *might* actually have some power. And she's connected to all of these different organizations. Now click on that tab. Fifth one," Steven said.

"I don't even remember opening this one." The screen flashed, some chatter from a social media site. "What is this? This is just people being dumb online."

"Anyone can say anything online, right? But when it all lines up together? It means something," Steven said. "There are a handful of dark web posts associating Ravencroft Foundation with a secret organization known as 'Advanced Idea Mechanics.' And if the business world—and nonprofit world—have taught me anything, it's that a cryptic organization can have a lot of fronts. But I'm guessing they're not just money laundering. Still," he laughed to himself, "as far as shady business practices go, A.I.M. probably isn't half bad."

Where does this put us?

"This puts us at the Pinkerton silent auction tomorrow. We'll need a tuxedo. It looks like they've rented out Top of New York Hotel for it. Art Deco, very nice."

Jake considered the dwindling wad of cash in their back pocket. A gala with a silent auction? Guess that was Steven's territory. Except . . . "Steven, your billions are in our reality. Unless you can do a wire transfer across universes?"

"No, no, no, it's not like that. I'll get us in there. But Jake, we're not bidding on it." Steven's voice turned into a whisper, though it got louder in Jake's head, as if Steven leaned forward— probably complete with an overeager grin. "We're gonna steal it."

Grand theft at a private auction for secret billionaires with nefarious goals?

Could be worse.

"Okay. You command the ship for that one," Jake said. "But one thing I still don't get—"

Stop talking about this now.

"What?" Jake asked.

"That's not exactly a polite way to be with your roommates," Steven said.

Don't you feel it? The beating in your left arm.

Come to think of it, Jake *did* sense a certain . . . heat or pulse or something from the arm, right at the scar tissue. He'd noticed a similar throbbing earlier, way back at Retrograde. But he'd just figured it was, like, carpal tunnel or something from typing longer than he'd ever typed before. "Yeah? So?"

It is the symbiote. It is Venom. We shall not discuss it anymore out loud, only in the Mind Space.

Jake and Steven locked eyes, like staring at the strangest mirror in the middle of the New York Public Library's main branch.

I fear Venom has been listening.

CHAPTER 16
VENOM

THEY HAVE LOCATED IT.

Your faith in them worked.

We will wait for them at this location, this towering piece of architecture, with its bright lights and excessive ornateness. It's one ugly piece of human ingenuity. We will let them lead us to the psi-phon. And then we will take it.

You resist. No, not resist. Not beg. Not fight back.

You are offering . . . a conversation.

What is this discussion about?

You don't have to do it this way, you say. *If you just tell me why this thing's so important, what you need to do, why you keep saying much more is at stake, then maybe we can find a way. I've already lost Steven and Jake once. I can't lose them again.*

Impressive. We thought we could push you down, squeeze you out. You connect with us in unexpected ways. Except what you are saying is different from what you are feeling. You are *plotting*—ways to possibly help them. Your exact thoughts, your true intentions, those stay obscured, an ability that we have rarely seen.

Is this your gift after having existed with Khonshu for so long?

No matter. You are still under our influence, our control. We understand that you think we are cruel, ruthless. You think we seek the psi-phon for power, for greed.

Do you really want to have a conversation? Do you really want to know what is at stake?

You say yes. You ask us to trust you.

And now, while we wait, we will open up our mind to you.

Do you see?

This is Earth in Reality113843. Or what was Reality113843.

A thriving populace, so similar to your own. In fact, identical to nearly every detail: the art created, the food consumed, the people spawned.

The only difference? He used it as a testing ground.

Now witness its final moments. There, that old man sitting on his porch, drinking coffee as the sun sets over San Francisco. His son approaches, pushing his own grandchild in a stroller. The old man stands to greet him, then he looks up.

See the moon, a bright full circle, seconds before now a smattering of glowing pieces, as if it imploded upon itself. And the stars in the dusk sky, they are no longer dots of light; instead they pop and sparkle like fireworks before disappearing forever. Even the sun over the horizon, it does the same thing as every other star in this universe—imploding, as if crushed by a gauntlet, all that heat and energy pressurized into its core before exploding outward.

The sun is gone. But before the man and his child and his grandchild can process the sudden change in temperature, the ground beneath them folds, one side of the street twisted vertically before everything drives down toward the planet core.

The old man, fortunately, was struck by debris before he witnessed more.

Now look at 113843—nothing. Every star, every planet, every nebula, every single object imploded upon itself and burst, all for the Whisperer to do . . . something.

One of his experiments for control and energy. He sees everything as experiment and result, a data point regardless of life or destruction. He is cold, calculating, ruthless. He shared this exact memory of this experiment as a show of power, as a way of demonstrating what he could do to the Hive Mind if we did not fall in line.

If we did not find *you*.

We don't particularly like him.

Do you see the potential of the Whisperer, what he plans to do?

Do you see his *power*?

Do you understand *why* we must recover the psi-phon, no matter the cost?

You, your body is the key. We don't know why yet, but the Whisperer sees that. The others, Steven and Jake?

They are in our way. And in order to save *everything,* we must give the Whisperer what he wants.

The psi-phon. And no witnesses, no survivors.

Got it?

CHAPTER 17

—

STEVEN

FROM THE OUTSIDE, IT LOOKED LIKE ANY OTHER DAY FOR THE TOP OF New York Hotel.

Except instead of bellhops at the front, two very large men in black suits and earpieces stood.

And the people walking in, instead of luggage and casual vacation attire, they arrived immaculately dressed.

"Your kind of people, huh?" Jake asked. They were, though that didn't necessarily mean that I liked them. I did, however, know how to work them. I stood, dressed in Mr. Knight's suit except for the mask, which stayed folded in my inner coat pocket.

That part was for later.

"Not necessarily. But they'll get us inside," I said, watching the arriving guests for the right situation. What that right situation was, I didn't exactly know. But years in off-the-cuff business situations had taught me enough about how luck often stemmed from simply being patient and open to opportunities. Every minute or two, one or two people arrived, a gradual trickle that culminated in guests presenting a thin card with a barcode, which the guards scanned before ushering them in. "A.I.M. must have rented out the entire hotel."

"Be nice to have that kind of money, huh?" Jake asked. "The people I know, they dream of staying at a hotel for one night. Your people, they rent out the whole damn hotel. They got no grasp of reality."

"Jake," I said, my gloved left hand balanced on top of the truncheon that doubled as a cane, "I'm going to need to pass as some-one who *doesn't* talk to voices in his head. So while I am usually up for a discussion on the issue of class disparity, can you be, you know, *constructive* right now?"

"Yeah, yeah." Jake went quiet, and thankfully Khonshu didn't chime in, either. "So what makes the right person?"

"Someone," I said, "trustworthy. Someone who knows me—or this universe's Marc. Someone who can pick up on what we need without being told explicitly 'get us into this place.'" Jake laughed at this list, prompting a quieter one in return. "Tall order, I know. The right person. Okay?"

"Right, right. Got it. Let you do your thing." Just as Jake said that, Khonshu also grunted an affirmative. Though they stayed quiet this time, I still felt their presence, kind of like how you just *know* when you have someone behind you on an airplane proba-bly quietly mocking the way you talk.

The right person, which meant, well, not the typical A.I.M. crowd. A.I.M. had a lot of fronts for their organization, and I'd noticed some of the people from all manner of industries: science, medicine, not-for-profit, government.

This was after all technically a fundraiser.

But then a few people stood out as having their own motives. "No, not him. Not her," I said, pointing at the duo that passed, a bulky man with silver skin in a matching suit and black doo rag on his head, then a pale blond woman, her flowing white dress cov-ered by an elaborate cape. Another tuxedoed man walked by, flecks of white sprinkled in his dark brown hair. He paused for a moment, steely eyes framed by gaunt cheeks and a large, jagged scar running down the left side of his face, then he turned our way, a brief eye contact before I looked elsewhere.

Definitely not that guy. Too creepy.

Right when I thought that, a new person strode into view.

It took several seconds to fully put it together—the last time I'd seen this person involved circumstances that were far from glam-orous, so the dress and shawl felt a little out of place. But she was as prepared and as reliable as I'd met—as *Spector* had met. More importantly, Spector innately trusted her with his life.

And she with him.

I took a calculated risk and assumed that it played out this way for this reality's Marc as well.

Layla El-Faouly.

She looked my way, first making eye contact with me, then tilting her head in amusement before digging into her purse for her invitation. "Perfect," I said, tapping my weapon-turned-cane. "Maybe fate's looking out for us."

Fate is something you humans made up.

"You sure you know her in this universe?" Jake asked, suspicious as always.

"Only one way to find out." So much for staying quiet. "That's the thing about these galas," I said under my breath. "Even if they don't remember you, they'll pretend they do. But I'm pretty sure she will."

I approached, a casual gait as I crossed the street, like I really, definitely belonged there. Part of the whole schtick of being a billionaire was simply acting like everyone expected you to, the outer layers completely different from the person who just wanted to stay home and deep dive into a rabbit hole of whatever topic caught my fancy—something Jake clearly did not understand.

Hopefully we'd have another chance to go over that after this was all over.

I trained my eyes on Layla, her dark curly hair and deep-red lipstick offsetting the layered gold shawl that sprouted like wings around the olive undertone of her bare shoulders.

"Invitation, please," one guard said.

"Of course," she said. Right when she held up her badge, I stepped forward. "Representing Scarlet—"

"Layla!" I said, arms wide.

She turned to me, irises sharp under her angled eyeliner. "Steven? Steven Grant?"

"You never know who you're going to run into at these things.

Oh," I said, patting my different pockets. "Where's my invitation?" I glanced behind us, where a bit of fortunate luck showed that no one waited in line, those nearby still lingering for arriving companions or deep in conversation.

The guard's scanner beeped to confirm Layla's, but she waited as I continued checking my coat. "Are you kidding?" I said. "Don't tell me I have to run back and grab it. In this traffic?" My arms gestured a little bigger than necessary. "I'll miss the whole opening."

"Sorry, sir. We need an invitation."

"Not to be rude," Layla said to the guard, "but this guy could probably buy everything being auctioned tonight. Anyone who's anyone here knows Steven Grant. And any fundraiser raises more funds when Steven Grant is involved."

The two guards looked at each other, one with crinkled eyebrows and the other with twisted lips. "I'm sorry, sir," the first one said, "but we have to scan an invitation."

"You know what?" Layla hooked her arm around mine. "He's my plus-one for the evening. Okay?"

I looked at the guards, then back at Layla's wry grin, an expression that took me right back to so many arguments about team tactics in the back of a cramped Karnak Cowboys van.

Simpler times.

"Guys, I wouldn't mess with her," I said, nudging her with my elbow. "I've seen what she's capable of." Murmurs came from behind, a small line finally forming up, and I looked over my shoulder to really point out that, hey, people were waiting.

The two guards looked at each other, then at the people impatiently craning their necks. "It's fine," one of them said. "Come on in."

I offered a nod in return, followed by Layla's big grin, which dropped as soon as we got to the revolving door. "You're actually Marc pretending to be Steven right now, huh? Lemme give you a tip, you're coming off as trying too hard. The real Steven isn't quite so 'look at me, I'm a billionaire.'"

"It's actually me. Steven, that is. Marc's . . ." My voice trailed off as I pushed the door and we walked in unison. "He's a little indisposed."

"Indisposed?" Layla asked. We stepped into the lobby, both waving at no one in particular, my best gala-appropriate grin on my face. "What's that supposed to mean?"

"You know how Marc's life is complicated?"

"That's putting it lightly," she said.

"It's, like, twenty times worse at the moment." My billionaire facade dropped, normal affect coming back to my words. "I'm certain I can trust you, so this is—"

"You know what? Right now I don't want to know." Layla put a hand up. "I'm here for a reason. Catch up the next time I'm in New York?"

"Oh man, you *wanted* to tell her," Jake said with a laugh. Which I suppose I did. It wasn't easy carrying the whole burden of this Multiverse-hopping, alien-parasite, Egyptian-god-in-a-dying-body state around. I shook it off, then turned back to Layla.

"Of course."

"I gotta check something," she said, examining her purse before turning to the signs displayed on the large panel: one arrow pointed at the auction, one at the reception, and one at the display exhibit. "You know who's sponsoring this whole thing?"

"Oh, I know." The urge to tell Layla *everything* still tugged at me. Her history with Marc included some wild times; if she could survive the realm of the Duat, this Multiverse business with Venom might not seem too unbelievable. But as we paused at the signs, Layla's stance, her stare, the way she scanned those coming and going, it was clear she had something—or someone—else in mind.

I respected Layla enough to abide by her wishes.

"Not your usual company, is it?" she asked, eyes still narrowed.

"Not yours, either," I said. "Where are you headed?"

"Not sure yet." She glanced at her phone, then looked at either side of the room. "Maybe nowhere for a few minutes. You on a hunt?"

"In a way." Years ago, we would have been on the hunt together. Or maybe in another one of those universes, we'd *still* be mercenary partners—and more. But here, that didn't quite line up. "You?"

She nodded, her eyes narrowing as she stared at the screen. No, actually—she looked *past* the screen. Slightly over it, as it was, her head turning gradually before snapping back ahead. "I'm looking for someone. Hopefully he arrives before sunrise. He's supposed to be here but I don't see him yet. Unless he's getting cocktails already. But that doesn't seem like his scene."

Cocktails. Now that I was here, now that other millionaires and billionaires and people who would be noted in a photo caption lingered all around, a new idea came to mind.

This could be my key to the psi-phon. I reached into my pocket, our lone Bluetooth earbud pressed against my palm, then looked at the person at my side.

Though we didn't have a long history, Layla El-Faouly was the type of person I could count on implicitly. More importantly, so could Marc—across any universe, apparently. And given that Marc dealt with more life-or-death situations than I did, I trusted his judgment. "I have a strange request," I said suddenly. "If you have a few minutes before your target arrives."

"You? Strange request?" Layla raised an eyebrow, a light tone in her voice. "I'm shocked."

"You in?"

"I don't know," she said, though the *way* she said the words showed that she did already know. "I seem to remember some things going awfully wrong when we worked for Karnak together."

"This will be easier, I promise. So," I said, pulling out the earbud, "I'm gonna give this to you. In ten minutes, find me in the reception and just give it back. Be as loud as you can."

Layla's head tilted, thick curls moving in step. She looked behind her, then all around. "As long as Harrow hasn't arrived yet, I think I can make it work. But *Marc* will owe me a favor down the line."

Her words presented the perfect opportunity to tell an ally— a *friend*—why that may or may not be possible, what sort of insanity they were up against. But with Venom likely nearby and a good amount of A.I.M. associates lurking *and* Layla on her own quest, this was the most I could ask for right now.

"Appreciate it," I said, putting the small device in her open palm. I closed her fingers around it, then glanced behind us. "Now," I said, starting my stride to the large double doors, "I need a drink. See you in a bit."

I WAVED. THEN WAVED AGAIN. THEN SAID A VERY ENTHUSIASTIC hello to a lanky man with wavy red hair in a white suit and oversized bow tie, before turning on my heel and offering a handshake to a quite large, quite unsmiling man, most of his face obscured by a large hat but hints of metallic tubes poking out from beneath the lapels of his coat.

I'd started these, circling the room as quickly as possible, all to establish to anyone and everyone in the space that *Steven Grant was here*. And with that, the ripple effect succeeded in raising the awareness I needed; a second lap around the room proved even more fruitful.

I knew because that time, people said hi to *me*. Enough that I took a moment to appreciate the foundation I'd built for this plan. Now I needed a drink—the kind I couldn't get walking through alleys with Jake—and someone official to talk to.

"Your scotch, sir," the waiter said, handing over a glass. Despite us being *really* low on funds, I reached into my coat pocket for cash. But before I could hand over a tip, the waiter left. Either A.I.M. paid the staff really well or upper-upper-management might be a little paranoid. I sipped, enjoying the cool burn of a quality drink, and scanned the room. "There," I said, nodding to the tall tuxedoed man standing by the large electronic sign displaying various auction items. "That's not a hotel employee. That person's working the auction."

"How can you tell?" Jake asked.

"He's a little too stuffy to be a waiter or a bellhop," I said.

Is your strategy to greet everyone in this room?

"That guy," I said, waving and nodding at anyone who passed, "needs to know that everyone here knows me." I made eye contact with him as I approached, catching his look long enough to announce my presence. He didn't move or react, lips pursed within a thin black beard, and his eyes drew away to looking *above* the crowd instead of at any specific person.

It didn't matter. He knew I was here now. I moved with more determination, saying hello to anyone who might listen on the way. "Steven Grant," I said loudly, reaching out over and over and shaking any open hands I passed. I paused as a young man with dirty blond hair and thin beard gave me a crooked look. "Good to see you again. We met at that exhibit, the—oh, what was it? Just a few weeks ago."

"Oh!" he said with the kind of laugh that gave away he had no idea what I was talking about, nor did he care. "Of course. The Rand Foundation fundraiser. But you know, everyone knows your work."

"I try," I said, hands out, sloshing my drink for extra good measure. "I'm looking at collecting some fine antiquities here tonight. I just—" I turned suddenly, turning my voice up a notch. "Oh, hello. Good to see you, too."

I kept going, moving from person to person, always opening with a greeting loud enough to catch the auction worker's eyes and ears. I checked the ornate metal clock on the wall, then glanced over my shoulder to catch a glimmer of gold at the entrance.

Layla kept a sharp watch on the time.

From across the space, our eyes met, and she walked with steady determination directly at me as I set myself in direct conversation with the auction attendant.

"Excuse me," I said, putting on my best, most confident, most *billionaire* front. "Steven Grant. What's your name?"

"Kamal Naran. Listing manager for the auction tonight. And, of course, we all know who you are, Mr. Grant. Everyone in New York does."

"Good to meet you," I said, clasping his brown hand in mine. "Actually, that's what I wanted to talk to you about. I can't get a down moment here." Our hands shook in my best imitation of a politician's greeting. "I've really wanted to check out some of the exhibits in storage before I bid. Is it possible to give me a tour of the area?"

"I'm sorry, sir," Kamal said with a headshake. "That area is off-limits. You must understand—"

"I get it, I really do." Was acting so *social* as easy for this universes Steven? I'd done my fair share of galas and junkets, but all of the grace and confidence displayed there came as a mask— probably more of a mask than Moon Knight. "But I can't even get to the displays in the other room without someone stopping me. You see—"

"Steven!" Layla's voice rose over the din of the crowd. "Hey." She approached with her hand out. "You dropped this."

"Hold that thought for a second." I took the earbud from her open palm, then put it in my pocket with a larger-than-necessary shrug and sigh of exasperation. "Of course I did. Silly me."

Layla looked over her shoulder, her posture straightening as she craned her neck. In the doorway stood a red-haired man with a bushy beard and weathered lines; he lingered for two or three seconds before slowly turning away. "There's my date. I gotta run. Some other time, perhaps?"

"Maybe some other place." I looked back at Kamal, an eyebrow raised to say it all for me.

"Works for me. See you around. Tell Marc I said hi," she called out as she walked away, a swifter purpose now emerging in her steps.

"You see?" I said, palms up. "I can't go anywhere without *something* happening." Kamal's lips twisted as he checked his phone, his watch, anything to probably try to get out of this conversation. "Come on. It's not like I'm going to do anything to mess with the stuff. Look, I'm Steven Grant, even if I *wanted* to do something to an antiquity, how could I possibly get away with it? Everyone knows who I am."

"That's a good line," Jake said, his voice a whisper in my ear.

The man's eyes narrowed in contemplation, and as he paused, I pointed behind him in a random direction and waved at no one in particular. "Good to see you," I said, flashing a smile.

"All right, Mr. Grant," Kamal said, a sigh as he glanced around the room. "Auction doesn't start for an hour, so ten minutes. Just a quick tour."

"Thank you," I said, shaking hands with, really, the only person that mattered in the room.

"Sometimes you actually know what you're doing." I couldn't tell if Jake's words were a compliment or passive-aggressive insult. Maybe both. I chose to ignore it as Kamal led us out the ballroom's side door and down a hallway to a service elevator.

Careful, Steven. I sense Venom is near.

The left arm. I felt the throb start, so subtle that I hadn't noticed while dealing with Layla and Kamal and the rest of the evening's shenanigans. But now it pulsed with a tangible pressure, signaling a warning. "How near is near?" I asked, keeping my voice low.

Unknown. But you should move fast.

"After you," Kamal said, holding the elevator door. I tapped my cane on the floor, gave him a knowing nod, and stepped inside.

CHAPTER 18

—

STEVEN

KAMAL HAD SAID THE TOUR COULD ONLY LAST TEN MINUTES. SO I kept my word. We just didn't discuss what would happen after. Ten minutes ago, Kamal and I arrived on the basement floor, which normally seemed reserved for hotel storage. Tonight, though, proved different.

My best "sociable billionaire" guise got a true workout, talking up all the details about the gala and auction that I could conjure, though when we got to the storage space's doors, I waited patiently as Kamal explained to the armed guards who I was and why I mattered. They'd nodded while I stood and demonstrated my impatience: tapping my foot, sighing, and generally acting like I really needed to be *somewhere,* and eventually one of them punched in the electronic access code to open up double doors.

The auction necessitated secure storage space, and things like extra chairs and other furniture were shoved off to the side while several dozen crates of varying sizes lay in neat order. I went to the first one and tapped the corner. "What's in this one?" I asked, full of inquisitiveness.

"Let me check," Kamal said, pulling out his tablet. And there it was—a complete digital list of everything in this room outside of hotel furniture and extra bedding.

I took a peek behind me, a sanity check that hydraulics and electronic locks sealed us off from the guards outside. Then I remembered that Jake had choked someone out at the Retrograde grounds.

Would I have that muscle memory? It seemed a little gentler than whacking him upside the head with an adamantium staff.

"Which item were you—" he started before I grabbed him from behind, framing his neck with my arm.

"More pressure on the carotid," Jake yelled. "Keep his chin against your elbow. Pressure! Pressure!"

The tablet dropped to the floor, its blue silicone case protecting its tumble. As for Kamal, well, the combination of Jake's shouted guidance, our body's muscle memory, and some dumb luck proved to be enough. I picked up the tablet and tapped through, the dimmed screen coming to life with the activity. "Look, it's in alphabetical order," I said, scrolling through the list of items. "There it is. Crate seventeen."

My shoes clacked on the smooth floor as I dashed through the stacks of mostly-in-order crates, even numbers on the left and odd numbers on the right. This whole thing came together way too easily outside of the little bit of choking, and it only took a minute to find the crate with a stencil-painted *17* on the top edge.

As for its lock? It proved no match for an adamantium cane.

Which brought me to this moment: My fingers slipped under the top edges of the crate, the hinged piece proving heavier than I thought. I flipped it open, the lid swinging back with a *thud* to reveal layers of bubble wrap knotted into a single ball, all resting on top of little bits of shredded brown paper. "Is that it?" Jake asked.

"I don't know," I replied, but something kept ticking in my brain, like Khonshu was pacing back and forth in there.

It is. Open it.

"How do you know that?" I asked, starting to peel back the bubble wrap and resisting the urge to pop a few pockets of air.

I sense it.

Khonshu liked being cryptic about stuff, and I wasn't going to argue with that. What I *was* going to do, though, was get fully dressed for the moment.

I paused with only one layer of bubble wrap remaining, then

stood and reached into my coat pocket. Seconds later, Mr. Knight's mask was neatly pulled over my face. I adjusted my tie for good measure, along with a final tug for comfortable tightness, then uncovered the evening's big prize:

The psi-phon.

Emmet's description proved apt: it looked like headphones. A metallic band connected two thick rectangular pads, pieces that would normally fit over the ears of a humanoid skull. On the left side, a small circle connected to the device's frame, probably some kind of sensor or transmitter that became active when it touched a forehead.

"This thing affected Moon Knights in different realities?" Jake asked.

It did. Moon Shade attempted to use the psi-phon to take the power of every Moon Knight.

"I don't remember anything like that," Jake said.

Your Spector was not involved.

"Wow." I leaned in, squinting at the seemingly innocent hunk of metal sitting in the crate. "I'm kind of offended by that. Are we not important enough of a Moon Knight?"

"The Multiverse," Jake said with a huff. "I'm leaving the complicated stuff to you. I got enough crap to deal with."

I feel it.

"Will you stop being so cryptic, Khonshu?" Jake asked. "How do we know you're not just feeling indigestion from our burrito?" Except I felt it, too—what "it" actually meant, I wasn't sure. But something changed the instant I held the psi-phon, like dozens of lightbulbs activated in a dark hallway.

Mind Space. Now.

"Yeah," I said. "I think you're right."

And with that, I closed my eyes.

WE STOOD TOGETHER IN THE LOBBY OF THE MET, MYSELF AND JAKE and Khonshu surrounding a single display pedestal with the psi-phon on it. "Wow, it's already here. Sure looks flimsy. Like it should come with some eight-track tapes," Jake said, tapping it with his fingernail.

I personally thought it looked like a prop from a low-budget sci-fi movie, but I didn't want to give Jake any more reason to devalue it. Wherever it came from, whatever it was made of, Venom pursued it—and that made it important enough that we could overlook its ridiculous product design.

It connects the Multiverse.

"Yes, we get that point," Jake said.

"But more than that," I said. "Right? It drains an individual's essence across the Multiverse."

Yes. That is what you felt when you held it. What I felt. The vibrations that echo throughout—

"Oh!" I said, smacking my forehead. "I get it, I get it." My laugh bounced off the large walls of my imagined Met. "'Psi-phon'— like, siphoning a liquid? Brilliant." I snapped my fingers. "I take back what I said earlier. That is excellent branding."

Look.

Khonshu tapped his staff, a rumble shaking its way through the room, and a long gloved finger pointed at The Met's large display. Where there was supposed to be images and informational displays and exhibits, where Venom's own point of view once played, now we saw . . .

Marc.

And me.

And Jake.

Just in many, many different configurations.

Moon Knight as we knew him. Moon Knight with shades of black woven into his suit. Moon Knight with silver armor. A female Moon Knight. A freaking pirate Moon Knight, complete with boat and sword.

Even a version of Marc running across a massive sand dune with Layla, Khonshu standing on the horizon.

"Look at them. They're us," I said. "That's *all* of us. The psi-phon is acting as a hub for *us*. Wow, we really missed out on this, didn't we?"

"I'll say one thing," Jake said, taking off his cap. "We've got great hair in all of the universes."

Though I agreed, I tried not to dignify Jake's comment with a response. Things were a little too serious for that right now. "Does this mean that we're, you know, draining the life essences of all of the other versions right now?"

I don't think so. The psi-phon is not activated yet.

"Well, how does someone turn this thing on?" Jake knelt down and inspected the device from all angles. "I don't see a plug anywhere."

"I don't suppose you just bring multidimensional tools to the hardware store," I said, matching Jake's pose. "Maybe they'll have a battery—"

A loud, sudden bang interrupted my words, prompting confused looks from each of us. Yes, even Khonshu showed surprise, despite having to work with a bird skull.

"What was that?" Jake asked.

What *was* that? Because it didn't come from outside our body, and it didn't come from one direction. It surrounded the space like a massive thunderclap hitting all surfaces of the Mind Space at the same time.

"It's not from the front," I said. Except something *had* changed about the front lobby. Normally, the space beyond the glass doors showed the larger steps and even larger columns that invited visitors in, often with people queuing or talking or simply lingering about—sometimes daytime, sometimes nighttime, but always Fifth Avenue.

Now only pitch black lay beyond the glass.

No, wait.

I squinted, leaning in that direction with my entire body, and blinked. Then blinked again, focusing to be sure.

The blanket of black *shimmered*.

"It's Venom," I said, words caught in my throat. "Venom is trying to break into the Mind Space."

My eyes snapped open, bringing me back into the reality of the storage room—no more posh museum digs, just harsh industrial lighting and storage crates with *really* expensive, rare, and possibly powerful stuff in them. With quickened breath and racing pulse, I told myself to calm down, focus, because while Marc would be assessing options and everything, he *wasn't here* to handle this sort of thing.

I still held the psi-phon, the headphone-shaped device gripped between my fingers. And though anxiety ratcheted the intensity on everything, an ache throbbed through my left arm.

It took a second before it hit me. And Jake, and Khonshu.

That throb had nothing to do with anxiety or circulation.

The drop of symbiote that remains. It must let Venom approach the Mind Space. I spun, now looking for any exit possible. To my left, rows of folded tables and stacked chairs. To my right, unopened crates, some much larger than the one that held the psi-phon. Beyond that sat the building's circuit breaker on the concrete wall.

And in front, the locked double doors. With two guards immediately outside. "We need to get out of here."

Run, Steven.

"Great idea, but *where*?" I asked. I shifted, psi-phon in one hand and adamantium staff in the other. Could the grapple work? Or maybe just brute force, smashing anything in our path—

Outside the door, muffled voices yelled unintelligible threats.

Then the distinctive *pop-pop-pop* of gunshots.

Then heavy *thump*s against the door.

Then silence, nothing outside of my breathing and the pulse in my left arm growing stronger. How much time had passed? It could have only been several seconds, yet time dilated like when we gathered in the Mind Space, the unknown approaching at a to-be-determined speed and intensity.

Bang.

It might have been a gunshot. Except the lights flipped off, possibly some sort of isolated electrical surge, leaving only complete darkness within the industrial space.

"That's never a good thing," Jake said.

"Pessimism isn't helping."

"Steven, we can't wish our way out of this—"

A loud *clang* interrupted the argument in my head, followed by piercing white light—enough to see the silhouette of two separate doors bashed off their hinges and sent flying, the light from the cleared doorway beaming into the space.

And another silhouette—a familiar one, a cape and cowl and two glowing white eyes as it stalked into the bright white. It stopped, exactly centered, and turned, stark black against immense white—a perfect shape in complete contrast.

Except it wasn't a silhouette.

No, Venom had somehow made the Moon Knight suit *black*.

A weak voice came from the hall, then another gunshot. Venom looked down, a casual annoyance in their posture. They shrugged their shoulder, the bullet making a ripple across the top ridge, and they stepped out of view for a moment before another crashing sound bounced off the hallway walls.

This wasn't going to be easy.

I ducked down behind the largest crate, palms pressed flat against the wood panel. "I don't see a way out of here."

The psi-phon. Use it!

"I don't know *how* to use it," I hissed. More clanging sounds came from the hall, then silence, then the faint taps of approaching boots on concrete floor.

"Steven!" Venom yelled. Or was it Marc? It *sounded* like Marc—but maybe more like when Marc got really angry about something.

Which, apparently, he was. I'd be angry, too, if I had an oily goo symbiote in me. A bird-skull deity was bad enough.

"Don't say anything," Jake whispered. Which was unnecessary, but I appreciated it.

"Give us the psi-phon!" *Us.* Okay, no way Marc would start using the royal "we." This was definitely Venom. I gripped the staff, then glanced down at the psi-phon.

Do not hand it over. It holds the power of the Multiverse.

"Yeah, well," I said under my breath, "our options are limited."

Even with my voice barely audible, it must have triggered Venom's radar, because a black tendril fired forward. Pure instinct pulled my head back, and the tendril lashed in front, barely missing my masked nose by mere inches. I twirled the staff, a full 360-degree spin, and smashed it down on the tendril. It snapped back, pausing in pain.

Pain. The staff.

Adamantium. Adamantium hurts Venom. Which made sense, because who wouldn't be hurt by adamantium? Except Venom was a gooey mass thing, and getting some bits chopped off probably wouldn't do anything more than slow him down. But still, that might be enough for now.

"We've got a chance," Jake said, probably piecing together the same thing.

As if to prove my suspicions, the tendril whipped back around, forming into a makeshift claw before gripping my neck, dagger-like ends digging in to squeeze the breath out of my chest.

"Give. Us. The. Psi-phon."

Slowing down was clearly relative.

I dropped the psi-phon for a moment and gripped the staff with both hands, the weapon now at a diagonal, and despite the awkward position—I was after all being choked by an oily stretchy hand—I bashed the adamantium staff into my captor. The claw loosened, droplets of the goo spattering off before being sucked back into form. I swung again and again, each time causing further damage, until it let go and I grabbed the multiversal headphone device, sprinting ahead as fast as possible.

Use the psi-phon.

"How?" I said, running in any direction possible. Movement offered at least *something*.

It needs power.

Power. What could produce power? Electricity?

I scanned the other side of the room: crates, stacked chairs, folded storage bags. But among the hardware and storage sat a possibility.

Jake must have seen it, too. "Oh no, Steven. Not the circuit breaker. Electricity and human bodies are a bad combination."

I twisted the staff, popping out the grappling hook, and aimed. Time and circumstance didn't allow for precision, but all I needed was a swift ride to the other side of the room.

With my right hand, I aimed the staff. With my left, I tightly held on to the psi-phon, forearm muscle throbbing from Venom's proximity. "Yes, the circuit breaker," I said as the grapple exploded from the staff. It soared to the back corner of the room, talons piercing the concrete wall, crumbled bits and chips dropping down. My arm pulled hard, soon followed by my body going diagonally faster than Venom could lash out. "You got a better idea?" I asked as we flew across the room.

"I tell you not to overthink things, but I guess you should really overthink things here."

"No time," I said. The grapple released, and I dropped some ten feet down, shoes impacting as I landed. The staff reassembled itself with a twist, and I dashed over, Venom's oncoming approach causing a growing intensity in my left arm, like a countdown to the drop of goo bursting out. "You better be right, Khonshu," I said as I ripped open the circuit breaker panel.

"No, no, Steven, never touch a—"

Technically, I didn't touch any of the circuit breakers. Instead, I bashed the psi-phon into them, figuring that somewhere in the mess, the skyscraper's electricity would arc into whatever alloy made up this *thing* that gave us all far too much trouble.

And then I floated. Kind of like the Mind Space, but not really.

Nothing actually formed in my vision; instead, it was more like swimming in some sort of ethereal goo, things blurring in and out of focus. You know how movies portray netherworlds? Kind of like that.

Except, for a moment, an infinite number of Marc Spectors filled everything and everywhere around me. And collectively, they winced, every version of them moving uniformly for a fraction of a second, the psi-phon seemingly grabbing a sliver of their essences.

Or so I assumed.

Me? I felt nothing. Maybe it filled up some hole in me, or maybe because I was actually *holding* the psi-phon, it protected me from that, whatever it was.

But Venom—or Marc—their proximity must have meant something. Instead of being a universe away, they stood only half a room down, and an unearthly howl came from the black-masked head of Moon Knight.

The Multiverse fell away and I looked over to find Venom on one knee, hands pressed against his cowl.

Run, Steven! Run!

No one had to tell me twice.

CHAPTER 19
VENOM

YOU ARE STILL REELING FROM THE POWER OF THE PSI-PHON.

Do you see why *he* wants it?

Do you see the danger its power can unleash across the Multiverse? Across something even as vast as our Hive Mind?

Stop moping on the floor. We must stand up.

Steven Grant is still close. Somewhere above us.

Move. Move your feet. Walk with purpose.

No. *Run.*

Over the bodies of the guards who shot at us. Smash your way through the stairs, through cement and piping, through floor. Embrace the chaos as you pursue the target.

You relent, we grow larger, more powerful, but in our connection, you cannot help your mercenary skills kicking in. You scan the throngs of people running past—all heading toward evacuation as billowing smoke envelopes them. Yet something pushes in the other direction, going upstream and slowing all it encounters.

There.

You move in pursuit, smashing your way through walls, tendrils lashing out to throw chairs and carts out of the way. Each step forward brings us closer, even through the billowing smoke of the fire somewhere on this floor. The oncoming emergency crew, the lights of fire trucks and ambulances outside, the oncoming chatter of "electrical fire" and "multiple floors," all of that catches your attention but you must ignore it and move forward. The backup generator must have activated to provide a path, but Steven's actions had their own consequences. We hear the echoes of the bursts and explosions, we smell the ash of the flames.

The safety of the people around us, that is not our problem. Our problem is that this mess has created much more chaos—noise, movement, crowds, all making it harder to track Steven. You press forward, and we are scanning the passing faces. Strangely, they do not cower or back away at the sight of us.

These people, they are the types that *understand* who we are. But they are not involved. You even recognize some of them. You have dealt with this one or that one, either by yourself or teaming up with someone else. You even pause to linger on the woman with curly black hair rushing by, the name "Layla" crossing our thoughts.

They are not a concern right now.

We sense Steven. No—you tell me that something has changed . . .

Jake. Jake has taken over. You *feel* it. You can even tell that Jake has paused long enough to pull the mask halfway on and put on his mustache. And as you feel their presence, we sense their location.

Up. They have gone up.

Past the lobby. The attendees, they scramble for the front door, firefighters and police officers directing everyone out. You march deeper, against the rush of oncoming bodies, past the closed kiosks and coffee shops and over to the main courtyard. What is his destination?

Scan the area. Look for the white suit. He is not hiding in the masses. No, he would want to get away . . .

The elevator.

In the middle of the courtyards are three glass elevators. Look in the middle one as it slides toward the sky. The white suit, huddled against the wall, staring at the device in his hands.

All of the electrical connections that surged with Steven's actions, fuses shattered and wires melted, it causes this facility to operate at a lumbering capacity. As you look up, you see the result: Jake's elevator stutters, rising and then pausing, rising and then pausing.

They are in our sights. Now, *pursue.*

No, you say, *there's no way. We need a grapple, a strategy. You can't just climb up an elevator track when the building is on fire.*

Yes you can.

You can when you embrace the symbiote.

A new instinct kicks in. You run through the courtyard, jumping over benches and shrubs. Your hands grip the side track that guides the elevator. And you *climb,* fingers gripping shards of broken glass as you pull yourself upward.

Up. Ten feet. Then twenty. While most people are evacuating the premises, some stop and gape at you. Do not mind them. Continue upward. The psi-phon is within our grasp, and then we can finally find a way . . .

Sparks burst, bouncing off of us, our black cape shielded by symbiote skin. You continue your ascent, muscles churning as you pull us up faster. Use the tendrils. They are your tools, stronger than any human limb. They fire upward, black lines shooting out of your shoulders. They attach to the bottom of the elevator, catching it as it rises, then they retract and pull us closer. Our combined weight slows the elevator, strains the mechanical cables and pulleys.

Now we are directly below. We can *sense* Jake. We can feel the drop of symbiote in his body. You reach back your arm, your fist in a symbiote gauntlet, and you send it through the elevator floor.

It pierces through, turning this blend of metal and composites into pulverized bits. Jake reacts, his adamantium staff now bashing away at what is attacking—first knocking away the symbiote shell, piece by piece, until your gloved hand is exposed.

You withdraw, still hanging from the beams and panels beneath the elevator floor. The entire unit begins rising again, and the groans of strained metal bounce off the passage. Sparks explode and litter off of us, and we swing around, then up, now clinging on to the outside of the glass.

In the glass reflection, you see yourself.

Your face, covered by the Moon Knight mask, glowing white

eyes peering out from a deep black void. You wince as the black shimmers, the symbiote oil constantly adjusting and calibrating to everything on and around us.

"Give us the psi-phon!" you shout out loud. "You don't need to get involved. You can just give it to us and leave."

Jake moves first. Psi-phon still in hand, he breaks the staff into two pieces connected by a chain. He whirls the nunchaku, causing the glass to explode outward. You swing to the side, hanging on by one girder framing the elevator car, then come back and use the power of the symbiote oil to fire a blast downward. It rips another hole in the elevator floor, larger than the previous one. Jake takes his adamantium weapon and smashes it across your arm. You react by pulling us into the elevator and punching the space immediately below Jake.

Now there's a third puncture in the floor, but the damage is accumulating, enough that an entire chunk of support panels falls downward. Jake starts to slip and his hands move quickly, reassembling his staff. It twists with a *click,* revealing his grappling hook, and that shoots into the elevator's ceiling, breaking lights and raining sparks as bits of metal debris fly down.

More groans from the elevator. Pulleys or belts or something are breaking, a snap and whip from somewhere above us. The entire elevator car shakes, dusting debris and glass fragments down to the courtyard below. You hold on, tendrils pressing against the remaining frames and panels.

But Jake does not. The grapple loosens and he moves to adjust, psi-phon still in his other hand. Yet another crack from above rattles, a lighting panel shaking before snapping, a jagged piece now dropping.

It smashes Jake on the head, catching him at an angle that snags the underside of his half-on mask, pulling it off.

You feel his consciousness. It is there, and then it is not.

His grip on the psi-phon loosens. It begins to drop.

As does Jake.

Reach out with your hand *now*. Grab the psi-phon before gravity destroys it.

It lands safely in your hands. Our mission is complete.

But you protest.

Only a fraction of a second passes. It is not just a protest; you scream and fight from inside. We feel the way you pound, like your fists can punch past our shared self into full control of our body.

No, that is not what you are doing. You are not . . . fighting us.

You are asking to be heard. Begging.

We will listen. You may speak.

Save them!

But why? In the scope of what is at stake, what the Whisperer plans for the psi-phon, what *we* must do to protect *everything*, what does one individual from another universe matter? No witnesses, no survivors. That includes them.

It's Steven and Jake.

You don't even know them. You even said that you can't stand your Steven and Jake, why do you care about these two?

We're all brothers! Save them!

All brothers? What a curious concept. When we first joined with you, their presence seemed like an irritant to you—any version of them. Now something has changed. This is more than your fear of being alone. The bitterness, the resentment at *your* alters, that lingers but the feelings have become much more complex. You do not just speak words, you communicate a *concept*, information moving faster than thoughts—a history, an understanding of your personal stakes against the rest of the Multiverse.

Much like . . .

The Hive Mind.

Steven and Jake are part of your Hive. In whatever form, whatever body.

Just like that, we understand.

The Whisperer wants them dead. But for now, we will abide.

And you let us, shifting the delicate balance within this body to our full control. We extend tendril, speeding down faster than the falling body. It grips Jake in mid-flight, some ten feet above the gnarled metal and glass draped across the ground, the jolt loosening the grapple base from his hand.

Jake is still unconscious. But we set him down, safe.

Thank you, you say.

What a curious reaction.

If we had time, we might ponder that, we might spend more time considering what that means. But our path is shortening, our goal in sight.

The Whisperer wants to know how to activate the psi-phon and use its full capabilities. He demands a test.

We might be able to use that to our advantage.

I think, you say. Suddenly, you are a chatty one. *I think I know someone who might be able to help.*

We trusted someone once, named Eddie Brock. We worked in unity. We accomplished many things together. Also, Eddie is a little more punk rock than you. You, the arguments in your head, have you considered that you may have anger issues?

Maybe try taking care of that when this is all through.

Yes, humor. When there is humor, there is trust.

Such a state of being had to be earned. By both of us.

And maybe we will trust you. If you will trust us.

ELSEWHERE . . .

AMERICA

WATCHING.

It was what they did.

It was what America was supposed to do.

"Intervention is never justified," they had said after the business with Wanda. "See that it doesn't happen again." Except that didn't really make sense, did it? Because right now she Watched, thanks to the power of cosmic windows. And what she saw?

She saw Venom join with Marc Spector to become a tool of the Whisperer.

She saw Venom and Marc sow chaos throughout New York City.

She saw another reality's Marc Spector try to stem that very tide of chaos. And, she might add, not particularly well.

In Venom, she saw that not all was as it seemed. Venom was tasked by the Whisperer. That much was certain. And the psiphon, it lay at the end of this collision course between Venom, this reality's Marc Spector, the other incoming Marc Spector, and the Whisperer.

So many variables. So many possibilities. Not just in those involved with the situation coming to a head at the Top of New York Hotel, but with the psi-phon itself. A multiversal device of some sort, perhaps the only one of its kind in existence across every reality, but knowing all of that still left a lot of blanks to be filled.

America steeled herself, floating in the ethereal space as she stared through a cosmic window down at the hotel. Chaos for sure, but with a purpose.

Purpose.

She glanced down at her jacket. Simply wearing it again helped her sense of identity resurface. For so long, she existed just to Watch, and while Watchers had duties across all of time and space, they didn't really get a lot done, did they?

America thought back to her younger self, the things she had accomplished, the setbacks she overcame, the friendships she made. All of that faded away as she became a Watcher, and for what?

All of the ability of a Watcher, yet without the most important ability of them all, regardless of species, age, or expertise:

The power to choose.

For now, America would Watch and not intervene. But that had little to do with the doctrine of the Watchers. Instead, this was a conscious choice to gather information, understand the situation with Venom, the different Marc Spectors, the Whisperer, and perhaps most importantly, the psi-phon. They all danced in a delicate balance, ripples across New York City, across this reality, across all realities.

Something was going to happen here. A breaking point would be reached. She would know it when she saw it. Once that played out, though, she would then hit a crossroads. Because the Multiverse itself would likely be at a crossroads.

Something would have to give.

Was America Chavez someone who merely observed? Or was she worthy of the jacket on her shoulders?

In that moment, America took a quiet breath and made a choice.

CHAPTER 20

—

JAKE

WERE JAKE'S EYES OPEN?

They felt that way. Small facial muscles flexed, the down-then-up motion of blinking. But nothing came into view. Instead, deep, unending darkness surrounded him, along with the worst headache he'd had in a while. And this didn't stem from one-too-many shots of cheap rum. He reached up to feel what certainly would be a bump on his head—

He tried to anyway. His arms hit . . . something smooth. Bendy, crumpled, and a little tight, like a small capsule loosely wrapped him. His weight shifted, low crinkling sounds accompanying his movements. "Jake?" Steven asked. "Jake, are you there?"

"I am," Jake said, flexing his toes still inside what felt like Mr. Knight's shoes rather than being barefoot or somehow winding up in Moon Knight's massive boots. "Where are you? Are we in Venom's goo?"

"Maybe?"

Jake rolled onto his shoulder, or at least tried to—the side-to-side motion caused a sudden jab in Jake's temples, enough to tell him to slow down, reset; it looked like whatever they were gonna do, they'd have to fight both this cocoon *and* pain. "What did he do to us? Did he trap us in something?"

Unsure. But Venom is gone.

Jake's left arm agreed with that sentiment, the throbbing pulse that once felt like it might burst now calm. "I can't see anything," Steven said.

"Huh. Okay, so that's weird." Hands still covered in Mr. Knight's gloves, Jake pressed against the barrier to gauge just how tight of a bind they found themselves in.

"Actually, I think it makes sense. I'm not physically anywhere, so if you have no sense of our place, then my personality has no foundation to build a notion of where we are. I can't even add Khonshu's abilities into it—"

"Hold on, hold on," Jake said. Stopping Steven had its benefits from a headache perspective, but it came with a silver lining of allowing other sensory details to flow in. As in, he actually heard what happened around them. "There's people talking."

It started as a murmur, steady cadences at even volumes, but definitely voices. These voices came across like office staff dealing with a work situation—calm, frank tones without laughter or anger or any other emotion. Multiple conversations, in fact, and the more Jake listened, the more he separated out the layers of sound. Talking, the clang of tools, the ongoing rumble of a large engine . . .

"Oh crap," Jake said. His hands moved quick, pressing out in all directions. The covering, whatever it was, it bent upon movement, a push above him causing the bottom to bend, too. "I think we're still at the hotel."

"What makes you say that?" Steven asked. "It's not like we're getting room service."

"Hold on, I think . . ." Jake started, fingers now searching for some sort of straight line in the middle of the material, a singular column that ran the length of this wrapping. "I think I figured it out." Near the top, at the seam where materials wove together, Jake found the smallest divot; he wiggled his finger in, pulling a small metal piece down just enough to get some leverage . . .

The whole thing unzipped. Jake sat straight up, now scanning his surroundings, the cool of the night air giving him a good slap in the face. "Ohhhh," Steven said, still only in his head. "We were in a *body bag*. That makes so much sense. And you're on a gurney; careful not to tip it over."

Jake tapped his coat pockets, then his pants pockets. "Where's the mask?"

"Well, let's take it one step at a time. Why did they think we were dead?"

"Oh my god," a voice said. Jake turned to see an EMT, her mouth agape before she started running their way. "He's been sealed up for an hour. Who checked him? Sir?" she asked, now pointing at him. "Sir, are you all right? Stay there."

"Easy, Jake," Steven said. "We don't want to draw too much attention."

Jake pulled one leg out of the body bag, then the other, then rolled his way off the gurney and back onto his feet. "Sir, please sit down," the EMT said, slinging her emergency bag off her shoulder and opening it. Out came a stethoscope, followed by some other stuff Jake didn't recognize, but suddenly a pen-shaped flashlight waved in his face. "Sir, can you please remove your jacket so we can take your blood pressure?" She looked over her shoulder, waving her free hand. "Hey! Who checked this guy?"

Jake. You must leave.

"Kind of difficult to do that right now," Jake said through gritted teeth. Another EMT ran up to the woman, eyes wide as he looked Jake up and down.

"I don't . . . I don't understand," the man said. "He wasn't breathing. He had no pulse. Literally no vital signs. That wound in his chest."

Jake. Get up and leave right now.

"Sir, please sit down." The man spoke while rummaging through a bag. "I am so sorry. I have no excuse, I just . . ." He held up his stethoscope. "May I listen? Just roll up your sleeve, I need to see where I went wrong. It's a miracle you survived your wounds."

Leave now. Before they do any more tests on you.

"Oh," Steven said. "I think people are starting to notice. We don't have time to get involved with this."

"You know what," Jake said, stretching his arms overhead, "I actually feel pretty good."

Good, Jake. Make your escape before more people notice. I believe I know what has happened.

"Sir, you've had immense medical trauma," the female EMT said. "It looks like you were standing under the elevator when its floor fell apart, and some of the debris hit you. Something gashed your chest."

"Oh, I feel fine." Jake put up a hand and began walking backward while trying *not* to wince at his pounding head. "Great. Seriously. I could go run a marathon right now."

"Don't do that," she said, putting a hand on his shoulder. "That might be the blood loss talking."

A quick look gave Jake the best exit route from the scene—in fact, during his pseudo-cadaver time, they must have rolled him out to the back loading dock of the hotel, next to the vehicles with flashing red and blue lights. A breeze tickled his hair as he squinted for further details—farther still stood TV vans and bright media lights, and beyond that, a small crowd of rubberneckers, probably looking at the wrecked elevator behind him. Police tape stretched in all sorts of directions, along with the constant coming and going of people on the scene.

"I'm just going to stretch my legs for a second, okay?" Jake said. "No marathons. Just to, um, what's the word . . ."

"Reorient yourself," Steven whispered, like the EMTs could hear him.

"Get my bearings." Jake held up his hands with a grin. "A little stroll that way," he thumbed back toward the courtyard and debris, "to avoid all those flashing lights. That's giving me a headache."

"Sir, that might be a concussion and—" the male EMT started, but the female one waved him down, mouthing something about "give the guy a minute."

"I guess I got people skills. Who can resist this face? Oh!" Did his mustache stay on? Jake's fingers pressed against his upper lip, relief washing over him when he felt the synthetic fibers still in place. Somehow it remained despite the basement escape, the rush through the crowd, and the battle with Venom.

And the drop to the ground.

"Think we can just walk right out the front?" Steven asked.

Go, before it's too late for us. We need to catch up to Venom.

"I don't know." Jake's pace slowed, an intentional act for the onlooking medical team until he managed to put some distance between them. "I'm pretty tired. And this thing that Venom stole, I'm starting to feel pretty pissed off about the whole thing. What's the big deal? I mean, we're from another place. Let Venom have the trinket and we can go disappear somewhere. Let's find a sandy beach while we figure out a way home. And no, Steven, that does *not* mean Egypt. This reality's Marc is a handy enough guy, right? I think—"

"Wait!"

Steven's voice no longer rang in his head, and instead Jake heard it behind him. Jake whirled around, only to find the sight of a tuxedo a good twenty or so feet away. Steven waved, an excited grin on his face.

A surge of adrenaline for sure.

"I found it!" he yelled, his voice so excited that Jake checked to make sure the EMTs didn't somehow hear it.

"Found what?" he asked, maintaining his slow pace. Steven kept pointing down at the debris, his phantom body standing over it but not affecting its balance. "Don't we have more important things than—"

Jake finally saw what Steven pointed at.

"Oh, good call, Steven."

"I think I'm actually getting a little control over this. It doesn't have to be panic that brings me here. Good things can do it, too." A huge grin came with Steven's hearty thumbs-up, and Jake knelt down to reach through several pieces of jagged concrete and bent rebar.

Mr. Knight's mask.

Jake took it, fingers brushing dust off the crescent moon symbol, then folded it neatly and put it into his coat pocket. But where
was their staff? Adamantium would surely survive a fall like that,
but maybe the police found it? Did they take that, too? "Do you
guys see the staff? It's been handy so far—"

"We might have to cut our losses." Steven pointed behind
them. "The EMTs have noticed you're taking your sweet time."

"Great." Steven was right—they now pointed at him. Jake fluttered his fingers in a wave, and perhaps that simple acknowledgment might stall them longer. "You know, maybe while we're here,
we should at least borrow one of their instruments to see why our
body is dying."

This is what you don't understand. You're not dying.

You are now dead.

"What?" The question came from both Jake and Steven in unison, and despite having the same vocal cords, Steven's distinct cadence prevented the word from perfectly overlapping.

"Well, that's a complication," Steven said.

"Hey, Khonshu, that's not possible. I'm moving." No words
came in return, only the distant noise of an emergency crew.
"Khonshu?"

"Oh, that's not good." Jake looked at Steven, or at least tried
to. His voice came at an appropriate distance rather than echoing
direct in Jake's head, but he no longer stood there. And if there
was ever a time when panic and adrenaline would bring him to
life, it would be now. "Steven, where'd you—"

Before Jake could finish, a deep pain bore into his chest, dropping him down to one knee. From within his left arm, the symbiote
oil raged, pushing against the muscle and skin like . . .

Like it was abandoning ship.

"Jake? Jake, can you hear me?" Steven asked.

Jake wanted to answer but nothing worked. One knee became
both, then he hunched over, hands barely propping him up. Every
movement burned, every breath weighed down like sludge, and
the world around them faded in and out.

Was this how it was going to be? Without the dignity of being in their home reality? Without ever getting to say goodbye to Marlene?

From his hands and knees, Jake collapsed farther, shoulder smacking the ground, and he rolled onto his back. He blinked at the blurry haze of bright fuzz against dark fuzz, then his eyes shut, everything dulling into nothing.

GET UP.

"What?" Jake asked, blinking as his vision returned.

Get up. Before they find you.

Everything *was* coming back into focus. Including the fact that Khonshu now stood over him. The bird-skulled god extended a hand, which Jake somehow took, and now Steven suddenly appeared as well.

"Did you resurrect us?" Steven asked. "Like you did with this reality's Marc?"

I did not. This body is too far gone. But I am using all of my strength to keep it going right now.

Now standing on his own, Jake let go of Khonshu's hand, and as he did, the hulking silhouette started to dissolve. Khonshu's voice, though, still echoed in his mind. *My abilities are limited. And fading.*

"*You* are literally fading," Steven said. "Oh my god, we're really dead. What does that even mean? People get resurrected, right?"

"I ain't taking 'dead' as a literal truth." Jake flexed his arms as his posture straightened. Sure didn't feel dead. Dead people couldn't make a fist. "Besides, we can't go out like this. We still need to get back to Marlene—"

"I think the gravity of the situation is finally hitting me." Steven's hands went to his temples, a sharpness and clarity to his phantom self that didn't seem to exist before. He must have been really, really stressed. "Khonshu? How did you resurrect Marc before? Is it, like, alien stuff? Or magic stuff?"

I won't be able to help you at all if you keep asking me questions. Look around you.

"Hey, Khonshu, I think it's best if you let me and Steven handle things in the real world." Jake glanced at Steven, who nodded at that—a milestone of rare agreement between the two. "You just focus on keeping all of us moving, okay?"

Khonshu didn't say anything, though the fact that he completely disappeared from view probably gave enough of an answer.

"Silver linings," Steven whispered. "It's creepy to see him just hanging out in a building or whatever."

I'm still listening.

Chatter came from afar, urgent tones that told Jake exactly what was happening. "Oh no, here they come. Walk faster."

The pounding in Jake's temples increased, but Steven was right—they had to go. "Sir!" the female EMT called out. "You really should come back."

Get ready to run. On my mark.

"Khonshu, this cryptic business is really a pain," Jake said, picking up his pace despite the worsening headache.

I have enough strength to get you out of here. I will cause a minor earthquake and distract those people. Get ready to run.

"Great, see, was that so hard to tell—"

A rumble interrupted Jake, prompting noise from *everywhere.* From the building, metal and glass rattled. From the rescue and emergency teams, yelling came in a wave. Beyond that, screams floated in from the sidewalk. Even the trees swayed in the courtyard, and the disturbance jostled the building's fragile electrical state to cause another loud *pop* from several floors above.

Despite the headache, Jake took the opening and sprinted, first across the courtyard and then back into the hotel's first floor, where emergency crews lingered with paperwork and equipment. Even with people coming and going, he kept pushing ahead, slipping between police officers and city maintenance workers seeking cover from the rattling. To his left, an emergency exit was propped open, and Jake broke through without any fuss. The rumbling settled, soon followed by the chatter and squawk of walkie-talkies, and he adjusted his coat and collar, quick footsteps clicking on the sidewalk as he left the hotel behind him.

"Marc!"

A voice from a side alley. And it didn't call out for Steven, as everyone at the party knew him.

Jake turned to see two figures emerging from the shadows between buildings, and even before they stepped into the light, he knew:

Gena and Frenchie.

CHAPTER 21

—

STEVEN

FROM THE ALLEY ADJACENT TO THE TOP OF NEW YORK HOTEL, WE'D dashed off, avoiding curious eyes and further oncoming emergency vehicles, even a helicopter with a spotlight on the scene. Frenchie kept track of it all as we moved in quick, short bursts, his phone app picking up chatter from the police band, all while he ran through the highlights.

Apparently we got people talking—not just the murders and destruction at Retrograde Sanitarium but also the mess here. Someone leaked footage from the former, where security cameras caught two very different-yet-similar people in the act: Moon Knight, except in all black, tearing through Dr. Emmet's office until a stray bullet from a terrified guard flew into her forehead. And Mr. Knight, at the same location, but this time taking down an entire hallway of guards.

"They didn't put it together," Frenchie had said when we got back to his car. "They see Moon Knight, they see Mr. Knight, people are arguing whether they're two different people. As if super heroes can't change their clothes! I mean, you both have a pretty distinct mask."

That footage led Frenchie and Gena to be on the lookout, and when the news hit that something strange was going down at the Top of New York Hotel, they got a hunch—though seeing a fully Venom-ed-out version of Moon Knight scaling up the track underneath a glass elevator kind of sealed the deal.

Once again, Frenchie and Gena swooped in when I needed help the most—just without Frenchie in the pilot seat of a helicopter.

And now I sat down for the best moment of my time in this reality—even with the whole "body is dying" and "Venom has the psi-phon" business lurking in the back of my head. Because for just a fleeting second, I could be totally Zen.

Pancakes helped that way. In fact, pancakes made *everything* better.

Which made sense, given that we'd only been in this universe for a few days, but with little cash and fewer friends, good food proved hard to come by. Of course, Jake had different tastes than me, so his choice of greasy bits from hot dog street carts still landed in the "avoid" pile. In fact, perhaps *that* was why our body died.

We sat, an hour removed from the mess at the hotel, now nestled into The Other Place, Gena's small family-owned diner in Brooklyn. Gena only flipped on a handful of kitchen lights to illuminate the space, and she kept the shades drawn—"evening janitor lighting," she said, though she told us to sit down and "figure it all out" while she started cooking up a storm.

"So this morning, Marc came to see us. Acting very strange. Then the NYPD had a press conference. Then the news came out about Top of New York. Put all that together and we knew something was going down." The phone on the table flashed as Frenchie slid a single finger across it to load a video: Venom stalking a room with orderlies on the floor, an intentional pace that brought the hulking figure directly into view—until the mask peeled back to reveal the face of Marc Spector. "He acted—Gena, how would you put it?" Frenchie asked, fingernail tapping the edge of his coffee mug.

"Marc seemed out of his damn mind," Gena yelled from the kitchen.

"So you're not Marc," Frenchie mused as he sipped from a plain white mug, "but you *are* dead?"

Dead.

What a strange concept to face. In so many ways, death acted as this big scary wall that ended everything. But we were still here. Khonshu even said that he'd *resurrected* this reality's Marc at some point, so clearly some work-arounds existed. My hand went to my chest, the place where if I felt close enough, my fingers would run over an incision wound about two inches long. How Khonshu kept it from bleeding out was a miracle I didn't want to ask about; maybe Egyptian gods knew how to magically induce blood clotting. Or maybe magic really was just magic.

It didn't matter. What mattered was the fact that death didn't necessarily seem to be the end, but the biggest obstacle in the way of everything remained Venom. Despite Jake's bluster—tantrum, really, though I wouldn't tell him that—the alien symbiote still represented the best chance of a ride home.

"Well, technically, I'm still Steven-in-Spector. Oh, and we've been calling our body 'Spector' to avoid confusing everyone. Including ourselves," I said, savoring the bits of bacon cooked into the syrup-soaked pancake. "And Jake's here, too. But the main thing is we are not your Marc." I let out a sigh at the thought. "That Marc is now hosting an . . ."

". . . alien named Venom." Gena finished my sentence as she brought another stack of pancakes, this time with bacon crumbles swapped for blueberries. "You have been through some weird, weird stuff, my friend. And I am still calling you my friend, because any Marc Spector is my friend. Even if you came from a different dimension."

"Reality, actually. There's a bit of a difference and—" I stopped as I met Gena's crooked glance. Friend or not, I knew better than to explain technicalities to Gena Landers. Especially when she made me a late dinner. "You're our friend, too, Gena."

Frenchie shook his head, teeth digging into his bottom lip. He still bore a large bandage across the side of his neck, wound narrowly missing his carotid artery—sometimes you were seconds away from death, but in Frenchie's case, he came centimeters away from death. He took another sip of coffee, waved his hand as Gena slid him a dish, though he did pick a small plate of crispy hash browns. "NYPD is going public with this. Since they're not sure who it is. Fancy black clothes and all." Frenchie slid over his phone, a press conference loaded up with a plainclothes man, his brown mustache bushy enough to be Jake's point of envy. At the bottom of the footage, the caption "Detective Flint, NYPD" flashed across the screen.

"Flint," I muttered. "Seems familiar."

"He worked with Marc on some weird homicide cases," Frenchie said. "In this reality, at least."

Flint spoke for a minute, his words lost without the volume up, but then it switched to black-and-white footage playing from an awkward corner angle. I recognized the location—the top of the rotunda, right by Dr. Emmet's office. Venom finished off a security guard, a solid kick sending the uniformed man over the railing, then the not-Marc alien turned, glowing white eyes against a jet-black mask.

"What did Marc say to you?" I asked, pouring more syrup over the remaining pancakes. If this body was dead, what did that do to our digestive tract? It still had to be *something*, given that we didn't have a pulse and apparently could remain for hours in an airtight body bag. Still, in all of my deep dive pursuits, experimental biology never caught my fancy the same way art or architecture did.

I supposed whatever happened would happen. It wasn't like Jake objected to my dining choices, and Khonshu didn't seem to mind, either.

"He asked if we knew anything about the thing he stole from the hotel. The psi-phon."

"And what did you tell him?" I asked as Gena set one more tray of food on the table behind us. Frenchie got only one foot out from our booth before Gena scoffed and nudged him to get back in. Plates clanked against our table as she set down more food:

fresh fruit, English muffins, sausages, and more hash browns for Frenchie, all of which combined for the best smell this side of the Multiverse.

"I told him the truth. That business with Moon Shade was a long time ago. I wasn't even involved, which I had to remind him. Just because he told me about it years ago doesn't mean I would know about it. Or how to power up the damn thing." Frenchie shook his head, then grabbed a strawberry from the fruit bowl. "Or know its history."

"Oh, he went on about that. Asking all sorts of very specific questions," Gena said, taking Frenchie's backpack off the cushion and putting it on the floor. She scooched in, settling next to Frenchie before taking a whiff of her own cooking. "You know what was funny, though, he went from 'psi-phon this' and 'Moon Shade that' to Marlene." She laughed, a hearty belt complete with shaking head and wagging finger. "Always coming back to Marlene with Marc."

"Any of you Marcs," Frenchie said, joining in the laughter.

"And any of you *in* Marc."

"Marlene," I said. In my head, Jake said the same thing, and I suppose Gena made the right call on that one. It *did* always come back to her.

But why?

Marlene was not involved with the Moon Shade business.

I guess Khonshu remembered. "If she wasn't involved, then that doesn't really factor in here. Why would Venom care?"

"I take it that Venom has no interest in wooing her back?" Gena asked.

Frenchie leaned over and bent a metal blind down enough to sneak a look at the passing traffic. "I don't think *that* version of Marc would charm anyone."

"Okay, so this isn't a personal call. There's no nostalgia or pining involved." Could symbiotes even pine for someone? That would be a good question if I ever came across one of the Avengers or someone who handled bigger problems than I did. "Why would he ask about Marlene?"

"Actually," Jake said, "*what* did he ask?"

I repeated Jake's question, though I wasn't sure if it was worth explaining that it came from the voice inside my head.

"He asked if she was still at her last known address or if she'd moved on." A crooked scowl formed under Frenchie's mustache. "Which was a very strange way to ask. Again, I told him the truth: Marlene lives under an alias right now."

"Either that alien is messing with his memories or he got hit on the head pretty hard." Gena sipped her coffee, then motioned both of us to eat more. "All I know is that whatever happened between her and Marc was bad—really bad. Bad enough to cut all ties with Marc in every way. It messed him up a lot."

"It still doesn't make any sense." Frenchie turned back to his phone, the screen temporarily dimmed until he tapped it again. "And besides, with all this stuff going on with Venom and Retrograde and everything else, why is he pining over Marlene? You know, when Marc told me about how it all went down with her, he looked me in the eye and said, 'Duchamp, don't ever bring your crap into the lives of the people you love. 'Cause even if they say they're okay with it, they're not. And they shouldn't be.' I don't know how having an alien parasite fits in there, but seems like that falls under 'crap,' you know?" Frenchie reached into his coat pocket and held up a small metal flask. "Maybe it's time for this? I've been saving it since our first few days at Retrograde. Smells awful. Definitely not quality." Gena's stern reaction prompted him to put it right back—she probably didn't want any of her hard work tainted by cheap booze.

Why Marlene, though? I closed my eyes, not to get into the Mind Space, but to simply unpack this new piece of information. "Let's start from the very beginning." I moved two pancakes off the stack, setting them side by side, then pointed at the left one with my fork. "Venom comes into my life on some mission from . . . *someone*. Hijacks Spector. Then transports this body over to here," I pointed to the right pancake now, "this reality because it has the psi-phon. If it exists in my world, I never heard of it, never dealt with it. Spector never had to fight Moon Shade. Maybe it can't exist in our reality? Because it's related to the Multiverse, perhaps only a single psi-phon exists in all of *everywhere*." I tapped at the stack of pancakes. "And Dr. Emmet's notes, she researched the history of the psi-phon. That's how she got her hands on it. In her notes, she mentioned Marlene's dad and—"

I stopped. And I no longer needed pancake visual aids to figure this out.

"It's *not* about Marlene," I finally said, pulling out Emmet's notebook from my inner pocket. "It's about her dad. I mean, look, Emmet wrote it down: 'He also claims it was created by an "interdimensional being" known as "the Magus" . . . I discovered some reference to the Magus appearing in ancient Egyptian lore from a paper by Peter Alraune.'" I spun the open notebook around for Frenchie to see. "Right there. Peter knew something about the psi-phon. He might have been one of the only people in the world to actually study it. Marlene wouldn't know how to power up the psi-phon—but she might have her dad's notes on it. *That's* what Venom wants. He's not trying to patch things up with her, he wants any notes she might have kept from her dad."

Gena blew out a whistle. "Your 'crap,' huh?"

"This isn't going to help Marc win her back." Frenchie squinted, then looked back out of a tilted blind. "I guess we have to get to her before they do?"

"Right, right," I said, taking a piece of bacon that did *not* represent anything in my food analogies. "So what's her alias?"

"My friend," he said, "you don't know?"

"I'm from a different reality," I said. "Like, ninety-nine percent of things are the same. But some things are different. Right now Marlene lives with us in the manor." Frenchie and Gena stopped and looked at each other, the same wide eyes and hesitant grimace on each of their faces. "So what's her alias?"

"Here's the thing, hon," Gena said softly. "We don't know. The only reason we even know she's using an alias is because you—I mean, Marc, Marc told us. And Marc said that he promised to keep her identity a secret. So he knows. Somewhere in that brain, he knows. But Venom?" She leaned forward, a sudden determination in her eye.

"I guess Venom doesn't."

CHAPTER 22
VENOM

THIS NOISE.

What is this noise?

What noise? you ask. This chaos of thoughts in our head. It has been there ever since we got hold of the psi-phon and left the hotel. With Eddie, things were different. We moved together, we understood. Our existence together is, well, let's just say we're a little clunkier with you than with Eddie. Even with that, something new has invaded, a buzzing noise that has only grown in the last hour.

It is as if . . .

. . . as if more voices speak.

But not the Hive Mind.

How many voices? you ask.

We cannot tell. Ourselves. You.

Something else.

Welcome to my world. You laugh. *Hey, you get used to it. You know, it's actually kind of nice. You're never alone.*

Why are you so *present* right now?

"I asked you to trust me. Guess that's just how we're learning to work together." You are talking out loud now instead of discussing in your mind, like you are simply having a conversation as we move through Spector Manor, past the unused furniture and ticking grandfather clock.

"Yeah, this is how I worked with Khonshu. With Steven and Jake, sometimes we'd talk out loud but sometimes we went to this place in our heads. It's trippy there; time moves differently."

You activate the security scanner, wait for it to whirl and beep confirmations, then move through the passage to the basement bunker. Lights activate as you descend, a computer voice greeting you. You move swiftly, psi-phon still in hand, and bring it to a scanning table and place it under the analysis machines. It groans to a start, then you turn to the central computer as it begins its findings.

"So am I a better co-worker than Eddie?" You ask that with a sudden humor in your voice. Like we are not facing extinction events.

"You said that with trust comes humor."

Besides, what do you know about Eddie?

"See, now you're changing the subject." Irritation colors your words. "Okay, I know nothing about Eddie. Other than you've mentioned him a few times." While the scanners examine the psi-phon, you tap away at the keyboard. Various charts and lists appear.

This is again different from Eddie.

"What, because he didn't like computers?"

Eddie was a journalist, he used computers all the time. In fact, he did a lot without excessive wealth to help him out.

"Ah, so you're touchy about him now. Got it."

What we are trying to say is that things are different. We cannot read all of your thoughts. We don't know why we are staring at this computer screen.

"You wanted to know more about the psi-phon. How it worked." You grin to yourself, but probably to smirk at us. Yes, we can still feel your facial muscles.

You said you knew someone who might be able to help.

"I do. I just wanna do my homework first. She's smart, I don't want to waste her time."

Your body temperature rises. Your pulse quickens. Your breath gets shorter.

Oh, it's one of *those* things.

"It's just complicated." You stop, tilt your head, and now your body temperature increases in a different way. "Okay, now you're just being difficult. Look, do you want to figure out how to turn this on or not?"

We do. But we want to know what you are thinking. Given how universes can implode, it seems important to be on the same page.

"Privacy is a good thing, Venom."

No, there is something else. We cannot tell because you are correct, your brain *is* different.

"See," you say, "I'm not trying to keep you out. But I think the way this brain, this body, works—we're all separate. Me, Steven, Jake. And Khonshu. We choose to share things, and some stuff bleeds through, but we all put our clothes in our own suitcases. You know? It's probably healthier that way. Sometimes I don't think Steven even likes me. And I don't always like Jake. But I'm starting to see that it's just part of the equation. Instead of actually using one another."

You stay steady, peering at list after list on the screen: security records, incoming alerts, equipment inventories. But you pause at a particular one.

Emergency Equipment Status is written across the top. And gray boxes surround several items.

Mr. Knight suit.

Adamantium staff.

Emergency comm phone.

Emergency Jake Lockley mustache.

Jake has an extra fake mustache in the emergency equipment? You really are different from Eddie.

We can read your next thought—*not gonna dignify that with a response*—and you move on. "Ah, you see?" You tap the screen, then click on a long window of text. "Steven and Jake—the other Steven and Jake. They *were* here. There's a whole security log. For some reason, their body is shorter than mine by nearly a centimeter and it screwed up the body scan."

No single person is identical across the Multiverse. Lived experiences create unique circumstances.

"Now you're a philosopher. Okay, so they grabbed an adamantium staff—"

We are very aware of *that* point.

"—and some other stuff. It makes sense. That's what they had when we tracked them." You stare at the screen for a moment, then open a new window, one with a number pad. "Venom?"

Yes, Marc.

"They have a phone. We can reach them."

Why would we want to do that?

"Look, you told me there's more at stake. You *showed* me—I don't quite get it all yet, but I know it's not just, you know, someone smuggling weapons or whatever. I'm better with Steven and Jake around."

That is a bad idea.

"More teammates mean more support." Your passive-aggressive sigh is very annoying. "Look, we're a team. Not just comfortable noise. You know, I probably should have realized that sooner."

More teammates mean more variables. We must be as inconspicuous as possible to the Whisperer. The Whisperer cannot read our thoughts but he is *monitoring*.

"I'm just saying, trust also includes trusting my intuition."

Suddenly, you're very agreeable. Why is this?

"Well, it's simple. I asked you to save Steven and Jake. And you did." A new window pops up, gradually filling in with a schematic of the psi-phon and a list of specifications. "That's called 'trust.' Or as Steven would say, team building."

You talk about trust. Yet we cannot read all your thoughts. With Eddie, there were no secrets.

"Okay, so I get that you're comparing me with your ex." You laugh in a strange tone. "Ironic, given the circumstances."

Eddie is not an "ex."

"Sure, Venom. I totally believe you." Your tone implies this is sarcasm. "But either way, all I'm saying is, my body is different. My *brain* is different. I've run a lot of missions and . . ." Now you pause as you study the screen.

This buzzing noise, it is louder now. What is that? Is that the wall between us?

"I don't hear a buzzing. Maybe you're just picking up on the computers doing their thing?" You click the keyboard some more, the schematics of the psi-phon rotating and zooming. "Come on, let's—"

You stop. You stay quiet for some time. Twenty-eight seconds, to be exact.

"It's nothing. I just had trouble hearing you for a second. Maybe it's my ears getting used to having symbiote in them."

It should not interfere with your auditory processing. Eddie never had an issue.

"You know, the more I get to know you, the more I feel like you'll always judge me against Eddie."

Eddie moved to San Francisco, which is nicer than New York.

"Harsh. Harsh, Venom. And quite judgmental. You can like both cities equally for different reasons. Good burritos there, though." You pause, head tilted, hands rubbing your face. "Look, if we're gonna be partners, can I stop explaining every single action to you?"

You may.

"Great. You know, this is very different from Khonshu. Khonshu was just kind of like this angry observer. Like the commentators when you watch sports. You, you're more like we're sharing the controller in a video game."

You're stretching the metaphors.

"Wow, you know 'metaphors.' Good vocabulary, Venom."

We told you, Eddie was a journalist. We probably know more big words than you.

"Fair enough," you say with a laugh—a genuinely agreeable laugh. "Look, here's our notes on the psi-phon. Granted, I'm not much of a *journalist*. But the stuff with Moon Shade was just plain weird so I had to jot it all down."

We do not care about Moon Shade. More engineering, less history.

Strange. You do not react at what we say. Instead, you hesitate.

Your pulse again quickens, though this time it is different from earlier. You squint, not at the inventory report or the psi-phon, but off into the distance. And right now your thoughts, your emotions, your *intentions* feel more distant than ever.

In its place, that buzzing noise has grown louder.

"Wait, what do you mean 'maximum power'?" you ask out of nowhere.

That's a weird thing to say. We do not understand.

Let us be clear: We do not wish to power the psi-phon yet. We must understand it first. We showed you what is at stake, the threat to the Hive Mind. Before we take any action with the psi-phon, we need a plan. We cannot simply *give* the Whisperer what he wants.

"You just said something. You said we need to figure out how to provide maximum power to the psi-phon." You scrunch your mouth in contemplation. "What do you even want with this thing? You still haven't explained that."

We said nothing of the sort.

"No, I heard you. Come on, I thought we were all about trust now. Stop using different voices, I'm *just* getting used to your weird growl."

Different voices? Are you hearing other—

The body seizes. Every muscle tenses. An electricity ripples through it, yet nothing is shocking the body. Instead, that buzzing noise comes back, an intensity and pitch that we cannot explain.

Except, this is not from you. Your presence grows, you grow in awareness, in agency, yet there's something more here—this buzzing comes with a malice that is not part of Marc Spector.

And then . . .

A voice. A sound that is clearly a voice, but the words are blocked by the buzzing noise.

Do you hear that?

"I know there's something more, because there's another voice yelling at me. I thought you just, you know, were trying to use a scarier voice. Khonshu sometimes gets in a bad mood and does this."

Something else is happening. Perhaps the psi-phon is causing interference. You may be hearing voices from other realms.

Marc.

Marc, are you there?

You have gone silent. Yet you continue to look at the psi-phon data on the computer. You type on the console, running commands to perform a power analysis, furrow your brow in frustration. We hear your voice now as you mumble, "There's got to be another way," but then your thoughts are gone.

We cannot feel your presence, your emotions, anymore.

Can you hear us?

Your movement slows. We watch through our shared eyes, and yet now we are disjointed, as if floating behind you.

"Yeah," you say slowly. You look around the room, but for a moment, we can feel you again. A tension exists, a flare of something. Not thoughts, but the inscrutableness of emotion. Your cheeks flush, your brow furrows, there is a burn in the pit of your stomach . . .

Is that guilt?

"I understand."

What is happening? Is this a trick from Khonshu?

"Venom," you say in a slow and measured voice, "I want you to know that I'm about to do something and it's for all the right reasons."

You asked us to trust you and we did! What are you doing with the body? Why can we not feel—

CHAPTER 23

—

MARC

MARC HAD THE BODY.

Holy freakin' crap, Marc had the body.

And he had the suit. After the incident at the hotel, Venom, well, Venom-ed out in totality, using tendrils and oversized limbs to move them quickly, Marc watching the whole thing.

All the way to Spector Manor. And then Marc had a little more control, getting them to the basement bunker and supercomputer. Still in the suit, still with the cape and everything, but mask off. Marc looked down, his chest, limbs, boots, everything back to the expected white Moon Knight color.

For the first time in days, he was more than just a passenger; this was like swimming through the thickest sludge to finally come up for air, clear and refreshing air. Well, that wasn't totally true— the past few hours offered more clarity, sharpness, an emerging sense of self. But still, nothing like being in total control of the body, a complete intake of sensory information. Even though Spector Manor's base of operations only offered meager ambient light, every blinking LED from servers and computer hardware exploded like a rainbow to Marc's eyes. The low hum of the ventilation ducts, the buzz of processors, all of it sounded practically symphonic compared to the weird netherspace where he'd been.

Venom had mentioned another host—Eddie. Did Eddie find some way to live a little more balanced coexistence with the symbiote or did he just get used to being stuck in a haze?

He'd have to figure that out another time. Because even though Marc controlled the body, he wasn't alone.

Someone else existed in his head, but this was different from so many of his previous experiences. With Steven and Jake, they may as well have been roommates in a too-small apartment. With Khonshu, he was more like the annoyed neighbor who banged on the door and yelled through the walls. And Venom—well, it took time for Venom to begin to trust him or even give Marc a little bit of agency back, so he couldn't really judge. For now.

This was new, though—strange, almost as if someone wire-tapped directly into his mind. This person, whoever it was, buzzed in and out, and he did so with a chaotic burst of turbulence, along with messages that Venom clearly didn't hear.

And this mystery person made a deal.

Marc knew better than to trust strange powerful entities that offered deals. But given that this person's threats created the biggest stakes he'd ever stared down before, he needed to change something.

Besides, he'd get Venom back soon. Once he figured this out.

"Are you there?" Marc asked.

I AM.

The person's voice came with a distortion that removed any nuance or tone and instead shouted directly into Marc's skull.

"Okay, well, we're here. You said you could squash out both me and Venom, but you wanted to talk to me. So let's talk. Who are you?"

IT DOES NOT MATTER.

"No, see, it *does* matter." How much could this person see into Marc's memories, his mind? No clear clues arrived about that, so Marc instead went with his gut, which told him that this person needed him more than they let on. "I said the same thing to Venom. If we're gonna work with each other, then we need to trust each other." That was a lie; Marc had begun to understand some of where Venom came from and why the symbiote went to such extremes. He didn't like it or necessarily agree with it, but he at least got it. And to be fair, he and Jake had their share of blood on their hands, so who was he to judge?

But this person—was this the mystery Whisperer that Venom mentioned, the one that somehow held the fate of the Multiverse? It seemed like it, given the scope of the threats made. Someone running a drug ring out of Hell's Kitchen didn't exactly have the means to obliterate an entire universe.

I DO NOT HAVE THE TIME FOR FRIVOLITY. TELL ME WHAT YOU KNOW ABOUT THE PSI-PHON.

What *did* he know about the psi-phon? Well, there was the analysis report in front of him—some basics about physical specifications, like weight and dimensions. And from the specifications, schematics with a circuitry diagram. Marc assumed that the computer gave that its best guess, since it's not like they could download the blueprints for the psi-phon off the Multiverse's website.

In fact, all of this seemed like a best guess, a foundation to consider the how and why of the psi-phon's inner workings. But to really put it together, they'd need whatever Peter Alraune had dug up on it.

"What I know," Marc said, "is that it was in the basement storage of the Top of New York Hotel." He made a decision right then to test this mystery person's capabilities—he clearly was connected to Venom, but did that mean this whole body? Or was the information between all of them tucked away into silos within the brain?

"Someone at the auction saw we were going for it and they tried to stop us." Marc went for the slightest of lies to see for sure. "A security guard, I think." One second passed, then two.

No response. No challenge or demand for further details.

Interesting. Not only did this person not have complete access to Venom's recall, he couldn't dig too deep into Marc's mind, either.

"And then Venom captured it."

YOU MUST ACTIVATE THE PSI-PHON.

"That's all I know, pal."

You lie. You know more. I sense it.

There it was. They weren't in a black-and-white scenario, but enough leeway existed that Marc could manipulate the situation—and protect everyone involved. "No, first you tell me who you are." Marc *almost* said it, but instead he withheld the information. This person couldn't know that Marc and Venom had worked out a kind of loose partnership.

You can call me "the Whisperer." And you must do my bidding. Tell me how to activate the psi-phon.

Marc's hunch was right. This was the person Venom of all beings feared enough to engage in subterfuge. That fear in itself carried enough weight to put Marc on edge; this person might not deliver on all of his threats, but he was clearly enough of a risk that even Venom pulled back from the normal level of chaos. What was the Whisperer's true potential? And did that make Marc capable of taking him on?

At this point, he didn't exactly have any other choice but to play along. Minutes ago, the Whisperer promised Marc the body in exchange for the one piece of information that might power the psi-phon. That was what he had at his advantage. "Or what?"

Or I will do what I must. Your reality means nothing to me. It is grounds for an experiment, and I need results. If you do not abide, first I will destroy this universe and then I will destroy Venom's Hive Mind. Which will ripple destruction outward across the Multiverse. Understand something, Marc Spector—if I cannot make the psi-phon work for me, then I will find something else that will.

Who suffers because of that is up to you.

Marc chose his next words strategically. "Well, so here's the problem. I *do* know someone who can help. It was in Dr. Emmet's notes—Peter Alraune. He studied the psi-phon." Marc hesitated for a moment, a plan emerging in his mind. A risky one, to be sure. And, really, it would piss Marlene off. Hell, it would probably piss *everyone* off. But it sure seemed like the only way to stay one step ahead of the Whisperer *without* the whole universe-destroying thing coming into play.

The entire deal with Marlene's alias came from the fact that she felt completely done with anything and everything Marc, Steven, Jake, *Moon Knight* brought into her life. She probably wouldn't forgive him for this. Though if she understood the whole "fate of the universe" stakes, maybe he'd get a pass.

If anything, she would hopefully at least think his plan was clever. "He died years ago. But his daughter has his notes."

BRING ME TO HER.

"I can't. At least, not yet. You see, there's a problem. She's not Marlene anymore. She assumed an alias. If you want, I can explain why. We've had a, um, rocky relationship. She told me her alias once. But I forgot it."

THAT IS NOT HOW THE HUMAN MIND WORKS.

"Sorry, I don't have a standard human mind. Here's one of the things about me—I used to have an Egyptian god named Khonshu stuck in my head."

YOU SHARE THAT MIND WITH ALTERS AS WELL.

Marc gave the Whisperer credit for knowing the proper psychological terminology. At least he was well read.

But did the fact that the Whisperer knew about the existence of alters mean that he also knew about the other Steven and Jake? Best to not let him in on it anyway; besides, who knew if that body even had much life left in it. Marc suspected Khonshu was doing something to help out with the massive chest wound from the crescent dart, but those types of things eventually caught up to people.

The less said, the better. For all of them.

"You're right, I got these voices in my head. But only one of them with helpful abilities. And thanks to Khonshu, I developed the ability to hypnotize people. And one time, I used it on myself."

Which was putting it lightly. In that moment, the process was more than just locking a secret away.

It was a choice. It was the *only* choice, and marked the last time Marlene spoke to him.

"I shouldn't tell you," she had said at the time. "A clean break is a clean break."

"Look, I promised I would keep you from my life of violence." At this point, Marlene had turned, only a hint of her long blond hair visible from her silhouette. "This is how I do it. In a perfect world, I'll never need this information, we never see each other again. But in order to keep that promise, I need to do this." Marc reached out to put his hand on her shoulder, but she stepped forward. "Please."

That discussion went back and forth several times, his logic ultimately winning over Marlene's emotions. And then she revealed her alias, on Marc's solemn promise that he'd hypnotize himself to lock it away. The only way to break it open? Return to that hypnotic state.

Marc snapped back into the moment with the Whisperer.

"Now, in order to do this, I need pure concentration. You may not be able to detect it but I can feel your presence. It's a weird bit of . . ." What would be the best way to describe how the Whisperer interfered? Granted, it stretched the truth a bit, but Marc was going to take whatever he could get in this situation. "It's a bit *loud*. And I can't control my mind in the right way with that buzzing."

Marc was winning. He knew it from the fact that the Whisperer stayed silent for a few seconds.

Whoever the Whisperer was, he was *thinking*. And that meant negotiations were in play.

WHAT DO YOU NEED FROM ME?

"Simple," Marc said, his mind racing through all of the possible strategies before him for this, hostage negotiations of the highest stakes. "I need you to stop whatever you are doing. Hang up your multidimensional phone or whatever it is you're doing. What *are* you doing?"

YOUR KNOWLEDGE HAS MADE YOU THE PRIORITY ASSET. I AM KEEPING VENOM IN LINE.

"With a noise?"

I KNOW HOW TO IDENTIFY WEAKNESSES AND EXPLOIT THEM. VENOM'S CONNECTION TO THE HIVE MIND CAN BE A CONDUIT FOR MY SONIC DRILL. YOUR WEAKNESSES WILL BE SIMILARLY EX-PLOITED IF YOU DO NOT COOPERATE.

None of that made any sense to Marc. And he had seen plenty of weird crap in his life. "Okay, lemme rephrase this. I need you to disconnect from me. I need a period of absolute silence."

HOW DO I KNOW THIS IS NOT A TRICK?

"I'm not exactly in a position to do that, right? But in case you don't believe me—if I don't provide you with the name by the end of this, then you do as you say. You obliterate this place. You de-stroy Venom's Hive Mind. And whatever else you plan to do." What were his options? Not many, really. The question was actu-ally more about what he *needed*. And how much time it took to get there.

If this was a negotiation, he would start high.

"Two hours." Two hours to get to Marlene, scan through her documents, and find a way to destroy the Whisperer.

TWO *MINUTES*.

"What?"

TWO HOURS GIVES YOU TOO MUCH TIME. ALL YOU ARE DOING IS UNCOVERING A NAME. TWO MINUTES. OR YOUR WORLD DIES.

The Whisperer had called his bluff.

Could he do *anything* in two minutes?

Possibly, if he truly was cut off from the Whisperer. Getting lost in his mind often provided a form of time dilation. And, really, the Whisperer was right—all he had to do was unlock the name.

The hard part was figuring out the rest.

Marc thought back to his U.S. Marine Corps training, the mode of thinking that had carried him through so much of his adult life, that had kept him alive through the darkest of mercenary missions and the most bizarre of Moon Knight struggles, a level of strategy and preparation that forged his will and pushed him to stay ahead of those that sought to kill him.

Even a distant voice buzzing in his head.

Marc took a single moment to confirm what he suspected. He stood, hands on the psi-phon just in case it amplified any of his thoughts to the Whisperer, and considered the one very specific thing that might push the Whisperer into an instant reaction.

When the Whisperer goes away, Marc thought to himself, *I'll activate this and destroy him before he even knows it.*

Marc waited. And waited. And waited some more, but nothing came—not a voice in his head, and no universe-ending catastrophe. Probably a good minute passed until the Whisperer said something, and even then, his words brought a surprising comfort.

Because they showed that Marc really did have a chance. Whatever the Whisperer did with Venom or *to* Venom, it still only affected Marc in terms of communication, like a commanding officer talking to an operative via an earpiece.

WHAT IS YOUR ANSWER, MARC SPECTOR? DELIVER THE PSI-PHON'S SECRETS OR LOSE YOUR WORLD?

The Whisperer had access to Venom. But this showed he did *not* read Marc's thoughts. Marc would leave logistics of physiological separation to someone else; for now, all he needed to know was that he could strategize in the small window allotted to him.

"I don't get it," Marc said slowly as he scanned the computer displays. Schematics and analysis for the psi-phon, that might help, but he needed to find some way to move the needle forward, to take that first step into subverting the Whisperer and helping Venom. "You're saying if I don't work with you, you'll destroy my world."

Circuit design. Weight, length, height. History with Moon Shade.

None of that would help. Spector Manor probably didn't provide the power to activate the psi-phon and it wasn't like he'd be able to reach Marlene, digest her dad's info, put it all together, and *still* power up the psi-phon in that span.

"But destroying my world also destroys the psi-phon. Isn't that self-defeating?"

YOU ARE SPECIAL, BUT NOT UNIQUE. THERE ARE OTHERS LIKE YOU. OTHER WAYS TO HARNESS THEIR ABILITIES.

Marc had no idea what that meant, but it didn't matter. The Whisperer gave a short speech about how both Marc and the psi-phon were tools but other ways existed to influence the Multiverse; Marc tuned it out and instead turned his focus to anything that might offer a way out of this.

And behind all of the psi-phon data, he saw it. The exact right type of hope: the people he trusted, the path he needed.

The inventory list. Marc scanned it, the list of things Steven and Jake took from Spector Manor before they disappeared. A suit, a weapon, yes, but also . . .

A phone.

That would work.

Everything was right there. He just needed to make sure it all got through.

STATE YOUR ANSWER.

"All right. All right, you win," Marc said, a map of steps forming in his head as if he planned an infiltration. "Two minutes. I'll try my best but give me a little bit of leeway? I'm going to set a timer for both of us to track." Marc shrank down various windows and tabs on the screen, dropping all of the psi-phon analysis and historical data off the computer's display to leave only the inventory report and a new clock app. "I need you free and clear of my head the instant I start this. We agree?"

AGREE.

"All right. I'm counting down." Marc's finger hovered over the keyboard's enter button. "Three. Two. One."

Marc pressed the button.

And in his head, the latent buzz of the Whisperer disappeared. Without that, without Venom, without Steven, without Jake, without Khonshu, the uneasy quiet of being *alone* tingled all of his nerves. But he didn't have time to dwell on it. The timer slipped from 2:00 to 1:59 and Marc shut his eyes in full concentration.

He arrived in a dim, foggy ether, the place that sometimes came decorated if things seemed right, but most of the time it remained like a blank stage. Jake didn't care for it, Steven applied his billionaire sensibilities to it, yet for Marc, he just needed a peaceful place to sort through the chaos of his brain. His mind focused, echoes flying by of harsh memories with Marlene, words and images blurring together faster and faster until he heard it:

"We'll have to find somewhere new and be careful."

And then she left.

In the ether, Marc saw her silhouette step out a doorway before the image faded, leaving only a box in its place, red frame and glass cover with the words *IN CASE OF EMERGENCY BREAK GLASS* printed in large letters.

And sitting neatly within it, a single folded piece of paper.

No time for nostalgia or self-pity. Marc's hand formed a fist, and just as if he punched someone in the name of justice, it flew through the glass. And while this all existed only within the brain of this body and its multiple occupants, for now, the jagged edges and broken shards pierced through his skin.

Somewhere new . . .

Marc shook off the bits of glass littering his bloodied hand and reached down.

. . . and be careful.

"I'm sorry, Marlene."

The paper unfolded flat, brushes of bloody fingerprints around it, and Marc stared at clear red letters in his familiar handwriting—not Steven's, not Jake's, but his very own.

Mary Sands.

Marc's eyes snapped open to find himself standing in front of rapidly changing digits on the computer screen.

Twenty-six.

He had twenty-six seconds to get a message to Steven and Jake. But *what* should that message be? Whatever happened after this, the Whisperer still had capabilities far beyond human abilities.

Even Venom feared him. And he clearly could exert some influence over Venom, enough that he'd squeezed Venom dormant, even temporarily.

No, only one message made sense. Marlene would have her dad's notes. And the Whisperer would pursue her.

Marc had to hope that Steven and Jake could intercept her before it was too late.

He tapped the computer's keyboard and highlighted the phone on the inventory list, opening up a sub-menu to send a message. His fingers flew as he typed out the name *Mary Sands* and pressed enter to launch the message across digital signals.

Seventeen seconds remained. The status bar at the bottom blinked steadily, only the message of "Connecting . . ." with animated ellipses lasting far too long.

Thirteen. Twelve. Eleven.

The status bar flipped to a display of *Sending data* as the adjacent timer went down.

Message sent arrived with four seconds left, enough for Marc to close out the inventory list and leave only the countdown timer on-screen.

Three.

Two.

A sudden epiphany came to Marc—*Venom* was the one locking away Steven and Jake, not the Whisperer. With only a second remaining, Marc reached out to the alters that shared his head, mind intent on conveying the message that somehow, someway, he'd eventually free them.

One.

An electronic chime went off the same instant the Whisperer's buzzing sound returned to his head. "I was successful," Marc said. "You will spare this place? You will spare Venom's people?"

I AM A MAN OF MY WORD.

"All right. Her alias . . ."

The world stopped, the weight of what Marc was about to un-

leash filling every nerve and muscle in his body. He looked down
to see the Moon Knight suit, its usual white hue across the bandages and cloth.

Could Marlene ever forgive him for this?

"Her alias is *Mary Sands*."

THANK YOU.

Marc fell to his knees. He didn't feel this, but he knew it, simply because he heard the clang of the floor, though any tactile sense
left him. The ground beneath him, the weight of his cloak and suit,
none of that registered. Even his vision began to blur, then fade—
soon followed by the sound, a nothingness swallowing all of the
whirs and beeps of the control room.

In its place came a voice.

Two voices.

The Whisperer and Venom.

And Venom, Venom was mad.

The last thing Marc heard before being completely crushed
within his own body was Venom's panicked questioning, a full-
throated demand to know what the Whisperer had done with
Marc.

CHAPTER 24

—

STEVEN

SOMEONE TEXTED US.

Which was really weird, because it wasn't like we gave out this phone number to anyone. Even Gena and Frenchie had to track me down outside of the Top of New York Hotel by foot. So one thing was consistent between universes: just like with Spector, this reality's Marc and his brain cohabitants kept security to a premium.

So why did the phone buzz in my back pocket? Why was the neat envelope icon sitting in the status bar?

"Thing was," Frenchie said, taking the last bite of hash browns off his plate, "I even asked you if maybe you should tell me Marlene's alias. A fail-safe. I wouldn't do anything with it except keep her safe. But if something happened to you, I could be there." He shook his head, crooked lips showing a hint of coffee-yellowed teeth. "You—Marc—refused. Said you made a promise that you wouldn't tell anyone. For better or worse. I don't think even Steven or Jake knew."

I nodded, though my eyes remained stuck on my phone's screen—on the message icon.

"What is it?" Gena asked.

"Someone texted me."

"Eh, probably spam. You know, they program bots now to sell insurance or whatever," Frenchie said with a headshake.

I tapped the icon, the lone message loading up to display something that made no sense to me.

MARY SANDS.

Frenchie leaned over the table to peer at the screen, and Gena smacked him on the shoulder. "Give the man some privacy," she said, but I held my hand up.

"It's okay," I said, spinning the phone over for them to see. "I don't know who this is." In my head, Jake grunted in agreement.

"Like I said, probably spam." Frenchie tapped a napkin to his mouth, then tossed it onto his empty plate. "We're running out of time, right? Let's find a computer and track down Marlene—"

"You don't think . . ." Gena started. She looked at Frenchie, then me, then the phone. "I mean, that couldn't be her, could it? Marlene?"

"That would be one hell of a coincidence," Frenchie said.

"It would," I said, nodding before picking the phone back up to stare at the screen. Could *Mary Sands* be Marlene's alias? Anything was theoretically possible; I'd only briefly read about quantum mechanics, but given some of the things I'd seen as Moon Knight—and given some of the things *Marc* had seen as Moon Knight, well . . .

Weirder things had happened to us.

"Who's the sender?" Jake asked.

"What?" My reply to Jake caught the attention of my present company. "Sorry. Jake had a question."

"Hello, Jake." Gena waved. "Do we get to spend some time with you?"

"Maybe, though this isn't supposed to be a social—" I stopped, Jake's question suddenly grabbing more of my thoughts.

Surprisingly, he was on to something. *The sender ID was blank.*

It wasn't obvious at a glance, since the phone didn't have any other texts to display for comparison, just this lone one with a woman's name in the message field. But now that I gave it a good look, such an oddity stood out.

"What is it?" Frenchie asked.

"Jake pointed this out." I tapped on the screen. "There's no sender listed here."

"So it *is* spam."

"Could be. But if the central computer at Spector Manor is set up the same way as in our world, these phones are for emergencies only. And the computer's messaging program," I said, wagging my finger as the pieces came together, "it was designed to blank out the sender. Nothing traceable. No clues in case it got into the wrong hands." I looked at my friends, their tired eyes and weary smiles the same wherever in time and space I encountered them. "Someone sent this to us from Spector Manor. And I think it's Marc. This reality's Marc."

Gena flashed a rare scowl for her. "Marc—Venom—just tried to throw you off a building."

"Something's not adding up here." I lifted my left arm and rolled up the sleeve, the scars and healing wounds causing Gena to gasp. "Part of Venom is trapped in here. Venom can sense our thoughts. I think so anyway. Because we can tap into a little bit of them. It was easier when we were close. Now?" I flexed my hand, the tightened skin showing a discolored lump the size of a fingernail. "I'm not sure. But if Venom knew to track us when we were at Retrograde, and then when we were at the hotel . . ."

"Venom was watching us," Jake said. "I felt it. Didn't you? We just didn't know what it was at the time."

Sitting here and filling our belly is not helping us get to the psiphon. Or Venom.

Jake's sigh filled our head. "That's not exactly helpful, Khonshu."

I'm a little busy trying to keep us alive. If you didn't remember.

"And we're trying to figure out what to *do* with our time being alive—"

"Will you two give me some space to think?" I looked up to see Frenchie and Gena carrying similar offended expressions. "Sorry. It's not you. I've got Jake and Khonshu arguing in my head."

"My friend," Gena said, "you live the most interesting life."

I supposed that was true. I mean, the Avengers traveled to space and fought aliens and stuff, but I had a cabdriver arguing with an

Egyptian god as part of my inner monologue, and Captain America couldn't claim that.

"Maybe Marc got control from Venom," Jake said, and I could practically see him nodding in thought as he spoke. "And is just trying to help us out."

Or this is a trap. Our loyalties are being played to lead them to Marlene.

"Here's the other thing I don't quite get," I said, partly to steer their arguments away. "Venom's after the psi-phon, right? But at the hotel, he didn't exactly throw me off the building. I mean," I flexed my arms over my head, "I don't have an adamantium skeleton. I should have all sorts of broken bones. Khonshu, you wouldn't have the strength to heal a completely shattered body, right?"

No, not in this state. This is hard enough as it is.

"Wait." Frenchie pulled out his phone and started tapping away until a video loaded. "Look at this footage. There's no clear angle. But here you are falling from the elevator. This is from the dark web." We all leaned in close, staring at a pixelated video of me dropping out of the bottomless elevator. Which was not something that makes you feel good about yourself. "Watch at the very end. From the top of the frame." Frenchie rewound it, bringing me back up like I'd been magically boosted before he played it again. "You see, there!"

The screen paused, and Frenchie pointed at the top of it.

At a black tendril coming down.

"I noticed it before. I thought maybe that was part of Venom's escape. But if you're falling straight down, you should be injured. This," Frenchie said, gesturing downward with a hand, "might mean that Venom *saved* you."

"Or *Marc* saved you," Gena said.

Marc.

Now, I couldn't exactly speak with any perspective or expertise on symbiote aliens that launched chaos into people's lives, though it felt reasonable to say that I was not exactly a fan. Pretty sure Jake would feel that way, too. But Marc, *this* Marc, somehow convincing Venom to pause all that destruction in order to save us?

Differences had to exist between this Marc and our Spector. It was only natural, given the divergences in our lives—after all, this Marc dealt with Khonshu, which had been a fairly unpleasant experience so far. But . . .

Would our Spector do the same for this reality's Steven and Jake?

An answer popped right into my mind, a clear affirmative, and I even heard Jake grunt in agreement. We were, it seemed, forever joined together, despite the difficulties and occasional arguments over the dumbest things. So yes, it made absolute sense that Marc found a way to help us. Because Spector would have done the same in return. Which meant that we all kind of owed each other as such, in whatever permutation or form.

Maybe when this was all over, Marc and Khonshu could help us find a way to rescue Spector as well.

"Venom said that we should just give him the psi-phon, that we didn't need to get involved, we could simply leave. It's all about the psi-phon. I don't think we matter. But Marc, of course Marc would try to save us." I reactivated my phone and looked at the name *Mary Sands*. "I think this *is* Marc. And I don't think it's a trap. I don't know exactly why Marc would give us this clue. But it's gotta mean something."

Frenchie started tapping on his phone again, though this time he shook his head with a furrowed brow. "Any public records for Mary Sands don't appear to involve Marlene."

"Wait, wait, wait," Jake said. "Marlene's smart. She knows how to work things."

So much for Jake giving me space. "You're right," I said. "She'd know how to stay hidden. If there are any records for a specific Mary Sands only on underground networks—"

"That sounds like her," Frenchie said with a nod.

"Hon, this is going to be messier than tangling with Venom." Gena let out a sigh big enough to fill the diner. "Marc promised her he'd stay away. I guarantee she is *not* going to be pleased."

Part of me wanted to ask what Marc had done to wreck things so badly with Marlene. This place's Marlene took actions far beyond a simple breakup or argument. No, their history hit a breaking point, a permanent fracture. Was it only one difference from ours that snowballed or was it *everything*?

"I don't think we have a choice right now," I finally said. In my head, Jake grunted in agreement, though his softer tone gave away a reluctance. "You know, in my home, Marlene is still by our side. It's one of the first differences we noticed about Spector Manor." Jake grunted again, a clear "ahem" to call attention to credit. "Jake noticed it first. He wants you to know that."

"Always trust the cabbie to have a sharp eye," Gena said, now with a smile and wink.

"All right, then. Mary Sands." Frenchie motioned to Gena, who gave him his backpack. He snapped open the clasp and pulled out a laptop that whirred to life. "I'm on it. Give me an hour to search my sources."

"Looks like we're going to need some more coffee," Gena said, stretching her arms over her head. "You do your job, I'll do mine."

"Khonshu," I asked, not just to address him but also to not confuse Gena and Frenchie, "how much time do you think this body has left?"

Unknown. I seem to be able to keep it—

Tire screeches interrupted the Egyptian god, and soon bright flashing reds and blues reflected off the diner's front windows. Gena scooted out of the booth and ducked down, and Frenchie's swinging knees collided with the table, his full body reacting as he reached into his bag for . . .

A gun.

"Frenchie," I said slowly, "I don't think a shoot-out with the cops is going to help anyone right now."

"Marc Spector!" a megaphoned voice yelled. "Come out with your hands up!"

"How'd they find us?" Gena asked in a loud whisper. "Why are they looking for you?"

"The security footage. At Retrograde." I pictured Venom walking up to the security camera, removing the blackened Moon Knight mask to stare right into the lens. "Venom was covering all possibilities to give them the advantage." Outside the window, I counted four cars, with possibly more coming in. I suppose I should have been flattered at gathering that much attention. Though, tearing through an entire asylum's worth of security would do that. Did they count *my* work in this or was I only being framed from the Marc-turned-Venom stuff?

Guess it didn't matter. Police car after police car pulled up, filling the street outside of The Other Place. Doors slammed, voices carried, and some very determined people wanted me. One look between the blinds showed many, many guns drawn.

I glanced at my friends, the way they put up with the insanity of Marc, Steven, and Jake—and Khonshu, for that matter. They'd dealt with enough, I couldn't let them face an onslaught of cops. And I was sure that this universe's Marc would agree.

"I'm gonna surrender myself." I stood up with my hands in the air.

"What?" Jake, Khonshu, Gena, and Frenchie all asked at the same time, for the most interesting of noises. Inside, Jake punched at his surroundings, but I held firm.

"Listen, we don't get anywhere with this unless we find Marlene." From my coat pocket, I grabbed Mr. Knight's mask and handed it to Gena. Her brow furrowed as she took it, and both of them watched as I slid out of Mr. Knight's coat and vest, folding them neatly on the chair. "I need you two to find her, and then figure things out for me." I shook my tie loose and rolled it neatly before putting it on top of the stack. "Keep these safe for now."

"What are you gonna do?" Gena asked as she creased the Mr. Knight mask.

I took in a heavy breath, then turned to the window, the slits between blinds filled with flashing red and blue lights. "I'm gonna be Marc Spector."

CHAPTER 25
VENOM

YOU WOULD NOT WANT THIS.

But you are not here.

Marc Spector is still present in our body, yet dormant. Instead, the Whisperer has done something to suppress you. As if you are locked in a room, with the Whisperer guarding it. He is here instead of you, in my thoughts and influencing my actions, a constant buzzing noise that spikes as he reacts or exerts his will.

With the morning sun creeping over the horizon, we arrive at Marlene Alraune's door, a small single-story home with several neatly trimmed shrubs in front of the porch. We are no longer wearing the Moon Knight suit, instead something that Eddie would have called "casual": a black T-shirt, loose gray pants, and boots. Though we cannot hear you anymore, we figured you would not mind us raiding your closet at Spector Manor to dress more appropriately.

You may not believe it, but we do have some understanding of your society.

We take steps up the porch, one hand holding a bag containing the psi-phon. The wood creaks under our weight as we approach. There is tension in this body—you may be dormant but you still echo throughout the body, and your anxieties are grounded in every muscle.

We knock.

And then, a voice—a small, tinny voice from above us. We look up to see a circular camera above the door.

"I'm not answering the door for you, Marc. This is way too early, even for you."

Now we must act as if we were you, as naturally as possible. Yet we do not know you on the same level as we knew Eddie. We do not know your history with Marlene Alraune, except for brief memories and emotions you shared with us.

We just know that you are not on the best terms with her. Which leaves a bit of a challenge, considering everything happening. And the Whisperer, he is here listening, projecting his will, telling us that one false move means the end of the Hive Mind.

He is not exactly being helpful.

So . . . we will try our best.

"Hello, Marlene." We raise a hand in a wave. "Can you talk with us?"

"Is this a joke, Marc? 'Us'? Like I want you *and* Steven *and* Jake arguing with me? Maybe you three should stop arguing first and learn to coexist in your head before you try coexisting with other people. At least stop blaming them for our breakup."

Our description of ourselves means something different to Marlene. The Whisperer buzzes with annoyance, causing a sharp pain in my eardrum that ripples through the internal symbiote. "I have a question about something your father was researching. Can you let us in?"

"No."

Nothing happens. No further words come from the speaker and the door definitely does not open.

In this moment, we wonder just what you had done to this person to make her so uninviting.

"Let us repeat ourselves. We need information about something your father researched. Can you—"

"No, I can't let you in." Her tone shifts into a clear annoyance. "So what happens now? I suppose you can just stand there. Can you roll out the garbage bins if you're going to be here? Collection is tomorrow."

"We are not—"

"They're on the side of the house. You only need to open the back gate." We look up at the camera and we feel Marlene staring right back at us. "Or you can leave me alone. You know, like you promised."

Perhaps it would be easier if we took over the body and used our abilities to rip the roof off the house. We think this as a bit of a joke, but you recoil at it. If you *could* break through the Whisperer's walls, we are certain you would have plenty to say.

Instead, we will simply try again.

"We need information—"

"Oh my god, Marc." Her voice now comes with a heavy sigh. "No, wait a minute. You're not Marc right now, are you? Dammit, what have you gotten yourself into?"

With that, we hear footsteps thump through the house. Then clicks as the door unlocks—more clicks than usual. Many more clicks than Eddie had at his apartment.

The door swings open and Marlene emerges, clad in a bathrobe and slippers, steaming cup of coffee in one hand. She takes one step forward onto the porch, then shuts the door behind her. "Security lock," she says, and the camera overhead beeps before all those clicks happen again.

She looks at us. Then the bag. Then back at us. We stand still and meet her eyes. And somewhere inside this body, we feel you shiver.

"What did you do with Marc?"

We attempt deception. "We are Marc—"

"I don't think Steven has gotten into the royal 'we' so let's just cut the crap." She points at the bag. "It's about this, isn't it?"

We pull the psi-phon out and let the bag drop to the porch. We hold the psi-phon up for Marlene to inspect.

"What is that thing?" Marlene leans in to look at the device up close, her tone darkening with her question.

"It is called 'the psi-phon.' An entity known as 'Moon Shade' once commanded it but we defeated him, and then it was lost. Now it is crucial and must be activated." We pause and wait, though her face does not show any recognition. "Your father studied it."

"Will you stop it already? I know Marc Spector. You," she said, leaning forward to tap our forehead, "do not sound like Marc Spector. Or Steven Grant, or Jake Lockley, for that matter. Are you Khonshu right now? Puppeting the person that used to know me best? You know, thanks to Khonshu, I can't even watch documentaries on Egypt anymore. That's how much that stupid bird has messed things up."

Her defiance is intense. Unexpectedly intense. She stands taller now, intimidating despite being clad in a light green bathrobe, all without blinking. She holds her cup of coffee like a weapon, like she may throw it on us at any moment.

The buzzing in our ear grows louder. It spikes, causing our knees to buckle as the Whisperer rages, demands more. The piercing noise interferes with the body for a fraction of a second, enough for our grip on the psi-phon to loosen.

And for Marlene to catch it.

"You're being weird over some headphones?" She pulls the psi-phon up and her eyes narrow as she looks at it closely. "What, do you need me to fix the Bluetooth for you again?"

Inside, you laugh. Or it feels like you laugh, a ripple of joy and bemusement within us.

We will try again. "We need your father's research on the psi-phon."

"Well, I'm not giving it to you. So now you go and leave and head back to wherever Khonshu is nesting at the moment. Unless you really are here to take out my garbage bins." She shoves the psi-phon into our hands, then takes a sip of her coffee. "And tell Marc and the boys that I said hello."

Something new is happening. A burning sensation, but not within this body. No, the buzzing gets louder, and across the Multiverse, it is as if a series of tiny drills go into every part of the Hive Mind. So small, so precise that they may not even notice.

But *we* notice. We know that is a first step, a fraction of what is threatened. Is it real? Or is it a message from the Whisperer? We cannot tell, not with the Whisperer in our head, only that he has plans to attack the Hive Mind. How much has he done? How strong are his capabilities? We do not know, but we cannot risk it. If the Whisperer acts on his threats, then all is lost. "We are begging you," we say, though the words struggle to come out. "There is much more at stake than you can possibly know."

"I've heard that before. You don't spend years with Marc Spector without hearing about some world-ending threat." She laughs and shakes her head. "You know, some of the time, it's actually true." Marlene steps closer, so close now that we feel her breath against our cheeks. "So which one is it? Real or fake?"

There is a door in our body, one that you are trapped behind. Except now we can feel you pounding on it, screaming and yelling. The buzzing noise gets louder again, and we finally understand.

The buzzing is as much a threat to us as it is a tool to drown you out.

The Whisperer does not want us communicating. In any way.

"It is true," we say. "And Marc is . . . dormant right now. But within." We tap our chest and let the body take a deep breath. "He is still within."

Marlene closes her eyes, though movement darts back and forth beneath her eyelids as if she is working out some deep, powerful idea. Finally, she opens her eyes. We wonder what you think of this, but under the shrieks of the Whisperer, we cannot hear you. We can barely control our own movements during this.

"We need information about—"

She shakes her head and mutters what sounds like a curse word under her breath before her eyes open and she stares right at us. "I know one way to get through to Marc."

Before we can respond, she pulls us in tight, her mouth pressed against ours.

The balance in our head feels different.

The buzzing goes away.

Where there was once the Whisperer's wall of sound, we feel a trust. Urgency, relief, panic, yet through that all, a trust.

You *are* here. Marlene has connected enough to push the Whisperer away, but for how long?

Perhaps not long enough.

We offer you control.

Yes, you say.

We relent. And you take over. "Marlene. Marlene, you did it. You broke through." Marlene's expression and posture soften, and though a clear divide exists between you and her, her relief is visible, even to us. "Listen to me. I don't have much time. I know I have put you through a lot. I know I have brought so much pain to you. I would not be here if it weren't really dire circumstances. And I know I don't seem like myself right now, and that's because I'm not." Now your mind is racing, a panic at the information you must convey in the little span you have. You feel the Whisperer fighting his way back in; we sense it, too.

The buzzing returns. Low, small, but there.

Whatever you need to say, Marc Spector, do it now.

"I'm going to disappear in a few seconds. Someone else will take over this body. The thing with the psi-phon, give them enough information to get started, but leave a vital piece out. Someone else is coming to help, but for them to get here, you need to slow everything down." Marlene shifts, her face hard and serious, like she has handled missions from Marc before. "This is a hostage situation and we need to buy time. Do you understand?"

She doesn't speak right away. Instead, her lips purse for a moment, then she nods. "Yeah, Marc. I do."

You sigh at that. Your relief is palpable. And now you start saying things that cause this body's temperature, heart rate, breathing, all of it to go haywire. "I miss you. I miss what we had, but I'm gonna keep my promise. I'm going to stay away. To keep you safe. Just," you say, your hands shaking, "get us through this, all right?"

This seems to confuse Marlene. Her facial muscles twitch and twist in ways we cannot read. And you, you react similarly. You two stand there in silence, as if neither of you knows what to make of this moment.

The buzzing grows. Louder, much louder—and fast. You speak quick. "And one more thing—trust Steven and Jake. They're going to—"

The body tremors. Now you are locked away again. That buzzing noise is back. Marlene looks at us, her eyes cloudy with tears while also narrowed in . . . frustration? Anger? Sadness? It is hard for us to know.

But as our posture shifts, she seems to understand. More importantly, you have put her through enough that she seems to take it in stride.

Now it is us standing with her in silence. Except in our head, the Whisperer asks what happened with Marc. We will tell him the truth. Enough of the truth, that is.

Marc experienced sentimentality. Emotions. Now he is gone.

The Whisperer is satisfied with that. And now Marlene changes. She is putting on a front. We know this because somewhere deep down, *you* can sense this.

"Look, Marc, I'll be honest with you," she says. "I remember the psi-phon. I mean, that deal with Moon Shade, that was wild. Wait right here."

She says a command to the security system and all of the locks protecting her plain wooden door unlatch themselves. She disappears into the house, and we wait.

The Whisperer waits.

And grows suspicious.

In our mind, he sends a message—an image, really. Of the Hive Mind. As we see it, we hear the buzzing get loud, loud enough to drown out the sounds of the rushing cars and passing airplanes and walking children around us. But this time, the buzzing comes with something else—the sense of flame at our hands, at the threshold of the Hive Mind.

The Whisperer demands results.

And the noise grows. The heat intensifies. We remain steady, strong on our feet, but the noise shakes our connection to the body, steals our strength, and then—

The door opens. Marlene returns.

We stand up.

"Here." Marlene holds up a folder of papers and waves them around before shoving them into my hand. "Take it and leave."

The Whisperer's noise is buzzing. It grows calm, steady. We scan the folder, knowing what Marc told her earlier, yet we push those thoughts aside. We cannot give the Whisperer any insight into what Marc has planned.

"This will work and—" we start. But a harsh sting stabs us from the inside. The Whisperer exerts control. We crumple to one knee before standing straight up, now a passenger as the Whisperer influences this body's movements, its actions.

"Something is missing here." The words come out of the body but are not from our mind. As the Whisperer pushes us further, the very fibers holding this body together burn, a pain that is equally paralyzing and electrifying. "What have you left out?"

Marlene remains steadfast in her posture. She looks at us and we remember what Marc said—that Marlene is smart. "My father researched this. Not me."

"This shows how to power the psi-phon. How to activate it. Not how to use it. It is useless without that."

As the Whisperer speaks, sweat forms along the body's forehead. It trembles and weakens, and our vision blurs in and out, the noise now screaming in our head. We debate ejecting from the host, yet doing so would be the end of the Hive Mind and we cannot allow that.

Everything that happens from here belongs to Marlene.

Her head tilts, her eyes narrow. She is watching, processing, and finally she straightens, an exaggerated sigh filled with annoyance. "Let me check one more place. I have a bunch of my father's things." Time passes, though for us, we cannot measure how much as the body stands there, the nerves and synapses of this body under duress as the Whisperer's ire grows. Marlene returns, another stack of papers in her hand. "I know you are not Marc. I know when Marc is himself. I remember things he said." She presents them and looks straight at me. "Here's the rest. Now go."

We look at it—a schematic, notes on connectivity and function. The Whisperer sees through our eyes and suddenly . . .

Relief.

Something else happens, something surprising:

We hear you.

Atta girl, Marlene.

It is faint, a flutter of thought that only we can pick up. You know something that we don't. We want to ask you what it is but we cannot reach you. Perhaps it is better that we do not know, to protect *everything* from the Whisperer.

Instead, we turn around. The buzzing has returned to normal. Our body movement, temperature, pain levels have all returned to normal. We move, the stilted gait recovering into a normal walk.

A surge from inside happens, a clear message from you. You are telling us something, and it is draining your last shred of will to get this through. *Do the Whisperer's bidding. He must believe you,* you say, *and you must trust them.*

All of them.

And then you are gone.

Only we remain in this body. Alone, with the buzzing.

CHAPTER 26

—

STEVEN

THERE WAS A FIRST TIME FOR EVERYTHING.

That's what I told myself. A bit of a coping mechanism, if you would. I mean, we'd certainly been through much worse if you put "how bad" on a bar graph. Getting into a scrap with Bullseye, dealing with Jack Russell's whole werewolf-ness, the ordeal—or ordeals—with Bushman, even a few days ago waking up in this place, massive arm wound while surrounded by flames. Those were all pretty bad.

This, though. Something about my innate sense of orderly respect tickled that certain wrongness that came with being inside a police interrogation room.

I would give the station credit, though. My surroundings were very, very neat.

Four walls. A door. A harsh fluorescent light in a stock industrial lamp overhead. Drab gray paint with little bits peeling off, and in the center, a metal table with metal chairs.

And then me. In my Mr. Knight pants and vest, no coat.

Oh, and my hands—cuffed. That was important. And my ankles, too.

The door opened, and Detective Flint walked in. He didn't sit; instead, he lingered as we made eye contact, then he put something on the table. "Do you remember me? We worked together once. Or, should I say, I worked with Moon Knight once. Just in passing. Helping each other out. Freaky homicides back in the day. Didn't know that you were"—he held up a paper with a mug shot and fingerprints—"Marc Spector, though. Either way, I've seen your brutality up close."

Jake let out a groan in my head. "Oh man, this reality's Marc is not going to like this. If we get through it all."

I shook off Jake's running commentary—that wasn't going to help right now. Though, really, if we messed up things in this universe for Marc, that was probably the definition of being a bad houseguest. I squinted at the object on the table, and it took several seconds to realize that it was a scrunched-up evidence bag. But inside of it sat a phone.

My phone.

Marc's phone. From the supplies in his emergency room, the same phone that received a single text with the name *Mary Sands*. Here, it sat wrapped in plastic, which Flint then slid over to me.

"You're a big fan of Retrograde Sanitarium, aren't you? Going there twice in one night. Had time for a costume change, though." He huffed, biting down on his lip. "Guess leaving Dr. Emmet for dead wasn't enough. You had to go back and take out some cops, too?"

To be fair, I *was* guilty of that last part. Assault, breaking and entering, theft. All valid charges.

But everything Venom did?

How did one explain that?

Also, Dr. Emmet's death was an accident, but I wasn't about to go off on that tangent. I needed to focus: How could I get out of here and reach Marlene before Venom did?

"Listen, Officer," I said, doing my best Wall Street schmoozing voice, "I think there's been a bit of a misunderstanding here. You see, I'm—"

"Oh, we know who you are." He tapped on the phone, the wrapped plastic bag sinking before crinkling back. "What I'm trying to figure out is what this is all about."

"No, I mean a misunderstanding with identity." I smiled like I was walking into a boardroom with the best quarterly earnings news. "I'm Steven Grant. I know of this Marc Spector, we look remarkably similar. Someone once sent me a side by side—"

"Nice try. Prints match up exactly with military records." He held up a sheet, giving it two quick taps before reading it aloud. "Marc Spector. Born March 9, Chicago, Illinois. Ex-Marine, dishonorably discharged. International mercenary. Lots of interesting stuff." The paper flapped as he waved it. "Your prints flagged the CIA right away. They were really helpful, *Marc*."

This body's dead state is taking its toll. My power is draining. I am losing the ability to drive this body's subsistence. Steven, we must take action now. We may only have a day left. Possibly less.

Flint leaned in close as he slammed the papers on the table. "So let's establish some facts here. Steven Grant is a billionaire. You're just some chump who got kicked out of the Marines. You were at Retrograde. Had some vendetta against Dr. Emmet. Looked good for the cameras. Then you tried to fake your way into the Top of New York Hotel as Steven Grant. Told everybody and anybody that you were Steven Grant, like they just *had* to believe you."

"I knew that was a bad idea," Jake grumbled.

"*Then* all hell breaks loose at the hotel. No one can really say for sure what was happening, but we know there was some expensive stuff in the basement, fancy collectibles for people with too much money and not enough taste. Am I right? So, what, are you an artifact hunter now? Big plans for the black market? I just can't figure out the connection to going to Retrograde. Or changing clothes, for that matter. But," he stood, hand propped up on the back of the chair for support, "maybe that's the point. You were *in* Retrograde for a reason, right?"

"I think," I started, choosing my words carefully, "you are underestimating the complexity of this situation."

"Oh, I am, am I? Let's try it this way. Records show that you escaped Retrograde not too long ago. Now, look, I'm no fan of what you did to the people there. But I hear things. I *know* things. Retrograde isn't exactly a resort. So maybe it's as simple as this."

Now he leaned forward, close enough for me to pick up his coffee-scented breath. "You got word of a job to rob this gala. I mean, you're a former Marine, you've worked as a merc, you've traveled the world. Perfect fit for a high-stakes job, right? Plus, you *look* like Steven Grant. Easy money. Problem is, you're stuck in a mental asylum. So the guy cutting the checks helps spring you out. Gives you a head start. But then an idea gets in your head. You think about all the terrible things they did to you at Retrograde and your anger grows and grows. It's justified, right? They shot you up with all sorts of chemicals, used electroshock therapy. Emmet, I saw her background, she's no saint of mental health. You think and you think and you think, and then *boom*." The table shook as his fist pounded on it. "You get mad. You get *really* mad, and then you put on this ridiculous hood and cape to go scare some people. Or maybe it's strategic, you know? Easier to hide in it. Whatever it is, you go there and you seek vengeance. You even get cocky, take off your mask for one good look at the cameras."

"Totally called it, Venom was framing us," Jake said.

"But then Emmet, she's not scared of you." A dramatic pause came, several breaths passing before Flint started a slow pace back and forth. "She even calls you out by name right in front of the security cameras. Smart woman. And that makes you snap. And *then* there's a mishap with a gun. Oh, I saw the footage. You didn't kill Emmet. It was an accident, and how infuriating is that? How absolutely infuriating? You *wanted* your vengeance and then someone else took it away. So you take it out. On everyone else. In fact, you go back for more, now wearing a white tux. Probably symbolic in a way, am I right? You take care of business and then you get yourself over to Top of New York, acting like everything's good. 'Look at me, I'm Steven Grant, not Marc Spector.' Except something goes wrong, a blown fuse or something in the basement and it starts an electrical fire." His fingernail tapped on the table. "Chaos theory, you know? Sometimes crap just happens, but you're still trying to get that payoff and you're climbing up this outdoor elevator shaft until . . . you can't."

"Steven," Jake says quietly. "I'm not a movie guy. But this is a good speech, right?"

I didn't want to dignify that with a response, but yeah, this *was* a good speech. It didn't help my predicament at all, but I at least recognized that.

"So I got a problem and it's this: I've got fingerprints, I've got footage, I've got eyewitnesses, I've got so much evidence that the scale isn't just tilted, it's goddamn broken at this point. So why don't you make it easier on us and just confess so we can all go back to our happy places."

"Damn. He's almost got *me* convinced," Jake said.

This would be the perfect moment to call for the Mind Space with the three of us, my ability to read people, Spector's ability to strategize, and Jake's street sensibilities—plus his quips. But without Spector, a key piece to our team went missing, leaving us with a giant hole in our tool kit and little time.

I took in a breath, then studied Flint. So many different paths emerged in my head—if we confessed, would that give us a way out? Was that better than stubbornly sitting in this room? At least there'd be movement involved.

I closed my eyes, taking in a breath, trying to conjure some direction out of this. If we did confess, that might activate a whole bunch of other police procedures, and who knew how long things might take? We needed to get to Marlene as soon as possible, *then* we needed to get to the psi-phon as soon as possible. Which meant getting stuck in handcuffs while being shuffled from place to place by escorting cops . . .

Well, that probably wouldn't work.

Except I couldn't get out with Flint stuck in this room with me.

I needed a third option. Which meant changing the game for now.

But how?

Flint's words played back in my mind—fingerprints, footage, eyewitnesses. But none of the eyewitnesses saw either me or Venom without the mask. In fact, the footage only had that very brief moment of Venom pulling the mask off and Emmet saying Marc's name. Fingerprints? Sure, I had the fingerprints of Marc Spector, but we certainly didn't take Mr. Knight's gloves off. And Venom likely kept the full Moon Knight suit on.

No fingerprints. No conclusive footage. No valid eyewitnesses. This cop was bluffing.

"I want to talk to my lawyer," I said.

"What?" Jake asked. "We don't have a lawyer. Don't say Matt Murdock, he hates us. I bet even in this universe he hates us."

"His name is Jean-Paul Duchamp." Though Jake only existed in my head, I felt him side-eyeing me. "Get me a phone so I can call him."

Flint remained still, a foul look on his face. He glanced behind him, and though his exterior remained tough, he let out the smallest of sighs, enough for me to know that his bluff cracked.

"I said, get me a phone. My name is Steven Grant, I have more money than everyone in this police station combined, probably everyone on this entire block combined." My voice grew in ire, the same sort of boardroom confidence that worked great in short, jarring bursts to anyone who saw it. I couldn't keep "it" up for too long, though.

It took a lot of energy being this much of a jerk.

"I'm done being polite. Steven Grant. Did you hear that? That's my name. Not Marc Spector. And I'm going to sue the pants out of everyone involved with this mistake. You're trying to bluff me into a confession for something I didn't do, something I'm not even involved with? I was at Top of New York for a good time and now I got this?" I laughed as I shook my head, trying for my best impersonation of Simon Williams on the set of the last legal thriller I produced. "Go ahead. Keep me here *longer*. Duchamp will love that. It's just gonna add to the list of things he'll do to burn the careers of you and everyone else too stupid to accurately connect the dots. Hey, while we're waiting for that phone, why don't you go down to the nearest corner store and get yourself an Avengers coloring book. Bet that's more your speed than solving crimes."

"Wow," Jake said. He shouldn't have, though, because his re-action caused me to chuckle. Though in a way, it worked, this brief burst of contempt punctuated with a laugh.

Flint turned silently, the door opening with enough force that a gust tousled my hair. And the slam when it closed, that must have echoed through the entire station.

"Frenchie?" Jake asked. "He watches the mission and flies a helicopter. When did he become a lawyer?"

"Just now," I said as I stared at the clock above the door, my eyes landing on the gradual rotation of the second hand. "But we need someone to talk to. And we need to get to Marlene."

Tick. Tick. Tick.

CHAPTER 27

—

STEVEN

THE HEAVY LOCK SET TWISTED WITH *CLICK*S AND *CLACK*S BEFORE the door swung open, revealing Frenchie in a rare suit jacket and tie. We met eyes, his mouth curled up beneath his thin mustache, and he stepped in. "Don't take forever," Flint said, before slamming the door shut.

"Frenchie," I said. "It is really good to see you."

About forty minutes ago, I got my one phone call—which, of course, Frenchie missed. It went straight to his voice mail, to which I'd put on my billionaire voice and said, "Duchamp. It's Steven Grant. They got me in a holding cell, mixing me up with this Marc Spector fellow. Get down here, I need my lawyer. Bring all the usual tools for getting out of messes like this."

As for those tools? Frenchie had a single briefcase with him, held up for me to take in. It landed on the table with a weighty *thud*, and he slid it my way.

"Which one am I dealing with right now?" he asked, a slight fatigue coloring his words.

"Steven."

"No, I mean, which dimension or whatever are you from?"

"Oh. Got it," I said, my voice returning to its normal not-impressive cadence. "Same guy who was sharing pancakes with you a little while ago. Steven and Jake in Spector's body."

"Just making sure." Frenchie leaned back in his chair, his legs pressing it into a small tilt. "You know, it's weird. Part of me is relieved it's you. Part of me wishes it was my Marc. So I could punch Venom out of him."

"Honestly," I said, "I'm not sure whose side Venom is on. But I need to find out. And that means—"

"Marlene. Yep. Don't worry, my friend. Gena and I dug into our archives of Marc's things. We got everything you need. Most importantly," he tapped the top of the briefcase, "check it out."

I pressed the two locks, their clasps flipping open, and I lifted the lid. At the very top of the stack sat a printout, all sorts of info on Mary Sands listed, including an address and a phone number.

"You're sure this is her?"

"*Mary Sands* is a pretty common name in the United States. But you isolate by region, you look at records that only emerged *after* she left Marc, you look at the underground activity in establishing things like DMV records and such. Yeah," Frenchie said, taking in a confident breath, "it's her."

"Great." I looked under the first sheet. Then the next, then the one under that.

Blank. Or mostly blank. A Chinese restaurant menu, some old receipts for rental cars, and some instruction manuals for power tools. "Frenchie, where's the stuff to get out?"

"What stuff?" Frenchie's eyebrow rose.

"I don't know, like weapons or something." In my head, Jake groaned, and if Khonshu had the strength, he probably would, too. "I thought you said you had a bunch of Marc's things."

"We do. Gena has them in the car." He pointed straight down. "It's downstairs."

One phone call. I had one phone call to get me out of here and I got a briefcase of old papers and some information on Marlene— valuable information, sure, but it put the cart before the horse, or whatever metaphor you wanted to use. My head sank into my hands, complete with a throat-rattling groan that would have done Jake proud.

"Steven, I don't know if this is how it works in your universe, but in our police stations we have things called 'metal detectors.'"

He thumbed over his shoulder. "That's a bit of a problem when it comes to trying to smuggle you weapons on short notice."

"But what about, I don't know," I said through my palms, "a lockpick or something?"

My reply was genuine, and yet Frenchie laughed so hard that tears leaked out the sides of his eyes. "A lockpick? You really *aren't* Marc."

"Is that a compliment or an insult?" Jake asked.

"Let's play this through, my friend. Let's say I brought in a plastic lockpick. A super-sturdy composite, as strong as metal. You pick the locks on your cuffs, then you pick the lock on that door." Frenchie swung his arm out, imitating a door opening. "Then you step outside and suddenly every one of those cops pulls a gun on you." Both of his hands held up, formed into finger guns directed right at me. "How is that going to help Marlene?"

"He's got a point," Jake said.

"Yeah. Okay, I get it," I said, closing the briefcase. "So we're not getting out that way. But then there's this other problem called 'concrete' and it's all around us. I don't know if your Marc ever told you this, but we can't exactly just punch through walls and stuff."

"Well," Frenchie sighed, "we know where Marlene is. Now what?"

"Maybe you go to her, tell her—"

"Wait," Jake said. My head tilted at the word, probably enough that Frenchie realized that a new conversation had started inside my head. "I got an idea. We'll need some time to hash this out. Mind Space, now."

"Mind Space? Look at you, Jake," I said. Frenchie shot over a confused look, and I put up a hand. "Hold on. I gotta talk to Jake for a second."

I NEVER FIGURED OUT WHY TIME MOVED DIFFERENTLY IN THE MIND Space. Jake didn't usually care, and Spector, he'd just shrugged it off when I brought it up. It probably happened because, in reality, the conversation came from synapses firing off inside our brain, true conversation at the speed of thought. Khonshu remained in the background, leaving only me and Jake to hash out a plan.

Which wasn't something we'd normally do. I guess we all shared a common trait of sticking to our lanes, but the fact that Marc had disappeared, we sat in an interrogation room, and we had no weapons or options, well . . .

It forced us to get creative.

I opened my eyes, and though it felt like ten minutes of discussion passed, the clock showed that only three minutes or so had transpired. Yet in that time Jake offered a very feasible idea—and I applied my grounded sensibilities to bash it into something that just might work.

Might being the operative word.

"I hope you were doing more than just taking a nap," Frenchie said as he rubbed his chin.

"Yeah. We got a plan. Just gotta get these pieces into place, and then we'll . . ." My voice slowed as it sank into the facts of the situation. Sure, we had a plan in place, and sure, we'd worked together a bit to get to where we were. More successfully at times than others. But right now?

Me. Jake. Khonshu. Frenchie. Gena. Marlene. This reality's *Marc*.

Even Venom.

We all had a part to play in this, knowingly or not. And that meant we all really, really had to trust one another.

In all of the realities that existed, was there a Marc Spector who chose the quiet life of, I don't know, someone who rescued animals and owned a coffee shop instead of being a masked vigilante? That would be ideal.

"We just need to work together," I said slowly. "Khonshu? Khonshu, are you listening? You were just lurking in the Mind Space."

I am. I am saving my strength.

"I need a favor," I said, and as I did, Frenchie leaned in, like he could hear the conversation in my head. Maybe he didn't need to, though. This would all be pretty self-explanatory in a second.

I am not exactly in a position to grant wishes right now.

"Just one thing. You said before that you sometimes helped Marc do things." *How* Khonshu did that, I'd love to know. But we didn't have time for science experiments. Maybe later. "Like, bursts of super strength. Or causing earthquakes. Right? You caused an earthquake at the hotel."

Quite the menu you're asking for.

"No, just one request." I held up my hands, the chain of the handcuffs jingling. "Cuffs on my hands and ankles. Can you give me a burst of super strength to break them?"

No reply came. Frenchie's eyes narrowed, though I couldn't tell if that was curiosity, amusement, or dread on his face.

Possibly.

"Possibly?"

I will try my best. But know this—afterward, I will have to stay silent to focus all my energies on keeping this body alive.

"Right, right." My head tilted back to stare at the flickering light above. "So what you're saying is—"

Go find Venom quickly and fix this.

"Okay." I nodded, both for myself and for Frenchie. "All right, just be ready in a second. Frenchie, here's my plan. We're gonna—"

"A plan!" Frenchie's laugh interrupted my momentum. "Are you sure you're not Spector now?"

"I don't know if Spector would come up with this, but it's our best shot. And if it doesn't work . . ." I said, the sheer ridiculousness of everything causing the smallest smile to tilt the corners of my mouth up. Just a little. "If this doesn't work, blame Jake. It was his idea."

"Thanks, Steven." Jake's voice was dry, but laughter followed his words. I'm sure one of our therapists at some time talked about levity in the face of adversity being a *good* thing, so why not now?

The side of my knuckle tapped the table, though given the

whole handcuff situation, that made both hands move. I looked down at the bits of metal links keeping my wrists connected—a fitting visual, given the way my life worked. "Okay," I said. "Here's what's going to happen. I'm going to give the body to Jake. Then Khonshu will grant whatever super strength he can. Jake takes over, breaks out of the cuffs.

"Then, Frenchie, we're taking you hostage and getting out of here. Out the door and down to Gena. Got it?"

Frenchie's eyes narrowed, a single finger up as he murmured to himself. "Wait a second, my friend. Let me get this straight. You," he pointed my way before tapping his own chest, "are going to take *me* hostage?"

"Not me. Jake."

This time it was Frenchie's turn to sink his face into his hands, followed by a groan that beat mine in volume. "You, Jake, that doesn't really matter. *I'm* the hostage?"

"Well, yeah," I said with a shrug. "I mean, I can't really take myself hostage, right?"

"I should have stayed in the car. Maybe I'll go open a restaurant when we're done. Seems easier than this." He pulled the suitcase over to him, then snapped it open. "Look, if Jake's gonna be doing this, we might as well do it properly." His hand rustled through one of the top pockets before holding something out for me to take.

But I wouldn't take it. Because it didn't belong to me.

That was Jake's mustache. It was *his* to take.

I closed my eyes and invited Jake to control the body.

CHAPTER 28

JAKE

JAKE, ARE YOU READY?

"I don't think I'm the issue," Jake said, looking at Frenchie. A crooked grimace sat on Frenchie's face, which was kind of weird, given the wide range of terrible situations he'd endured with Marc and company. The guy had airlifted Moon Knight out of exploding buildings via helicopter, and this tickled his nerves?

Maybe acting as a human shield—even as a ruse—put the danger in a much closer, more personal context.

Too late now, though. The plan was in motion.

"But yeah, I'm good. Juice me up."

I will likely be fully dormant after this. My remaining strength will focus on keeping this body alive. If we are successful, I may leave this body for Marc's. Any parting words?

Steven paced behind me, a phantom filled with muttering and nervous energy. "How about 'It's been fun, let's not meet in a burning basement next time'?"

Very well. Good luck, Steven and Jake.

"Luck," Jake mused to himself, but then things began to shift in the strangest way. His muscles didn't swell out or anything like that; instead, he just got a sense of everything becoming lighter and easier. He turned to Frenchie with a knowing nod, then looked at the mustache waiting between them. "Here goes nothing," he said, balling his fingers into fists and taking a deep breath.

Jake flexed his arms out.

And the chain linking the cuffs snapped.

"Wow," Frenchie said. "New Hulk in town. Watch out, Jen Walters."

"Not quite," Jake said, snapping the metal pieces off his wrists. He bent down and pulled the ankle cuffs off, then tossed them aside, the metal bits jingling off the walls. "I guess we know they're not watching us, huh? Would have been ten cops in here by now."

"Attorney/client privilege." Frenchie stood and held up the briefcase. "See, I'm getting good at this lawyer stuff."

Jake reached down for the mustache and pushed it into place, smoothing it over several times just to make sure. As he did, a heat surged through his body, followed by a tingling and a sudden sense that things began reverting to his normal tough-but-not-super-powered state. "I'm losing Khonshu's boost," he said to Frenchie. "Help me find a weapon before I'm back to being just me."

WITH THE LAST BIT OF KHONSHU'S STRENGTH, JAKE KICKED THE door as hard as he could.

It worked, even better than he'd expected. The metal door flew out, smashing against the hallway wall and leaving dents in the brick, bits of wood scattering across the floor from the frame. Voices echoed down the hallway, followed by a clamor of foot-steps.

"This better work," Frenchie said, a makeshift bit of metal pressed up against his throat, the opposite side of his earlier injury.

"It will," Jake said, and alongside them, Steven nodded.

"I'd peek around the corner but it feels like my range is limited now that Khonshu's asleep," Steven said. "I can still chat your ear off, though."

"Thanks, Steven," Jake said, nudging his fake hostage forward. "I'm sure that'll get us past a wall of cops."

"Drop the weapon!" a woman yelled as a duo appeared around the corner.

"Oh my god, how'd he do that to the door?" the man behind her asked. "Is he a super?"

Flint appeared next. "I don't know about that, but he is ex-Marine. A mercenary. Be careful. Marc," he yelled out, "I don't know what your lawyer did to piss you off, but we don't need to do this. Drop the knife."

It wasn't a knife, exactly. More like a bit of hardware-turned-shiv courtesy of Jake's remaining super strength tearing the leg off a metal table. He stepped ahead, Frenchie moving with little resistance and Steven trailing him. "How do we get to Gena?" he whispered.

"Elevator to underground parking."

"They might be waiting there," Steven said. "Or if they realize we're going to Gena, they might stop her car."

"Stairs," Frenchie said.

"Shut up," Jake yelled, probably a bit too loud, but appropriate for the role. He twisted the shiv into Frenchie's skin, Steven apologizing for them all the while

"Take it easy, Marc," Flint said. The gathering officers slowed their approach, a wall of uniforms lining the drab office. "No one's gotta get hurt here."

"Yeah, you see what I did to that door?" With his free hand, Jake thumbed at the interrogation room behind him. "Go check it out. I'm not what you think. If you don't believe me, take a look at what's left of the table in there."

They moved down the hall, every step forward matched with the police backing off. Was this the most guns Jake ever had pointed at him in his life? Possibly. Marc definitely had seen more, though.

"Don't kill me, please!" Frenchie cried out in a voice far whinier than Jake—or Steven, for that matter—had ever heard. His arms and legs flailed for an instant, prompting shouts of "Calm down" from the police and "Don't you move" from Jake. "Don't shoot! Please!" The most ill-timed chuckle formed, and Jake bit down on his lip to stifle his reaction to Frenchie's theatrics. "He's superhuman! He can deflect bullets!"

Steven's head tilted, his eyes going sideways to Frenchie. They swung over to Jake, who gave a quick shrug while keeping his hostage up. Then back to Frenchie. "Good improv work," he finally said. "Oh wait, you can't hear me."

Jake shook Frenchie, a quick bit of roughing up as if to show a tiny amount of "you gave away my super-powered secret" irritation, which caused Steven to look away again.

"Everyone back down!" Flint called out. "That's Moon Knight. I've seen his work up close."

"Tell me where we're going, Steven," Jake whispered as they turned the corner, the hallway now opening up into a wide space filled with detective cubicles and workstations. Most of the officers gathered by Flint, who kept his hands up while he directed foot traffic, though a few lingered around. "Khonshu, if you got the juice to give Steven a look, that'd sure help right now."

Low voices floated through the space, Jake picking up on bits and pieces, everything from time checks to weapons speculation, though he did hear the specific question of "when did he get a mustache?"

"Okay, just give me a second here," Steven said. "I'm looking, I'm looking." He sprinted, dashing around desks and chairs to get better views. "There's a big green EXIT sign. Down that hall. That's gotta be it."

They shuffled through, an ongoing call-and-response between Jake and the assembled cops, Frenchie doing his best—or worst, really—overacting in the hostage role. Jake scooted them over to the stairwell, a flood of voices going back and forth, and despite the noise, Steven's running commentary somehow cut through all of it. "Over here, over here, watch your step," he said, clearly ignorant of Jake's growing annoyance.

Behind him, Jake leaned into the emergency bar of the stairwell door, then pushed the door open. He stood, one foot in the musty hall and one in the office. "Frenchie, we're gonna keep this up until we get to the ground floor," he whispered. "Then we run like hell to Gena. Got it?"

"Got it, but no more stabbing, please," he whispered back before returning to a convincing wail.

Jake kicked out behind him, his heel gauging the space between the doorframe, the door, and the textured floor. "We're gonna go through here," he said for one final call. "Then we're going down the stairs. No funny business or he gets it. A clear route out. All right?"

Flint nodded and was about to respond when another officer interrupted him with a whisper in his ear. To which he waved several other officers over.

"Uh-oh," Steven said before dashing over to the cluster of officers. Jake held Frenchie tight, and they both stepped into the stairwell, the door now propped open only by the tip of his boot. "There's been a Venom sighting. Apparently heading north, to the Long Island shore. They don't know his destination. So now they're really confused."

"You can hear that?" Jake asked with a quick hiss.

Steven glanced back and forth several times, then shrugged. "I think so? But we need to go now. Either they think you are actually Moon Knight or they don't. It might slow them down. Or it might make them more aggressive."

Frenchie tensed under Jake's grasp. "I'm assuming you're having a heart-to-heart with everyone?" he asked under his breath.

"Steven says we need to move." Across the hall, the small huddle broke and Flint began his approach. "Not a step closer!" Jake yelled. "No followers. No one in the lobby. And no one gets hurt. I'm leaving now."

The door slammed shut before Flint or anyone else could respond, but the fact that the police didn't fly through every possible entrance meant that they bought it, at least for now. The shiv remained at Frenchie's throat, though Jake let up on the pressure as they awkwardly marched down the steps, the rattle of metal stairs echoing while they moved. They made progress slowly, passing floor after floor, Jake taking a moment at every landing to check that no surprises awaited on the other side of each door, until they got to the ground floor.

"Do we even look in the lobby?" Steven asked.

From above, the sound of a mechanical latch filtered down, soon followed by shouts. "I think they changed their minds," Frenchie said.

"Okay, no more of this." Jake let Frenchie go, then kicked the door to the lobby all the way open. Its hydraulics began peeling the door back, a hiss coming with the gradual decline. "Maybe this will throw them off. Let's get to Gena."

The stairs shook, Jake taking two at a time behind Frenchie as they sprinted down to the second floor of the station's underground parking lot. Thick, stale air greeted them as they burst into the space, and Frenchie moved with an athlete's pace, turning at the third row of cars. "Gena!" he yelled. "Start the car!"

Car lamps came to life, followed quickly by the roar of an engine from too much gas, the sudden shift in noise enough to catch the attention of a young couple walking the other way. Frenchie jumped into the passenger side of Gena's car while Jake dove into the back seat, body curled up as tight as possible. "Go fast." Someone—probably Frenchie—threw a coat over Jake as the car pitched back in reverse, then jerked forward. Steven was likely there somewhere, maybe sitting on him in that phantom way, though the coat completely cut off Jake's vision. The car jolted and bumped, Gena taking the exit ramp far rougher than she should have, and soon the familiar honks and groans of New York City streets came back.

"If anyone's following us, they're way behind," Frenchie said. "Take as many turns as possible and get on a highway. We need distance."

The car tilted with one aggressive turn, then tilted the other way for another, honking horns from angry drivers cutting through the air. The engine revved and Jake stayed under cover, leaving all of this up to his friends.

"You can't see this," Steven said, "but Gena pulled some bad-ass moves."

"Jake," Gena said over the roar of the engine, "glad to see you."

"You too, Gena." Jake lifted the edge of the coat up for a quick peek. "It's been a while."

"We brought a present for you," she said, thumbing over her shoulder. "In the trunk. Thought you might need them."

"Pancakes?"

"Better," Frenchie said, a toothy grin emerging under his mustache. "A Moon Knight suit and some crescent darts."

CHAPTER 29
VENOM

WHAT HAVE YOU SET IN MOTION?

We cannot know. There is a sense of something in your slumber. You remain buried, blocked out by the Whisperer. We exist in your body, you are a part of us, your gifts and instincts absorbed into our own.

We showed you the horror of the Whisperer. What the Whisperer is capable of, how he can reach across the Multiverse.

When we first found you standing in the rain, we knew you were special, important. Don't get an inflated ego back there, that's what the Whisperer said. Not any Marc Spector, but *you*. For what reason, it was not fully revealed, only that the psi-phon was key to transferring your life essence to the Whisperer. This entire journey has been part of our plan to stay ahead of the Whisperer, to lull him into a false sense of security—a trick, a way for us to turn at the very last moment and rip away his power and save the Hive Mind.

Even now we wonder—have you betrayed us? Have we betrayed *you*?

Yet more becomes clear with each step toward our goal—much more easily because the Whisperer's buzzing is silent for the moment, though it is sure to come back after he finishes attending to his plans.

He knows that the end is near. But whose end? Ours? Yours? The other Steven and Jake?

The Multiverse?

We think back to the destruction of 113843. To the Whisperer's power, a buzzing noise that infiltrates us and emits the exact frequency to cause us harm. To his ability to somehow use us as a conduit, bringing that noise to the entire Hive Mind.

Do the Whisperer's bidding. He must believe you, and you must trust them. All of them.

That is what you said. You must have sensed our plan. Well, not quite a plan. We did not get there yet. It was more of a hope, an understanding that the psi-phon should not fall into the Whisperer's hands. That at the very last moment, something must be done to thwart him, but only after we have secured the safety of everything: this world, the Hive Mind, the Multiverse.

Also, we would like to kill the Whisperer. That may not be possible. But it would give us great pleasure.

The Whisperer's bidding? If that is the goal, then we are nearly there: four tall stacks towering above a series of box-shaped buildings, all beyond a wall of barbed wire and a security gate.

Roxxon Power Station.

If he is to believe our actions, then we must be ruthless, powerful, and swift. If we get some of our frustrations out during this process, that will work as well.

Though we remember the rules we set with Eddie about *not* hurting the innocent. We will abide by that, the best we can.

If you were here, we imagine you would laugh at that point. We might, too, but perhaps for different reasons. Keeping that pledge is not as hard as you might think.

The part about trusting *you*, though. That does not come easy to us.

To *me*.

But we feel you are an okay person, Marc Spector.

The more we have gotten to know you, the more we feel certain about something: Eddie may not have liked you. But he would have respected you.

And because of that, we will respect your wishes. We will carry out the Whisperer's bidding.

And we will trust in the others to do what needs to be done—and make it believable.

Our body grows, the full power of the symbiote coming to the fray. The Moon Knight suit becomes one with us, completely enveloped in black, from the top of the hood to the toes of the boots. Our chest glows with a crescent moon, and as we march toward Roxxon Power Station, four police cars swarm in from all sides. We roar, our layers of teeth bared and our tongue lashing.

Guns draw on us. A mouthy man yells at us to stand down.

We turn, a tendril shooting out from our back to wrap around one of the police cars, squashing the glowing lights atop it. The impact shatters the windows and bends the frame, then we flip it over, crunching the rest of it.

Gun explosions flash, a wave of bullets soaring through. We form a symbiote shield, a large square of black that absorbs the bullets mid-flight before dropping them to the ground, each pinging metal against pavement.

"We're gonna need backup!"

Yes, tiny cops, you will.

We turn, and with one lash of our fist, the metal gate knocks back at its hinges. We walk in, knowing what we must do.

Which we shall. Because we are Venom.

I am Venom.

CHAPTER 30

—

STEVEN

IN THIS WORLD *AND* MY WORLD, MARLENE HAD LIVED IN SPECTOR Manor, complete with its somewhat excessive number of rooms and large outdoor sitting areas and underground vigilante bunker. Though in the universe I came from, she still resided there. In fact, she probably sat in that bunker now, hunched over reports while reviewing the latest surveillance footage with Frenchie, in a desperate search for how and *why* Spector had disappeared.

Maybe she even saw the Venom symbiote goo overtake Marc for the first time.

Here, though, Marlene chose to escape the vortex of Moon Knight for a life without those related complications and entanglements. She traded away luxuries as well, and as the sun blazed high behind us, Gena pulled the car up alongside a sidewalk in front of a very ordinary, very livable suburban home technically belonging to one Mary Sands.

"The sun is shining, there's a nice breeze," Frenchie said, tapping away at his laptop. "We're totally going to ruin her day."

Five hours had passed since we escaped the NYPD 17th Precinct at sunrise, and most of that time involved extending the relatively short distance to Marlene's new place, driving around in random turns and highway stretches to lose any potential visitors before "borrowing" (Frenchie's term) the first eligible (also Frenchie's term) parked car available and making our way out here. Outside of a very brief sanity stop at a donut shop, strategy had consumed our focus, the early-morning light turning to bright sun as we monitored the police band via Frenchie's laptop.

Including word that Venom had been spotted going northeast, toward the Long Island coast.

As for me? Us, I suppose?

Well, this was the weird thing. Since we technically died, I didn't exactly feel tired anymore. Neither did Jake. What that meant, I didn't know, especially since we ate a bunch of stuff at The Other Place last night, so I guessed we'd find out what bodily functions worked or didn't work.

In most cases, this would freak me out, make Jake mad, and Spector would do something to calm us both down. Here, though, I at least told myself to enjoy the warm colors of the sun.

Little things that made a difference.

"If I know Marlene," I said, adjusting in my seat, "she probably is already digging into the news about Venom."

"You think Venom came here?" Frenchie asked.

"Good question," Jake said in my head. "I don't see a trail of destruction. Even the lawn is neat."

"Well, first," I said, holding up one finger, "we know Marc sent us her alias."

"We don't know that. We *suspect* it," Gena said.

"Fair point. We suspect that, and we suspect that Marc or Venom or both of them saved us. And there's nothing weird here. See," I said, holding back my grin at Jake's eventual reaction, "even the lawn is neat."

"Hey, that was my line," Jake said, but I kept going like I didn't even hear him.

"It's not like we have a choice," I continued. "We roughly know where Venom is heading but we don't know why." I scanned the scene. The blinds remained down, no movement behind them.

"She wouldn't peek through the window," Jake said.

"Should we just knock?" I asked.

"She's got cameras," Frenchie said. "Look above the front

door. One on either side of the awning as well. Probably the back, too. Complete surveillance."

"Well," I said, adjusting my clothes. Beside me sat the folded Moon Knight suit brought by Gena and Frenchie, and while I still had my Mr. Knight shirt and pants, dust and debris from the hotel incident had turned the clean white color spotted with bits of grime. Carbonadium could only do so much against falling out of an elevator. "I guess then we won't be *too* much of a surprise."

"I'll keep the car running," Gena said. "Frenchie, you should go, too."

"You think?" Frenchie asked.

"Venom wouldn't have a Frenchie with him." Gena's laugh filled the small sedan. "Besides, she may be mad at Marc and company, but I'm pretty sure she's not as mad at *you*."

EVERY SINGLE DETAIL ABOUT THIS NEIGHBORHOOD FELT EXACTLY out of a painting or a 1960s sitcom, especially with the bright noon sun. Other than the occasional car passing by, the only noise came from a random dog bark and the sounds of sprinklers spraying across front lawns, most of the community's residents at work or school. Yet when we got closer to Marlene's porch, it became clear that she'd made some of her own upgrades.

Cameras, as Frenchie pointed out. And on the door itself, a wide strike plate was installed along the jamb, and a series of motion sensor lights spanned the entire run of the porch. Plus a large BEWARE OF DOG sign.

Years and years with Moon Knight in all of his different forms did that to a person. A pang of guilt rippled through me; even though our Marlene didn't take these steps to separate herself, it still fired up countless what-if questions in my head. It's not like the toll of being Moon Knight–adjacent hit differently wherever you existed.

I shook my head, though; that part didn't really matter if we didn't get home. Or fix the fact that this body was dead. Or that we needed some way beyond Khonshu to keep it going.

"Should I pretend to be Marc?" I asked as I took the first porch step. "We do talk a teeny bit differently."

"You didn't think of this already?" Jake asked.

Behind me, Frenchie shook his head. "Honesty is the best policy and all that."

"It's just, this Multiverse stuff is kind of hard to explain and—"

Before I could finish my sentence, the slides and clicks of locking mechanisms interrupted. The door swung open to reveal a very tired Marlene Alraune dressed casually in loose jeans and a T-shirt, hair tied back in a ponytail. She held a giant mug of steaming coffee, and I guessed that wasn't her first today.

"Marlene," I said, doing my best Marc impersonation. "I know I shouldn't be—"

"Save it, Jake. Or Steven. Whoever you are," she said, eyeing us. "Hi, Frenchie." She offered a hug to him, then squinted at the car. "I heard everything you just said."

"Oh." I blinked, then glanced up at the camera. "Oh, right. Cameras. Got it, got it," I said, relaxing back into my normal cadence. "Well, that's good. We don't need to recap things—"

"You talk different from the Steven I know. Did Marc tell you that?" Her mouth tilted with bemusement, which meant she wasn't just shoving us away. "My Steven's a bit more . . . I don't know, confident?"

Jake's laugh filled my head, and I tried not to react. "Well, different life experiences and all that."

"Uh-huh," she said, finally waving at Gena in the car. "Are you trying a slight British accent? That's weird." She stepped aside, then nodded to motion us in. "Come on in. I've been expecting you."

———

ABOUT TEN MINUTES PASSED, MARLENE GIVING US A CRASH COURSE in the odd visit with Venom/Marc. Which confirmed a lot of my suspicions—first, Venom was *not* trying to kill us, and second, Marc had bought us some time. "I've seen anger. I've seen rage. I've seen control," she said. "I know those things when I see them. I know them when they're directed at me or someone I love. This was different. Venom clearly felt those things, but his *fear* was for something else. I'm just a bystander to him. To Marc, though . . ." Her voice trailed off and her eyes fell for the briefest of moments. "You don't love Marc Spector without learning to be concerned about him all the time. And I'm concerned. This is weirder than the usual Moon Knight business."

"The police scanner said Venom is headed northeast, to the Long Island coast," Frenchie said. He tapped his laptop screen. "Not a lot there except for strip malls and suburbia. And Roxxon Power Station."

"To activate the psi-phon," Marlene said, her voice deadly serious despite her cozy attire. "It requires a *lot* of power. I mean, think about it—if it's pulling from across the Multiverse, it's not like a few double-A batteries will do the trick. No, Dad actually commissioned an engineer to examine it. Didn't tell her what it was about, of course. But she did some scans and built a theoretical schematic." She patted a folder on the coffee table. "The device's power system is delicate. But it's not like we had a chance to test it." I thumbed through the documents, angling them for Frenchie to see as well. "This is what's important. Marc knows I left something out but he doesn't know *what* it was. It all happened so fast, I just had to make a decision and go. They have notes on activating the psi-phon, using it across beings, across the Multiverse. But the direction of the transfer, it works a little differently if you're absorbing across universes. If you have two multiversal beings," she said, pointing at me, "in close proximity, there's an additional polarity configuration to determine who gets what. It's all in the schematics. At least, that's our best guess." Marlene took a long, deep sip from her mug. "Like I said, it's not like Dad had another version of himself to test things out."

"I think we may be able to get Venom to cooperate," I said, staring at the different sheets before passing the diagrams and specifications to Frenchie. "Or Marc. Depending on who we're talking to. If we can catch up to them."

"This is complicated," Jake said with a sigh, though I shook my head at that.

"No, it's actually pretty simple," I said, catching Marlene and Frenchie's looks. "Sorry, Jake's doing a running commentary. What I mean is if we can control the direction of transfer, if we figure out who is *supposed* to get what—then maybe we can work around that."

"If Venom cooperates with this," Frenchie said, "then *we've* gotta be careful. We can't reveal that we're all working together. There's someone else behind this."

"Right, exactly. Whoever Venom's working for can't know that he's being double-crossed," I said. "Marc would have a plan right now. I think for us, we have more of a direction to go."

"Good enough for now." Jake's gruff tone practically came with a doff of his trademark cap.

"Wait." Frenchie tapped the laptop keyboard, the volume gradually getting louder with the squawk of police band activity. "Did you hear that? They said Roxxon Power Station. Confirmation. Venom's there."

Marlene stood up, probably her polite way of saying that she'd done her part. I took the cue, nudging Frenchie with my elbow, and we moved in a polite scoot to the door. Frenchie got a big parting hug, one filled with the weight of both good and bad times. For me—us—though, just a nod and a "good luck."

I supposed that made sense.

From the porch, Frenchie waved at Gena, who brought the car back to life. He trotted off, open laptop still balanced in his hands, and I had made it one step down the brick walkway when Marlene called out. "Steven?"

I paused, whirling around. And if I could see Jake, he likely would have held the same pose.

"In your home," she asked, brow furrowed in thought, "did we . . . I mean, have we figured this out?"

I glanced over my shoulder at the running car. Beyond that, the bright sun burned through light cloud cover, a very ordinary day.

But not for us.

"We are still together," I said, facing her again, "if that's what you mean."

Marlene leaned against the doorframe as she considered her next words. "Is she happy? With everything that happens?"

Was she? I left out the part about how our return was in severe jeopardy. "A week ago, I would have said yes. And genuinely believed it. But after all this," I said, gesturing around, "and seeing what happened to you and Marc here, I don't know. Maybe less than she lets on."

"You two. Steven Grant, Jake Lockley. It's nice to see you all working together. And working it out with your Marlene." She bit down on her lip, eyes narrowing before she sighed, a full-body exhale that seemed to release her layers and layers of defenses. "You know, Marc blames his Steven and Jake for our breakup. But it's not them. It's not just him, either. Or," she paused for a laugh, "Khonshu. It's *all* of that. It's Moon Knight. It's the way none of it ever balances. It's a vortex that takes over and sucks in everything around him. How do you do it?"

Inside, I heard Jake shift. And I knew what Spector would have said had he been there. Guess I was speaking for all of us.

"It wasn't easy," I said slowly. "A lot of unpleasant conversations. Self-reflection. Therapy—for all of us. Jake didn't want to go." Marlene chuckled at that, which I soon matched, and even Jake did as well. "You know, the biggest difference between us and your Marc was Khonshu. Now Khonshu's . . ." I chose my words very purposefully. "Khonshu is helping us out. Other than the freaky bird skull and loud voice, I don't have too many complaints about him. But maybe Khonshu brought out the best and worst in

Marc. When you're operating only on extremes, sometimes it becomes too hard to find the right balance."

Normally, Jake would insert a snarky comment. Khonshu might have even complained, if he was listening. In this moment, though, we all remained silent, letting that massive divide between our reality and this reality just *exist*.

"Be good to her, Steven. And you, too, Jake. She's been through a lot." Marlene's words came as barely a whisper, but her posture changed again, a stoicism draping over her as she straightened up and strength returned to her voice. "Now, if you'll excuse me . . ." Marlene brushed past me before I could respond, her voice shouting a greeting as she went over to the car and pulled Gena out for a hug.

"You didn't tell her we were dead," Jake said.

"She's not our Marlene," I said, watching the two friends embrace. I gripped the folder in my hand and took in a steadying breath. "In here, I don't think she wants to know."

CHAPTER 31

—

JAKE

JAKE TOOK OVER THE BODY AS THE CAR APPROACHED ROXXON POWER Station, assuming control and talking with his friends even before he fully planted the mustache on his face.

He wasn't one to feel nerves—that was usually Steven's department—but seeing the oncoming four enormous smoke-stacks, white and red stripes looking like the most menacing candy cane, that fired off all sorts of disquieting feelings. Not the structures themselves—the stacks nor the buildings they towered over—but simply knowing what was inside: Venom, with the power of Marc Spector and under the direction of some other entity, probably wreaking havoc. While Venom wasn't necessarily straight-up diabolical in his actions, collateral damage didn't exactly feel like the symbiote's concern based on the overall track record.

And if Venom had to appear like they were focused on getting the psi-phon to their boss, well, Jake prepared to see that collateral damage up close.

The car slowed on a two-lane road surrounded by dirt and fields with a simple turnoff toward Roxxon—and at the end of that turn, about a quarter mile down, flashing red and blue lights blinked, so many that Jake couldn't quite count the number of vehicles parked there. Above, a police helicopter circled through the early-evening sky, the *whip-whip-whip* sound thunderous enough that it echoed through their "borrowed" compact sedan. Gena slowed enough to catch the attention of a uniformed cop standing along the main road as he waved a long flashlight and pointed toward a detour. The flashlight beam penetrated the window long enough that the cop gave away that he was scanning the vehicle's passengers; Gena kept her eyes straight while Frenchie shot a polite nod to the authorities.

And Jake? Still clad in the remnants of Mr. Knight's garb, he offered a shrug, though with his head turned. Even with NYPD's finest probably focusing on Venom, he didn't need to give them any reason to slow them down.

"Just drive a little bit," Jake said, gesturing farther down the road at the trees and shrubs lining it. "I think I might have to infiltrate on foot."

"I know Moon Knight's supposed to symbolize all this stuff, you know, being a beacon that strikes fear in the hearts of criminals and all that," Steven said, "but it really is making our attempts at sneakiness a tad difficult."

"It's getting dark quick," Gena said, pointing at the sky. Brakes squeaked as the car rolled to a stop, and she pulled the parking brake into place while Jake sorted through the folded Moon Knight suit next to him.

Frenchie reached into his bag and grabbed a pair of binoculars. "Looks like a lot of fence. Barbed wire across the top," he said. He leaned over to hand the binoculars to Jake, teeth digging into his bottom lip. "It's not going to be easy. I should have brought more equipment."

"Pretty sure if you tried to fly me in on a helicopter, we'd get shot down," Jake said. He blinked, eyes adjusting to the magnified view from the binoculars, the flashing lights skewing his count of moving silhouettes.

"There's always a way with a helicopter," Frenchie said with a laugh.

Actually, Jake realized that it didn't matter what mode of transportation they used. No way through the front door.

"You know what?" Jake said, starting his thought without consulting Steven. "You two go home."

"Um," Steven's disembodied voice said, "are you sure about this? Don't you think support is a good idea?"

Frenchie and Gena looked at each other with a quiet pensiveness, the only noise coming from the police band chatter on Frenchie's laptop. "We're your backup," Frenchie said, a dry gravel to his voice. "Whether you're Spector or Steven or Jake. This reality or another."

"With the police all out here like this? I don't think you'll do anything except put yourself at risk. And I can't ask you to do that. *We* can't ask you to do that." Jake didn't know exactly how Steven reacted to that, but he decided to run with it, adding his next thought for emphasis. "Steven agrees with me." Jake gave everyone a moment to object, including Steven. But the combination of Steven's silence and solemn glances from the front seats told Jake that, like usual, his gut was right on this. He looked next to him at the various pieces of the Moon Knight suit, the familiar tall white boots on the car's floor in front of it. "If Marc is really in there and Venom really is trying to do the right thing, then we might have all we need right here."

"There is one thing we can do." Gena pointed toward the flashing lights. "We can at least distract them for a few minutes when you start your break-in."

"Play dumb. Lost innocent tourists. 'I'm sorry, monsieur, I'm just a poor lost foreigner who cannot speak, uh, what do you say, English?' " Frenchie's mustache rose in a grin as his accent intensified. " 'How does one get to the Empire State Building?' " Outside, a tap on the windshield: a single drop of rain falling, before another and another arrived. "This is why I always carry multiple IDs, you never know when you're going to need them. For you," Frenchie stretched down and held up a grappling hook loaded into a black pistol. "Not your color, but I thought you might need it. Oh, and for luck," Frenchie said, reaching into his jacket pocket. "I was saving this until we were all together and safe."

Between his fingers sat a small metal flask, the very same one he stole out of Retrograde. The slight odor from it tickled Jake's nose; he knew good whiskey when he smelled it, and this particular one wasn't the best.

Sort of expected, given that Frenchie had lifted it from the back pocket of a Retrograde orderly. But quality or not, that flask *meant* something. Because where it came from mattered.

"You take this, my friend," Frenchie said, handing it over. "You hold on to it and when we get back together, we'll have a drink. It'll be horrible. Sometimes freedom tastes that way, and you enjoy it regardless."

Jake held the flask, a cheaply manufactured bit of stainless steel. Of all the equipment he'd bring in with him, this might be the most important.

"An excellent callback," Steven said. "I mean, we are dying, so it might be wasted, but—"

Jake groaned, the type that told his brain-neighbor to shut up. And to his credit, Steven listened.

"We should drop you off over there," Gena said, pointing to a row of tall trees lining the fence. "It's dark. There's a path around the perimeter."

"Probably some security cameras." Frenchie squinted, eyes narrowed in thought. "But at this point, I don't think that will matter too much."

"Yeah," Jake said. He undid the top button of his now-worn, somewhat dirty shirt. "By the time they realize it, I'll be long gone. And they've got bigger issues at the moment. Let's head out."

The parking brake clicked as Gena released it, headlights cutting through the growing downpour of rain.

HOOD. CAPE. SUIT. CRESCENT DARTS.

Mask.

And Frenchie's flask stowed safely away.

As he stood alone, the blanket of tree branches and shrubs protected him from the last gasp of daylight, though if he looked hard enough between them, the reds and blues of police lights still poked through despite the distance. Jake assembled the Moon Knight suit piece by piece—Steven didn't say much during this, though his presence carried a weight of observation, an acknowledgment that they were in this together no matter who drove the body.

The carbonadium flexed, the tight, protective molding moving lighter than its bulky appearance let on. Jake stretched his arms and bent his fingers, the *feel* of being Moon Knight familiar, yet foreign. Was it the suit? Frenchie did say it was a backup one that he'd stored for Marc. Or was it this universe, all of the small differences accumulating into the strangest sense of discomfort in the face of the seemingly familiar?

Or was it the fact that this body wore this suit without Marc Spector?

"I think that's it," Steven said.

"So you're listening." Jake attached the cape, though he kept the hood down for now, bits of rain getting into his hair. He fastened the few crescent darts on his belt, then checked his boots for appropriate tightness.

"I can't always. But sometimes it's obvious. And loud."

"Right. Well, I guess we just gotta get over it." Jake stepped to the perimeter of the thicket and assessed the fence standing about twenty feet away—and the four stacks still looming in the distance, each lit from the base for some illumination against the gradually darkening sky. His focus pulled closer, away from the grandeur of the facility ahead and more to the practical part of infiltration—Marc's specialty, but this would have to do. "See that? That's a security camera. I think we're probably out of range now, but as soon as we walk, oh, about ten feet that way, this whole thing begins." Jake stroked the fake mustache on his face, the thin layer of adhesive pulling on his skin. "What do you think happens to us after this?"

"I'm trying not to go there, honestly." Steven huffed in his ear. "It's an anxiety management technique."

"Alien parasites, cops everywhere, our body is freaking dead. I don't get what you're worried about." Jake laughed as he adjusted the pouches on his belt, a laugh that Steven soon matched. "You're probably right, though. For all we know, we could wind up in yet another place after this. Maybe with a Greek god instead of an Egyptian one."

I heard that.

Khonshu's familiar growly voice came in faint, its weakness revealing itself in volume rather than tone, like someone turned down the sound rather than the last gasps of a dying being. "Try not to insult our host while he's keeping us alive," Steven said. "Like, literally alive."

"Right, right. Sorry, I meant 'Khonshu is the best and I hope he keeps us alive.'" Within the body, Jake heard an amused grumble but left it at that. No need to drain Khonshu's energy any further. "Right. Well, I guess there's just one thing left." Jake gripped the Moon Knight mask, staring straight at the blank white slate. His fingers instinctively stroked his mustache, except as he did, a strange calm came to him, and with it, a realization.

Jake tugged on the fake mustache, a light sting across his upper lip as it tore off.

"Now's a strange time to decide to shave," Steven said.

"It's one of the things that makes me different from you two." He held it up, this cheap bit of costuming that lived so close to the core of his identity—his own self, whatever space it took up within this overcrowded body. "But right now, I don't think I need to be me." The mustache fell to the ground, lost somewhere to the blackness of the night. Jake took the mask and adjusted its tight width, stretching it out in all directions.

Then he put it on.

And unlike his usual look, Jake didn't leave it halfway up to expose his mouth and chin. Instead, he pulled it fully over, just like Marc would have, just like Steven would have.

"We," he said, "need to be Moon Knight right now. Me. You.

Whatever is left of Spector in us. Because we're going it alone. I feel weirdly calm about this."

Which was true. Of all the strange things thrown their way over the recent days, the sight of the massive facility ahead didn't intimidate him, despite the weight of their task at hand—even with the stakes between realities.

Jake took a breath, the air coursing through their shared dead body, and somehow never felt more ready for a challenge.

"Well," Steven said. Something was different this time, though it took several seconds for Jake to figure out what it was:

Steven's voice wasn't in his head.

It came from behind him.

Jake turned around to see Steven, decked out from head to toe in spotless Mr. Knight regalia, from the crescent moon on the mask's forehead to the slick white shoes and piece of finely tailored material in between. He adjusted the tie around his neck, then held out a hand. "Don't go hogging all the glory for yourself."

Jake walked up to him, then pushed a finger into Steven's shoulder. It disappeared effortlessly, absorbing as easily as it would into a hologram.

Which, Jake supposed, Steven was.

"What are you doing?" Steven asked, his head tilted.

"Oh. Well, I just thought maybe with all the weird stuff happening, you'd somehow popped out of our mind." Jake sliced a flat palm through Steven's phantom, enough that Steven stepped away, complete with an annoyed huff. "Is this a fear response? Or are we more amped up on adrenaline than I thought?"

"I'm not magical. Still a phantom. When *you're* in control. But I just thought," Steven said, tugging on his coat, "this might help."

"You chose to appear?"

"Yeah," Steven said, tilting his head. "Not panicked. Just wanted to be here for us. For moral support."

Moral support. What they needed was more equipment, an honest talking-to with Venom, an understanding of just what the crap actually was going down, and maybe some allies from the NYPD. Outside of that, though, moral support would do.

Jake rested his right palm over his left forearm, where despite the layers of protective fabric from the Moon Knight suit, a tangible throb rippled through.

Venom was near. Somewhere within that mass of metal, concrete, and technology, doing who-knows-what, for whatever purpose—nefarious, noble, or something in between.

Jake pointed toward the Roxxon facility, the property's evening lights beginning to activate, a beacon at the end of the wide stretch of dark between Moon Knight and Venom. "Lead the way," he said to Steven.

CHAPTER 32

VENOM

THE BUZZING RETURNS.

Strange, after all this time with Marc, this buzzing now overtakes cleaves him from me. This is a lonely cacophony. He is there, somewhere underneath it, though we can no longer read him or hear him.

Instead, we have you.

The Whisperer.

You have gone silent, though. Only the buzzing remains, as if that sound, that *threat* is all you want me to hear.

It increased, from the moment we stampeded through the road ahead of the Roxxon Power Station to the few seconds it took to swat away the police officers, their pistols firing useless bullets against us. Once past the main gate, we vaulted over the fence, and the noise intensified, a frequency on the cusp of being unbearable for a symbiote.

We climbed up the building wall, tendrils and formed claws ripping into the brick exterior until arriving at the large window on the main building's left side. As we smashed it open, the human screams came from below, the remaining workers now evacuating against a flow of incoming police.

We infiltrated. We got through. And now we are here, a trail of carnage through hallways and rooms.

The transformer room. Rows of metal boxes and thick cables tying them together, all to do some primitive change from high-voltage currents coming in to low-voltage currents flowing out to the population.

That power, that is what we need.

That is what *you* want.

We hold the psi-phon up, this flimsy bit of technology that somehow transfers life essences across universes. We rip cables from the large metal boxes, follow your instructions to connect the psi-phon. Then we pause to take it in, this mess of technology bridging dimensions and whatever else your larger plans might be.

Your voice cuts through the noise:

EVERY ACTION YOU TAKE IS ONE STEP CLOSER TO FINISHING THIS.

THE BUZZING STOPS. FOR JUST A MOMENT. THEN THE INFORMATION comes in a flash, but with a force that burns into my thoughts. Are you making a point about your power? Questioning our abilities? Do you simply not trust that we will remember exactly what to do?

Perhaps all of the above. You send a message into our minds, wrapped in that same buzzing noise, but it creates clarity, a tangible and visible packet of details.

YOU WISH TO PROTECT THE HIVE MIND? THIS IS WHAT YOU NEED TO DO.

THE MARC SPECTOR OF THIS UNIVERSE, THE ONE WHO HOSTS THE SYMBIOTE, HAS A SPECIAL ESSENCE THAT I CRAVE. THE PSI-PHON CAN TRANSFER THIS ESSENCE FROM OTHER MULTIVERSAL VERSIONS OF A BODY INTO THE USER—OR IN OUR CASE, FROM MARC SPECTOR'S BODY INTO THE SYMBIOTE.

I WILL ARRIVE SHORTLY. BRING THE PSI-PHON TO ME. THEN EJECT FROM MARC SPECTOR AND JOIN WITH ME.

THE PSI-PHON WILL COMPLETE THE FINAL STEP: TRANSFER-RING THIS ESSENCE FROM THE SYMBIOTE TO MY BODY WHILE WE ARE JOINED. WHEN THIS TRANSFER SUCCEEDS, THEN—AND ONLY THEN—WILL I STAND DOWN THE THREAT ON THE HIVE MIND.

This ends with one final message, a clarity of thought that leaves no doubt:

ALWAYS REMEMBER THAT I AM IN CONTROL.

Indeed. For the Hive Mind, we will oblige.

And with that set in place, we flip the switch on the largest transformer module. Machines *click* and *pop*, heat radiates, a low hum starts up.

As the psi-phon begins coming to life, a ball of glowing yellow forms around it.

We wait. The buzzing returns, louder than ever. You tell us to await your arrival, to have everything prepared for the transfer.

Next to the modules, another station sits, several monitors with graphs and data scrolling across. We watch and think of how much time it will take for all those charts to peak, for the psi-phon's faint radiating yellow to become fully possible.

And what might come next.

As if on cue, something changes. We feel it.

Part of the symbiote remains, a single drop living in another body. A pulse, a subtle measure that only a native symbiote could detect. It tells me all we need to know.

The other Moon Knight has come. Just as Marc predicted.

We concentrate, shielding our thoughts and feelings from the Whisperer.

I shield *my* thoughts and feelings.

I remember what Marc said: *You must trust them. All of them.*

And to myself, I think: *Whether that is Jake Lockley or Steven Grant controlling the body, the time has come for all of us to connect, to find a way through this and defeat the Whisperer.*

That is what Marc wants. That is what Marc would have done.

CHAPTER 33

—

JAKE

IT ONLY TOOK A FEW MINUTES FOR SECURITY TO NOTICE MOON Knight.

Steven actually figured it out first. "What's that noise?" he yelled as Jake sprinted through the tall grass and weeds. Jake kept going, getting to the paved concrete square framing the buildings.

"What noise?" Jake replied, almost instinctively, but then he heard it:

The distinct whirr of helicopter blades.

Followed shortly by a blinding spotlight blasted directly down on them. "Oh, whoever's doing the spotlight's having a hard time holding it steady," Steven said.

"Thanks, Steven." Jake's yell dripped with annoyance. "I'm sure they're being graded on their performance."

"Attention, intruder." The loudspeaker voice broadcast downward, powerful enough to be heard over the hovering helicopter. "Stand down."

"I guess they'll be here soon," Steven said, Mr. Knight keeping pace with Moon Knight in a physics-defying way. "Do we know where Venom is?"

"Somewhere inside," Jake said, pointing at the large rectangular building sandwiched between the stacks and the smaller office building in front.

"I can't tell if you're being sarcastic or not."

"A little." Legs pumping hard, Jake ran between the two rectangular buildings, and the strangest thing happened. He'd gotten used to Khonshu talking with them, as well as a phantom Steven Grant just hanging out.

But this thing in his arm—the pulse that punched harder the closer they got, like radar detection that grew from a blip to a scream—that took some getting used to. "I don't think I need a map. Can't you feel the arm, too?"

"Not as much as you, apparently."

"I can sense Venom's proximity. Even some of the obstacles ahead. Like," Jake huffed a breath as he continued to dodge the helicopter spotlight, "I sense Venom encountering a bunch of security right now and—oh, never mind, they're taken care of."

"The next time I'm driving, I'll give it a try. But first . . ."

Steven pointed around the corner, where four uniformed police officers rushed into view. From behind, Jake looked up and saw what might have caused the throbbing in his left arm—a second-story hole in the wall, likely where a window and concrete once sat.

It looked like Venom's path into Roxxon.

Too bad they weren't the first ones to discover that.

"Freeze," a voice called out, and with that, four guns drew on Jake. From above, the helicopter spotlight stayed on him, and Jake considered how Marc would strategize through this. His own instinct called to run at them, beat the crap out of all of them with reckless abandon, and then forget about it. Of course, that was usually against underworld goons, but this was the NYPD standing between him and his goal.

Jake ducked back around the corner and checked his equipment—a few crescent darts and Frenchie's grappling hook, though not much else, and he didn't want to waste his few adamantium weapons now, not with Venom ahead. "Jake, we don't have time to fight them," Steven said. "Who knows how far Venom has gotten with the psi-phon?"

Jake looked ahead at the gradually approaching police officers, the distance between them closing. Brutality worked in worse situations, but this wasn't the time for such a course of action. Above, the helicopter lowered until it maintained a height of, what, two hundred feet? Three hundred? Oh hell, Jake didn't know. But an idea suddenly popped into his head, and without consulting Steven, he pulled out Frenchie's grappling hook and aimed it high.

It couldn't be that different from the truncheon, could it? Or at least firing a gun?

"Wait, Jake, what are you—"

Before Steven could finish, the gun exploded with a *pop* and a flash, the grapple now soaring through the air before latching onto the helicopter's base. "Holy crap, it worked," Jake said as they soared upward. The thick metallic cable whirred as it retracted, pulling him upward, and within seconds, he got his best-ever view of Long Island—though he made a note *not* to tell Frenchie that. Duchamp would probably take it as a personal affront to the Mooncopter.

"Well, we're way above them," Steven said. "Now what?"

Jake answered by letting go of the grapple gun.

They dropped, a frightening speed to their descent. Jake turned to his left, only to see Steven falling alongside. "Are you going to tell Frenchie you lost his grappling hook?"

"Not our concern right now," Jake yelled against the soaring wind. "I got this." Wind pressure whipped against the mask, the armor, the boots of Moon Knight, and Jake threw his arms out, cloak now hooked to his wrists. The cloak billowed out and stiffened, giving him enough glide to navigate, gravity handling the hard part about maintaining speed.

Actually, *gaining* speed.

"The building is arriving a lot faster than seems safe," Steven yelled, his phantom floating alongside. "This is why Spector should handle this part!"

"Hold on," Jake yelled back. Which, of course, wasn't exactly necessary, though he'd blurted out whatever came to mind first. Steven was right, though; smashing into a wall instead of a hole in the wall would be very bad. Spector had practiced this the most among them, which made sense given his usual command over infiltration.

If they survived this whole ordeal, Jake was going to have to talk with him about balancing out their skills.

"I'm trying," he shouted, adjusting the glide up and then down, a rolling wave to take the edge off the speed before tilting his shoulders to aim. "I'm gonna go for it."

Steven said *something* in response, but a combination of wind and probably Steven's own anxiety muffled it. No matter, given that Jake had enough on his plate. His arms burned as they held the cape, fighting the steady pull against the tension of oncoming wind. A little down, then farther up, then a little to the right, then a rotation to bring him in line with the second-story opening.

And in they went. Mostly.

Jake's feet caught some debris, smashing bits of concrete against his boots, causing his body to roll in response. His arms tucked in, the cape with them, and they skidded forward until slamming against the side of a metal workstation. Several seconds passed by as Jake oriented himself, ignoring the set of pencils and pens that rolled from the desk and bounced off his chest. "A little more tricky than landing on a roof," he muttered.

"I'm not sure if that was faster than fighting those guys," Steven said as Jake straightened himself up and set forth.

JAKE FOLLOWED HIS INSTINCT, OR AT LEAST THE GROWING PULSE IN his left arm. Though the trail of destruction made for some pretty significant markers—from the property damage to the unconscious, possibly dead people strewn about. In fact, the wake of Venom's destruction made the interior of the building surprisingly easy to navigate.

At least until they got to metal double doors, a large sign stating DANGER: TRANSFORMER ROOM—HIGH VOLTAGE.

And in front of that sign, seven police officers. All with guns drawn.

Well, almost all. Behind the spread of cops stood a single one, his gaze still on the far door. At first, Jake thought the door was simply painted black, an odd choice given the otherwise drab industrial grays and whites. Steven probably had opinions, though he kept them to himself.

But then the black shimmered, as if it were a muscle that flexed, causing the lone officer to gasp and step back. This caught the attention of the others, enough that they all turned or glanced enough to get a sense of what was going on.

Jake readied himself, looking ahead and considering the distance between him and the officers, the way they spaced apart in a line, the height of the ceiling and the width of the walls, all things that would impact how this might all go down. Because unlike the last group he faced, no grappling hook would swoop him out of this one. And when bullets started flying, the mix of metal lockers and concrete walls would create all sorts of ricochet possibilities.

Jake dropped his weight, knees bent, left foot in front of his right, body carrying forward, and though his hands were now fists held up in a ready position, he considered reaching down to grab a crescent dart and toss it through as an opening salvo. On the edge of his peripheral vision, Steven stood, the same ready position despite the fact that he existed solely as a phantom of their shared brain.

Equipment in this room and the previous hallway clattered with industrial clicks and buzzes, and from the ceiling, the ventilation system reverberated with the shaky metal of creaking ductwork, though through that noise, Jake even heard the labored breath of one of the officers. From beyond the black door, a clattering escaped, then a noise somewhere between a growl and a shriek.

Actually, that might have been one of the officers. Because despite the low light, Jake saw a tendril form out of the bottom of the door, wrapping itself around the nearest officer before slowly elevating him. The man's muffled screams came through, grabbing the attention of his fellow uniformed officers.

And then a loud *pop*. And a bright flash.

Followed by a drop of a metal shell casing.

Jake saw a divot penetrate the black tendril, pushing a hole inward before it popped a bullet out, the bit of metal rendered inert on the floor, next to its casing.

"It's active, shoot—" one of the officers started before the tendril swung the trapped man directly into him. They collided, bones crunching against bones, then the tendril dropped its captive, two bodies now limp on the floor. The other officers opened fire, a barrage of explosive flashes as the tendril slithered into a shield-like form, absorbing the bullets. Jake backed down, shielding himself with his cape as the officers concentrated on Venom's weaponized appendage; the oil shook and vibrated with the impact, but it twisted and then lashed out, hitting all the remaining officers in a single swoop.

One flew back, an audible grunt as she hit the wall. Several others simply fell over, like bowling pins against a perfect throw. The remaining officer struggled from his knees, a slow push to stand up before the tendril formed a tight tail and whipped him aside.

Jake stood up as the tendril pulled back, then the black melted off the door, pooling at the bottom before slithering away. As it did, the throbbing in Jake's arm took on a strange new pulse, a rhythmic double beat that felt ready to burst through the muscle and skin and past carbonadium to get back to Venom.

Finally, a single *click* came from the door's locking mechanism.

"I think Venom wants us to enter," Steven said, ear against the door. He waved Jake over, then looked again.

Jake walked, even and measured steps, his grip tightening on the crescent dart. "Adamantium," he said slowly. "Remember the hotel. It slows Venom down. It's the best option we got right now."

"Maybe we shouldn't start with violence," Steven said, straightening up. "I have a better idea."

"Yeah? What's that?"

Steven huffed, and Jake swore he felt a push of air from the phantom's movement. "Trust Marc."

Trust Marc.

Jake moved, glancing at the floor as he approached. From what he could tell, the downed officers still breathed—and hopefully, it just meant they'd wake up with soreness, maybe a broken bone or two.

Venom could have killed them. But he didn't.

Which also meant that Venom probably could have overpowered him. But he didn't.

Jake's fingers wrapped around the door handle. It pushed down easily, the pressure of springs and hinges giving way to open the latch, then Jake pushed in, swinging the heavy door open.

He stepped inside, letting go of the door handle, the *hiss* of hydraulics guiding it back shut with a *thud* and a *click*.

Before him stood Venom. Bigger, more menacing, more *Venom* than before.

When they'd last come face-to-face, Venom had taken over Marc's Moon Knight suit, giving it a black sheen over its signature angled hood and flexible armor.

Here, Venom was . . . different. More alien for sure. And taller. Rather than matching each other's height—more or less—Venom towered over Jake by nearly two feet. The basic shape of the Moon Knight hood persisted, but the mask's usual sharp glowing eyes were distorted, now slanted white orbs, menacing in their clarity over rows of too many sharp spike-like teeth. And on the chest, the familiar crescent moon now glowed white against the black of the rest of Venom's body. Jake wasn't sure if this was a trick of the light from the rest of the shimmer that occasionally rippled across, or if Venom just found a way to make the icon look extra cool.

"How do we start?" Steven asked, standing side by side with Jake. "A friendly 'hello'?"

Jake shrugged, and whether or not the alien noticed it, he wasn't sure. But it was an easy place to begin. "Hey. Is, um, Marc in there?"

Venom remained still, and only now did Jake notice that behind the alien's imposing figure sat the psi-phon, hooked up with wires and cables and other electrical stuff that went far beyond fixing carburetors in taxis.

"Maybe he didn't hear—" Steven started, but a tendril whipped out from Venom's shoulder, wrapping itself several times over and around Jake's upper body. It squeezed, pushing air out of him; his arms shimmied back and forth, struggling against the imposing grasp. The tendril tightened again, then began to pull, Jake's heels digging in to resist. His fingers searched his belt until they felt the familiar curve of a crescent dart; he grabbed the weapon, and though his shoulders remained locked in Venom's grasp, Jake thrust the crescent dart up from his elbows. He stabbed into the symbiote's tendril, once, twice, and a third and a fourth time, each causing the tendril to flinch and loosen.

With enough give, Jake tensed his arm, then ratcheted it upward, the adamantium blade tearing through the symbiote. Venom recoiled, head tilted and mouth agape with a howl that rattled the room.

And a massive whip-like red tongue.

Another tendril shot out from Venom, but before it got to Jake, he leapt up and sliced outward with the crescent dart, a diagonal slash that cut the tip off. Venom tried again, another one whipping out; Jake tumbled to the ground, using his cape to help smooth into a roll, then he swung the blade upward, cutting into the tendril. "I thought we were on the same side," Jake yelled as he dashed across the perimeter, Steven keeping pace the entire time.

A tendril whipped out, grabbing Jake by the ankles. It tugged hard, knocking him off-balance, though as he fell, he jammed the crescent dart into the room's hard floor. The adamantium dug in and he gripped it with both hands, anchoring Jake enough that his body pulled in two directions. Venom's limb continued to pry him away from the crescent dart, his entire lower body now several feet off the ground. Jake's grunts mixed with curse words, and his body jerked back as one hand let go, one quick swipe to grab another crescent dart off his belt . . .

. . . and throw it at Venom.

The crescent dart soared through the air, twirling in flight. It flew in a general direction, not enough time for Jake to use any precision with his aim, but luck guided it to pierce Venom near the shoulder, just away from the moon on the suit's chest. Venom recoiled, massive tongue lashing out in pain. Jake dropped to the floor, his entire body landing with a *thud* that echoed through the room. His hand wrenched the crescent dart out of the floor and he twisted to reach down and slash the tendril around his leg. Venom let loose another howl, and Jake cut into it again, severing it clean off. The remaining tendril unwrapped before deforming into a pile of goo, and as Jake got to his feet, it wriggled back to the main symbiote body.

"I'm looking for a way out!" Steven yelled, but as Jake turned, something shocked him, putting him on his knees.

No, not a shock. A burning pain, from deep inside—

The symbiote drop in his left arm.

His arm throbbed, a fire radiating out of it, and this time it was *his* turn to recoil in pain. He got back to his feet, though the burning spread, not just stabbing at him from the inside, but slowing him as if . . .

As if it tried to control him.

"We're too close to Venom," Jake said. "He's trying to—"

Three more tendrils wrapped around Jake, around his shoulders, then waist, then ankles again. They pulled in unison, the burning now in every vein and every fiber within, and though he pushed and pulled, nothing could overcome the combination of it all. He approached Venom, drawn in closer and closer, and when the symbiote had him within arm's reach, another layer of black spread out, wrapping both Venom's imposing figure and Jake himself.

They existed within this strange cocoon, the noise from the power plant muffled out, and Venom's neck angled until they looked eye to eye.

Venom spoke:

"Close your eyes."

The words came in a menacing growl, yet they were so unexpected that Jake needed a second to process it.

"Close your eyes!" Venom said again. "Now!"

Jake continued to struggle, his shoulders flexing and twisting within the confines of Venom's hold. "Did I," Steven started, panic swapped for confusion in his voice, "hear him right?"

"It sounded like 'close your eyes' to me," Jake said through grunts.

"Close our eyes . . . Why would Venom . . ." Steven's voice came from outside the cocoon, but now he burst inside, his phantom penetrating the cloak of black without any resistance. "Jake, do it!"

"What?"

"Close your eyes. Go to the Mind Space." Steven now floated in front of Jake, his body half cut off by the cocoon's perimeter.

"I don't even use the Mind Space! That's *your* thing!" Jake sucked in what air he could grab. "You're right here. In front of me."

"I'm part of your brain, too; I'll guide us."

"It's a trick," Jake managed to get out. "Venom's tricking us—"

"No, think about it." Steven's words moved at a quick clip, unhindered by massive tendrils squeezing the oxygen from him. "Remember, Venom saved us at the gala. Marc has to be somewhere inside him. We're connected with him in our left arm. Close your eyes."

Jake grunted in defiance, though Steven's logic made a little sense. Not complete sense, but enough to try, especially given the fact that they literally had no other choice.

"First time for everything," Jake muttered to himself.

And he closed his eyes.

CHAPTER 34

STEVEN

I STOOD IN THE LOBBY OF THE MET. EXCEPT IT WASN'T EXACTLY MY usual Met. Closed, lights dimmed, wrapped by the darkness of night. Cracks ran along and through the ceiling as bits of rubble dropped to the floor, displays lay knocked over, and even my brochures scattered on the floor.

And in the middle of it? A giant-sized Khonshu stood, arms pressed against the crumbling ceiling, a soft glow around his gloved hands.

Guess he really *was* keeping us alive.

The fact that Khonshu's struggle against death was represented so literally here was a bit surprising. The theatrics must have come from my time as a movie producer. Jake looked surprised as well. No longer in the Moon Knight suit, he stood in his familiar cap, jacket, and trousers. As for me, I arrived in my usual tuxedo. Khonshu remained completely still, more a reminder that, yes, he was involved and, yes, he was indeed doing what needed to be done.

"Okay. We're here." Jake looked around, then scuffed his heel on the debris-ridden floor a few times before walking over to me. As he passed the front desk, he pulled some of the scattered brochures and held them up. "How come my Mind Space looks like yours?" he asked, head tilted upward at all of the details of the lobby: the dormant video screen on the wall, the few glass-cased displays that remained standing, even the sign to the permanent Egyptian exhibit.

I sucked in a quick breath and straightened up, letting a brief bit of smugness enter my tone. "Maybe next time you can put the energy into crafting one yourself. You might find the experience rewarding."

"Ah," he tossed the brochures back onto the desk, "I'll use Spector's next time. Easier that way." He took another look around, then stroked his mustache. "We're here. What does this have to do with Venom?" His boots echoed on the tile as he walked up to Khonshu, giving him a deliberate poke on the oversized leg, to which the Egyptian god didn't react.

"Well, maybe just give it a second. Time moves differently here, it could be like when you're waiting for someone to connect to a Zoom call or—"

My musing got interrupted with a thunderous clap that rattled the space.

"That was Venom," Jake said. "Oh, now we've done it."

The noise hit again, a sharp and sudden banging that arrived to my right, Jake's left. I turned to face that direction, and Jake matched my look, our eyes tracing over to . . .

The front doors.

The noise came one more time, this time with a louder urgency. And then I noticed it—the lights were indeed dimmed, but that was *not* the night sky past the door.

Instead, the pool of black that lay beyond the front entryway was the viscous liquid of a symbiote.

Just like before, Venom had wrapped around the entrance. And just like before, Venom wanted in.

The only difference in this moment lay in how we reacted.

"Venom's *knocking*," I said. Jake instinctively tensed up, halfway into a combat stance, but I held my hand up. "Remember, Marc's been, I don't know what you call it, joined? But Marc is somewhere inside that mass of goo." I turned to Jake with a sharp, quick breath. "I think we have to let them in."

Another *bang* crashed through, the impact hard enough that the front door rattled and the floor shook. The remaining displays jolted, too, and the sign for the Egyptian exhibit tipped back and forth until eventually coming to rest.

"Yeah," Jake said, lines of concern forming under the brim of his cap. "You can do the honors."

I walked across the lobby, passing the large promotional banners and entry desk, walking until I got within arm's length of the front door. Through the glass, I finally saw Venom up close, the way the oil clung to the outer glass, a complete smothering of outside light, and as I leaned closer, a shimmer rippled diagonally through the black.

I gripped the deadbolt's turn piece between thumb and finger, the weighty, slightly stuck piece of metal ready to go with just one push. And even though we existed only within the brain of this body, my heart—not Jake's—galloped at a quick, rhythmic pace.

The door unlocked with a *click*.

Venom, though, did not burst through. Instead, everything remained still until I did the polite thing: I opened the door and waved him in.

From the doorway, the wall of black once pressed against the entrance now pulled downward into a slither, a purposeful movement that oozed into the lobby. Behind it, the view of Fifth Avenue gradually came back, like shades being drawn from the top down.

The symbiote moved in, sliding around the front desk until it began to take shape, the form of two arms, two legs, and a head transforming into a slick, humanoid creature with the same fierce white eyes and rows of teeth of the one we'd just fought.

But this time without Moon Knight's hood or cape. And though Venom cast an intimidating figure, something proved less inherently threatening.

"Hey." Jake put up a hand in a wave as I dashed back to him. "I'm Jake. That quiet big fellow is Khonshu. You've already met Steven."

"We are Venom." The symbiote's voice still came with a low, unearthly growl, but at least I didn't feel like I was about to be eaten by a semisolid alien thing.

We. Did that mean Marc still resided somewhere in there?

"I got a question," Jake said, and maybe he thought the same thing. "Why do you got a spider on you?" He pointed at Venom's chest, which had changed from the adapted Moon Knight crescent out in the real world to a white insect-ish shape.

"Actually, I thought it was kind of like a dragon," I said under my breath.

"Why do you have a bunch of junk on display in your brain?" Venom asked, and despite the distortion in their voice, a clear snark came. A black finger raised, nudging an item just enough off the display block: a clapper board from my last Hollywood production. It slid off and began to fall before disappearing and resetting to the display.

"Fair point," Jake said.

Venom's head angled before turning and looking my way. "We really don't have time for this. The Whisperer is watching. He must believe we are in conflict."

"So hold up," I said, forming a T with my hands. "One, who is the Whisperer? Two, if he is watching, how can we all be here?"

"This place is safe. The Whisperer only knows that we have fought and trapped your body." Venom looked around, though I wasn't sure if they were taking in the detail of the Mind Space's other exhibits. "Part of us exists in you. In this proximity, we can psychically connect."

"The left arm. I knew it," Jake said with a clap. "Hey, you know, that thing hurts when it throbs."

"We find your body equally uncomfortable. Perhaps you should consider taking a shower at some point."

"Wow," I said, taken aback by what was apparently a new level of symbiote humor. "It's not like we had a chance but, you know, point taken."

"Marc told us about this space within your mind, how you use it to communicate amongst yourselves."

"Marc." Urgency now laced Jake's voice. "Is he in there?"

"He is. Dormant. Before the Whisperer neutralized him, he

told us to do the Whisperer's bidding but trust all of you. You two, at least." Venom pointed at Khonshu, who probably would have presented an irritated beak if he could. "We're not so sure about that one."

I shot Jake a look, which he received with a single raised eyebrow. "Why did Marc want you to trust us?" I asked. "You saved us at the elevator. Was that you or was that Marc?"

Venom turned to me, then Jake. "Both. Much like you are both right now."

"Both," Jake said. "You trust Marc. And Marc asked you to trust us. But also, you killed us."

"You are dead?"

"Not dead yet." Jake pointed to the spot where the gash from the crescent dart would have been in the physical world. "Khonshu's keeping us moving. And our Spector's gone."

"We acknowledge there has been collateral damage along the way." Jake and I looked at each other—was that the symbiote's way of apologizing? "The Whisperer has threatened our Hive Mind." I took that as some sort of, well, hive-like setting, similar to how bees worked. Given our limited time and scope, now would not be a good time to ask for an encyclopedic explanation. "Unless we deliver the psi-phon to him. As well as activate it. Beyond the Hive Mind, he can also destroy your universe. Many universes. He has gained immense power."

Jake scoffed, muttering to himself as he counted off his fingers. "Hive mind, our universe, many universes." His lips slanted in a frown. "This guy sounds like a jerk."

I couldn't quite read Venom's expression—were they expressions? The whole slimy black semiliquid goo body made it hard. But the bright white eyes narrowed, layers of teeth parting just enough to give a hint of the long red tongue.

Then the massive shoulders started to bob—slight at first, but then it came with a guttural, rhythmic noise, something both familiar and yet very, very alien.

Was Venom . . . laughing?

"Yes," Venom said. "The Whisperer *is* a jerk."

That triggered Jake's laughter, which then triggered *my* laughter, and I swore even Khonshu's large bird skull vibrated a bit. We all stood there, the fate of multiple universes in our hands—no, in our *heads*—and here we were as mind phantoms within a makeshift Met. Did Venom even know where The Met was located?

"Okay," Jake said, wiping away tears, "okay, I get it. I get it. You're double-crossing the Whisperer."

"While trying to keep all of our universes alive." Venom shrugged, a ripple shimmering through the black oil. "No pressure."

"So," I said, in my best Producer voice, "You need to stay ahead of the Whisperer. You have the psi-phon. Is the Whisperer listening to us now?"

"No. His powers are limited to our body, not yours." Venom turned, pointing . . . somewhere. Relative to The Met, the direction had no meaning, but the finger probably traced to something in the real world. "The psi-phon is powering up right now."

"Okay, let's think this through," I said. "The psi-phon is charging. The Whisperer does not know we're working together. What else do we know, what are the facts? What are you going to do with the psi-phon?"

"He views Marc's body as having a special life essence." Venom held up a hand, and a phantom of the psi-phon materialized—an impressive trick that made Jake and me exchange glances. "We are unsure of what that means. He wants the psi-phon to transfer this ability from Marc to the symbiote, then from the symbiote to him. At which point, he can exploit it and turn it into his own."

I followed the trail of actions, one thing rolling into the other, and it suddenly clicked for me, all of it. "Oh, I see. So you're like escrow for super-powers."

"We do not understand *escrow*," Venom said with a grunt.

"It's like when you buy a property and the bank—"

"No one cares, Steven," Jake said, stepping forward. "I think we've got everything we need."

We all turned to Jake. Even Khonshu. Well, as much as he could, but I swore I saw the massive bird skull tilt slightly enough in Jake's direction.

"Look at this. We know something the Whisperer doesn't— what Marlene told us. The psi-phon's calibration is off because two Marc Spectors are here. It's supposed to just have one user, one Marc Spector to pull in juice from the other Marcs across the Multiverse. The Whisperer has jimmied it up to transfer the power in that body to your . . . um," Jake waved his hand, "alien self."

I don't know if Jake caught Venom's angled glare at that.

"There's a hole in his plan," Jake continued. "You know how to power the psi-phon but Marlene kept a detail from you. It was *Marc's* plan, he asked her to do that, to give us an advantage. It needs precise activation because there are two Marcs in one reality, that's *not* supposed to happen. So we have two bodies in Moon Knight suits. We know a secret about the psi-phon that the Whisperer doesn't. And the Whisperer doesn't know we're working together." Jake tapped his chest, then pointed around the room. "Me. Steven. You."

"What about him?" Venom pointed to Khonshu.

"Well, I guess he's kind of like your Marc. He's a bit dormant right now. See, we're technically dead and Khonshu's keeping us—" I stopped abruptly, and when Jake inhaled to say something, I put up a finger. "I think I've got it. I think I've got it." Spector may have been our team leader when it came to things like planning mercenary ops, but my boardroom experience lined up with my expertise at doing practical sleight of hand. "There's just one really, really big caveat," I said, looking directly at Jake.

"Wait. Before we get into that." Venom tapped the white icon across the large black torso. "About this, on our chest. You were both right. And you were both wrong."

"What does that even mean?" Jake whispered as he leaned over, and while I also wondered how a symbol could be both a dragon and a spider, we had more pressing things to discuss.

CHAPTER 35

—

JAKE

JAKE OPENED HIS EYES.

And like the last time he came face-to-face with Venom, he found himself wrapped in black. But unlike the claustrophobic, stuffy confines of a body bag, this felt as simple as a warm bath, but without liquid soaking through to his skin.

Then he fell, the black shell suddenly dissolving. His back slammed against the floor of the transformer room, a thud that rattled the metal grates across the floor.

Not the most welcome return to the real world. And definitely not as cozy as Steven's Mind Space—their Mind Space. Jake rolled over, the Moon Knight cape getting caught underneath him. His muscles tensed, ready to push himself back up and fight—except then he remembered Steven's plan. *The* plan, the one that they'd all agreed to join in. Despite Jake's own reservations at, well, pretty much everything.

Steven's plan asked a lot of both of them. But when the fate of the Multiverse was at stake? He had called it a "cost-benefit analysis."

Jake had told Steven it was "the least crappy option of a bunch of crappy options."

The floor continued to rumble as Jake slowly got up, a random thought coming to mind:

He was like a boxer throwing a fight for a big payday.

Of all the ways to go out, he supposed it could have been worse.

Venom approached the psi-phon, suddenly being much more

vocal about what was happening. Wasn't the Whisperer in psychic communication with the symbiote? Probably to give Jake some cues about when to do things. Too bad he didn't have any acting experience like Steven did. A yellow glow surrounded the psi-phon, electricity dancing in constant bolts while sparks flew off, leaving tiny singe lines across the floor. "The psi-phon is nearly charged. It is absorbing everything this power grid can give. We will activate the psi-phon when it is ready and transfer the body's essence to the symbiote. We await your arrival."

The Whisperer's *arrival*? Venom hadn't mentioned that part. In fact, Jake only had, like, two steps left to do. This seemed like a relatively easy plan until the multiversal apocalypse bringer arrived.

Steven suddenly appeared alongside him, kneeling in full Mr. Knight suit. "Am I the only one having second thoughts?" he asked.

"It's heroic, isn't it?" Jake whispered, watching as Venom pulled several cables out of the psi-phon's band.

"Just remember what Marlene told us."

"It is time," Venom announced. He gripped the psi-phon, one hand on each side of the multiversal power-transferring headset. "The power transfer begins now."

Jake shuffled to his knees, then stood up, settling himself back into a balanced fight stance: knees bent, hands up, weight slightly forward. "Venom!" he called, a full-throated yell he hoped worthy of a performance in one of Steven's movies. "You're not going to get away with this!"

"Oh dear." Steven's lament was one of the last things Jake heard as he dashed forward. He leapt, both hands extended, and he did exactly as Marlene had prescribed, placing white Moon Knight gloves over Venom's black fingers.

Electricity ripped through Jake's body. That was, if multiversal energy across space and time counted as electricity. Whatever the specifics, the damn thing zapped Jake, first burning his fingers and hands before his muscles felt like they were being punched from inside *and* outside at the same time. His teeth chattered and his joints burned, but he girded himself, taking the pain moment by moment until his boots grounded beneath him, holding him as sturdy as possible. And though Jake kept his eyes open and focused on Venom, the yellow energy grew in blinding waves until it burned everything else out and his vision held only a single, intangible brightness.

Then nothing.

Then they simply existed.

Jake and Steven stood, Moon Knight and Mr. Knight. And in front of them, a gray haze—but through the haze, a mess of images, layers upon layers of—

Jake couldn't figure it out. Steven leaned forward, probably creased with wrinkles underneath the Mr. Knight mask as he likely squinted. "We are in the psi-phon," Steven finally said. "I think this is . . . everywhere."

"Everywhere?"

Figures surrounded them, variations of Moon Knight in ways both familiar and super freaking strange. One guy looked like them, but with a dark mask. Another Moon Knight stood in a familiar suit, but instead of Marc Spector, it was a woman, long white hair pouring over her shoulders, her face visible but with a crescent moon branded on her forehead. Even . . .

A dinosaur? A freakin' T. rex in a white hood and vest?

"The Multiverse." Steven pointed at the images flying by, like an old-time film reel spidering off in every direction.

"So many places," Jake said, pointing to the dinosaur. "That's us? Even *that*?"

"Infinite possibilities," Steven said, gesturing wide. "In the strangest, wildest ways. I don't think we're getting any powers from any of the other Moon Knights. Not right now. But in a way we are. *Knowledge* is power. And look at all this knowledge being transferred to us, all these memories and . . ."

Steven stopped as a vision played out, something more than a memory. Unlike the glimpse they got through Venom dealing with

Emmet, these moments locked in through every sense—the smooth floor under their shoes, the stale air in the room, the dim light casting shadows from the tall ceilings downward.

And metal, cool metal against warm skin—the metal of a photo frame holding a picture of this universe's Marc and Marlene. Together, Steven and Jake experienced every sensory input, every flood of emotion as Marc packed the frame into a storage bin. He brought the lid down, clasps clicking into place, before shoving it into the corner of the same empty Spector Manor that sat on a private Long Island estate.

"Why would Marc give us that?" Jake asked as the ether snapped back into a deluge of *everything* from the other Moon Knights.

"Maybe," Steven said slowly, "so we could understand him. Just a little bit more. In the . . ."

"What?" Jake turned to the now silent Steven, then looked back at the flowing images. "What? What am I missing?"

"It's . . ." Steven thrust his hands up, and suddenly everything froze, leaving them with a look at the Spector Manor bunker.

"It's our computer. Not this place's." Jake pointed at the massive screen, various maps and reports across its display. "So what?"

"No, it's more than that. Look at those windows." Maps, security details, police reports, public CCTV footage, and other such details sat scattered across the screen. To the left, one larger window with the names MARC SPECTOR, JAKE LOCKLEY, and STEVEN GRANT across the top, each heading a column with constantly scrolling updates of tiny text. "Just wait."

"Wait for—"

Jake's words came to an abrupt halt as the shadow of a woman came into view.

A sigh, a yawn, and then Marlene sat, holding a steaming mug of coffee up to her lips, though she didn't sip. Instead, she just stared, yet her eyes didn't track to any particular bit of information.

She just *looked*.

Another figure came into view, blurry at first, but then the obvious half smile of Frenchie emerged from the shadows. "You should take a break, Marlene. Get some sleep. Marc goes off the grid all the time."

"Not like this." She finally sipped her coffee, though the gesture seemed more out of defiance than anything else. "There's always *some* trail. Data transmission. Money transfer. Voice identification, facial recognition, even in the most obscure place. Not like this. These searches," she said, pointing to the large window with three columns, "there's nothing. He's just *vanished*."

"No, no, no, Marlene, we're *right here*," Jake yelled, punching the air like it was a pane of glass to be smacked for attention. His fist hit nothing, the lack of physical impact deflating his shoulders.

"No, we're not, Jake." Steven put a hand on Jake's caped shoulder. "We're dead. Remember?"

Jake turned to Steven, glowing eyes from their masks lining up. "Yeah," he said with a heavy gulp. "I remember."

They both turned back to the moving image, except something had changed:

Marlene stared right at them.

Was it a scientific miracle of the psi-phon? Or simply the most eerie, most wonderful coincidence? Jake didn't know, and Steven didn't spout out any explanation, though he seemed present enough in the moment to react, which was more than Jake could do.

Steven held up a single hand, tilting it quietly with a wave. And with that lone move, all of the distressed creases framing Marlene's face softened, her eyes glistening and mouth moving for the smallest smile, a gesture that likely would have been missed by anyone who didn't deeply know Marlene Alraune.

"Let's transfer this to Marc," Steven said. "So he can understand us back."

Jake nodded, and Steven did *something* to make that happen—whether it was his nod or the way he waved his hand or maybe just his thoughts, Jake wasn't sure. The only certainty he had was that their sliver of the Multiverse got passed along to Marc.

Suddenly, they snapped back into reality. The yellow whipping energy of the psi-phon. The hulking body of Venom. The cold industrial walls of the Roxxon transformer room.

Jake remained, hands still gripping Venom's as the symbiote held on to the psi-phon, beams lashing out of the device. Jake's left forearm throbbed, a different kind of pain than the crackles and sparks from the psi-phon. Instead, a pressure came from within, a burning that melted through the fibers of muscle and ligament and even the carbonadium of the Moon Knight suit, until the drop of symbiote goo burst out. Jake's hands remained locked on to the psi-phon despite the pain, and he watched as the black blob floated through the air until it landed on Venom's shoulder and disappeared, now absorbed back into the whole.

The black, symbiote-covered Moon Knight then changed, the dark liquid peeling off and ejecting upward, leaving Moon Knight face-to-face with Moon Knight as the psi-phon began an energy discharge, chaotic bolts reaching all four corners of the room and everything in between, even the floating hulk of symbiote known as "Venom."

CHAPTER 36

VENOM

I AM FORMLESS.

Beneath me, the two Moon Knights stand face-to-face, engulfed in a swirl of yellow energy. Between them is the psi-phon, both sets of hands on the device.

I hover, feeling the burn and pressure of the psi-phon. It pulses through, energy seemingly traveling through all of time and space and then back again, a closed loop in ways that few had foreseen. The bolts whip and curl, crawling up and down each Moon Knight, a transference of power driven by the only device in all of the universes capable of such an act.

And then?

The energy absorbs. Its glow softens, the aura around the two Moon Knights fading, first from their feet, their legs, their torsos, all the way to their hands. As if from the inside out, it dissipates from the hands directly gripping the psi-phon.

The yellow is gone. Both Moon Knights collapse. The Whisperer's arrival is imminent. The time has come.

Jake and Steven had talked about how Marc was the planner, that he usually sorted things out. Steven offered analysis; Jake, well, in different circumstances, Jake could be a lot of fun—the chaos we could create. But here too much was at stake, and with the Whisperer coming at any moment now, I reined in my worst urges and followed the plan.

I AM NOW WE.

We are Venom, back in the body of this reality's Marc Spector, the same body taken off New York City streets days ago. The same body that stormed the Retrograde Sanitarium, that recovered the psi-phon from Jake Lockley halfway up an elevator shaft. We activate the body, moving its limbs and pushing it forward, despite the fact that the psi-phon's energy surge has kept Marc knocked out.

The other body, the one of Jake Lockley and Steven Grant, the one we hijacked from Spector's native universe to this one, it slumps on the ground, face still hidden behind the Moon Knight mask.

We await the Whisperer.

First, the buzzing noise returns. Is it a threat to see this through or simply a precursor to the Whisperer arriving in this world? Seconds later, a different flash arrives, a brilliant and blinding purple that bleeds into a core of white. From the white, a silhouette emerges, a hood over square shoulders and a flowing cape, arms and legs covered in some kind of mechanical armor.

We consider this moment, the possibilities. Who is the Whisperer? Does the answer really matter? Could we strike fast enough to end all this now? As if the Whisperer hears this, the buzzing intensifies, like a blade hanging over the Hive Mind.

We move forward with the original plan.

"We are ready," we say, though things are not in place yet. Inside, we growl and yell at Marc, trying to bring him to the surface in time to execute our plan.

"Bring me the psi-phon," the Whisperer says.

And with that, time runs out.

Inside our head, we yell at Marc one more time to wake up already. We use some language that probably isn't too polite, but desperate times call for greater urgency. Then we hold the psi-phon, gripping it tight, much like before. Except this time, we turn and offer it to the Whisperer. He takes it, head tilted in observation, and then he puts it on his head. An energy shock wave swells outward, causing his cape to billow out, and we catch a hint of dark green in the cloak.

The yellow energy returns, bolts crackling all around as the psi-phon charges up. We await the Whisperer's reaction, holding firm on to the knowledge passed to us by both Moon Knights.

Everything must play out with exact precision.

"You've done well," the Whisperer says. His voice is broken by electronic distortion, and the shadows over his head show that no mouth moves, everything hidden behind an obtuse metal mask. "We had an agreement and I am a man of honor. Now join with me and we shall take the final steps. I will search your mind to confirm you are not concealing anything from me."

"We have nothing to hide," we say. And there we sense Marc finally coming through. Is he ready to take on what lies ahead? We are unsure, though it will have to be enough, as the Whisperer awaits our next move.

We eject out of Marc Spector. For a moment, that body stumbles, falls to one knee, his white cape draped over his body.

"Once you fulfill your pledge, I will stand down against the Hive Mind and activate the psi-phon." The Whisperer stands at attention, ready to become my host. I descend, the symbiote wrapping around him, even as he stands, his form nearly obscured by the bright pulsating portal. We intersect with his body, becoming one with him.

Yet unlike Marc, unlike Eddie, the Whisperer is in complete control. I try to look deeper into his mind, except something about the Whisperer prevents I from becoming we.

No true joining occurs. Instead, I remain an observer, like when he pushed me down and awoke Marc. The Whisperer extends his right arm, the limb covered in a metal gauntlet; he taps a series of controls on it, causing two chrome wires to extend and snake up his shoulder before they connect directly into the psi-phon. Above the gauntlet, a readout projects, the words CALIBRATION and TRANSFER ISOLATION flashing above a rapid series of numbers. The psi-phon's glow intensifies again as it charges up, and all around us, bursts of yellow flashes sprint up and down, blending into the brightness of the portal. Inside, I feel the Whisperer's mind racing, almost machinelike in his calculations but a pure organic sense of emotion underneath all of the cool, distanced processing. This echoes across us, an awareness that remains distant enough that I cannot determine what lies beneath, who the Whisperer really is.

No confirming details. Only a sense of bitter dread, an unsympathetic logic, and an ambition too large to comprehend.

The gauntlet remains connected as the psi-phon processes, and the Whisperer watches the floating holographic text. I wait, time ticking by as I look over at Marc. He struggles to his feet, a loose wooziness to his stance, but steady enough to show that he is actually present. Then he straightens and turns, the glowing eyes of Moon Knight now bright and brilliant.

Nice of Marc to finally join the party.

Marc turns, the dark figure of the Whisperer likely even more striking than usual due to the change caused by hosting a symbiote.

And the data streaming through the gauntlet's holographic display, it grinds to a halt. New words form above it, first a blinking CALIBRATION ERROR, and then TRANSFER ISOLATION ERROR.

The Whisperer roars, and I become we, but not like with Marc. This is the Whisperer forcing his way through my mind for some clue as to what might be wrong. His mind opens up to mine, and I experience his internal fury, a rare state of simply *not knowing*— something nearly impossible for him.

Under all of the science, under all of the brilliance of calculation, inside the Whisperer is screaming at the sheer lack of *control*. He grasps at the fibers that join our bodies together, but that is the one thing that he cannot manipulate. Even movement slows for him, his thoughts of defense, attack, vengeance incapable of executing because *something* has poisoned him from within.

As he stares at the message of TARGET ESSENCE NOT FOUND, I eject upward, a floating mass of shapeless, formless symbiote, though I create a mouth for long enough to say one thing. With a smile, of course.

"Something wrong?"

I dash downward, not into the Whisperer but to rejoin Marc, his

Moon Knight suit now encased in a shimmering black. As his body intertwines with mine, I feel a new presence, one that I have yet to acquaint myself with.

Me. Marc. Khonshu.

Our bodies and minds intertwine, a fully integrated combination of Marc's skills and experience woven through the powers of the symbiote. Our hand clenches, and from that black-gloved fist bursts a flare of symbiote oil, a new kind of muscle flexing before returning to its ready position.

You good?

Welcome back, Marc.

Khonshu grunts a short affirmative, and we prepare for what awaits.

We are Venom.

And we are Moon Knight.

CHAPTER 37

—

MARC

THE STRANGE SENSATIONS CAME IN WAVES, KNOCKING MARC OFF-balance. Did this happen every time someone accepted a joined existence with Venom? Contradiction after contradiction arrived: being wrapped but feeling lighter and more powerful; a nausea at the physiological changes, yet a sudden sense of invincibility.

And a voice. Even after all that time together, Venom's voice still proved to be a little more disconcerting than the usual roster of shouting and arguing in his head.

Venom rooted into him, a black sheen now over the Moon Knight suit, though for perhaps the first time, they truly moved as a team, a unified front on the final steps of a plan built by multiple versions of himself.

Would it end the Whisperer? He wasn't sure about that—none of them were. But they were definitely going to try.

Marc grounded himself, small rumbles rippling through the floor plating of the transformer room and absorbing into his boots. His gloved hands gripped into fists, and his weight adjusted, an instinct to get into a ready position. Except when he looked up, he saw he didn't really need all that.

Instead, he could take a minute and simply execute things step by step.

Because the Whisperer, obscured by the blinding light of his portal, fell to one knee, shoulders slumped over and psi-phon still on his head. Marc dashed over to the transformer controls, tapping away to complete the final steps. A low rumble grew, and all around the psi-phon, its familiar yellow energy began radiating.

"What have you done?" the Whisperer yelled, his distorted voice struggling. As Marc glanced over to find the Whisperer stretching his trembling left arm slowly over to reach the gauntlet on his right, Venom barked out a command:

The Hive Mind. Quick, we must stop him.

Instinctively, a tendril whipped out from the top of Marc's shoulder. It split in two, a Y formation, with one holding the Whisperer's free hand in place and the other wrapping around the gauntlet. Under the Moon Knight mask, Marc's brow furrowed with intention, a gesture coming more from Venom than him, and with it, the gauntlet smashed into pieces under the tendril's pressure. Sparks and charges flickered off of it, residual energy discharging and leaving the gauntlet a broken, lifeless piece of technology.

And with that one gesture, the buzzing noise—the thing that pierced at a frequency specific enough to put Venom on edge—simply ended. For Marc, it felt like a post-blast tinnitus that disappeared. But for Venom, Marc sensed the relief, one that turned into a sudden urge for swift vengeance and chaotic fury.

Venom was ready to get murdery with the Whisperer. Marc flexed whatever thread connected human and alien, a signal to rein in Venom's worst impulses. Would Jake have done that? Did Eddie do that for Venom? Marc wasn't sure, but for now he stood at the helm of this body—and after several tumultuous days, Venom respected him enough to heed the call.

Part of Marc *wanted* to pull the Whisperer forward—not for the throttling that Venom wanted, but just to see who the person behind this interdimensional threat actually was. His best mercenary sensibilities kicked in, minimizing risk by keeping his target weakened and at a distance.

Distance would be especially important given that Marc started charging the psi-phon again. Doing so was the only way to save *everything*. That thought lingered, both for himself and for the symbiote joined with him.

The Hive Mind is safe for now. We must finish this.

"You think playing hero with an alien and an Egyptian deity makes you powerful?" the Whisperer asked, the question coming with a clinical coldness despite its threatening tone. "Whatever you plan to do, whatever you've done, it's insignificant at best and—"

"I'm gonna stop you right there," Marc said, turning back to the control panel, though the tendrils kept the Whisperer's hands bound. "So you probably are wondering why your body just doesn't want to move right now, huh? Here's the cool thing we found out about the psi-phon. If you know what you're doing with it, you can actually direct the transfers. Between multiversal versions of yourself." Marc pointed to Jake's limp body on the ground. "Or even a symbiote. They're a bit of a wild card in the process. Our two bodies each gave something to Venom. From me, he got the ability to block off the different voices in his head. We can do that, you know. I don't know everything Steven and Jake do, and they don't know all of my stuff. Relevant," Marc said, tapping the side of his head, "if Venom didn't want you to know something. By the way, he did hide a little bit from you. Jake and Steven over there? They're dead. But they had one drop of symbiote in them, a little bit of death that passed to Venom. Which he passed to you." Inside, Venom's otherworldly cackle almost took over Marc's body, but he stifled it and checked the control dashboard again. "Sorry you feel so bad right now."

Let's hope it stays that way.

Marc kept Venom's taunting in his head for now. No need to get into a protracted battle of snark with an interdimensional scientist. "It's pretty cool, this exchanging of powers. I got something back. You called him 'an Egyptian deity.' We're not always the best of pals, but I certainly do appreciate him right now."

Different screens on the control panel flashed, some charts filling all the way up and others with blinking text about exceeding limits.

Safety warnings? Power capacity?

They were almost there. Just a few more seconds.

"Oh, I almost forgot. All these different voices and different bodies, hard to keep things straight. One more thing got transferred. That life essence you wanted from me? Sorry, I don't have that anymore. I passed it to them." Marc pointed to the limp body on the floor. "Remember, that body is dead. Kind of hard to transfer it back to you now. We," Marc said, with full intention of representing himself and Venom and the other Moon Knight, "give you a heartfelt apology for missing out. Guess you couldn't read that from Venom, either."

Despite the shadows draped over his face, the Whisperer reacted in a way that Marc didn't quite expect. Usually, telling a madman that their master plan got derailed caused at least a little bit of a rage response. And while the Whisperer's posture didn't exactly project joy at Marc's explanation, the way his head tilted seemed more filled with curiosity than anything else. His mechanized voice spoke, barely audible over the cavern of machinery around them.

"So the ability *does* transfer."

Marc's gut sank at the realization that the Whisperer might be one of those really annoying people who had layers of backup plans built into their strategies. Which meant there was only one way to truly finish this.

A loud *thunk* rattled the wall of machines and monitors, and seconds after, the monitors themselves blinked to dark before restoring with their status graphs and charts.

The psi-phon is almost powered. Move now.

If the graphs and charts on the control console didn't reflect the psi-phon's power status, then the light radiating around the device gave it away. Distorted grunts and groans came from the shadowy figure, the purple portal still framing the Whisperer, but around his head the psi-phon's yellow glow eclipsed it with a heat and intensity palpable from twenty feet away. Lightning fired off the device, striking the wall, the floor, the ceiling, each bolt carving in and causing further destruction. At the center of the spectacle, the device singed through the Whisperer's hood, scorch marks visible on his mask or helmet or whatever metallic thing hid his face.

"Let's do this," Marc said to Venom. "Do you wanna tell him or should I?"

We do enjoy a good taunting.

Marc nodded and considered the way Venom used *we*. At first, it had felt distant, otherworldly, like a way for the alien to exert control over him. Maybe it started that way, a puppet under control from his puppet master. But now, as the Whisperer struggled against his bonds, Venom and Marc moved as one, joined in a common purpose, cause, and intention.

Indeed, they both enjoyed a good taunting.

"Here's one more detail about the psi-phon," Marc said. "All this power generated is now in that tiny headset, ready to pull across the Multiverse. But what happens if you *don't* actually activate it?"

His voice took a sudden shift, now a full-throated growl tinged with Venom's own words. "It becomes a bomb."

More than just a bomb—Marc had spent his share of time working with explosives and thinking about things like blast radius and detonation velocity. But when an entire power plant funneled into a bomb?

Well, Marc figured it would be pretty damn big. Three scenarios played out in his head: push the Whisperer through too soon and the psi-phon would incinerate whatever innocents lived around where he landed. Too late and they'd take out the Roxxon Power Station and a good chunk of the surrounding Long Island coast.

Just right, though, and the explosion would be contained by whatever was in the interspace void, eliminating both the Whisperer and the psi-phon as threats. "Timing's gonna be tight on this," he said, looking around them, watching the monitors.

Just a second further.

A harsh, sudden tug pulled on the tendrils from Marc's shoulders, and a quick look showed that the Whisperer now moved. No longer completely immobilized, his shoulders shuffled enough to pull himself backward. He came to a full stand, the portal's purple light now casting a threatening shadow that seemed to grow stronger by the second. He twisted again, and this time an arm broke loose.

And a searing pain shot through Marc—through both of them. Inside, Venom howled, and now the Whisperer extended a free arm, curved blades sticking out of the remaining gauntlet on his left hand.

The piece may have been more armor compared to the functional technology they'd just crushed on the other gauntlet, but it still had one thing just as dangerous to a symbiote:

Adamantium.

The Whisperer's movements regained speed, somehow freed from the poisonous essence they'd transferred to him. He swung his bladed gauntlet at the other tendril, and Marc felt Venom stifle through another adamantium slash. The tendrils dropped to the floor, and right as that happened, all of the monitoring stations flashed, the brightness from their screens fading away. Above them, the industrial lamps shut down, each clicking and popping as they fell dark, stealing the room's illumination until all that remained came from the Whisperer's portal and the sparking halo of yellow from the psi-phon.

The psi-phon is ready! Do it now!

The stumps on Marc's shoulders reabsorbed into his body, and the cut tendrils on the floor wriggled back, leaping upward to meld with the whole as he began charging forward.

All except one. Marc sensed it, Venom directing one lone bit of symbiote oil to go past their body and snake across the ground to absorb into Jake Lockley.

Ahead of them, the Whisperer raised an armed fist, then stepped forward with a heavy, awkward movement, as if freeing himself from cement. He reached up, a deliberate gesture while still fighting off the effects of the psychic poisoning, and wrapped one hand around the psi-phon's middle band.

One hit is all we need. Smash him into the portal!

Marc pushed himself forward, legs churning with whatever additional strength Venom or Khonshu granted him—or perhaps it came from the very desperation of the moment. The Whisperer continued, now his free arm up and taking hold of the psi-phon's other side. He let out a harsh, desperate groan, a sound made all the worse by the electronic distortions in his voice, and as Marc covered the distance, the Whisperer began lifting the psi-phon off his head. The yellow energy now saturated the space, a thick heat growing with every approaching step, and the Whisperer pulled, the intensity of the psi-phon dragging molten strings of metal off his mask—enough that if Marc took just a second, he might be able to get a look at who lay beneath.

But there wasn't time. Four steps away, then three, then two, then Marc leapt into the air, pushing off his front foot. He twisted his body, angling his other leg up and out until it soared forward, the momentum colliding with the Whisperer's chest—as clean a hit as any he'd ever done as a soldier, as a mercenary, as Moon Knight.

Except the Whisperer didn't fall backward into the portal. At least, not enough for him to vanish into another dimension or wherever it led. Instead, he grabbed on to Marc's leg mid-kick, the momentum carrying them both. The Whisperer stumbled then steadied, groaning as the psi-phon shot off sparks in a way that seemed to lock the device to his head.

Venom's tendrils whipped from Marc's shoulders, but the Whisperer now moved with regained agility and speed, slashing away with his gauntlets of adamantium spikes. Each stab into the tendril rippled pain through the joined body, and while Venom slowed from the injuries, Marc pushed their human side forward, going with old-fashioned fighting techniques.

The Whisperer still held Marc's foot from the failed kick, but

Marc launched himself upward, swinging his free leg to collide with the Whisperer's head, boot connecting with the helmet or mask, even part of the psi-phon—in fact, heat from the overburdened device ate away part of his boot's outer layer, leaving a smoking burn across the toes. The impact knocked the Whisperer hard enough that he let go of Marc's foot; as Marc fell to the ground, symbiote tendrils shot from his arms, whipping out to lash the Whisperer back. The Whisperer countered, quickly balancing to his feet and raising his arm just in time, adamantium gauntlet spikes intercepting the tendril. With the symbiote limb still pierced, the Whisperer yanked his arm back, pulling Marc close.

Marc swung, landing a clean blow on metallic armor, and despite the Venom-powered force of his attack, his hand bounced off, the armor seemingly impenetrable. The Whisperer countered, a gauntlet spike coming directly at Marc's head, and Venom detached part of the symbiote body to create a dense black shield. The adamantium spike pierced it, a gradual cut through Venom's body; it pressed farther and farther, until the spike made contact with the Moon Knight mask. Marc twisted his neck to angle his face away, but it was no good—the Whisperer, through whatever means, was simply too brute of a force for both Venom *and* Marc Spector.

The symbiote shield trembled and rippled, strengthening its form to try to hold the Whisperer in place, but the spike pushed more, the tip of it now cutting through the cheek of Moon Knight's mask. Pain stung Marc, the pressure of an adamantium spike making his skin bleed, when suddenly, the tension released.

The spike went limp, and Marc stepped back, tendrils retracting into his body. With the Whisperer still silhouetted, the psi-phon's yellow radiating glow lit the space enough to reveal what tipped the scales in their battle.

Through his armor, a crescent dart lodged in his chest.

Adamantium.

The Whisperer's gauntleted hand moved to the embedded weapon, fingers feeling the blade before pointing. "You," he said, a marked weakness to his voice that wasn't there seconds ago.

His pointing didn't target Marc. Rather, Marc traced its direction, turning his head to see Jake on the floor, propped up on one elbow. Jake looked at Marc, then the Whisperer, and though his words strained to come out, Marc heard them loud and clear—both in the room itself and in his head, connected by the loose symbiote oil that found its way over.

"Not . . . dead . . . yet."

Funny what a little bit of the symbiote could do for a few seconds—even for someone who was dead.

Marc's fingers balled into a fist, a shell of symbiote bluntness layering on top. "Remember what you told Venom?" Marc asked, faces flashing through his mind. Steven and Jake, Frenchie and Gena, *Marlene*.

Even Venom.

" 'No witnesses. No survivors.' " Marc threw his arm forward with all his weight, punching his target square in the chest. The Whisperer flew backward, the glow from the psi-phon tipping into ignition right when he flew into the sea of bright purple light.

The portal snapped closed, both silence and darkness blanketing everything.

CHAPTER 38

—

STEVEN

EMERGENCY LIGHTING FINALLY KICKED IN, A LOW RED GLOW GIVING the transformer room a hellish look.

Which was made worse with Jake lying on the floor.

I suppose that meant that I was on the floor, too. Except I wasn't. I still wore my Mr. Knight suit as I knelt next to Jake. Marc/Venom stood in front of me, their Moon Knight suit draped in all black.

Until it wasn't.

Venom drained away, peeling oily layers down until lines of symbiote threads crosshatched across Marc's boots. The pool trailed over to Jake's raised hand, then wrapped around it, and in that moment, I felt it.

Guess that meant Jake felt it, too.

For what little burst of strength or adrenaline or *life* Venom gave us, everything became brighter, sharper, clearer, *louder*, despite it all staying the same. Marc leaned over, gently guiding Jake's mask over his chin before fully pulling it off. I did the same, removing Mr. Knight's mask and letting it drop away into nothingness, before putting my hand on Jake's dying body.

Dying? Or dead?

Just about dead. But we're doing what we can.

"Whoa," I said. Jake looked up at that, his eyebrow arched in similar response.

"I heard it, too," he said, his voice barely audible. "That's not Khonshu, that's—"

"Venom," Marc said. From behind him rose a black snake-like form, two massive white eyes and rows of sharp teeth now hovering at his shoulder height. Marc then did the impossible:

He looked at *me*.

"I don't know how much time you two have," Marc said before turning his head. "The three of you, I should say."

With that, Spector came into view, fully dressed in the same black proto-military gear he wore when Venom hijacked him and brought us all over to this reality. He knelt down and leaned over Jake's other side.

With a now fully formed mouth, Venom spoke without yelling in our head. "As we fought the Whisperer, he cut one of my tendrils with adamantium. Rather than re-form with the symbiote, we sent it over to your body. It sustained you for moments. This should give you a little extra time. But there's no healing you. Your body has been dead for too long."

"And that," Marc said, pointing to the symbiote tendril wrapped around Jake's arm, "is why I can see you all. I don't pretend to understand it. I'm just appreciating it."

Spector met Venom's white eyes, lines forming across his face. "You."

"Yes," Venom said.

"You killed me." Spector tapped his chest, then looked over at me.

"I did. It was not my favorite decision," the alien said. And despite the growly nature of Venom's voice, I detected the slightest hint of regret in those words—maybe that was all a symbiote could express.

"You killed to get the job done and save your kindred." Spector's face dipped with a solemn nod before turning back to Jake. "I understand. I've done the same." On the ground, Jake groaned, then turned to Spector, possibly finally realizing that the three of us were reunited. "And worse. Ask my brothers, they'll tell you all about it."

"The Whisperer," Jake asked through harsh breathing. He pushed himself up even though standing probably wasn't a great idea right now, and another tendril came from the symbiote pool to support him. "He's gone?"

"The portal is closed," Venom said. "There is no way to know if he is alive or dead. But your worlds and my Hive Mind are safe for now."

"Our world," I said, a different image now in my head, and for all of the terrible things the psi-phon had brought into our lives, it at least parted with a little gift for us. "Marc, I don't know what happened between you and Marlene here. And I'm not telling you to fix things or even reach out to her. She wants space for a reason. But for your own sake, know that despite everything, she still cares about you. I think that she cares so much that she needs that space."

Marc reacted with silence, unblinking eyes locked on mine. Even Venom pulled back, a strange bit of empathy from an alien beast that seemed hellbent on chaos—even the good kind.

"Hey," Jake said with a weak cough, "don't forget that I saved you today."

"Always count on Jake Lockley to do the dirty work," Marc said softly, to which laughter caught on around the room: Marc, then Jake, then me, then Spector, then even Venom.

I don't think I could ever get used to alien laughter.

"You saved more than me. And this guy." Marc thumbed to Venom.

"The Whisperer cheated." Venom's eyes narrowed. "He wasn't supposed to have adamantium."

Marc shook his head again, then gestured wide around us. "The Multiverse. Everything could have been destroyed. So many people will never know it was you two." Marc took Jake's hand, and through either a dying brain's imagination or the power of the symbiote oil, I placed mine on top of theirs. And I *felt* it. Spector stood back at a respectful distance, and I wondered if maybe he gave *us* this moment since we were the ones who went through the whole ordeal. "But I will. Right now I'm seeing *your* memories. All of them. I'll always know."

"Ah," Jake said, and his fingers fumbled as he opened a belt pouch. "Then you'll know what this is." His huff turned into another groan, and he held up one shaking hand for Marc to see.

"That's Frenchie's," Marc said quietly, taking the flask from Jake.

"Take it. Go celebrate." A grunt echoed off the chamber's metal walls, followed by Jake suddenly collapsing to one knee. Venom's tendrils shook as Jake fell farther, his weight giving out. Though I remained a phantom of our brain, a momentum tugged at me, pulling me closer to the body. Venom guided Jake to lie on his back, and I anchored enough to keep a kneeling watch over him.

"Dammit," he said, his tone now more rasp than speech. "Out of time." Venom retracted, re-forming the snake-like being floating above a pool of black, while Marc knelt down with him. "It's funny," Jake turned to Spector, "going out as me. I always figured there was some rule or something that we'd go out as you."

Marc met my eyes, then looked at Spector before returning to Jake, the stoic whites now carrying the slightest layer of glisten. His face shifted, a quick inhale of epiphany. "No, Jake," Marc said. He slid the flask away before popping open a different pouch on his belt, then reached inside and pulled it out:

A fake mustache.

"I forced Venom to take this. I knew it would come in handy." With that, Marc put the mustache on Jake's upper lip, giving it one good push to make sure it held in place. "You're the one taking them home."

As Jake closed his eyes, I found myself transported to The Met's lobby, back in my tuxedo, with my brothers for one last time.

CHAPTER 39

—

MARC

THESE TWO, STEVEN AND JAKE, THEY WERE DIFFERENT FROM THE usual duo Marc lived with. This Steven proved a little more neurotic, and this Jake cursed a little less, but Marc very much recognized the core of who they were.

There was a reason why they didn't always get along. Probably because they each represented pieces the others lacked. Most people had their own versions of Marc, Steven, and Jake in a way, a mode of thinking for dealing with family or work or that one jerk who always hung around in their lives.

For Marc Spectors across existence, theirs was just a little more extreme, a little more delineated.

A little more *interesting*.

And for the Marc in this reality, he finally understood that he'd had it wrong this whole time. For so long he'd viewed Jake and Steven as necessary evils in his life, sources of conflict that also helped him get the job done. Hell, he even blamed them for all the trouble with Marlene. When the truth was, they each owned the fallout from their lives together—and if Marc could accept that, then maybe he could start being better about *everything*.

At least a little bit.

The thought lingered as Marc alone stayed by the fallen body of Jake Lockley, the phantom of Steven Grant and the other reality's Marc Spector now vanished. How much time had passed? He wasn't sure. The silence, the stillness as he stood over the body of his fallen brothers, felt like minutes, the same way time was distorted in the Mind Space. "We can't just leave them here," he finally said.

Now fully separated and independent, Venom turned to him, a floating face at the end of a string of black. "Sentimentality will get us killed. The police are still outside. They could come any minute."

Marc looked up at the door, a sheet of metal dividing everything out there from everything here. Then he turned, now taking in the space carved by the Whisperer's portal. Whatever that purple energy was, it incinerated a trail behind it: twisted bits of metal and shattered rebar rods mixed in with crumbling concrete, burned edges glowing from the absorbed heat. He leaned in, the tunnel's path leading to an unknown patch of black.

"Guess that's our way out." He turned to the floor. "It's going to be difficult carrying him out. I'll figure—"

A strange noise came from Venom, an almost hiss-like sound that interrupted Marc. But it came without malice; rather, the strangeness may have stemmed from the fact that it was one of the very few moments, possibly the only one, where Marc heard the symbiote express empathy.

With that, its oil slid under the still body before dozens of tiny tendrils lifted him up. "I will take them. Back to their home." The tendrils now wrapped around the body, mummy bandages in the form of symbiote liquid. Venom's floating head turned to Marc. "I will carve a path." En masse, Venom slithered to the start of the industrial cavern, head now rising above Marc's height, and Marc was relieved *that* Marc had come back at the end, even for simply a final breath with Steven and Jake. "It will feel good to smash some stuff right now." A large tendril extended outward, whipping away hanging bits of debris. "We go up. To the roof."

"I appreciate that. I—"

Something has changed.

It took Marc a second to realize that the booming voice in his head wasn't an alien symbiote, but an Egyptian god.

"Khonshu. You're back."

Emotions churned through Marc, both relief and uncertainty at the realization. Khonshu had given Marc many things across his life, and in many ways, the god was the reason why his life was this way—for better or worse.

But given everything that just happened, Marc wondered if he might be able to take a little bit more control back in their messed-up collaboration in the future.

I am. I am not at full strength yet. Getting Jake and Steven through this was tougher than expected. I was not fully prepared for how much of an ordeal those two would be. My restoration is gradual.

Maybe Khonshu had learned some humility across this crisis as well. "Good to have you back, Khonshu," Marc said. "You know, the last time you said something changed, this whole mess began."

I am aware of that. Something is different. I am sensing that the connective tissue of the Multiverse has suddenly shifted. As if someone poked a hole and sewed it back up.

"The Whisperer." The mention of him caught Venom's attention, pausing his destructive lashes in the tunnel, and Marc looked the symbiote right in its angled white eyes. "He's the type to have backup plans, isn't he?"

Venom's head tilted, the rows of teeth coming together in a frown. "I sense it, too. A ripple through the fabric of everything."

"Venom," Marc said, a sudden dryness in his mouth. "I don't think that explosion got him."

"I'm not surprised." Venom paused, looking upward before turning to the symbiote-wrapped body in tow, then to Marc. "We should hurry. The Whisperer is a tricky bastard."

Venom seemed to ignore the sudden bemused smirk Marc gave at the unexpected cursing. Mark took a moment to consider what life must have been like for someone who'd spent more than just a brief flash living with an alien symbiote. Whoever this Eddie was, he must have had a lot of patience.

Of course, Eddie might have thought the same thing if he'd spent a week with Khonshu.

We should follow Venom on this quest. I can give you the strength and speed to tear through whatever remains.

"What then? How do we stop the Whisperer again?"

Venom shook his head before gesturing for Marc to move. They began, starting with the burned tunnel carved about fifty feet deep. "That may not be up to us. For now, you keep watch here, in your time and space." The symbiote led them through a diagonal path upward, past the occasional sparked wiring or cracked pipes dripping water. The cavern finally ended, and Venom formed a large fist-like shape and began slamming through the layers of materials to get to the roof. As he did, Marc stood alongside, heaving chunks of debris out of the way by hand. Venom turned to him, a quieter version of that familiar growl. "I must return to the Hive Mind. As long as the Whisperer is still out there, he remains a threat."

"Breaking up with me already? You know, when we first met," Marc said, finding a handhold in the debris in the dark, "I thought *you* were the bastard."

"I *am* the bastard." Venom continued to tear through the structure. A symbiote tendril hammered away, chips of concrete dropping in layers before a single draft of wind blew. Another blow, and finally the smallest hint of moonlight. "Didn't I make that clear?"

Marc shook his head, his laugh probably inaudible underneath his mask. At least they could agree on that, given that their friendship, or partnership, or whatever this was called—all started with Venom sucker-punching him on a New York street. But here, Venom did lead the way, taking the torched path from the Whisperer's portal energy and pushing it farther until they emerged at the roof of the central Roxxon building. They stood side by side, Moon Knight and Venom, the most unlikely of pairs. Marc turned to say something, but Venom had already launched skyward, a mass of dripping black blob with a snake-like head on one end. Trailing behind it, the symbiote dragged a dark cocoon carrying the body of a fallen friend.

Venom disappeared skyward without a trace or salute or friendly farewell. It just *left,* on to somewhere else in space and time.

"Just us, huh, Khonshu? We may as well be stuck in the desert together."

Outside of the groan of rooftop air-conditioning units and the carrying voices from an emergency crew on the ground, no sounds came.

"Khonshu?"

Nothing.

For a moment, Marc's pulse quickened, a sudden panic at losing Khonshu just after getting him back—and right after losing Venom, and the uncertainty surrounding *his* Steven and Jake. But he settled himself, grounding his sense of weight and presence where he stood, and with that, clear thinking returned. Khonshu must have still been recuperating, particularly after granting Marc that final burst of strength.

Khonshu would be back. When, Marc wasn't sure. And as for Steven and Jake?

Marc tried not to think about it.

Now, on top of Roxxon's east wing office, Marc was alone, truly alone for the first time in . . .

Well, pretty much since he was a little boy.

No Venom. No Khonshu. No Steven or Jake.

Nobody.

Above him, the waning moon poked through the clouds, a sliver of dark clipped away from the celestial body's right side. Ahead of him, the landscape of nearby suburbia had gone dark, the final victim of the psi-phon's power absorption. Though Marc still saw the flashing reds and blues of police lights far below, he knew what they would ultimately find: a mix of unconscious security and staff, hopefully not injured too much.

All leading to the transformer room, where their forensics team would have to deal with a combination of interdimensional en-

ergy, symbiote brute force, and debris courtesy of an Egyptian god
and a suit made of carbonadium.

Marc stood, the altitude's high winds billowing his cape out,
and closed his eyes.

To his surprise, he didn't go into the usual smoke-filled void.
Sometimes, he'd wind up in different locales, but that took intention, like the time he took Steven, Jake, and Khonshu on a fishing
trip. But this?

This was different.

"What the hell?" Marc said, his footsteps echoing against tile.
He twisted his neck, then spun around, taking in the details both
near and far.

A checkerboard tile. A large video display on the far wall. A
front lobby desk, displays with exhibits seemingly pulled from
throughout his life. Was that a stack of brochures on the counter?

The Met. From the other reality's Steven Grant.

Apparently the psi-phon transferred some unexpected things
from the body as well.

Marc walked from wall to wall, marveling at the detail crafted
by Steven's mind or his mind or perhaps both, from the statue of a
gold figure holding a balance to the fine print in the brochures.
Was this what the real Met looked like or was it the version in
Steven's world? Or was it just the version Steven *wanted*? Regardless of authenticity, the specifics came to life; even the video wall
played a fully produced trailer with voice-over and music while
images dissolved into one another. And in the corner, just on the
edge of a hallway, stood Khonshu, half-faded in what was likely
his dormant, regenerating state.

Yet as Marc continued, examining each display and sign, the
space provided little solace. Despite the specificity and sharpness
of everything within the lobby, it was still nothing more than a
room with only himself.

Until a *bang* shook the space.

And another one. Followed by a pause, and then three more in rapid-fire succession.

But it wasn't a threatening rumble or something raining destruction from above. Instead, Marc realized:

It was a knock at the door.

He turned to the front double doors of The Met, the brightness of a full sun on a New York morning obscuring the two figures at the door, their identities hidden in silhouette.

What did people even do in this situation? Shouldn't The Met have some sort of automated locks? It wasn't like one of the biggest museums in the world would have a simple key lock. But then, no one ever explained the rules of this place.

Marc cleared his throat, then looked again at the two figures, one in a neatly tailored suit and the other casting a frumpier shape as the person adjusted his flat cap.

Could it be?

"Come in," he said, making his voice as loud as possible. And with that, the doors clicked, locks adhering to whatever mechanisms belonged to the Mind Space. They swung open, a gust of air coming in, along with noise from city streets that he'd rarely traveled in real life.

In walked Steven Grant and Jack Lockley.

"Are you . . ." Marc started, trying to think of a right way to phrase the question. But from the way they stopped several feet in and examined The Met in wonder, Marc *knew*.

This was not the duo that had gone on a quest to recover the psi-phon and defeat the Whisperer. These were *his* brothers, the ones hidden away as soon as Venom crashed into his life. If any doubt remained, Jake's mustached sneer triggered an impulse in Marc to punch him in the face, and as if he detected it, Steven rolled his eyes.

Definitely them.

"Do you understand what happened?" Marc said.

Steven and Jake looked at each other, then they walked in equal steps to meet Marc. Steven put his hand on Marc's shoulder, then spoke. "We saw everything," he said, and unlike the Steven who had tangled with Venom, this voice carried the familiar confident tones Marc had heard all his life.

Jake gave a solemn nod, a gravel to his words. "We remember *everything*."

Marc stood, a silent appreciation for the fact that these two, for better or worse, were a part of him.

CHAPTER 40

—

MARC

AMBULANCES AND FIRE TRUCKS JOINED THE POLICE CARS AT THE front gates of Roxxon Power Station. Marc moved swiftly, scaling down the back side of the office building, the property's lights knocked out by the psi-phon's power drain. Branches whacked against his shoulders, and his feet kicked up dirt and rocks until he got to the back fence, where he leapt over the formed iron and barbed wire with a quick up-and-over move.

He landed, brush and grime crunching beneath his boots, and he looked ahead, moonlight showing a sliver of a lake through the thicket.

Where to for now? Marc laughed to himself, shaking his head as he considered *why* he didn't ask Venom for a lift back. Even halfway home from Roxxon would have helped. For someone who constantly considered options and plans, that one had slipped past him. For now, he took a moment to consider his circumstances and understand his surroundings. Even from this distance, the rumble of idling fire trucks persisted, the occasional honked horn still audible. And over that came the familiar whipping of helicopter blades; he took that as his cue to get moving, especially if emergency crews called in further medical choppers.

Except this copter didn't linger around the Roxxon buildings or land by the mess of vehicles by the front gate. It came closer, its whirling blades growing louder, and soon enough, Marc looked up to find it directly above.

In fact, it even began descending.

The helicopter maneuvered to the edge of the shoreline, landing skids setting down on wet dirt, its blinking red and white warning lights reflecting off the water. The door swung open, and though Marc couldn't make out the details of the pilot, he recognized the voice that called to him:

"Marc! Get in!"

Gena.

Her silhouette reached out and waved, then she called again. Marc sprinted to the vehicle, already knowing who sat in the cockpit.

Of course Frenchie flew the damn thing, but where the hell did he get a helicopter?

"*Monsieur*," Frenchie yelled over the noise. He adjusted the headset on his ears as he offered a knowing nod. "Sorry it's not the Mooncopter. Got it on short notice."

Gena and Frenchie did the thoughtful thing of bringing a change of street clothes—strategic, as it probably would catch some attention if Moon Knight was spotted casually strolling through an airfield. Though it also sat more comfortably, for sure, plus the cape didn't get in the way.

The copter ascended just as Marc settled into his seat, the *snap-clip* of the belts locking him in, when his eyes caught Gena's beaming smile. "We were worried we'd never see you again," she said.

Frenchie leaned over from the front cockpit. "Yeah, after you dropped off the grid, we looked everywhere."

These two—always there when Marc needed them.

Except, what did Frenchie mean by *off the grid*? Only hours had passed since the transformer room, and before then, they drove Jake and Steven to Roxxon themselves. "You mean, while I was with Venom? And you were helping Steven and Jake?"

Gena and Frenchie turned to each other in sync, a mutual confusion between them. The copter floated forward, the rhythmic vibrations of the vehicle rattling the headset hanging above the door. Marc grabbed it and put it on, a wholly different experience from the similarly shaped psi-phon.

"Steven and Jake?" Frenchie asked, his voice now coming through the headset.

"You were with who?" Gena asked, her head tilting as her brow crinkled. She adjusted the speaking mic, the movement seemingly to conceal the worried look she shot over toward the pilot seat. "Did you say *Venom?*"

Maybe she couldn't hear him over the noise of the helicopter?

"Sorry, it's been a long, strange few days," Marc said slowly. His mind was used to piecing things together, little hints and clues of different lives and dreams, at least until he'd learned the delicate balance needed to unify a life—or lives. Perhaps his time with Venom caused him to regress? "Refresh my memory, when was the last time you saw me? Or, um, Steven or Jake?"

"After the sewers. You led us out of Retrograde Asylum," Gena said. "The orderlies chased us, Frenchie got injured, you fought them off, and then you disappeared."

"Did you go do this 'venom' thing?" Frenchie asked. "You should have called me in for backup. The Mooncopter's still busted, but you saw how fast I got this."

Marc considered his next words, a strategic way to probe without seeming too out of the ordinary, even for him. "Did you see the news about the Pinkerton gala?"

"The elevator failure? No one got hurt, fortunately," Frenchie said.

Elevator failure—not a hulking, black-tinged cape fighting a masked fellow in a white tuxedo? Marc looked at his friends, pieces coming into place, and though *everything* bordered on suspicious after what he'd just gone through, he leaned toward trusting his friends. "Marlene—her place in the suburbs?"

Gena gave a quick *tsk tsk* before shooting a dirty look over her shoulder. "Come on, Marc. You promised her you'd leave her alone. Is that where you went?"

"No, I've been here. There was an incident. Um, Venom—"

"Marc, you're going to have to explain what this 'venom' thing is," Frenchie said as he tilted the yoke to push the copter forward. "Is it like S.H.I.E.L.D.?"

Marc leaned back into his chair, mind racing at the possibilities that suddenly opened up—none of them good, but some certainly worse than others. "How did you know to pick me up?"

"Back at Roxxon?" Frenchie thumbed over his shoulder at the power plant now shrinking away in Marc's view. "The tracker in your suit. I just got a ping that you were here. We've been looking for days."

Marc rubbed his fingers in thought, the details of Jake and Steven's time with Gena and Frenchie coming into his mind, shared memories appearing like a book he'd just read. He reached over to the folded suit and opened up one of the belt pouches. "Right before you dropped Jake off, you gave him a flask. The one you stole from Retrograde. Remember that?"

"You must have gotten hit pretty hard on the head. I'm saving that for the right moment. I've got that right—" Frenchie reached into his coat pocket, then paused. He patted the other pocket of his coat, then his pants. "Wait, where is it?"

Many, many moments came in Marc's life where he questioned his recall, his sanity, his complete state of existence. But pulling the flask out from the Moon Knight suit, he *knew* all of that had happened. It was real. Venom was real. Steven and Jake from a parallel universe, they were real.

And the Whisperer? *He* was real.

Khonshu himself said that something had changed again. And Venom seemed certain that the Whisperer was not defeated, but instead managed an escape before the psi-phon's explosion incinerated him. Fitting for a being so powerful that even Venom feared his ability to threaten the Hive Mind.

Marc blinked, thinking back to the vision of the Earth in 113843 collapsing in on itself. Venom had shared that catastrophic vision, the specifics of destruction vibrant and terrifying: the crack of rock and pavement, the sudden burn of explosions, the piercing cries of panic.

But this?

This was almost worse.

They had destroyed the psi-phon. They saved this universe. They protected the Hive Mind. Yet somehow the Whisperer still had done *something* to affect this place, either stealing memories or altering perceptions or somehow just making people forget that he ever pulled strings here.

Why? And would that spur the Whisperer to do even worse things?

More importantly, was there anything Moon Knight could do about it?

For now, Marc knew the answer to that—he would do the only thing he could, and that was protect the people and community that he loved. If fate—or the Multiverse—pulled him into battle against the Whisperer again, he'd be ready.

Marc held up the flask. "You looking for this?"

Frenchie turned, the movement pulling at his shoulder seatbelts, and he squinted at Marc's hand. He glanced down, patting his jacket pocket, then he turned back to Marc. "How'd you get that?"

Outside the small window, light from the waning moon provided a beacon, a bright hue over a landscape darkened by the psi-phon's power drain. In the distance, reds and blues still flashed as specks of light, all centered around the Roxxon facility. Marc inhaled slowly, so many thoughts and explanations coming together that he needed a moment to sort through it all. As he did, streetlights and lamps in windows flickered to life, first in the immediate vicinity of Roxxon's rural surroundings, then block by block, electricity coursing through the different paths to bring neighborhoods and communities back to life.

"It's a bit of a long story," Marc said, glancing at the folded Moon Knight suit in his lap.

"Well," Gena said, "I'm sure we're all starving. How about you tell us while I fire up some pancakes after we land?"

CHAPTER 41
VENOM

I AM UN-JOINED, BUT NOT ALONE.

I lurk among the Hive Mind. Less fully enmeshed and more wrapping and binding them. It's complicated. The metaphysical symbiote realm isn't exactly as simple as an Earthbound highway network.

But there is a reason for my floating in this form. The Hive Mind connects symbiotes, but also contains our layers of existence: the primary space, the void, the UnBeyond. It's a bit of a tourist trap for the multidimensional—and let's not discuss Eddie's stint as the person in charge here. None of that interests me now.

Because somewhere out in the Multiverse, the Whisperer still lives. Where, when, that is unknown.

So I stand guard. I watch.

It's boring, but in this case, boring is good. Boring means safe.

Until a silhouette fades into view.

Despite being in a non-corporeal dimension, my teeth gnash and tendrils form, all of my senses on alert.

I get ready to fight.

The silhouette comes into focus, and though I hadn't uncovered the identity of the Whisperer, I know immediately this isn't him.

For one thing, the buzzing noise doesn't accompany this person. For another, the person wears a faded denim jacket and hoop earrings rather than a cape and armor, no gauntlets or adamantium spikes. And around her neck, a set of headphones with padded earpieces.

Definitely not the psi-phon.

The woman approaches, hands up, the hint of tattooed stars on her arms. I remain on guard, teeth still on full display, though instead of lashing out with tendrils, I wait.

"I know what you've done," she says, gradually coming closer. "With Marc Spector on Earth."

"Brave of you to start with that. Instead of saying who the hell you are."

The natural growl of my tone startles her at first, but then her head angles and she laughs, her disarming smile telling me that she agrees. "Right, right. Sorry about that," she says, slapping her forehead. "My name is America Chavez. I have been Watching."

"Watching what?" I ask, a little annoyance sneaking into my question. I am in no mood for cryptic statements.

"All of it." Even though we float in this metaphysical realm, she straightens up. "The Whisperer has left quite the track."

"The Whisperer." Tendrils retract into my shoulders, and any menace in my face leaves.

"He's doing all sorts of experiments." America crosses her arms, brow now furrowed. "Long story. But for this one, I couldn't figure out the purpose. Why Marc Spector? Why *that* Marc Spector? And having a symbiote get involved? Seems overly complicated just to get a set of headphones." She taps her own headphones resting around her neck, quiet beats playing from them, a slower, more melodic rhythm to the sound compared to the noise Eddie preferred. "I mean, these only cost twenty bucks and they sound just fine."

"The psi-phon transfers essences of an individual. But he could not directly transfer between Marc Spector and himself. The psi-phon needed a symbiote as a conduit." I laugh, a low chuckle that probably sounds strange to the uninitiated. "Steven Grant called it 'escrow.'"

"I . . ." Her voice trails off into a quick laugh. "I don't know what that word means."

"Neither do I," I said, "but what I do know is *that* Marc Spector was key. It couldn't be any Marc Spector. His life essence was specific only to that particular universe."

"But what was this essence?"

"Unknown." Now my arms cross, matching America's pose. "But the Whisperer needed a power that he could not create himself. He needed to steal it from someone else. Someone special. He needed to find it, then identify some means of transferring it."

"Someone special." America closes her eyes, now in deep thought. I leave her be, waiting for her to put the clues together and offer some brilliant epiphany that might easily solve this whole thing. Instead, she whispers to herself, so quiet I barely hear it. "Like Loki. And Wanda. A power that crosses infinitely." America's eyes snap open. "A nexus?" Her head angles, and she looks at me, the sharpness of realization in her gaze. "The power. It made its way to you at the very end. Didn't it? With *three* beings, something must have gone awry when you and Marc tried to transfer it to the other body."

Now I tilt my head, a gesture that I must have picked up from hanging around humans for far too long. "I feel no different from the time before Marc Spector. What would this even involve?"

"Never mind. It's just a thought." America shakes her head, a sudden shift in her posture. "Either way, we're just lucky the Whisperer was fooled . . . or satisfied. You should focus on your task here." She now looks around, taking in the vastness of this realm. "I used to think someone was trying to draw me out. But it goes far beyond that. There is a purpose to the Whisperer's targets." A small smile comes to her face as she tugs on the lapels of her jacket. "I hadn't worn this in a while. Forgot how much I like it." She then gestures around us, back beyond the Hive Mind. "Do you have any clues to his identity?"

I think of what I saw in Roxxon, what Marc saw. Flashes of light, shadows over armor, his voice changed by electronics and his face covered by a mask. "He remains hidden. Even when we fought him up close, we couldn't decipher his true identity." One moment, though, stands out, the instant he realized that we had fooled him and his fury caused his guard to drop. "But when I joined with the Whisperer, some of his thoughts emerged. He was careful, elusive. I could not confirm much about him, but there was one thing I intercepted." America leans closer, her eyes narrowed with an intense stare. "A single word, projected clearly, like it was essential to his very being:

"*Doom.*"

Seconds pass as America takes in this information, and the word causes everything in her to shift: her eyes, her mouth, her folded arms tightening their pose. "That changes everything."

More of that cryptic stuff. "How?"

"I need to go." She begins to drift back, her eyes dropping for a moment before locking with mine, a new certainty emerging in her face. "Take care of the Hive Mind."

And then she disappears.

ACKNOWLEDGMENTS

—

I have been around publishing long enough that the business of books rarely surprises me anymore, and yet, I can still remember the moment that my agent Eric Smith called with the news that Marvel wanted me to write a book for their new What If . . . series. We heard early on that Moon Knight would be involved in the series, but when I got word that Marc Spector would be a host to Venom, well, it was a genuinely surprising publishing moment. So much so that I actually said "Holy $#!^" out loud and felt like my brain exploded with possibilities.

Of course, an offer to write a book is one thing—getting a pitch actually approved is another. And this really awesome idea came with a bit of a logistical hiccup. After all, how the hell do you write a narrative with Marc, Steven, Jake, Khonshu, and Venom all in one body?

The answer is that you don't—you split them up. And though I worried about pitching a Multiverse story, it made the most sense to actually break up these voices into distinct characters that could physically push one another in new and interesting ways.

With that being said, a huge thank-you to Gabriella Muñoz at Random House Worlds for leading this project, with an assist by Elizabeth Schaefer. Both were instrumental in helping form the narrative into a story that focused on the odd-couple pairings while honoring established lore. The Marvel team of Sarah Singer, Jeremy West, Jeff Youngquist, and Sven Larsen answered many questions about character history and details. Perhaps most important, they approved my use of Layla El-Faouly, which I am still kind of in disbelief over. Related—they also approved the Arthur Harrow cameo, and I really, really hope one of you readers out there has picked up my *Before Sunrise* joke I snuck in. Yes, I was a '90s teen, can't you tell?

The tone, aesthetics, and characterizations in this book were largely inspired by the 2016 Moon Knight run by Jeff Lemire (writer)/Greg Smallwood (art) and the 2018 Venom run by Donny Cates (writer)/Ryan Stegman (art)—with a huge shout-out to Oscar Isaac for being a great Moon Knight.

Kelly Knox and Alex Segara provided some answers to early lore questions. Wendy Heard and Diana Urban helped out with the non–super hero side of things with practical crime/thriller vocabulary and police procedures. Fonda Lee, who writes the best fight scenes in literature, discussed a little bit of her process with me, as well as actual fight logistics about stances and weights. Sierra Godfrey was there for me to discuss plot beats when I felt like they weren't making sense or the stakes weren't high enough. Finally, Peng Shepherd answered a lot of my dumb questions about New York City locations, distances, and cabs.

Shoutout to my friend Kamal Naran, who is the biggest Marvel fan I know and thus has earned a little cameo here working at the gala. Kamal knew I'd get to work in a few cameos, so he suggested Random, Cyber, and Arcade.

Finally, thank you to my wife, Mandy, who sat through several rewatches of the *Moon Knight* MCU series with me and let me bounce ideas off of her. Tough gig being a writer's spouse, I know.

THE VASTNESS OF SPACE
AMERICA

AMERICA CHAVEZ HAD WATCHED.

She Watched Loki grapple with the untimely—and unnatural—death of his brother.

She Watched Wanda Maximoff endure losses she should have never had to face.

She even nudged the arc of time, reaching out to Peter Parker and Stephen Strange.

That pissed off the Watchers. And then she backed off.

She Watched as the Whisperer inserted himself, across galaxies, across realities. And in some cases, the Whisperer destroyed them. Even the symbiote Hive Mind, something so vast and powerful that it both existed and didn't in the physical realm, the Whisperer managed to cobble together a device putting them mere seconds away from extermination. What had he used to threaten the Hive Mind? A sonic drill for sure, and some properties of the M'Kraan Crystal, and probably more.

America wasn't an engineer or a scientist. She couldn't understand what exactly the Whisperer used to augment his armor and tools in such a way that they could threaten the Hive Mind. Nor did she grasp how the psi-phon worked. All she knew was that all of this involved different universes and power—and the ability to transfer power.

For an uncertain, shapeless time, America lived by the title of the Watcher. But that lacked action, purpose. She had

Watched, a cosmic window tracking as Venom joined with different versions of Marc Spector to locate and destroy the psi-phon, to even put a stop to the Whisperer's plans. Marc and his differing identities didn't usually tackle gods and magic and galactic threats, even in different versions of Moon Knight across the Multiverse. No, Marc, Steven, and Jake made a difference in their communities—even now, she saw Marc had moved forward from the fallout of the Whisperer to establish the Midnight Mission in one of Manhattan's forgotten streets.

Though one very small, subtle thing was different:

Now Marc Spector leaned back into a cozy green chair, dim light throughout the small room. A dark-skinned woman walked by, her pensive cheeks framed by short black hair and intense red eyes. Marc nodded to her, then stared at the object in his hands.

A flask.

A simple trinket. But with it contained knowledge that the balance of reality was at stake. When, America wasn't sure. But soon.

Marc didn't just watch. He took *action*.

He *chose*.

Just like Venom chose to stand guard over the Hive Mind. The symbiote now have the power coveted by the Whisperer . . . right? America sensed it, and it seemed feasible given the final chaotic struggles involving Venom, both Marc Spectors, and the psi-phon. If she went back to watch the whole thing closely, she could probably pinpoint the moment it happened.

Watch. America laughed at the irony of that thought. Perhaps she would eventually return to that moment, if she ever needed to confirm her hunch. For now, she let it be—Venom had enough to handle with the Hive Mind.

As for America, she had her task. And her choice. Now, primed with the knowledge passed along by Venom, America understood.

For America Chavez, noninterference, observing, *Watching* no longer worked. The time had come to take action.

She paused for a moment, feeling the weight of reality, a countless number of living beings all weighing on this moment—and the one word that Venom passed along. She fixated on it, her thoughts reaching out through the Multiverse along timelines, the shadows and silhouettes and hints from her observations coming together until her head tilted in epiphany.

Doom.

Doom was not a feeling or a sense.

Doom *was* the Whisperer.

America moved swiftly, breaking through from reality to reality, staying mere steps ahead of the Watchers while sensing the trail of *broken* left by the Whisperer until it centered—not just on a universe, but on a single person who represented the next inflection point susceptible to the Whisperer's plan:

Bright red hair. Brilliant green eyes.

And fire in the shape of a phoenix.

"Jean Grey," she said to herself, before balling her hand into a fist. It surged with star power, a vibration that rippled up and down her arm as she prepared herself for the next step. Such a move would anger the Watchers, possibly draw them into pursuit and punishment. But it didn't matter.

Some things needed to be set right.

America punched into the ether, releasing energy in a brilliant spark of every color imaginable. She hit it again and again until the colors dissipated, leaving only a path to another dimension.

Time to go.

AMERICA CHAVEZ WILL RETURN IN THE NEXT . . .

MARVEL

WHAT IF...

FALL 2025

ABOUT THE AUTHOR

—

MIKE CHEN is the *New York Times* bestselling author of *Star Wars: Brotherhood*, *Here and Now and Then*, *A Quantum Love Story* and other novels, as well as *Star Trek: Deep Space Nine* comics. He has covered geek culture for sites such as Nerdist and The Mary Sue, and in a different life, he's covered the NHL. A member of SFWA, Mike lives in the Bay Area with his wife, daughter and many rescue animals.

Follow him on
X, Threads, and Instagram:
@mikechenwriter